The
HIDDEN
FLAME

ACTS *of* FAITH, BOOK 2

The
HIDDEN
FLAME

DAVIS BUNN
&
JANETTE OKE

BETHANY HOUSE PUBLISHERS

Minneapolis, Minnesota

Published by Bethany House Publishers
11400 Hampshire Avenue South
Bloomington, Minnesota 55438

Bethany House Publishers is a division of
Baker Publishing Group, Grand Rapids, Michigan.

Printed in the United States of America

Library of Congress Cataloging-in-Publication Data

Bunn, T. Davis, 1952–
    The hidden flame / Davis Bunn and Janette Oke.
        p.   cm. — (Acts of faith ; bk. 2)
    ISBN 978-0-7642-0557-6 (hardcover : alk. paper) — ISBN 978-0-7642-0742-6 (pbk.) — ISBN 978-0-7642-0741-9 (large-print pbk.)
    I. Oke, Janette, 1935– II. Title.
    PS3552.U4718H53   2010
    813'.54—dc22

                                                     2009035938

This book is dedicated
to all our friends
at

Bethany House Publishers

with heartfelt thanks for
the wisdom, care, and
creativity with which
you bring our stories
to the world.

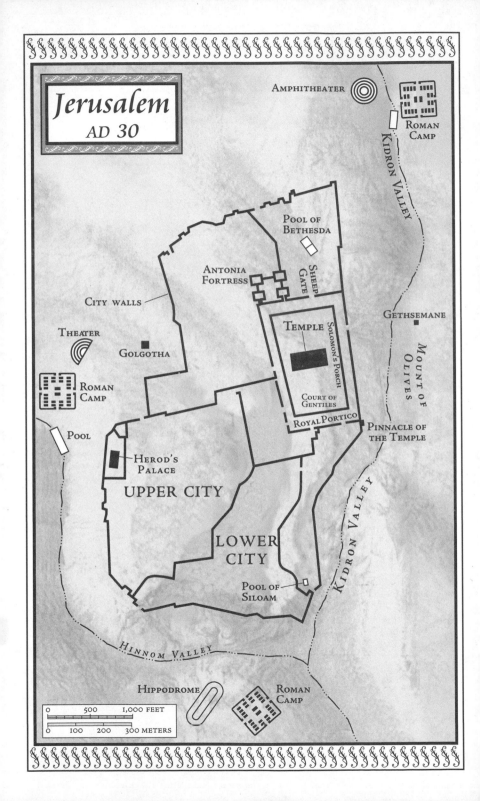

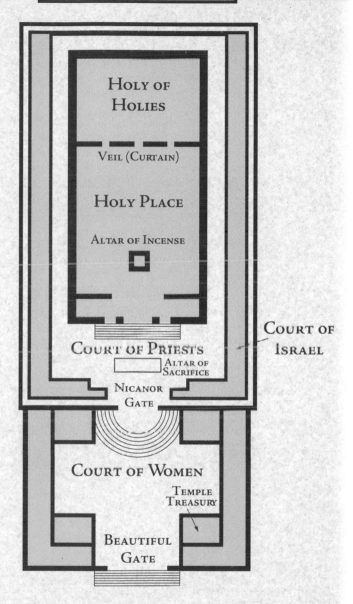

HOLY OF HOLIES

VEIL (CURTAIN)

HOLY PLACE

ALTAR OF INCENSE

COURT OF PRIESTS

ALTAR OF SACRIFICE

COURT OF ISRAEL

NICANOR GATE

COURT OF WOMEN

TEMPLE TREASURY

BEAUTIFUL GATE

SOLOMON'S PORCH

Jerusalem, AD 33

ABIGAIL QUIETLY WITHDREW from the celebration and limped into the shadows' coolness. Her leg throbbing, she eased herself down onto a stone bench by the courtyard's outer wall. Around her hummed the gaiety of wedding revelers. Never had she witnessed such joyous festivities. She felt as though the tension, the anguish, the uncertainties of the past weeks had been transformed. The group was not merely celebrating the wedding of Alban and Leah. There was a far greater reason beyond the joyful union of these two new followers of the Way.

They all rejoiced in the truth they had believed but that now had been confirmed. Their leader, the rabbi Jesus, had indeed risen from the dead, and there were eyewitnesses to the fact.

Abigail watched twelve-year-old Jacob as he danced back and forth among the merrymakers with a fervor bordering on hysteria. Abigail was still marveling that her brother was alive—whole and well. The time since the massacre of her family had seemed an eternity. A lifetime of feeling lost and alone. And just hours ago, she had caught a glimpse of the boy across the courtyard, and it was as if he too had been resurrected—a miracle that seemed like a dream. The very thought brought tears to her eyes once again.

Jacob must have felt her looking at him, for he turned as though seeking her. When their glances connected, he ran over to her, concern in his dark eyes. "Why aren't you dancing too, Abigail? Are you not well?"

"I'm fine, Jacob." And she was. Her injured leg hurt rather a lot, but just then she could feel nothing save the joy in her heart. Her beloved friend Leah danced with her new husband, Alban, in the circle of believers, and her brother stood before her. Her *brother*. "I am only a bit weary," she assured him.

"Shall I bring you something?" He glanced at the wedding banquet table spread with flowers and greenery, all ready for the feast to come.

Suddenly she needed to touch him, just to assure herself he was not merely an apparition. She reached up to his shoulder with a tremulous smile. "Perhaps some water. Thank you."

When Jacob dashed away, her attention returned to the jubilant crowd filling the little plaza. *Could it be only six weeks past that our Lord died?* The group of followers, already under suspicion, had locked themselves away, whispering solemn and frightened words to one another, checking anxiously about whenever they needed to enter the Jerusalem streets.

And then Jesus had appeared to them, afterward rising up into the heavens, only to have the Lord's own Spirit descend among them in a most stunning fashion—in wind and fire.

And now here they were, faces flushed, eyes bright, voices blending into song. The music of tambourines and flutes swirled upward once more, setting feet to dancing—a wedding festival for sure, but also a celebration of their Lord's resurrection and his parting gift to them of his unseen but unmistakable presence.

And the return of Jacob, Abigail whispered to herself with a little smile as she fanned her face with a palm leaf. How good it was to have so many reasons to celebrate. *If only my leg did not hurt so.* She reached discreetly beneath her robe to rub it. She would have loved to be among those dancing. She would whirl on and on around the courtyard. . . .

"Here you go, sister!"

Abigail couldn't help her little shiver of joy at the familial address coming from a lad she had thought lost to her forever. She smiled her thanks and took the earthenware mug but was unable to drink because her throat was closed up tight with emotion.

Jacob turned back to watch the clapping, singing throng. She nodded and motioned for him to go and join them. She could tell he was torn, but she gave his shoulder a little push. "Go, Jacob. Dance for both of us," she managed to say through tears of joy.

He was gone in a flash, and she watched him join hands to weave in and out among their friends. Her dear friend Hannah was among them, a circlet of white flowers wreathing her head. Leah and her bridegroom had already slipped away to their bridal chamber.

Abigail roused herself. She should be assisting Martha and Mary, who were now bringing platters of roast lamb to tables stretching along the opposite wall. Sounds of laughter caught her attention above the general hubbub. One of the fishermen from the Galilee must have been telling an amusing tale. Though she did not hear the words, she couldn't help but smile again as the man slapped his companion good-naturedly on the back and they roared together.

She sighed and attempted to rise as she saw the women carrying earthen bowls of plump red grapes and ripe olives. She had helped prepare the dipping sauce made from dried chickpeas along with a dish containing fresh spring onions and coriander and mint. Inviting fragrances filled the cooling air.

"Abigail," Martha called over to her. "Come and take your place at the table." Though the voice was direct and curt, Abigail knew the heart. It was love that spoke.

"I should be helping—"

"There are many more hands to do it. I saw you limping earlier. Now sit and eat."

As Peter rose from his seat to bless the food, Abigail moved reluctantly to a place at the women's table. She loved to hear him pray aloud, words addressed to Jehovah but ones of such comfort and insight.

Scarcely had she settled into her seat, however, when someone plucked at her sleeve. Nedra, from Herod's household, was crouching down beside Abigail. This was astonishing, for despite Leah's entreaties, Nedra's superior, Enos, had refused to permit her to attend today's celebration. "Oh, Nedra. Leah will be so happy to hear that Enos relented—"

But Nedra was already shaking her head. Panting so hard her breath puffed against Abigail's face, she leaned close to gasp out, "Enos does not know I have come. They must leave. At once."

Abigail felt the words jostle in her head. "Who do you mean?"

"Leah, Alban. They must go *now*." Nedra's eyes were wide, fearful.

Laughter spilled over them from the table's opposite side. The woman's agitation did not fit into the day. "But Leah and Alban, they're—"

"Now! You must hear me." Nedra's fingers tugged at Abigail's robe. "There is *no time*."

"You don't understand, Nedra. They have gone to the bridal chamber—"

"Herod has already dispatched his guards." Nedra's eyes looked wild.

A voice from Abigail's other side said, "Is something the matter?"

She was relieved to find Martha standing behind her bench. "Nedra tells me there is a danger. But I was trying to explain—"

"And I am telling you, they *must flee*." Nedra was on her feet, her arms waving wildly.

A young man named Stephen was suddenly beside them. Abigail could see the fine lines in his dark complexion as concern creased his forehead. Yet in spite of Nedra's obvious consternation, he exuded the most remarkable sense of calm. "Please . . . Nedra, is it? Please tell us—"

"If Enos realizes I am gone, he will have me killed." Nedra wiped her brow with a shaking hand.

"Then we can't allow that to happen. You must thirst if you've run all this way. Martha, bring her a drink, please. Now then. Tell us what has happened."

Abigail saw the woman's shudder. "Herod is dispatching his guards," she repeated hoarsely.

"For Leah?"

"And Alban. Herod continues to seek vengeance on them both. They are to be brought in and given a hasty trial. And then . . . and then he will put them both to death."

"You are sure?"

"I overheard the plans."

"Is there anyone we can appeal to?"

Martha arrived with the cup, but Nedra only held it.

"No," she said. "Pilate has left for Caesarea. Which is why Herod is acting now." Nedra's breath returned to its frantic spasms. "I must return. Every moment I stay is added danger—"

"Of course you must." Stephen lifted his gaze around the

courtyard. "Jacob," he called. "We need your help. Will you see this lady safely and quickly back to the palace?"

The lad might have been young, but he responded immediately. He must have sensed the danger. "I know the secret passages. Come!" He beckoned as he turned toward the gate.

"Good lad." Stephen nodded and smiled at Nedra. "You were right to come."

"Tell them I am sorry. But they must hurry." Nedra allowed Jacob to grip her hand and pull her away as her last words trailed over her shoulder. "Tell them to make haste. Give them my love. And prayers."

"Our own go with you. Now hurry." Stephen turned to Martha. "We must tell them."

Abigail realized the music had stopped, and the group was watching them. "Could we not hide them?" she asked, her voice sounding choked in her ears.

Martha responded quickly, "Nedra is not given to undue panic. She has risked her life to save her friends."

"If Herod has already ordered his guards out, we must hurry," Stephen added. Not even the emergency could erase his innate calm. "Alban and Leah are in grave danger. There is no place here for them to hide—not from Herod's ire, not in this city. Nedra is right. They must flee."

Abigail found strength she did not know she had. She turned to Martha. "I will go to warn them. Would you collect some food in a sack for them?"

Stephen was already moving away. "I will see if we can manage a horse."

As Abigail rushed frantically up the wooden steps to the chamber that she and Hannah called their own, the one they had decorated and offered to the bridal couple, she heard a woman's soft laughter. She had never heard Leah laugh before. *And now, how quickly the moments of joy must end.* Her eyes filled with tears as she stood at the room's door.

She was about to call to them when the door opened. Alban stood with his arm about Leah's waist. "What is it, Abigail? I heard running footsteps—"

"Herod." The word tasted foul on her lips. "His troops are coming for you. Now. There is no time—"

She halted because Alban was now gripping her arm.

"Steady," he said. "Now tell me again."

"Herod is sending his guards. Nedra slipped out from the palace to warn us. He intends . . ." She could go no further.

Leah whispered, "What are you saying?"

"Pilate has left the city," Alban explained, his tone grim. "Herod sees this as his chance to retaliate for thwarting his plans."

Abigail flung herself against Leah, the tears turning to sobs as she wrapped her arms around her friend. "You must flee. The troops—"

Leah's arms felt warm as they tightened about Abigail's shoulders. "Grab your things—you and Jacob. We must hurry."

"The guards are not after Abigail and Jacob, Leah." The steel in Alban's voice helped steady both women. "It is far too dangerous for them to accompany us. We will move more swiftly, less noticeably, alone."

"But—"

"Leah, if the guards are already hunting, we must go *now*. After we make it to safety, we will send for them."

"Jacob has taken Nedra back to the palace." Abigail wiped her face. "Alban is right. And my leg . . ."

Leah gripped her more tightly still.

Gently Alban eased Leah away. "We must go."

"We will send word as soon as we can," Leah said over her shoulder as she was hurried down the stairway. "I promise."

15

Abigail sank down on a step, face in her hands and tears running through her fingers. "O God, give them speed, protection" was all she was capable of praying.

———

The only animal Stephen could locate on short notice was the donkey they used for transporting firewood from the valley. Abigail could see from Alban's expression that this was not what he had hoped for. Fear of capture showed in the depths of his eyes. Thankfully, Leah was too busy embracing the women to notice. By the time she had climbed onto the donkey's back and looked once more in her beloved's direction, Alban's features had resumed their grim strength. "We must leave."

"Where will you go?" Abigail asked.

"It is best you do not know. If you have no knowledge, you cannot be put in a dangerous position."

Even stoic Martha was fearful. "That donkey will not get you far."

Alban gripped the lead rope and started forward. "We have little choice."

As they reached the plaza's gate, the sound of hooves rang up the narrow passage. Abigail was close enough to see Alban reach to his belt, but his fist gripped empty air. He turned to Leah and said, "Prepare to run."

"I will *never* leave you!"

Alban began to argue, then turned toward the horse and rider racing furiously up the little street. "Linux!" he called as he and Leah wheeled into place in front of him.

The soldier's face was grim. "Herod's men are fast on my heels!" Linux slipped from his horse. "Take my mount, and run like the wind!"

The two officers embraced. Hesitancy quickly turned into a firmness that bespoke military colleagues who had become friends. Then Alban flipped up onto the horse's back and pulled Leah up behind him. Stephen and Martha pushed quickly gathered bundles for the journey into their arms. For one brief instant the pair stared around at the gathered throng, a silent moment too full for words. Then Alban spun the horse about and dug in his heels.

Abigail twisted a corner of her shawl and lifted it to wipe the tears running down her cheeks. Fear nearly compressed her chest, and she wondered when—*if*—she would ever see them again.

She felt eyes observing her and realized that the soldier, Linux, was not watching his friend depart. He was looking at *her*.

A chill ran through Abigail. She had noticed the handsome Roman officer before, as well as his boldness. She tightened the shawl about her face, covering all but her eyes, and turned away to watch the fast-fleeing mount carrying Alban and Leah disappear around the corner.

As the sound of their racing gallop over the cobblestones faded away, Abigail moved her head to see the entire community of believers standing in stunned silence. No longer the wedding music. No longer the laughter and camaraderie, the dancing and feasting. Once more their world had abruptly changed, and they were reminded of who they were, *where* they were. Aliens in their own land. Judeans, certainly, yet viewed as enemies by both their own religious leaders as well as the Roman conquerors.

Out of the silence came a confident voice. Though little more than a whisper, it resonated through the silent courtyard, a prayer that came from the heart and soul of the former fisherman of the Galilee. "Go with God," breathed Peter.

"Go with God" echoed throughout the group, as though the entire gathering took a fresh breath. Yes. After all, God was with

17

the two now escaping for their lives, as he was with those left to face the hunters.

———

Abigail was still reeling from the dramatic events of the last moments when a panting Jacob tugged at her shawl. He could scarcely voice his question. "Are they hidden?"

Abigail clutched his shoulders with both hands. "Did Nedra—?"

"We made it," he puffed. "I don't think Enos knew she'd ever left."

"Thank God," breathed Abigail.

"Where's Alban?"

"Gone. They—"

"Gone? What do you mean? Where?"

"They've left. We can only pray that their escape will be successful."

"But . . . but how could he leave without me? I was to go. He promised he'd never leave me."

Abigail looked at her brother's stricken face and realized what he was trying to say. "He couldn't wait, Jacob. Alban and Leah were in danger. You know that."

Even as she spoke, they heard the sound of horses' hooves— many of them—clattering upon the paving stones coming up to the courtyard. The hunters had arrived.

"Quick!" Abigail pushed at Jacob. "We must hide before they enter." When he resisted she pulled him forward. "Run, Jacob!"

He half turned to look at her. "Run where?"

"Behind the wash tubs. Out back. There's an alley that leads to the back streets."

They hurried across the courtyard just as prancing mounts

snorted and stomped their way into the enclosure. Leah heard the crude shouts of soldiers, the clanging of steel blades. She pressed Jacob into the shadows behind her, afraid that any movement would get unwanted attention.

"The man Alban. Where is he?" came an angry shout from the obvious leader of the soldiers.

"He is not here." It was Peter's voice that met the demand.

"We were informed he is in this compound. You deny this?" The voice was harsh.

"I do not deny that he *was* here. It is his wedding day. We celebrated the claiming of his bride, and—"

"I am not interested in your celebrations. Where has he gone?"

"He did not say."

The soldier released a volley of curses. "We'll see if you know how to tell the truth. Men, dismount. Search every corner of this foul place from top to bottom. If this uncouth man here is lying, he'll soon mount a cross. Along with the rest of his followers."

Abigail pulled in a deep breath and pressed more firmly against Jacob. Amid the noise and confusion in the courtyard, they would not likely be noticed. "This way," she hissed over her shoulder. As they ducked into a passageway toward the back of the compound, she prayed. *Please, Father God, help us . . . help us all. Lord Jesus, direct our steps. Holy Spirit, be with us. . . .*

Jacob, who knew the warren of back streets and alleyways of Jerusalem like his own hand, soon took the lead in their headlong rush to safety.

———

Later that evening, in the back of a shed attached to the shop of a fishmonger who belonged to the followers' community, Jacob again plied Abigail with questions. Where were Alban and Leah headed? What were their plans? How soon would they send for him?

Over and over her answers were the same. "I do not know."

His patience quickly came to an end. "Then what are we to do?"

"Wait," responded Abigail.

"Wait!" Jacob attempted to scoff but was near tears. "It was not to be this way. I need Alban now. I did not even get to say farewell. To receive instructions of what I am to do. How can you say wait? For what? For whom? What if they don't make it? How will we know?" His words tumbled over each other, a litany of his frustration and grief.

"If they do not make it, Herod will be boasting of it from here to Rome," Abigail finally said, trying to rein in her impatience. "Even if they do make it, he might claim they did not just to save face. There is nothing that we *can* do, Jacob, but wait. They will send word when they can. They will send for us when the time is right."

But Jacob failed to be convinced. Abigail could feel him withdraw from her in the blackness of the night. It hurt deeply. Had she found Jacob, merely hours ago, only to lose him in his sorrow over Alban? She prayed not. But for the moment her heart felt even colder than the night's chilly arms encircling them.

CHAPTER

Two

Caesarea
Twenty-five months later . . .

THE SIGHT THAT GREETED LINUX as he stepped once more upon Judean soil was of children playing. Two youngsters raced along the top of the stone harbor wall. Linux was instantly transported back to his brother's villa. The two girls Linux had left behind in Umbria were both blond, and these scampering children were dark haired. Yet both pairs shared an impish laughter and an ability to find joy in chasing a butterfly or a dog through dust and sunlight. Linux had dreamed of his twin nieces almost every night since leaving Umbria, his country of birth, for Rome, and from there to Judea. Another committed bachelor might have considered it a recurring nightmare. But after what Linux had discovered while in Rome, he felt the dreams contained his one tiny shred of hope.

"Linux! You are indeed a sight for sore eyes!" The harbor master was a former ship's captain from Tyre. Horus liked to claim he had skippered a Phoenician pirate vessel, but Linux knew he had served Rome long and well, both on sea and land. Some years back, a ship's timber had pinned Horus to the deck during a storm. As he walked toward Linux with hand outstretched, the harbor master's gait rocked like a ship in heavy seas. "What news of Rome?"

"The women are as lovely as ever." Linux dredged up the sardonic grin the harbor master would have expected. "And much lonelier, now that I have departed."

"And the husbands breathe much easier, I warrant." Horus slapped Linux on the back and steered him toward the stone hut from which he supervised the comings and goings of all vessels in the harbor. "You and I will share a glass."

"My belongings . . ."

Horus pointed to his assistant. "You. See to them. Come, Linux. I must hear of all the wailing ladies."

But once inside the hut's shadows, the harbor master's humor vanished like the mist on the Mediterranean at dawn. "Wine?"

"Tea. I have much to do before sundown."

"I can imagine." Horus stuck his head out the cabin's door and bellowed, "Where is that scurvy dog!"

"Here, master!"

"Tea! Good food!"

"Just tea," Linux corrected.

The harbor master looked at him askance. "You have been at sea for weeks, my man!"

"Almost two months," Linux agreed. "Two weeks since our last landfall."

"We received fresh bread from the baker not two hours ago—"

"Just tea. With my thanks." Linux ignored his growling belly.

Horus gave his servant the order and slouched into his chair. Linux noted the table beneath the window piled high with charts and scrolls. The man's badge of office, the emperor's seal, held down an unfurled manifest, no doubt awaiting his calculation of the duties to be paid.

Horus asked again, more subdued this time, "What news of Rome?"

"Are you sure you want to hear, old friend?"

"Everyone in Caesarea is feasting on rumors, all of them dreadful. The truth can hardly be worse."

"I would not wager on that."

"So it is true. Sejanus is in trouble."

Linux sighed and stared out the window. Since Emperor Tiberius had retired to his palace on the island of Capri, Rome had been ruled by his deputy, Sejanus, whose only official title was head of the Praetorian Guard. Tiberius remained officially the ruler of the empire. But the emperor was increasingly interested only in his own pleasures. What was most troubling to Linux was that many of Rome's powerful and wealthy citizens were following Tiberius's example, letting whatever gratification caught their fancy sweep them away into increasing debauchery.

"Sejanus battles constantly with the Senate," Linux finally said. "And he is losing."

The harbor master scowled. "This does not bode well for the likes of you and me."

The servant appeared in the doorway. "Tea, master."

Linux accepted his mug with a nod of thanks and said, "Let us walk."

"The sun is blistering," Horus protested.

"To remain hidden away is a danger for us both," he murmured.

Horus followed him out into the afternoon light. "You are so fearful of spies?"

"I do not yet know for certain what we face," Linux said, his voice still low. "I can only tell you what I found upon my arrival in Rome."

"Then tell me."

Horus was an old friend and one of Linux's most trusted allies in Caesarea. Linux also knew that whatever he told Horus would make its cautionary way through the garrison's ranks. News traveled fast in a provincial capital. And the information thus carried provided the only hope of survival.

Fourteen months earlier, Linux had returned home to northern Italy. His brother's first wife had died, and Castor was remarrying. Linux had received an official summons, his older brother using the opportunity to test Linux's loyalty. Linux's visit home had not gone well, he freely admitted to the harbor master. The only part of that experience Linux failed to share was how he spent much of the time playing with his nieces, his brother's daughters from the first marriage. The little ones missed their mother terribly, and now with their father giving his attentions to his new young bride, the girls felt totally adrift.

While in Umbria, Linux heard of events further south in the capital. The old emperor, Tiberius, seemed incapable of focusing on anything other than his pleasure gardens on Capri. His deputy Sejanus repeatedly came into conflict with the Roman Senate. In defiance of Sejanus and Tiberius, the Senate ordered Pontius Pilate's return from Judea in disgrace. In his stead, the Senate had appointed a trusted ally as replacement consul to Judea, a man named Marcellus.

Fortunately Linux had not been caught up in the unfolding political turmoil. Nor had he been included when the orders arrived, commanding Pilate to present himself before the Senate. Since Pilate could be banished, or even executed, along with his entire cadre of senior officers, Linux's exclusion from the whole sorry scenario was a very good thing indeed.

But what Linux had found awaiting him in Rome so disturbed him that even now, nearly five hundred leagues away, his gut still clenched in the telling.

Horus stared silently out over the crowded Caesarea port, though Linux doubted his old friend actually saw very much at all. Finally the man muttered, "How is a simple officer of the sea to survive all this?"

Linux repeated what an ally in Rome had told him. "Be extremely careful in everything you say, everything you do—maybe even everything you think."

"When does the new prelate arrive?" Horus leaned on the stone wall circling the harbor.

"He was to leave the week following my departure. I was ordered ahead to . . ." Linux waved that aside. It would not be appropriate to further discuss imperial business with the harbor master. He said instead, "We were struck by two storms. There is no telling when his vessel will dock. Or at which port."

The two youngsters chose that moment to come racing up. The stone wall placed the boys' smiling faces at eye level with the two men. "Uncle, come play with us."

"Can't you see I'm busy here?" But Horus's growl contained a genuine fondness. When the two ran away, laughing, Horus muttered, "Young scamps," though his pride was apparent.

"You're their uncle?"

"In a manner of speaking. Their father was a mate of mine. His ship went out three winters back and never returned. I have been adopted by them. As have half the men who work under me. They are delightful one moment and rascals the next."

Linux leaned forward so as to watch as they raced to where an old sailor repaired a fishing net. The shorter of the two boys took up one of the arrow-shaped shuttles. The ancient mariner fitted his large hand around the smaller one and helped him weave the rough twine as the other child watched silently. On some unseen cue, the two boys started singing about fishing on a summer's dawn and the ladies who waited back home, clearly a song taught to them by seafaring men around the harbor. The sailor leaned back and laughed out loud, the sound rusty with disuse.

Linux suddenly asked, "Have you ever thought of marrying, Horus?"

Horus turned from the wall toward the stone hut. "Women and the sea are like oil and water. They do not mix."

Linux fell into step beside him. "I have heard the same of soldiers and wives."

Horus's eyes grew wide in obvious alarm. "Don't tell me your heart has been stolen by a lass back in Rome."

"In Umbria," Linux confessed. "Two of them. My brother's daughters. They laugh like those two there."

"Can they cause the same mountain of mischief when they have a mind?"

"No doubt." Linux looked back at the boys, his heart twisted by the memory of his last day with his brother's twins. He had entered their room to find the girls arguing over a tiny carved wooden doll. He had gently teased them into reconciliation, bringing laughter to their eyes. It did not last long. They had wept inconsolably when Linux had told them he was leaving for Rome.

Linux kicked at a small stone with his scuffed sandal, shrugging to hide his deep emotion, and dared to murmur to the sun and the hot summer wind, "I do miss them."

———

Two days later, Linux left Caesarea for Jerusalem in the company of a mounted troop. He had not planned to travel so. But orders had been issued from Bruno Aetius, tribune of the Jerusalem garrison. Without a governor in place, the tribune commanded all Roman troops in Judea, and Bruno Aetius's order was that all Roman soldiers taking to Judea's roads must travel in strength. So Linux attached himself to a troop assigned guard detail and set forth.

He was not sorry to see the back of Caesarea, which was very odd, for it was the only truly Roman city in the entire province. And Linux held no love for Jerusalem, none whatever. But perhaps at the moment Jerusalem was preferable. Caesarea, the Roman capital of Judea, was at present a boiling pot. Rumors swirled, and the people fretted. *And the news from Rome* . . . Linux shook his head.

Their first night on the road, they camped in the very same ruined village where Linux two years past had escaped a late-season rain in the company of a stranger who became a friend.

Around the fire that night, Linux asked the troop's commander, "Did you know the centurion Alban?"

"Knew of him." The officer was a hard-bitten man of middle years named Cyrus, suggesting someone from a far-flung province still holding to the Greek ways. "He was a friend of yours?"

"Perhaps the best it has ever been my good fortune to know."

Cyrus took no ease by the fire. He did not sit in the camp chair so much as crouch at its edge. His eyes constantly surveyed the perimeter, out where light from the soldiers' three fires was swallowed by the night. "Is it true what they say, the centurion went native?"

"He married a Judean. He gave up his commission. That much is true."

"I meant no offense, sir."

"None taken. And on the road, I am Linux." He studied the officer across the fire from him. Linux would have expected a more relaxed demeanor at a campfire after a decent enough meal, especially with a double guard posted. "Do you expect trouble?"

"On these roads, always. Much has changed while you've been away."

"I thought it bad enough before I left."

"Bad then—now worse."

Linux nodded.

"I'm not talking about changes at the top," Cyrus said. "Governors come, they rule for a time, and they go. My concern remains with the men under my command."

"My friend Alban might have voiced the very same words." When the other officer continued to study the night, Linux went on, "Pilate had planned to banish the centurion for failing him in a duty. Though in truth Alban failed no one. He merely reported news that Pilate did not wish to hear. But before he was to depart for his new posting, Alban—"

Linux stopped when Cyrus leapt to his feet. Linux rose and gripped his sword, listening intently, but he heard nothing. The night was utterly still, without a breath of wind. Their fire crackled, sending cinders flying up to join the stars overhead. "What is it?"

"Perhaps nothing." Cyrus replaced the sword Linux had not even seen him draw and gradually lowered himself to his seat. "What was the news your friend brought back to the prelate?"

"That the Judean prophet known as Jesus of Nazareth, the one who was crucified, was . . . alive."

The officer focused fully upon Linux. "I have heard this rumor. His followers are growing like a wildfire."

"Alban is one of them."

A high-pitched shriek pierced the darkness, and a soldier just on the edge of the nearest campfire collapsed into the dust. Cyrus leapt forward, hollering, "To arms!"

The night was suddenly filled with a whirring sound. Linux rolled and came up beneath his shield as arrows rained down upon the campground. Two hammered into the wood of his shield. Linux crouched more tightly, drawing his head down to where it almost rested on his knees. Around him, he saw that even the legionnaires who had been fast asleep now hunkered behind their shields. Clearly these men had been attacked before.

Once again arrows hammered against his shield, one thumping down within inches of his shin. Another soldier shouted in pain. Cyrus shouted, "They're hidden in the rocks to the west! Attack!"

Linux roared with the others. He unsheathed his sword and raced for the rocks.

He leapt upon the stone to the left of Cyrus. But all they found was empty sand turned silver in the starlight.

"Squads of three! Spread out! Search every defile!"

But Cyrus sheathed his sword and motioned for Linux to follow him back into the camp. As Linux helped him tend to the pair of wounded men, he asked, "Should I search with your scouts?"

"My men won't find anything, but I gave the order to be safe. These attacks never vary. They come with the night, they strike in stealth, they slip away and vanish." Cyrus patted one of the soldiers. "These are just flesh wounds. We'll bathe and bind them. You'll both ride tomorrow. The surgeons will leave you with some scars for the ladies to admire."

Cyrus lifted his head and called his men back. They returned facing outward, a tactic so ingrained their officer needed to give them no instructions. Linux knew none would sleep again that night.

"Who were the marauders?" Linux wondered.

"We know nothing for certain."

"What, you have not captured any?"

"Not in eight months of such attacks."

Linux recalled the troubles with bandits he and Alban had faced. "Parthians?"

"Not this far west. Though we hear they have grown bolder

on the Damascus Road. No, this is trouble that has grown up here in Judea."

"Do they have a name?"

Cyrus swept the night with his gaze. "They call themselves Zealots."

CHAPTER

THREE

EZRA ALWAYS FELT A VAGUE SENSE OF ENVY when visiting Gamaliel in Jerusalem's Temple Quarter. A broad avenue ran from the Temple to the citadel, from one center of Judean power to the other. Most priests who served on the Sanhedrin, the Temple Council, lived along this road. But it was not Gamaliel's position among the Temple priesthood and the larger Judean community that sparked Ezra's jealousy. It was something else.

"Welcome, old friend. Welcome." Gamaliel, elder Pharisee and long-time mentor to Ezra, received his childhood friend in the main room overlooking the courtyard. A central fountain cast rainbows that were being scattered by the afternoon wind. "How was Alexandria?" Gamaliel waved Ezra toward chairs adjoining a small carved table.

Ezra sighed and nodded as he seated himself. "Filled with chaos and confusion, like the rest of the empire." He was a senior merchant, whose trading empire had stretched out from Jerusalem as far as Damascus on the east and Rome to the west. He nodded his thanks as a servant washed his hands and feet in the traditional manner. He accepted a silver goblet and tasted the fruit-flavored water. The priest certainly lived well, Ezra noted as he gazed around the large room. "What is new in Jerusalem?"

"So much has happened. . . ." Gamaliel's voice faded at the sound of footsteps hurrying down the side passage. Both men turned toward the arched opening.

"Ezra!" The woman moved quickly across the room, almost tripping in her haste and joy. "How dare you stay away so long!"

"There were difficulties, Miriam. I do apologize."

"Your son and daughter are well?" She sat down on a wooden bench situated near the chairs.

"They seemed to thrive upon the journey, unlike their weary father."

"They are young. They are free of tutors and boundaries, off on an adventure with their beloved father. How could they not enjoy such a trip? Our own son wailed inconsolably when he learned you had taken the children."

"Next time he may come as well."

She waved her finger. "If you even dare mention such a thing, I will give you—"

"Shah, Miriam," her husband chided, though he smiled. "Shame."

Ezra listened to the woman discuss her and Gamaliel's children, then join in with her husband to describe the changes in Jerusalem—the dismissal of Pilate and the awaited arrival of the new governor, Marcellus. Then there were the rumors that the tribune of the Judean garrison, Bruno Aetius, was to be sent back to Damascus. Some of the news Ezra had heard in Alexandria. Other items were new. He tried hard to pay attention, for these were two well-connected, intelligent and trusted friends. But his envy formed a cloud of pain and remorse in his mind and heart, such that it was difficult to follow the conversation at all.

Miriam and Ezra's late wife had been best friends. Miriam and Gamaliel's two children were almost the exact same age as his own, four and six. Yet their home was complete and full of the constancy of love. While his own had been torn to shreds.

Two years earlier, his beloved young wife had slipped on a wet tile floor and fallen. It had seemed like nothing—a bruise on her elbow, another above her temple. A bit of pain, but not so much as to cause alarm. That night, however, she had said she had a headache, felt a bit dizzy.

By morning, she was gone.

Ezra's inner agony had lessened over time. He had found some healing for the deep sorrow as he turned to the needs of his two small children. But his heart still ached for all that he had lost. And he felt it nowhere as keenly as here. In the peaceful home of his oldest friend.

The children were brought in, their excited questions answered, and his heart felt the loss more keenly still. Finally Miriam left with them and the maids, and Gamaliel ordered the other servants to leave and shut the doors. The room was enclosed in shadows as thick as the priest's sudden scowl. "There is trouble."

"The Zealots?" Ezra asked.

"No. Well, yes. Them too."

"I have heard their attacks have grown impossibly daring."

"The attacks—yes, they are a scourge. But what is worse is their popularity among the common folk."

"I heard songs about them around the caravanserai campfires," Ezra recalled. "One was very appealing, in a simple fashion. Something about a new Judean David fighting the Roman Goliath. My son has taken to singing it as he plays."

"The people are oppressed, and they seek heroes," Gamaliel said. "It is a natural enough reaction."

This was one of the man's most remarkable traits. Ezra knew that most men, as they rose to positions of genuine power, became increasingly rigid in their opinions. Their ability to question themselves or see another's point of view became lost. Gamaliel, however, was a mediator. He calmed the waters by truly seeking to understand what motivated another. It was a gift, this skill of listening and studying and respecting someone else's perspective.

Ezra, however, held no such illusions. "They are a threat to us and our position within the community. The Zealots will destroy everything we hold dear. The Romans will win in the end, and they will crush us along with the Zealots."

"Are you suggesting we help the Romans?" Gamaliel's voice was low, but his meaning clear.

"I am tempted. But I, for one, cannot condone that step."

"Quite. Judeans aiding Romans to kill Judeans. It is an appalling prospect."

"The Sanhedrin have done it before." Ezra's eyebrows arched pointedly.

Gamaliel was silent.

"I am speaking of the crucified prophet, the one they call Jesus of Nazareth."

"I know of whom you speak." Gamaliel rose and crossed to the window. "They have adopted a new name."

"Who?"

"The dead prophet's disciples. They call themselves followers of the Way."

The window's heavy drapes cast his friend's features in soft desert pastels. But Ezra could see he was very worried indeed. "What difference does it make to us, the name a handful of Galilean rabble take for themselves?"

"They are no longer a handful, and they are not just from Galilee. Some put their numbers at three thousand, others at five—or more."

"Impossible!" Ezra rose to his feet.

"Perhaps. But I trust my source." He named a senior priest at the Freedmen's Synagogue, a gathering place for many freed slaves, especially Judeans from outlying regions of the empire where Greek was still the predominant language. "He says they are spreading like wildfire, most especially among the Jerusalem poor."

"Just like the Essenes," Ezra murmured, sitting once again.

"Yes and no. The Essene movement has certainly gathered momentum over the past ten years. It is said there are somewhere around fifty communities spread throughout Judea. Some number a few dozen members, others as many as a thousand. One of the largest lies east of the Mount of Olives, another on the Dead Sea's western shore. Some are celibate and restricted to men, others populated by entire clans. They are united in their loathing of the Sanhedrin and the Temple priesthood, which they consider corrupt. But they've been a peaceful lot, electing to remove themselves entirely from the general population, waiting for the Messiah to come and rescue their nation. But in the current political and religious upheaval—"

"I don't understand," Ezra cut in. "You think even the Essenes might now preach violence?"

"No. At least not yet. They claim many astonishing things," Gamaliel replied, still facing the window. "But violence is not among them."

"Have these—these new disciples of the dead prophet joined with the Zealots?"

"No. They too speak of peace." The priest gave a shudder. "If they changed . . . What an appalling thought."

"I still don't—"

"No, nor I." Gamaliel strode back over to his chair. "All I can tell you for certain is that these followers of Jesus are growing faster than any sect we have ever faced. And the stories I hear grow with them. They still claim the prophet Jesus rose from the dead, walked among them, and then went up into the heavens. They claim he is the true Messiah. They claim . . ."

"Yes?"

"Miracles," Gamaliel said. "Signs and wonders. Things which enflame the passions of everyone within reach. Either the listeners join, or they become enemies. Talk of them is everywhere. If anything sways them—diverts them—I fear a storm of such force that everything might soon be swept up. And away . . ."

Ezra shifted uncomfortably in his seat. "Were this anyone else speaking, I would cast it aside as nonsense."

"But it is I who talk with you, old friend, and this is not nonsense. How long were you gone, four months?"

"Almost five."

"So in five months the followers have grown into a force that must be reckoned with."

"I would think the Sanhedrin would be very disturbed by all this. What does it propose to do?"

"The Sanhedrin members are pulling their beards, looking down at the floor. They thought with the prophet dead, the rabble would soon disperse. They are only beginning to accept that this is something new. And many more are coming to believe that this dead prophet is in fact the long-awaited Messiah. It is growing into a powerful force within the community. One that must be confronted."

Ezra caught the new tone. "You have an idea, do you not?"

"Think of it. They have no allies in the power structure. I want you to go speak with their leaders."

Ezra couldn't believe what he was hearing. "You cannot be serious. I'm just a merchant—"

"Precisely. They have nothing to fear from you." Gamaliel picked up a parchment from the table. "Here are the names of their leaders we have managed to identify. Apostles, they are called. The street names are where local followers have opened their homes to the group. Some have given land which has now been set aside for their encampments outside the city gates. Go and meet with them. They are clearly poor. Build for us an ally. Offer them Temple gold if need be. See if they can be trusted. Find out their intentions. And report back to me, old friend, and no one else."

———

Ezra was a man of many talents. Son of a merchant from Tyre, he had traveled to Jerusalem at age twelve to study with a Pharisee scholar. Some said this man had been the finest living teacher of Torah anywhere in the world. At the time of Ezra's arrival, Gamaliel had been studying with the same teacher for almost two years. Gamaliel took young Ezra under his wing and helped him adjust to the alien worlds of the Temple, the city of Jerusalem, and applied study. Ezra soon became aware that the Jerusalem scholars were already speaking of Gamaliel in awe, for the young man's mind absorbed verses and commentaries like a sea sponge. Gamaliel could either read or hear a text one time, then recite it back perfectly. They were already calling him a *tzaddick*, a man apart, one set aside by God for special purposes.

Ezra had never possessed a scholar's mind such as Gamaliel's. Nor did he much care. The eldest son, he had come for this time of study because it was a family tradition. His father had done so, as had his father's father, and on back through the seven generations since the Maccabees had redeemed the Temple and the scholars had returned to Jerusalem. Before sending Ezra south, his father had set two tasks before him. Of course he was to study the Talmud, and obey his teacher, and bring honor to the family name. But there was something more besides. Ezra was also to establish allies within the Temple hierarchy and the city of Jerusalem. His father assured him that such friendships, forged early and strong, would bear great fruit, even beyond financial ones, in the years to come.

Ezra had eventually expanded the family empire. He had sent his younger brothers to establish new centers in Cyprus and Tarsus and Damascus. His sisters had wed, and through these marriages Ezra had forged further powerful alliances. He had recently renewed contact with far-flung relatives, extending the family's trading reach as far as Spanish Gaul to the west, and now to Alexandria to the south.

His father had been correct, of course. The friendship with Gamaliel had borne great fruit. Ezra for some years had been the priest's largest benefactor. As Gamaliel had risen through the ranks to finally become one of the Sanhedrin, Ezra's power had risen with his. But there was more. Ezra possessed far-flung alliances forged in secrecy and maintained through utmost discretion.

These were perilous times. The Roman empire was in foment, especially here in the east. The Zealots were growing in power, their reach extending much farther and faster than even Gamaliel realized, for the priest had not left Jerusalem for years. In the provinces, talk of the Zealots was everywhere. More and more young men, infuriated by the foot of Rome upon their necks, were dropping their shepherd's crooks and their tools and leather aprons to slip away from farms and shops and forges, taking up the swords and the cause of the Zealots. Their families said *kaddish* for them, the prayer of the dead, because it was an accepted fact that they would never hear from their loved ones again. Once a man entered the

Zealots, his only possibility for opting out was through death—in battle or by a Zealot's sword as a traitor.

Several young servants and workers of Ezra had already followed the call of adventure and glory and duty. Early on, he had realized that trying to stop them was futile. So he had let it be known that he wished contact with the leaders. Not to negotiate. Simply to offer assistance. He became one of the first merchants to grant the Zealots a tribute. As a result, his caravans were never touched, and he was often the first to receive news of any development. As with his other astute business decisions, he profited greatly.

Now with this new group, these followers of the dead prophet Jesus, Ezra's plans were simple. If they were growing as fast as Gamaliel suggested, he needed to forge another alliance. Yes, of course, he would assist Gamaliel with news and such. But what harm was there in some gain for himself? He was, after all, the son and grandson and great-grandson of successful merchants.

So he tucked away the names that Gamaliel had offered him, and did as he had done so often in the past. He let it be known through his employees and his allies that he sought an audience with the leaders of this group. He assured them that he was curious. Nothing more. He sought to gain, to learn, to give assistance. He came in peace.

What was the harm in that?

CHAPTER

Four

THE DAY WAS ALREADY TOO HOT, even though the glow from the sun was barely visible above its eastern bed. Abigail brushed at the persistent fly disturbing her sleep, hoping to sink back into the blissful comfort of slumber. She fanned the air above her, both to get some movement into the stillness and to scare away the pest.

Her simple motion served to pull her further into the morning and into the responsibilities and challenges facing her. She stirred. What would this day hold? Simply another round of toil? Further revelations about their Messiah to one or another of the group leaders? Longed-for news from Alban and Leah? Threats from those who did not accept the truth? Or maybe even Messiah's return?

Abigail rolled from her pallet, now totally awake. After Leah and Alban's harrowing escape over two years previous, she and Jacob had returned from their overnight hideout to her quarters among the followers. Later they had moved to the small lean-to at the back of the fishmonger's shop, and Jacob had settled into his Hebrew studies with varying degrees of cooperation, depending on the opportunities for adventure that day, while she continued her duties among the women.

She heard no movement from the tiny loft above the room they called home. Jacob was either still asleep or had already left without her. They met each morning with a group of the followers for a time of thanksgiving and supplication, a practice maintained by members of their group throughout Jerusalem.

Abigail rolled up her pallet and pushed it to the side of the small room. "Jacob, I fear we are late. Didn't the rooster crow?" she called.

She had always depended on their neighbor's fowl to rouse her from her bed. "Jacob!"

The muffled reply drifting down from above brought an unconscious sigh. Jacob had truly accepted neither the reality nor the reasons for Alban's sudden departure without him. Though Jacob did not speak of it, she could feel his sorrow, his discontent. She knew Alban's leaving had left an enormous hole in her brother's life. She also knew he did not enjoy his work assignment among the carpenters since his bar mitzvah. She had observed him sitting at the end of the day, saying nothing, just staring at his roughened and blistered hands. Abigail was sure she could read his expression. *These are not made to be handling rough wood, gathering splinters, forming callouses. No, they were made to clutch a sword. To signal an order to those under my command. If only Alban . . .* Some days Abigail felt she was losing her brother, one day at a time. He was becoming more silent, more withdrawn, and there seemed to be nothing she could do or say to bring him back.

As many times before, she whispered a prayer as she prepared herself for the day. "Dear Father, may this be the day we hear from Alban. And keep Jacob . . ."

She heard shuffling steps as Jacob slowly descended the ladder from the small loft over her head. His hair was tousled, his jaw set in a grim line. He said nothing. Not even a morning greeting.

"Did you sleep well?" she asked cheerily.

He merely nodded.

"We must hurry. I overslept. I didn't hear the rooster—"

"Maybe we've been blessed and it died."

Abigail cast a quick glance his way. His expression had not changed.

They soon left together, Jacob lingering a step behind. Already the streets were crowded, though the merchants and stall owners were not yet displaying their wares for barter or sale. In the half light, no Roman soldiers paraded prancing horses over the cobblestones. A slight wind shook the leaves of the palm branches overhead, offering a breath of refreshing air that Abigail knew would soon become stifling with the day's heat.

"I wonder who will lead prayers this morning," she mused aloud, hoping to engage her brother. "I believe Peter and John are both away."

"Where are they this time?" grumbled Jacob.

Abigail turned toward him, new sorrow and regret filling her heart. A desire to protect this beloved brother welled within her. He was still young in her estimation—not yet fifteen, and already doing a man's work, though this certainly fit with their traditions. Day in and day out he carried and sawed and shaped and planed heavy pieces of olive or cedar or pine. From dawn till dusk, he toiled at work that brought him no personal reward. Abigail knew there were men who loved the feel of the wood as they ran their calloused hands over the intricate grain. They understood just what it was as God had formed it, envisioned what it could become under skillful shaping and building. And also what it had been in the Carpenter's hands. Not Jacob. To him it was merely a task. Tedious and unrelenting.

She replied, "Visiting some of the brethren, I've heard."

He merely shrugged.

The walk to their meeting place was enough to cause her leg to throb with pain once more. She tried not to limp as Jacob's stride brought him abreast and then steps ahead of her. Her accidental burn from the scalding wash water had healed over, but the skin across the wound remained tight and sensitive to any stress or bump or bruise. And her days were often filled with such incidents. As she hoisted heavy clay jars or worked with other women in the close quarters of the kitchen, she often moved or stretched in a way that bumped against objects, causing a bruise or small tear in the scar. Normally she said nothing, simply waiting for the new injury to heal itself. She had never been one for complaining. In fact, she would much rather sing, even on the worst days. But there were times when she could not hide her limp or conceal the discomfort that no doubt showed on her face.

Jacob looked back at her, then slowed his pace.

The simple act brought tears to Abigail's eyes. In spite of his moodiness, he still sought to assist her. To protect her. He always seemed to sense when her injury was causing her pain.

They caught up to fellow worshipers heading to the courtyard. With brief greetings they joined step, their voices hushed as they moved forward. It would not do to draw attention to the growing numbers that gathered each day.

A familiar shiver of excitement ran through Abigail. *Will this be the day?*

When first the Lord had departed with the promise of his return, they had begun every day with that question on their hearts and lips. Later they greeted one another with the unspoken question in their eyes. Gradually they steeled themselves to accept that the Messiah might have other plans or there might be some unknown reason why he was delayed. Certainly their numbers were expanding daily. They had been charged with spreading the Word, to bring in others, to be his witnesses there in Jerusalem, in Samaria, and throughout the world. Was that not sufficient reason for him to prolong his coming?

Gradually the group endeavored to put aside their yearning for his swift return and to reach out to those who still needed the truth of his first arrival among them. But Abigail, in spite of her longing to be a good follower, often found herself hoping that this would be the day. Doubts and fears and threats—and pain—could all be left behind when their Messiah was once again among them in person. She had felt his healing touch once already, lifting the deep sorrow in her mind and heart. And maybe this time her leg . . .

She glanced again at Jacob. She was sure that when the Lord returned, Jacob's unhappiness would once again be turned into the joyful exuberance she loved. She would gladly suffer the rest of her life if that could be so.

———

Abigail was busy scrubbing cooking pots with sand and rinsing them for the next meal when Martha hurried into the kitchen, back straight, lips firmly pressed together. Abigail sensed immediately that all was not right but held her tongue.

The older woman stopped, took a deep breath, and brushed her arm over her forehead, sweeping back a few strands of delinquent hair. She looked flushed and weary with the day's work and the afternoon heat. *Body and soul weary*, Abigail thought, but she did not speak. She straightened from her task and reached for a towel. Her eyes sought Martha's for an answer.

It did not come quickly. It was as though Martha was carefully sorting through her words.

"If only I were a younger woman," she murmured at last.

"Why don't you sit," Abigail invited. "I still have fresh water here from the well."

Martha sat down, her back remaining straight, chin lifted in a stubborn set.

Abigail went to dip a cup of the cool water. Martha accepted it without comment and drank long and deeply. She passed back the empty cup, seeming somewhat restored.

Abigail quietly took a place on the bench beside the woman. Martha would talk when she was ready.

But after several moments, Martha still had not said a word. Abigail decided she had waited long enough.

"You would wish to be a younger woman, you said. Why is that?"

Martha shook her head and lifted her shawl to wipe her face.

"Could it be a young man has caught your fancy?" Abigail added with a smile.

Even the stoic Martha, after a shocked glance at Abigail, could not suppress a laugh.

"A man," she mused, dabbing again at her warm brow and damp hair. "And a young one, you say. Now, whatever would I want with one of those?"

Abigail shrugged. "You would need to explain it to me."

"Such foolishness," Martha said with a shake of her head, but there was no edge to her tone and her chin had lowered. She fanned at her face with the edge of her shawl.

"So—?" prompted Abigail.

Martha shook her head and sighed. "How are we ever to keep up with the work load? There are more and more people coming every day. Peter rejoices with every new face. As I do. But *Peter* does not feed them. He does not spend every waking moment bending over hot stew pots or scrubbing dirty dishes. No, not Peter. He just calls them to come on in." Martha waved a hand as though welcoming whoever might be at the door.

Abigail said nothing. She indeed knew that dear Martha was as eager as anyone to see new members joining the community of followers. But the older woman was obviously weary, overwhelmed with all that must be done. And she needed to express her feelings without criticism.

"Do we again have additional—?"

"A good two dozen of them. All tired and hungry, I expect. Peter has just ordered them fed and bedded. Do you see any more food in the pots? Any empty spaces where we can spread out mats?" Martha's arms swung through the air with her rhetorical questions.

Abigail stirred. "I think we may have some bread and goat cheese left. There are a few grapes. Will it feed so many? God has blessed loaves before—"

"Of course. And I have not forgotten it." Martha stopped fanning and lifted her shoulders. "I'm just a tired old woman, speaking without guarding my tongue. I should be ashamed."

"You have been on your feet all day in this dreadful heat, serving countless souls. You have no necessity for shame. You—"

"If I were a younger woman . . ." But this time she smiled at the thought.

"If you were a younger woman you would not have the wisdom and fortitude and skills that it takes to do the job. Now, Martha, you sit here and rest a spell. I will call some of the younger ones, and we will see that the newcomers are fed. Then somehow, miraculously perhaps, we will also find a spot for them to roll out their mats." Abigail hoped to coax another smile from the woman.

Martha began to rise from her seat, but Abigail put out a hand to press the woman back in place. "You must rest. If you don't, we will no longer have your wise counsel. Then what will we do? We need you. You keep us all going in the right direction, Martha, in an organized fashion. You guide us in our doing and in our praying. We can't do it all without you."

Tears came to the older woman's eyes. She reached out and took Abigail's hand. "I don't know what I would ever do without you, Abigail. Even with your painful leg—oh, don't look surprised, I see you wince when you think no one is looking—you still manage to do the work of two people."

Abigail *had* been surprised. She'd thought she was hiding her injury. But she should not have thought to fool Martha. The woman had sharp eyes and a tender heart.

"You sit," Abigail said gently. "I will see to what needs to be done. I have watched you, and I will do the same."

Martha nodded, her eyes still glistening.

———

Abigail was astonished to be summoned the next morning by the followers' council. When she arrived, there sat Martha, eyes fixed firmly on the leaders. Abigail entered quietly and nodded her greeting before taking a seat beside the older woman.

"It has come to our attention," began Peter, gazing at the two, "that the work is becoming overwhelming. With the daily increase in our numbers, we need to organize better in order not to overlook anyone or overtax our workers."

Heads nodded approval.

"It seems that one of our biggest needs is the care of the widows and orphans. If they were kept separate from the rest of the assembly, it would be easier to meet the needs of all."

Murmurs of agreement and more nods.

"We have had some discussions here, and we feel we need to set up a distribution site where those who need daily rations can come and receive their allotment. They can then take the food back to their own homes or tents and cook it there. This will greatly reduce the food that needs to be prepared here. Martha proposed the plan, and it is a good one. We should have thought of it sooner." He stopped and looked at Martha in recognition.

Why was I brought here? Abigail was wondering. *Martha is well able to handle things. I am needed in the kitchen—*

"It has been noted that you, Abigail," Peter said, turning his head slightly, "are most capable and efficient. It has been suggested that you oversee these new distribution tables."

Martha was on her feet, her face pale. "But—but I need Abigail in the kitchens."

"We will train other girls for the kitchen."

"We?" repeated Martha, arching her brows. "We? I don't believe I can recall your presence in the kitchen, Peter."

Peter may have turned red, but his beard hid it. He chose to laugh. A hearty laugh. "You are quite right. I will be doing no training. But you are most capable of that, Martha. After all, you trained Abigail, did you not?"

Martha reclaimed her seat, mumbling as she did so.

Peter turned to Abigail. "Are you willing to serve in this way?"

Abigail swallowed, then nodded. *Yes. Yes, I am willing to serve.* But the very thought of such a significant responsibility frightened her half to death. And yet she too was an orphan, and was sensitive to her companions' needs.

"I am willing," she heard her own voice declare. Her mind was already scrambling to determine what needed doing, where she would begin.

"Good. Then it is settled. You will talk with Stephen. He is in charge of the supply rooms. He will advise you on what is in store, and he will work out with you the processes of the food distribution. If you have questions he cannot address, Stephen will bring them to council. And choose two or three of the younger women to help you as you see need."

Peter looked satisfied with this solution, and Abigail nodded dumbly. She assumed she was now excused and rose from her place. Already Martha was a few steps in front of her.

They were almost to the stairs when Martha spoke over her shoulder. "Now, haven't I just served up a day-old fish? I was seeking to *ease* our load—and what happens? Peter goes and dumps more on your shoulders than anyone should need to carry. I'm so sorry, Abigail. I never should—"

Abigail reached for her arm. "Don't trouble yourself so, dear Martha. I don't mind. Really I don't. I am happy to serve the widows. And orphans. It's a task that with the Lord's help I can do. It's an honor to participate in this way."

Martha shook her head, her expression saying she refused to be comforted.

"I will miss working alongside you," Abigail hurried on. "But we will still see much of one another. I will be in and out all day long. You'll get tired of me meddling in your kitchen. I will—"

"That's enough now," Martha said. "I know you are just trying to make the best of the situation. I interfered, and I am reaping the harvest. And that's final!"

"Actually," Abigail dared to add, "once I am used to the idea, I think it is a good one. It does take much of the work from the kitchens. It also lets the widows and their children feel like families even in their difficult situations."

She hesitated. "And I do think that once I learn how to do it, I will love serving in this way."

"Humph" was Martha's response.

"You know," said Abigail, tilting her head, "I've got a feeling this new duty might be even better than the wash tubs."

Martha "humphed" again, but this time there was a twinkle in the eyes that turned to meet Abigail's.

———

It wasn't until the quiet of the night that Abigail was able to think through what had just happened. She was to be an overseer—in an important role. Oh, not a true overseer perhaps. There would still be those above her. Stephen in charge of the storehouse. The Council. Peter. But still, she had just been given a significant task.

The idea challenged her. Even frightened her. Could she do it? It was a large responsibility. What if she failed? The widows needed daily rations, as did the children without parents. There were many who had no remedy for their situation except for the community of believers. Daily she had noted these two groups as they came and went. Daily her heart ached as she watched them.

Sad, empty faces, with babes in arms or young children clutching at their skirts. Or children totally on their own. Even as their faces lightened as they worshiped, she still saw their grief. They grasped for some sign that would give them hope.

She felt honored, deeply honored, to be asked to serve in such a way. Perhaps, with the Lord's help, she would be able to bring some comfort, some encouragement, to those who came for help.

"O Lord God," she breathed fervently, "may I be able to serve as you served when you were with us. I will joyfully lend my hands, my heart to the task before me, in your name. Strengthen me to serve. Give wisdom. Supply the means to meet the needs. Make me a blessing to all whom I touch, I pray with thanksgiving."

CHAPTER

FIVE

THE TWO WOUNDED SOLDIERS slowed down Linux and the troop considerably. They did not approach Jerusalem until just after sunset on the third day. Jerusalem at dusk was stunningly beautiful. Torchlight and twilight's final glimmer turned the city walls the color of molten gold. A rising moon in the east washed the Kidron Valley in silver and stark shadows. Somewhere within the Temple compound, a trumpet sounded the signal for evening prayers. The city seemed to float upon its hilltop, a lustrous crown to the fading day. Despite the beauty, however, the troops did not ease their hands from their weapons until the first rider saluted the sentry guarding the Sheep Gate.

Linux returned to the chambers he had shared with Alban—seemingly a lifetime ago—above the fortress stables, though he certainly could have commanded more auspicious quarters. The Antonia Fortress was the first major structure completed by Herod the Great, father of Herod Antipas and the man responsible for the rebuilding of Jerusalem's Temple. Linux left his respects with the night duty officer, glad he did not have to deal immediately with the gruff commandant, and made an official request for troops to be placed at his disposal the following morning. One glimpse of the scroll with the imperial eagle he carried was enough to have the commandant's aide saluting and promising that all would be as Linux requested.

He ate a leisurely supper and lingered in the baths attached to the fortress, soaking away the dust and the bruises. Then he began his quest.

Linux tried to tell himself that all he wanted was to determine the location of his friend, the former centurion. But in his heart he knew otherwise.

The fortress was a brooding hulk, separated from the Temple's western wall by a lane that was always in shadows. That night the lane was so empty Linux's footsteps echoed off the stone underfoot and the walls to either side. But up ahead the major thoroughfare connecting the Temple entrance to Herod's Gate teemed with activity.

Linux felt his heart rate surge as he approached the packed avenue. The Zealots' attack was fresh enough for him to be more aware than ever of the danger the city held for a Roman walking alone and unarmed. But Linux could not bear arms and go where he wished that night. So he accelerated his pace until he was a half step off running. He glanced at every passerby, every shadow.

He was neither challenged nor threatened, though he felt eyes on him everywhere. Linux feared he might not even find the place he sought, for his three visits had been over two years ago. And he had never made the trek at night. Nor could he ask directions, as he did not know the square's name, if it possessed one at all. What was he to say to a suspicious Judean? That he, a Roman, sought the courtyard where the followers of the dead prophet gathered?

Linux walked until he feared he had missed the turning or

had taken the wrong route entirely. The city's poorer quarter was a stone-lined warren where even Temple guards walked in threes, and rarely at night. He was about to turn back when the familiar stairs appeared to his right, as broad as the fortress lane, scarred by centuries of feet. The steps climbed to just beneath the city's interior wall. He arrived at the pinnacle and surveyed the empty plaza. Linux had only seen it teeming with people and burnished by the desert sun. But he knew he had arrived.

The first time he had been there, an intense discussion had swirled from every side. How these Judeans loved to talk—about news of the day and politics, but mostly about their religion! Linux recalled that momentous day when he had led Alban to meet his fate. Pontius Pilate could well have demanded the centurion's head. Yet Linux's friend had walked alongside him, speaking quietly of the Judean prophet.

Linux took a deep breath of the night's dry, dusty odors. The early spring rains were long gone. The worst heat was still ahead of them. It would not rain again for six long months.

As his thoughts continued, Linux felt as though Alban had moved up alongside him. He heard anew the questions for which there were no answers, about forgiveness and love and a living God. The words resonated inside his head as he looked around him for signs of life.

Then he heard quiet conversation and saw the glimmers of light around the edges of a door.

Linux walked over to the tall double doors, obviously locked. Up close he heard the sound of many voices. The last time he had been there, these doors had been wide open, the crowd so dense the plaza's air had seemed compressed. The prophet's followers had been celebrating the wedding of his friends, and Herod had sent his guards to arrest them. Four days later, Linux had been ordered back to Italy. He had heard nothing of Alban since then.

Linux knocked on the door. Instantly the conversation inside went silent.

A small portal at face level was unlatched. The door, about a foot across, was laced with iron bars, preventing a sword or spear from stabbing through. A bearded face studied him for a moment, then demanded, "What is it you want?"

An unseen man from within hissed, "Who is it?"

The bearded man squinted through the barred portal as he replied, "A Roman."

Linux said, "I come in peace."

The man was as tall as Linux with the features of a worker. Or warrior. "It is late, Roman. What do you want?"

"I mean no harm to any of you," Linux said, raising his empty hands. "I come seeking word of a friend."

The man was dubious. "This friend, he is a follower of the Way?"

Linux had never heard this term before. But now was not the time to inquire about its meaning. "His name is Alban. He is married to Leah."

From behind the man, a woman's voice said, "The Roman speaks of my guardians."

The man did not take his eyes off Linux. "He speaks of the God-fearer?"

"The same. May I have a word with him please?" The voice trembled a bit.

The bearded man frowned his reluctance at Linux, then slowly stepped away.

At first glimpse of the young woman who replaced the man, Linux's heart began to thump.

The iron bars framed an exquisite face. And the eyes . . . As she drew the covering up over her lower face, a single curl of brown hair emerged from the traditional Judean shawl. "Forgive me, sire, I have forgotten your name."

"I am Linux." She was far lovelier than he recalled. The dark eyes frankly met his gaze, the voice sounded musical even when turned shy by this stranger. "Forgive the intrusion. I come in peace, seeking word of Alban and Leah."

"They are not here."

"Are they safe?" His voice was rough with emotion, as if he had run a fierce race.

"They are." She smiled, and her face grew lovelier still.

Someone from within said, "Abigail?"

She backed a step.

"My lady, please, can you at least tell me where they are?"

"We do not speak . . ." Her name was called again, more sharply. She swiveled the small door shut, saying, "I must go."

Linux stared at the closed portal. The young woman had left behind the scent of lemons and some spice, perhaps myrrh.

He whispered the name. "Abigail."

Reluctantly, he turned away, shoulders sagging in defeat.

CHAPTER

SIX

THE NEWS EZRA SOUGHT came from the most unexpected source. "My own *sister?*"

Sapphira was the youngest of their clan. "An unexpected jewel," his mother had always called her, which was how the name had been chosen. Sapphira had married into a family of Jerusalem merchants. It was from their compound that Ezra did business whenever he was there in the city. He sat now in the chamber he had taken as a headquarters for himself, and stared across the table strewn with documents and samples of wares, and tried to come to terms with what he was hearing. "You? A follower of this dead prophet?"

"If you ask among the followers, my brother, they will tell you he is not dead."

"Who? Who says such a thing? The man was *crucified*. By the *Romans*. You think suddenly these masters of death and mayhem made a *mistake?* Or changed their *minds?*"

Sapphira was not an especially attractive woman. Ezra also considered her rather weak willed. But their parents had doted upon her like they did their grandchildren, refusing her nothing. As a result, she had grown up expecting her every wish to be fulfilled before it was hardly uttered.

But this. Ezra was aghast.

Her husband, Ananias, sat next to her. He was a smallish man with constantly moving eyes. As though whatever deal he might just have negotiated, he suspected that an even better one lurked somewhere around the next corner. Ezra demanded, "You too?"

"They are accomplishing signs and wonders. I have seen them with my own eyes."

"This is your answer? I can walk you down to the Temple gates and show you a dozen mendicants who claim such powers!"

"These miracles are real," Sapphira declared quietly.

Ananias added, "Didn't you tell us you were interested in making contact with them yourself?"

Ezra rose from the table and walked toward the wide balcony doors. His attention was caught by the hand-polished mirror he had purchased for his late wife. Most religious Judeans considered reflections an unnecessary temptation. The finest mirrors were also extremely expensive. But Ezra had wanted her to see how beautiful she truly was. They used to stand before it together, and he would point out all the features of her beauty.

Nowadays, he rarely gave his reflection a glance. But today Ezra found he could not turn away. He stared at himself and noted the traces of grey in his neatly trimmed hair and beard. There were also circles under his eyes, so deep not even the tan from his travels could disguise them. He was in his forties, and though he still thought of himself as young and vibrant, he could feel the first winds of wintry age sweep about his spirit. As Ezra studied his reflection, he realized he was coming to resemble his father.

With a calm he did not feel, he changed tack. If he wanted information, he must feign an interest in the beliefs of this new sect.

Success for his assignment depended upon it. He turned back to the seated couple and said, "You are right, of course. Forgive me."

"As you wish to do, I went the first time out of curiosity," Sapphira said. "I had heard so many things. I merely wanted to see for myself."

His sister had always been a lover of the markets and the tea-houses, Ezra reflected. Gossip was as vital to her as breathing. He knew he was being uncharitable, but he could not help himself. Hearing that his own sister was a follower of this nonsense left him wanting to distance himself from her.

Ananias nodded. "I went because she asked me to come. She asked and she asked."

"Ananias, please."

"It is true." He turned to the woman. "You would not leave me alone about this."

And you, Ezra amended silently, *were born to follow.*

Ananias was also the youngest sibling of his clan, just like Sapphira. Ezra had been against the marriage. The father of Ananias had been the first of his line to deserve the title of merchant. The grandfather had been a simple caravan driver. By dint of hard work and harder bargaining, the family had lifted itself into the class of traders. Now they owned a dozen stalls on Jerusalem's main avenues.

Ezra returned to his chair and inspected the wispy-bearded man seated across from him. If Ananias did nothing else his entire life, this alliance with Ezra's merchant empire justified his position within the clan a thousand times over.

Ananias reiterated, "You pestered and you begged, and so I went."

Ezra asked, "And now?"

For once, the man's restless eyes were stilled. "You have not witnessed what is happening among them. I have."

"And what does that mean?"

"You see them as a growing sect. You wish to know who they are. You think perhaps an alliance might be of benefit."

Ezra was unsettled by the man's intuitive summation. "Is that wrong?"

"We are merchants. It is our way. I am merely saying that things are not as you expect. Judea is filled with sects and people claiming to possess secret knowledge. This is not such a group."

Ezra inspected the man more closely. Perhaps there was more to his rather furtive brother-in-law than Ezra thought. "How can you be so sure?"

Ananias looked at his wife. "Tell him what you told me."

Sapphira said, "I heard a friend speak of . . . of miraculous things. It seemed like an afternoon's entertainment to go and see for myself. I confess this now. You see, I too had my reasons for wanting to know them, all of which were wrong."

Sapphira spoke in a rush now, like she had as a child. Eager and excited and full of the moment's desire. Yet Ezra heard something new. A strength he did not recognize, an intensity that suggested a deeper passion. "You are saying I am wrong to wish to know them?" he suggested.

"No, brother. What I am saying is be prepared to confront things which you cannot understand."

"Either you are with them or you are not," Ananias said. "If you are among the followers of Jesus, he will work within you."

"But the man is dead!"

The two of them shared a secret smile, which unsettled Ezra more than anything he had yet heard from them. Sapphira pointed to her heart and said, "He lives. Here. Now."

"Accept it or not, it is your choice," Ananias added. "But it does not change the facts. Jesus died, and yet he lives."

Ezra clamped down hard upon his first impulse, which was to

stamp and rage and argue. He took a few moments to swallow away his contempt. "This I must see for myself."

Sapphira beamed. "And I will arrange it for you, dear brother."

Ezra spent the next hours in a state of wary expectation. He remained unsettled that Sapphira had become one of the dead prophet's followers. He tried to find out more about them, sending a trusted servant into the marketplace with instructions to ask around, offer bribes if necessary, but bring him information to clarify the situation. Surely if he could discover what he wanted to know on his own, he would not need the illusionary help of his sister and brother-in-law.

But what his servant brought back disturbed him even more.

"Signs and wonders" was the expression the servant repeated. The way the man spoke, Ezra knew he was reciting what he had heard from others. Apparently the market was as conflicted over this group as Ezra was. Some dismissed them as outcasts. Jerusalem was filled with followers of one person or another, shouting to the heavens how their rabbi held a special understanding of the truth. Ezra had expected this. In his youth, he and Gamaliel had been among those outside the Temple, proclaiming to other students how their own teacher was the finest Pharisee who had ever lived.

But this was different.

According to his servant, actual miracles were taking place. The leaders of this group, now referred to as apostles, or holy teachers, were gifted with powers that had once belonged only to the prophets themselves. Or, more likely, it was all a ruse.

Ezra hid his unease from the servant, who had only done what Ezra had requested. Yet when the man departed, Ezra found himself unable to return to his work. He paced the room, arguing internally over the notion that little Sapphira would have given her allegiance to one such as this.

A knock at the door halted him. The servant returned to announce, "A woman is here, master."

"She was sent by my sister?"

"She did not say, master. But I think not."

"I do not . . ." Ezra then noticed his servant's barely concealed smirk. "What is it?"

"I am certain you will wish to see her, master."

"Send her in." Mystified, he waited in the middle of the chamber.

As soon as the woman appeared, Ezra understood.

She wore the trailing robes of a Greek temple priestess. Elongated cheekbones stretched down to a truly enormous nose. Her skin was mottled, yet she had rouged her cheeks like a brazen young girl. The effect was ghastly.

"I bring you greetings, Ezra bin Simon."

He responded with a courtly nod and said to the servant, who was openly smiling now, "Bring refreshments."

"Greetings," the crone repeated as Ezra motioned her to a chair. "From one of the finest families in all Judea."

"I am honored," Ezra replied.

"You should be, sire. Oh my, yes. You should be honored beyond the powers of speech to convey. Shall I tell you why?"

He walked around the table and seated himself. "Please, continue."

"Because this family has a daughter, sire, the likes of whom you have never seen. How do I know this? Well you may ask, sire. I know this because if you laid eyes on this beauty, you would be blinded to all but your desire to wed this young woman and claim her as your very own."

The servant proffered the crone a gilded tray. The hand that reached for the goblet was as ancient as the rest of her. She took a noisy sip, and continued, "You have two children."

"That I do, yes."

"And they miss their mother. No doubt you also long for your departed wife. A tragedy, your loss. I see her absence still embedded in your features. But the time for mourning is over, sire. I come as the herald of a new dawn."

His servant lingered by the door, watching the woman as he might an actor upon the stage. And she was very skilled, Ezra had to admit. He had met enough matchmakers over the months to know that this one was indeed a professional. "Does this new dawn of mine happen to have a name?"

"Gloria."

Then the family was Greek, the term the locals used for any Judean clan from beyond Israel's borders. "From which clan?"

"Isaac. Of Athens. And Caesarea."

He knew them, of course. They were a shipping family. Of good repute. "Her age?"

"A truly beautiful sixteen. Fresh as the dawn, this child, and with a voice that brings to mind the soft cry of doves."

As the woman continued to sing the young lady's praises, Ezra leaned back in his chair and gave this the serious consideration it deserved. The Isaac clan possessed ships, which his own trading empire lacked. He had dealt with them for years. He had in fact journeyed to Alexandria on one of their vessels. He suspected they were not particularly religious, which was the norm for most Judeans who lived in Caesarea. This did not disturb him overly much. They were known as an honorable clan, and Ezra had found them harsh but fair and true to their word. They would know of his own standing within the religious community, and if they were offering their daughter's hand, it would mean that the young woman knew how to run a *kashrut*, religious, household.

His mind darted back to the meeting that Sapphira was setting up, which returned him to the question of what to do about
his sister's newfound allegiance to this sect. Suddenly he was too
unsettled to remain in his chair. He bounded up so swiftly the old
woman stopped in midsentence.

"Forgive me, lady. Do continue."

The woman stretched her features into the semblance of a
smile. "Clearly the gentleman is taken with the young woman, yes?
And well he should be, for her skin is as fresh as . . ."

Ezra found himself standing once more before the mirror's
polished surface. He was not a bad-looking sort. A bit craggy, and
still very dark from the months upon the open sea. Ezra stroked
the silver in his short beard and wondered what a young woman
would think of him.

But what the old woman said was true. The time of mourning
was coming to a close. The children needed a mother. And he a
wife.

He realized that the woman had asked him something and was
waiting for a response. "Could you please repeat that, my lady?"

"I asked whether the gentleman might wish to have me
approach the family on his behalf."

"You were the one who came to me," Ezra countered. Clearly
this woman sought a betrothal payment from both families. "The
family sent you, yes? Which means you are here on *their* behalf."

The woman gave a satisfied smile. Ezra had not refused the
offer outright. "Indeed I am, sire. Indeed I am."

———

His sister arrived just as the matchmaker was departing. By
the time his servant had seen the old woman out the front door,
Sapphira must have put together all of the pieces concerning the

old woman's visit and wore the same smirk as his servant. "Are you ready, brother?"

"For what?"

"For what, he says. Look at the man. He has not even met the young lady, and already he is thinking of bringing her into his home."

Ezra felt his face grow hot, which only caused Sapphira to laugh. Even his servant hid a chuckle behind his hand. Sapphira took his arm and said, "Come, we are expected."

"You have arranged for me to meet one of the sect?"

"We do not consider ourselves a sect, brother."

"I meant no disrespect. How should I refer to them?"

"Within the gatherings, we now call ourselves followers of the Way."

He heartily disliked hearing his sister claim allegiance to this group, whatever they might call themselves. Ezra hid his grimace by squinting at the sun. "The heat is fierce this afternoon. Shall I order us a cart?"

"It would be unseemly to arrive in such a fashion. Besides, we are going into the old quarter."

Ezra bit back a complaint. The old quarter was how the poorest section of Jerusalem was known. He had not been there in years. He doubted it had improved since his last visit. He motioned to the two sentries standing by the entrance to the compound. "Accompany us."

Sapphira clearly disliked the armed protection, but did not voice objections. Instead she went on, "Among those who do not follow, but who hold us in respect, we are known by the town where Jesus was raised. Nazareth. Nazarenes."

Ezra faltered, leaning against a nearby wall. The word in Hebrew was *Hanozree* and held powerful significance among religious Judeans. The word signified the highest form of denial of self, rejection of sin, turning away from temptation, and earnestly seeking the Lord.

"Is everything all right, brother?"

"Yes, I'm fine. So you are taking me to the home of one of the leaders."

"The apostles come mostly from the Galilee. They reside here with other followers who have homes in Jerusalem."

This time he could not hide his scowl. To the religious of Jerusalem, the Galileans were only a tiny step above Samarians. "Really, sister, this is too much. You have taken up with riffraff!"

Sapphira, unaccustomed to having anyone in her family criticize her ways, turned sullen, and instantly Ezra was taken back to earlier days, when such looks would have melted their parents' hearts. She said, "If you are going to talk to me like that, we may as well turn around and go home."

"Forgive me, sister. That was unnecessarily rude."

"You were the one who wanted this meeting."

"Indeed I was. Tell me more of this group."

Sapphira turned cheerful once more, but her account now was laden with tales of miracles and events which simply made no logical sense whatsoever. She described the group's growth at an impossible rate. She spoke of how people shared what they had, and no one within the community lacked for anything. She related how the Master himself had fed five thousand from a single basket of fish and a few loaves of bread, and how this same miracle often appeared to still happen as daily needs were met.

Ezra could not stop himself from asking, "How much of our family's money have you given to them, sister?"

The sullen pout returned. "We share with those who need."

Ezra guessed that his family's hard-earned gold—gold that his own efforts had increased significantly—was now feeding the poor who flocked to this new sect precisely because there was free food to be had. His food. His gold. No wonder the sect was growing.

They walked the rest of the way in silence.

C H A P T E R

SEVEN

THE SCENE THAT EZRA FOUND at the apostles' gathering place was nothing like what he had expected.

There was no swelling crowd of the poor, gathering like crows around anything for the picking, no hordes of beggars grasping for alms. Ezra and his sister Sapphira entered a square like a hundred others in the city, populated with a modest number going about their business. Water in the unadorned central fountain trickled from a simple clay pipe and fell into a narrow trough. The surrounding dwellings were poor but not unkempt. Shutters remained closed against the late afternoon heat. A single donkey ate from a feed sack. A woman filled a clay pot and nodded a greeting to Sapphira before stepping back through high double doors and out of sight.

Sapphira was subdued. "We should not have come."

Ezra was tempted to agree with her. Yet a growing curiosity held him. Sapphira was not unintelligent. Nor was she gullible. She enjoyed buying things at the market stalls, and loved to boast of her new perfumes and brightly colored scarves. But she had never been one of those women who let gold drip through their fingers like water. Something clearly had affected her. The sect must have touched her in a significant manner.

Ezra said, "I will address them with respect."

She showed him anxious eyes. "You truly will do that?"

Again he was impressed by how important this was to her. "I give you my word."

"Come, then." As they passed through the open portals, she said, "This was where the Master appeared after his crucifixion."

Ezra opened his mouth to correct her, but caught himself and merely nodded.

"The room at the top of the stairs was where Jesus celebrated the Passover with his apostles. It was the last meal before he died."

"This was before he returned, do I understand what you are saying?" It was very hard not to object to her preposterous assumptions.

"That is right, brother." She spoke with a firmness that unsettled him even further. "He died and he returned, and then he left us again, so that the Spirit might arrive."

"Where did he go?"

She looked at him, seeking assurance that he was not mocking her. "Back to his Father. In heaven."

Unable to think of a suitable reply, Ezra nodded again, more slowly this time.

"He was taken bodily into the sky. The apostles were there. They saw it happen."

Ezra busied himself with a sweeping inspection of the inner courtyard. It held far more activity than the square beyond the high doors. Yet it also carried a remarkable sense of calm. He saw a scene hearkening back to his earliest days in Jerusalem, when he lived with his teacher's household. Under this scholar's tutelage, he had been both student and servant. His family had paid for his studies, of course, but he had also been expected to work hard, and some of his payment had gone to help impoverished young men of intelligence and promise. Gamaliel had been such a young man, full of passion and fire, though from a very poor background. Which helped explain why Gamaliel had grown to appreciate life's finer things—good food and a nice home and grand robes. All this flashed through Ezra's mind as he surveyed the courtyard.

Perhaps two dozen people, mostly women, were busy with any number of chores. He smelled lamb roasting, seasoned with both garlic and thyme, he was sure. Two tables were being laid out in the shade, as would happen in most religious households where women and children were segregated from the men whenever strangers were present. The women he saw all wore the most modest forms of veils, long shawls wrapped about their shoulders and discreetly covering their lower faces. They clearly were not wealthy, yet neither were there signs of extreme poverty.

What impressed Ezra most of all was the calm—a certain peace, the same impression he had found within his teacher's home and maintained through religious study and prayer and worship. Of all the things he might have expected to find within this new sect, the serenity of his early years was certainly not one of them.

He started at a sudden noisy clatter behind him. Ezra turned, and held his breath at the sight.

A young woman had dropped the armful of wooden bowls now scattered across the ground. The end of her traditional veil had fallen away as she bent over to retrieve them. "Forgive me. I am so sorry for my clumsiness."

"Here, let me help—"

"No, no, sir, you mustn't. I will do this."

Ezra had no interest in doing a servant's duties. He wanted

a closer inspection of this woman, to see if his initial impression was correct.

She was even lovelier than he had thought. As she restacked the bowls in her arms, a face of astonishing beauty was revealed. A refined loveliness, and beyond that, an inner strength and content- ment that he had not seen in such a young woman before.

Ezra's mission in visiting the compound had changed its focus in an instant. Everything he heard and saw was now sifted through his fascination with the young woman. Every time she came back into view, the rest of the world faded into the distance.

Sapphira looked at him for a long moment, then drew him over to the courtyard's main table and seated him in the shade. She said something indistinguishable to him, then left for a moment. When she returned, whatever she said further also fell upon deaf ears.

Then the young woman was before them with a clay goblet. She held it out, saying, "Here is the cool water you asked for, Sapphira."

Sapphira said, "Thank you, Abigail," and motioned toward her brother.

Ezra took the water and smiled but did not speak. A single man would not respond directly to a maiden in conservative households. But who was to say what rules might govern this place? Ezra tasted the woman's name with the water. *Abigail.* It rested lightly upon the senses. A good name.

He then saw a slight limp as she departed. The businessman's side of his mind noted that the young woman might be genuinely flawed. A physical imperfection serious enough to cause lameness would be grounds for canceling a marriage contract. The Judean laws regarding this were very clear. A visible defect, particularly one that affected either the face or a person's ability to walk, was considered in the same light as ritual uncleanness. Such a person was forbidden to enter the Temple.

Ezra sipped his water and watched the followers go about their business, constantly searching for another glimpse of the young woman. He dismissed his mental appraisal with a shrug. He simply did not care. He wanted this woman. Her beauty of face and form would surely offset the physical deformity if the physicians had been unable to correct it.

He and his sister stayed as long as was polite. Ezra held back from his desire to speak directly to Sapphira of his new aim.

She waited until they were back on the main avenues to ask, "What did you think of them?"

Ezra paused a moment, then began, "I was wrong in my assumptions."

"You thought they were all beggars who came for free food and shelter."

He glanced over, surprised by her observation. She had not usually been so perceptive.

Sapphira went on, "I know because I thought the very same thing. That they wanted me to join because they knew I was from a prosperous family, and they wanted my money."

"And they do," he shot back.

"But they do not *ask*." She added, "It is not about the money, brother."

He wanted to argue. But he knew now was not the time. So he turned away from that and said, "The young woman, Abigail. You know her, yes?"

He could see she was attempting to hide a smile. "You astound me, brother."

He curbed his impatience. "Tell me about her."

"She is an orphan."

This was unwelcome news. An orphan was almost as low on the social scale as a freed slave. To be an orphan meant there was no clan to claim her. No wealth or position to back her name. "How did she lose her family?"

"I have heard there was an attack on their caravan. Only she and her brother survived. He is apprenticed among the followers as a carpenter. She initially served in a household that came to know the risen Lord. Now she is part of the community here and serves—"

"What about her limp?"

"I have heard there was an accident. She was washing clothes, and hot water . . ."

Ezra tuned out his sister's voice. The more he learned, the more he knew he should dismiss all thoughts of this Abigail. The very idea of a merchant of his standing seeking to wed a servant girl, a washerwoman, a member of this rabble sect, was absurd. But he was held by the vision of her lovely face.

"Brother?"

Ezra realized his sister was no longer walking beside him. He turned around to discover she stood by the street to their home. "Do you no longer remember where I live, where you have your office?"

He walked back and said, "I wish for you to speak to her clan on my behalf."

"I just told you, Ezra—the girl has no clan."

"She has been adopted in all but name by this . . . this group, yes?" He had almost said *sect* but caught himself in time. "Speak to the leaders for me."

Sapphira studied him, her expression full of amazement. "You truly seek *marriage* to this woman?"

He felt his whole being burning with desire. "I own two parcels of land. If you will act for me, one of them is yours this very afternoon."

Sapphira's mouth parted and her eyes stared upward into his.

Land inside the city wall was as valuable as a field of precious jewels. "You are serious, brother?"

"The other will be yours the day I wed her," Ezra said. "Now tell me if I am serious or not."

CHAPTER

EIGHT

LINUX AWOKE AT DAWN to a desire that clenched his soul with a force both painful and exquisite. He had no choice but to murmur the woman's name. "Abigail."

A voice from the front room called, "Did you say something, sir?"

As he rolled from the pallet, he searched for the name of his new manservant. "Julian?"

"There's tea and fresh bread, sir. A bit of goat's cheese. Dates."

There were always retired soldiers hovering about any main fortress, looking for work or an ally or simply a connection to the former life they had loved. Linux had met Julian in years past when he had served one of the officers sent home with Pilate. Linux went into the front room to find the manservant bent over the breastplate worn by Roman officers on parade.

"Why, pray tell, are you bothering with that?"

"Word came this morning, sir. The legate will see you." The man was using a mixture of old paraffin and sand to scrape away two years' worth of grime. The breastplate was beginning to gleam like polished silver. "I wanted to let you sleep as long as possible, after your being away until late." He polished more fiercely still. "Alone."

"I was looking for a friend, a former centurion."

He was clearly accustomed to the ways of Roman officers, for he sniffed his disbelief. "No doubt the lady you visited was married."

Linux started to correct him, then decided it would make no difference to the old man. "Have you any word of your former master?"

"Nary a whisper since he left for Rome with Pilate. Which does not bode well." Julian scrubbed vigorously along one edge. "There's rumors enough around the fortress. How every officer is to be sent home in disgrace. Or worse."

Linux thought of the reason behind his request for a meeting with the legate, and stuffed his mouth full of bread and dates.

"Times've changed since you were away," Julian went on darkly. "The legate's ordered all Romans to travel in force whenever they go out after dark."

"What, here in Jerusalem?"

"There've been incidents. Most have been hushed up, on account of how nobody wants to give the locals reason to think we're going soft. But a couple of soldiers went off drinking and never came back. Gotten the lads nervous."

———

Linux emerged from the stable's shadows wearing a legionnaire's dress uniform. His breastplate, helmet, buckles, and scabbard gleamed from Julian's thorough work. As expected, a young officer awaited him. If the subaltern found anything odd in a senior officer emerging from the fortress stables, he did not let it be known. "Commandant's compliments, sir. He wishes to have a word."

Linux motioned with the scroll he held in his left hand. Even in the lane's perpetual gloom, the imperial eagle glowed with unmistakable intensity. "Lead on."

Antonia Fortress was a functional and charmless place. When the Romans took it over as their garrison headquarters, they buried the courtyard gardens beneath heavy stone tiles. Where flowers once bloomed, soldiers now paraded and trained and gambled. The halls were bare of adornment, the sounds brutal and masculine. Linux followed the young officer up the broad central stairs, nodded in response to the guard's salute, and entered the commandant's quarters.

"So you're back."

He snapped off a parade-ground salute, then bowed low. "Linux Aurelius at your service, Tribune."

Legate Bruno Aetius was just as Linux had recalled, a bull in leather and gold. "When exactly did you arrive?"

"My ship docked a few days ago in Caesarea, Tribune."

"You had some trouble on the way to Jerusalem?"

"Not much, thanks to your men. They handled themselves well."

"They'd better, or I'll show them just how rough I can be on soldiers who don't." Bruno settled into the leather-backed chair behind a massive table. "I suppose you've heard of the new pestilence sweeping the Judean plains."

"I understand they call themselves Zealots."

The tribune nodded as his aide placed a mug of something hot by his left hand. "Will you take tea, Linux?"

"Thank you, sir, but no. I just ate."

"These Zealots are determined that Judea will once again be ruled by Judeans, united under a name from the distant past. 'Israel,' they call it. Legends are springing up about them. Songs are being sung in the local taverns."

Linux recalled the hum of death flying out of a desert night. "And you have yet to capture any."

"The Zealots are neither strong enough nor stupid enough to attack my troops head on. They prey upon lone riders and small contingents of soldiers."

"Not local merchants?"

"Not many Judean caravans are hit, which leads me to suspect they pay tribute. Or the Zealots resist attacking their own. But our own merchants and Herod's are suffering losses." The tribune showed a brief glimpse of humor. "I find it hard not to agree when they call Herod their enemy."

Linux gave a sardonic grin in answer, then asked, "Are you suffering casualties?"

"Some. We have not had reason to mention them in official reports. But, yes, we've had some casualties."

Linux heard the unspoken concern. "More than you would like, I'm guessing."

"I dislike losing any men. Speaking of which, whatever happened to that friend of yours, that former centurion—what's his name?"

"Alban, sir. I was hoping you could tell me."

Bruno Aetius turned to his aide, who remained stiffly at attention by the side window. "Do we know?"

"Haven't heard a thing since he resigned his commission, sir."

"Hate losing good men," Bruno Aetius repeated. "From all I heard, he was a fine officer. Wouldn't you agree?"

"One of the best I have ever served with, sir."

"Even if he was a Gaul." Bruno eyed him with a commander's wisdom. "How did you find things in Umbria?"

"Much the same. My brother has grown fat."

"I recall Castor from my days in Rome. Your brother was always on the heavy side."

"Now he is obese. I doubt he can any longer tie his own sandals." He felt a trace of the old bile. His brother had married a girl half his age and a third his weight. She had wept on her wedding day. As had Linux's nieces, who were hoping for a mother. But it would not do to relate such things to the legate. "My days were brightened by the company of my brother's two daughters. They are growing up to be as lovely as their late mother."

Bruno's eyes glimmered with a smile he did not release. "They stole your heart, I wager."

"I would have given anything to have brought them back with me."

"You did well to leave them in Umbria. Judea is suffering through perilous times." The tribune finally deigned to notice the scroll Linux held. "You have brought something for me?"

"Yes, Tribune."

"Can't be good news, the way you're holding it as if it were a viper." He gestured across the table. "Let's be having a look at it, then."

Linux handed over the scroll and resumed his military posture. The tribune broke the seal, unrolled the parchment, and read in silence. He then rose and walked to the side window. His aide risked a single glance, his expression full of concern.

Bruno Aetius announced to the arched opening, "I've been ordered back to Damascus."

Linux said nothing.

"I and my entire officer corps. Sent off as if we'd been caught stealing from the emperor." He planted two fists on the windowsill. "I suppose I should be grateful for the chance to leave this pestilent city. But to be sent off like a . . ."

Linux remained standing at stiff attention, his eyes upon the wall behind the tribune's desk.

"I assume you met this new prelate."

"I did, sir. In Rome. Just a few weeks after his appointment became public. I went by to present my compliments, as any officer would to a new commander. To my surprise, Marcellus asked to see me."

"What do you make of him?"

Linux replied carefully, "He is most definitely a man of today's Rome."

"Yes, I've heard all I need to know about what is happening at the heart of our empire." Bruno returned to the chair behind his desk. "Sejanus is said to be digging his own grave, fighting with the Senate and demanding to be named consul. What help is he receiving from our Emperor Tiberius?"

Linux hesitated, then confessed, "The emperor rarely emerges from his pleasure gardens on Capri. Sejanus stands alone against the Senate."

"Then I warrant he is not long for this world." He lifted his head to stare into Linux's face. "When does the new prelate arrive?"

"Marcellus was scheduled to leave Rome soon after I did, sir. We were delayed by some vicious storms. If he missed the bad weather, he could be here any day."

The tribune toyed with the scroll unfurled across his desk. "Well, all I can say is, if Marcellus is anything like what I've heard of the people running our empire, Damascus will not be far enough away from Rome for me."

———

The Temple trumpet sounded just as Linux left the fortress. He had rarely given the Judean rituals any thought when he had been posted there in the past. The city was full of the Judeans' religious fervor. Every Roman officer was certain this intensity was behind much of the antagonism shown toward their Roman masters. Linux returned the salute of the officer awaiting his appearance. "You have the legate's staff?"

"Yes, here, sirc."

The imperial eagle at the top of the gilded staff glowed with the same power as the bird on the end of Linux's second scroll. "It's a nice day for a stroll, don't you agree?"

The soldiers all grinned. Linux's sardonic air was well remembered among the Jerusalem garrison.

Linux took the reins from the soldier tending his horse and slipped into the saddle. "Let's get this over with."

The air held a dense mixture of sunlight and heat and dust. Linux rode alongside the subaltern, the only other Roman who rode. Their way forward was made easy enough, for not even the most surly Judean was willing to obstruct the imperial eagle. The staff held by the soldier who walked ahead of them signified to all that they rode on the emperor's business. Any who stood in their way would be treated as though insulting the emperor himself. Such processions only took place under very special circumstances, as when a governor was traveling under official business, or when the emperor sent a royal decree to a local ruler. Such as now.

Linux held to the mask of Roman authority that every officer in Jerusalem was forced to adopt. The lead guard shouted for the people to make way, while a pair of soldiers walked on either side, armed with long staffs to prod away any man or beast. The avenues were crowded, as always. Many of the looks cast their way held dark fury. But no one threatened their progress.

At the first major turning, the lead guard glanced back. Linux motioned them to the right, away from the Temple. The subaltern frowned, clearly wanting to make as public a display of Roman power as possible. But Linux had no desire to confront the mobs clustering around the Temple entrance. From the glances the foot soldiers shared, they clearly agreed with him. Their way took them north toward the Pool of Siloam, then along the main thorough-fare bisecting the upper city. This route was further but much less crowded. They made good time.

Linux found himself thinking about the Judean lass, Abigail. The horses' hooves offered a gentle cadence to his reflections.

He felt as though his spirit were being torn in two. One side of his reflections, the Roman side, shouted like a commander facing enemy battalions. *Marry a Judean?* His brother, Castor, would be utterly delighted by the news. Linux knew Castor had always feared his seizing power. Many Umbrians made no attempt to hide their preference of Linux as their ruler. Marrying a Judean would hand his brother a sharpened sword, one Castor would not hesitate to use against him.

But the other side of him, the lonely wanderer, hungered for a woman he scarcely knew at all.

———

The Jerusalem palace stood upon one of the city's highest points, overlooking the western valleys and the Jaffa Gate. Herod's father had chosen the location both to be as far as possible from the Temple Mount and to proclaim his rule as an opposing force against the high priests. The palace was so large that seven years earlier it had been split in two, with Pontius Pilate residing in one side and Herod Antipas in the other.

Linux presented himself and was granted entry. His men dismissed the palace guards with a single glance. Herod's guards bore the weak faces of men born to loiter and were dressed in finery that looked absurd to the Roman foot soldiers. The palace interior, however, was another matter. The troops stood at the top step of the entrance hall and gawked over a garden as large and verdant as an enclosed forest.

Linux recognized the man scurrying toward him as Enos, personal aide to Herod Antipas and head of the palace staff. Clearly the man was too frightened, however, to realize they had met before. His bow was so low his robes swept the floor, and his voice shook as he said, "Your most loyal servant greets you, sire."

The instant the man's eyes fell on the scroll, Linux realized that Enos knew. It had been said that Herod's spies were the finest in the realm. "I bring word from the new governor for your ruler."

Enos bowed again, most likely to mask the shiver that wracked his frame. "My sincerest apologies, sire. King Herod is still at his residence in Tiberius."

Linux knew his men were listening intently. "In that case, perhaps we should have a word in private."

"Of-of course, sire. This way." Enos led him inside with yet another deep bow.

As Linux followed the man into the lavish formal chamber, he recalled the last time he had been there. Alban's betrothal ceremony had taken place at the chamber's far end, with thronelike chairs placed on the raised dais by the garden doors for Herod and Pilate's wife, Procula. Linux had since learned how miserable Leah had been on that day, dreading marriage so intensely she had actually considered complicity in taking Alban's life. How she had intended to do that, Linux had no idea, but he suspected it included the help of Herod's sweating and slippery head servant.

Linux allowed himself to be bowed into a gilded chair, and reflected that things had certainly changed between Leah and Alban since their betrothal. The Gaul had charmed the lady so thoroughly she had shone with an unmistakable joy at their wedding.

Pity this servant's master had managed to shorten those celebrations and send the two on a flight for their lives.

"My . . . my Lord Herod will indeed be most sorry to have missed you, sire. But we received no notice of your honor's arrival."

Other than the word of spies, Linux privately amended. "It is of no consequence."

"Will you take refreshment, sire? Food, perhaps? We have fresh figs plucked just this morning."

"Nothing. But my men wait outside in the heat."

Enos turned to a hovering maid. "Fetch a pitcher of cooled water, and scent it with rose petals."

Linux waved his hand. "That is not necessary."

"And with lemons," Enos added. "Sire, are you certain there is nothing—"

"Water then."

"It will be my sincerest pleasure." The head servant vanished.

Linux stretched out his legs and glanced about. The room was much as he remembered, large and richly furnished in an outlandish fashion. His mind went back to the last time he had seen Alban and Leah. On the day of their wedding celebration, Alban had announced his decision to leave the legions. It had come the same day Linux had received his brother's invitation to present himself. Their two responses could not have been more contrasting. Linux had seethed over the letter's wording, a rude command that was meant to mock and belittle. But what had shocked Linux was how Alban had responded to his own crisis. His friend had every reason to be furious, for Alban had spent his life preparing to lead men into battle. Instead, while Linux feasted upon bile and dreams of revenge, Alban had spoken once again of this Judean God, the joy he and Leah both knew because of this faith. Linux had scoffed at the time, then grown even more angry when Alban refused to argue with him.

Though in truth his anger had little to do with Alban at all.

While passing through the outer gardens shared with Herod, Linux had overheard plans to turn the wedding celebrations into a tragedy. Linux had not given a moment's thought, nor had he hesitated. He'd ordered a subaltern off his horse, claiming urgent business on behalf of Pilate himself, and raced for the Lower City.

Three days later, he had departed for Italy. He had spent much of the ensuing months worrying over the fate of Alban and his new bride.

Enos scurried back across the chamber bearing a golden goblet on a golden tray. But when he saw the scowl on Linux's features, he quailed. "Forgive me, sire, is something—"

"I was recalling the last time I entered this room," Linux said. He lifted his helmet and rubbed his sweat-stained hair. "I stood as witness for Alban at his betrothal."

"To Leah. Of course, forgive me, sire, I remember you now." Enos's voice shook in time with his hands. "But this day—"

"Do you have word of where they might be?"

"I have heard nothing since Leah's final day serving Procula, sire." He handed the goblet to Linux. "But if you were to give me a few days, perhaps I could learn something."

"Any news would be most welcome. You can reach me in the quarters above the fortress stables." Linux drained the water, set the goblet back on the tray, placed his second scroll next to the goblet, and rose to his feet. "Prelate Marcellus arrives from Rome in a few days. He expects Herod to make this palace his gift of welcome. Have your men break down the walls that divide the palace."

"I will— It will be as you say, sire." Enos bowed to the scroll as he would the emperor himself. "And King Herod—"

"Would be well advised to remain in Tiberius."

"When . . . well, when can he be expected to be summoned?"

Linux deliberately turned on his heel and departed, the question hanging in the palace air behind him.

CHAPTER

NINE

ABIGAIL'S ARMS ACHED, even though she kept shifting the market basket between them. Once again she'd had to go to the market for Hannah, since the woman was ill. The afternoon heat was making her feet drag and her entire body long for some respite.

Once again she set the basket on the cobbled street and molded herself into a shaded corner. If she could just cast her shawl aside and catch the breeze whispering faintly around her . . . She fanned the exposed part of her face with the end of her shawl. She still had some distance to go before reaching the compound, and the women waiting to prepare the evening meal would be looking for the produce she carried.

She pulled the shawl's corner more securely over her face, thankful that for today her leg was not causing as much pain as it had recently. Perhaps it was again on the mend.

As she reached down for the basket, a work-roughened hand lifted it before she could. Her head swung around. "Jacob!" She was both surprised and relieved. "What are you doing here? It's not nearly—"

"Just heard some news," he said, "and I couldn't wait to tell you." His face was split by a big grin.

She realized she had to tip her face upward in order to look him in the eye. How quickly he was growing to full manhood. His face glistened with perspiration, and he was panting slightly. She wondered what news would bring him in such haste. "Good news? By the look of you it must be good indeed."

"It is. Great news." His eyes shone with merriment as he waited, the grin firmly in place.

When he offered nothing further she prompted, "And?"

"Alban is coming!"

She grabbed his arms and shook him gently. "You wouldn't tease?"

"Not about this, I wouldn't."

They had been waiting for such word a very long time. They eventually had learned that Alban and Leah had arrived safely to wherever their sudden escape had taken them, though they had not said where that was, no doubt in an attempt to protect them all. But Alban had also promised they would send further word when they felt it safe to do so. Now two years had passed, and Abigail and Jacob had begun to despair of ever hearing further.

The only response she could manage was, "When?" as relieved tears filled her eyes.

"Soon. Alban has hired himself out as a caravan guard."

"How did you hear? Who—?"

"A wood supply just arrived at the shop. The man who made the delivery is one of us, and he got this from a trusted caravan master, also a believer." Jacob thrust his hand into his tunic and pulled out a small roll of parchment.

"A letter? Oh, please, will you read it to me? Quickly!"

" 'To our beloved Jacob and Abigail,' " Jacob began, his tone triumphant. " 'Greetings in the name of the Lord our Savior. I trust this finds you both well. I have been seeking for some time for a way to contact you without jeopardizing our safety and yours. We are well. My Leah sends her love and regrets that she must wait before seeing you again.' "

Abigail stopped Jacob with a hand on his arm. "Leah is not coming?"

Jacob read on. " 'She is unable to accompany me, as she is with child—' "

"A child—imagine, Jacob, Leah a mother. Oh, I do wish I could see her!" She motioned for him to continue.

" 'The caravan that I will be guarding, with God's help, expects to arrive sometime within the month if all goes well. Because of my responsibilities, I will not be able to come immediately to you in the city, so I pray you visit me. The caravan master traditionally resides in the south camp. It is within a Sabbath day's journey. I will send a messenger with word of my arrival.

" 'I anxiously await our reunion. You may need to look carefully for me, as I no longer look as I once did. Purposely so.

" 'Until we are able to see one another, may our God guard you. We have prayed for you both every day and long to be united once again. A.' "

Abigail carefully rerolled the letter. "You are sure this is not a hoax? A way to—"

"Like I told you, the trader who brought our wood is a fellow believer. He would not deceive."

Abigail's legs trembled with her excitement. Did they dare share the news with the others?

Jacob answered her unspoken question. "I don't think we should say anything to the others until we have talked to Alban. He must suspect there still is danger."

Abigail nodded, though realizing how difficult that was going to be.

Her eyes fell on the basket Jacob was holding. "Oh my, Jacob," she exclaimed, "we must get these vegetables into the cooking pots for supper."

The two stepped out quickly, and Abigail staggered as she felt a searing pain up her leg.

"Are you all right?" Jacob asked quickly.

Abigail took a breath and smiled her thanks. "I am now." She pushed her shawl slightly back from her face. The lane ahead was momentarily clear, and she could chance a bit of air. "I don't think I've been better in my entire life."

It was hard to continue through the rest of the day without talk of Alban's upcoming visit, even though they were long used to guarding their tongues and holding close their secrets. Yet Abigail and Jacob both wished for an opportunity to share with others the coming visit.

Abigail managed to fill her time with overseeing food distribution while Jacob occupied a bench in the shade or paced the courtyard by turn.

Evening prayers followed the meal, seeming to be longer than usual. Abigail knew there was much for which to thank their Lord, along with many requests for wisdom and direction for members of their fellowship. But her thoughts kept drifting no matter how tight a rein she tried to maintain.

She understood Jacob's restlessness even though she was not seated beside him. His bearing exuded an energy he obviously found hard to contain.

At length they were free to go. The two were about to leave

the compound when Jonah, a member of the newly formed council, approached her.

"I wish to speak with you," he began without preamble. "A meeting of the Council this afternoon included this request from Sapphira—do you know Sapphira, the wife of the man Ananias?" At Abigail's nod, he continued, "She spoke on behalf of her brother. Ezra, the merchant. It seems the man is desirous of a union."

Abigail frowned. *A union?* She was not in any way related to business or commerce. "I . . . I don't understand," she said.

"He wishes a betrothal. With a marriage in short order. He is a widower and has two young children in need of a mother. . . ."

Abigail was certain the man was continuing on, but she was no longer listening. She had no objection to caring for children. But could that not be done without a marriage? She felt her heart pounding. She reached for Jacob's arm. Her lips refused to move. She wasn't sure she even breathed. Her entire body felt numb.

It was Jacob who answered for her. "That is impossible," he said with no hesitancy. "A betrothal cannot be arranged without permission of our guardian. He may have already made plans for her future."

Relief washed over Abigail with Jacob's first words. As he continued with the possibility that she might already be promised, she sucked in some air to try to keep her head from spinning. Surely Alban would not have made plans for her without her knowledge. But Jacob was saying, "Our guardian is to be in touch with us . . . shortly. We will pass the man's request on to him when he comes. Until such time, I trust the man—Ezra, is it?—will bear patience."

As Jacob made as though to depart, Jonah nodded. "I suppose that is as it must be. I shall inform Sapphira, and she can let her brother know that the request has been relayed and will await a hearing."

Jacob nodded in a manner far beyond his years and experience, and Abigail was both astounded and reassured. She heard Jacob muttering but could not make out the meaning of his words. Was he as troubled as she?

They were safely out of earshot before he whispered fiercely, "I know this Ezra. He has come into the carpenter shop. I think only yesterday. He is a pompous old man. Not suitable at all. Have nothing to do with him."

Abigail shivered. "You know I will have no say in the matter." She tripped over an uneven paving stone and would have fallen had Jacob not grabbed for her arm to steady her.

"We will convince Alban. He would never agree to your being passed off—"

"We will pray," Abigail put in. "We will pray intently that God's will be done."

"Alban is not an unreasonable man. Just because this Ezra is wealthy does not mean—"

"He is wealthy?"

"Enough that our master carpenter himself bowed the man into our shop." Jacob studied her. "You would marry for wealth?"

"Of course not," Abigail was quick to respond. "But . . ." She looked away.

"But what?"

"Think of the needs," she said, looking back at him. "Money could do so much for so many followers."

"Are you saying you would give yourself to him for a few bowls of soup?"

Abigail was now near tears. Her lips trembled, and she was glad for the concealment of the shawl. "Jacob, don't," she pleaded. "You know I would not willingly give myself to someone for any reason. But think what it could do for you. You could be trained in something you love instead of . . . instead of working as a carpenter, which you do not—"

"*I* am not a part of this arrangement," Jacob again interrupted. "The man is not intending another one to rear. Besides, I already know what I want to be. And when Alban gets here he will take the steps to work it out for me."

"Hush," Abigail whispered. "We are not to mention his coming, remember. Even the walls have ears."

They turned the corner leading to their small quarters. Abigail could already detect the odor that continually hung over the area. At first she had often covered her nose with her hand when entering the street. She had now become familiar enough with it to make it bearable, but she still detested the strong smell.

Jacob loathed the place. "I cannot wait to leave this place and begin my real work," he said now, his mouth twisted in disgust. "I taste raw fish throughout the day. When I become a legionnaire, I will live on fresh bread, sweets, and—"

"You know you can no longer follow that path, Jacob. Many of our leaders say that being a soldier is not compatible. Soldiers must take up arms. They must—"

"You think I don't know what soldiers do?" he burst out. "Why do you think I want to be one? I know they do their *duty*. That's what. Have you ever met a finer man than Alban?"

"No," Abigail agreed quickly. "But Alban did not remain with his troops. I think you may find him saying that life no longer fits with our way. Think on that, I beg you, my brother. What if your desire displeases Alban? Think what he has done for you. He only wants what is best. He loves you like a son."

Her voice had gradually risen from the whisper that they were trying to maintain. She checked herself and switched to a softer tone once again. "He would be so disappointed. He wants you to become . . ."

Jacob moved away from her. Even in the shadows of the twilight she could see his eyes shone with a different intensity. Was it pain or anger that passed over his face?

"Jacob—please," she begged, but she knew that her brother had once again shut himself away. There was no use to talk further. He would not be listening. She felt tears sting her eyes. They were almost home, but it would not be an evening of camaraderie. Even before they reached the door of the small abode, she knew that Jacob would be retreating immediately to the loft and his camel-hair bed. There would be no further discussion of Alban's upcoming visit. There would be nothing left for her to do but to pull out her musty pallet and spread it out on the floor. She, too, would retire—and pray.

———

Abigail arose earlier than usual the next morning, but Jacob did not respond to her call. After three further attempts, Abigail climbed the shaky ladder made of scraps Jacob had gathered here and there and peered intently into the darkness of the small upper platform. There was no form on the pallet. Jacob had already left.

Her heart sank as she climbed back down to the dirt floor. It was all she could do to keep her tears in check. Had he merely left early for his work? Had he been so angry with her for her strong words that he had decided to disassociate himself? She couldn't bear to think of the possibility of losing him again. He was all she had for family. She wanted to cling to him. To protect him—and be protected, as he had done for her the previous day. What if he had found some way to join the legion without the help or consent of Alban? What if she had driven him to it? She would never be able to forgive herself.

With a heavy heart Abigail prepared herself for the day. She would be attending the morning prayers alone. But she began her own prayers now. Prayed that Jacob might already be at the compound waiting for her. Prayed that she would be able to control her tears if he was not. Prayed for wisdom in what to do next.

She pulled her shawl closely over her face as she closed the lean-to door and propped a stick against it to keep out straying goats and chickens. She wished she could also cover her red and swollen eyes.

The sun was not yet up, though the pink flush on the eastern sky was assurance it soon would be. A bird sang in a tree and was answered by a mate resting on a stone-built wall. Somewhere nearby a baby cried. A man cursed angrily at a skulking dog. And the strong odor of raw fish assailed her nostrils.

She paid little heed to any of it. Her thoughts were still of Jacob.

———

The long day dragged to its end. Abigail had heard nothing from Jacob. He had not been at the morning prayers, nor at the evening meal. As she wrapped her shawl about her for the journey home, she prayed that when she arrived at their humble dwelling his few belongings would still be there, indicating his planned return.

As she crossed the courtyard, a tall man stepped from the shadows. Her weary heart accelerated when she recognized the Roman soldier, Linux. His dress uniform gleamed where the setting sun reflected off the polished brass. She could not help but notice that he did make an impressive figure. Abigail took a deep breath and would have brushed by had he not stopped her.

"Please." His voice sounded more entreating than commanding. "If I could have only a few words."

Abigail had no recourse, and she nodded, her fingers twisting themselves in her shawl and drawing it more closely about her. She was relieved when he motioned for her to step into a shadowed doorway where she would not be seen in conversation with a Roman soldier.

"I remain much concerned over Alban. I have made numerous inquiries, but I have heard nothing."

"Please, sir," Abigail dared to say, "do not ask about him any further. It could put him and Leah in great danger."

"There may still be enemies?" He stopped, then added, "But of course. Herod no doubt harbors thoughts of revenge."

"I fear so. Some memories are long when they are filled with bile."

"Then I shall indeed remain silent."

"Thank you." Abigail made as though to depart, but he stopped her again.

"Could you at least allow me to ask if there has been any word?"

Abigail paused, then nodded. "Yes."

He gave a deep sigh. "Then they are still safe—and well?"

She merely nodded again.

"I am relieved."

"As are we all."

A third time Abigail moved forward. But again his words halted her. "May I ask if he will be . . . joining us soon?"

Abigail wished not to answer. Yet no doubt her own eyes betrayed her. She could no more conceal her anticipation of seeing Alban again than she could deny his coming.

"He will. But in secret. I can say no more."

"I understand. And Leah?"

"She will not be traveling."

"Is she not well?"

"She . . . she is very well, I gather." How much should she say? "She . . . is with child."

She was totally unprepared for the expressions that crossed his face. A smile. A longing. Then a smile again. But he said nothing. Just looked at her. Deeply. In a way that unsettled her more than she could have expressed. What did he mean by such a daring study of her half-hidden face?

Her thoughts suddenly flew back to a market day of long ago. She had gone on an errand with her mother, when she was young enough still to pay little attention to what might be happening on the streets around her. But her mother had noticed something that made her hiss, "Cover your face," giving the girl a firm nudge. Abigail had quickly complied, wondering, even as she obeyed, about other girls her age with no covering.

It wasn't until they were back within the confines of their own courtyard that her mother offered an explanation. Of sorts. Abigail did not fully understand it. "You must always cover your face when you are in the streets. Men—even older men—look at you. If they think you are bold, they will be bold in return."

"But other girls do not—"

"There are evil men who admire beauty far too much," her mother was quick to cut in. "Once they see it, they must possess it. Your father and I will make the proper arrangements for your betrothal when the time is right. We will choose a man who wishes more than a beautiful face. For now, you must cover your face to keep any of those bold eyes from evil desires. Always. Whenever you are in the streets or market. Do you understand?"

From then on she had been careful to obey her mother. But now she did not have a mother or father to make the proper arrangements for her betrothal. How was she to know if the eyes that met hers conveyed honorable intentions?

This Roman officer's expression sent an undeniable shiver up her spine. Whether from fear or something else, Abigail could not explain. She knew only one thing. She had to escape. With no further words she pulled her shawl tightly to her face and rushed past him. She would not stop if he tried to speak further.

At the next corner she risked a quick glance over her shoulder, but she saw no one.

When she opened the door of the lean-to, she hardly dared look in the loft. But she climbed the ladder to some relief that Jacob's clothing was still strewn about, though there was no sign of him.

CHAPTER

TEN

THE DUTIES OF THE MORNING called for Linux to make a trip to a silversmith's shop. Some infraction had been reported to the garrison, and he was assigned to investigate. He'd been offered an armed escort but shrugged it aside. He knew the shopkeeper—many soldiers bought trinkets for their women from him, though Linux had never had occasion to do so. There was no reason to think the matter could not be worked through by simply listening to the merchant's case.

As he walked his thoughts were on Abigail. How was he, a Roman, to make an approach, beginning with this strange sect to which she had attached herself? He knew little of these people and their ways. No doubt Alban could help him with that. If the man would be willing to act on his behalf when he made his visit to the area . . . Considering their past friendship, he was sure Alban would find a way to contact him when he arrived, and they would discuss the matter.

As Linux turned onto the main market thoroughfare, he paused by a shop whose interior was being rebuilt. Workers crammed the tight space, raising as much dust as noise. Linux's thoughts were on Abigail. If only . . . He thumped the new wooden post by which he stood. He must find a way to make Abigail his.

Linux felt eyes upon him. It took him a long moment to recognize the tousle-haired young man grinning at him. "Jacob!"

"Greetings, sire!"

"You've grown so I doubt your own mother would recognize you. What are you doing here?"

"Working—"

"You're doing no such thing, unless your job is to prop up that wall."

Jacob displayed calloused hands. "I'm learning carpentry."

Linux detected a resigned tone. "This is not something you chose? You wish for a different craft?"

"I . . ." Jacob must have caught sight of someone behind Linux.

He turned to find a bearded Judean with mallets for fists and a square face glowering at the lad. Linux assumed an officer's demeanor. "Good day to you, Master Carpenter."

The man nodded abruptly. "Roman."

"I have need of this young man for a time."

"Let us hope you can gain more work from him than I've been able to." The man turned back to his work.

"Come." Linux led the boy up the heat-drenched street. Jacob was a head taller than the last time they had met. In the full sunlight Linux noticed how his shoulders had filled out. His dark hair was flecked with sawdust and his face was ruddy from working in the sun. When Linux was sure they were out of earshot, he said, "You do not wish to be a carpenter?"

"You are correct. I hate it."

"What do you wish for yourself?"

Jacob paused, then said, "I want to be a legionnaire, sire."

Beneath the lad's matter-of-fact tone Linux detected a very real longing. "I recall you saying the same thing to Alban when we first came to Jerusalem."

"Nothing has changed." Jacob kicked at a rock in the road. "That is, nothing has changed *for me*."

"Ah. I think I understand." Linux walked alongside the boy up the rutted road to where it joined the street of shops. "Alban does not wish for you to become a Roman soldier?"

"How can I know, since I have not seen him in two years? But Abigail is against it. She and our leaders."

Linux's heart leapt at her name, but he kept his voice steady. "Does she say why?"

He kicked at another stone. " 'Ours is a way of peace.' That's all I hear when I talk of my dreams."

"Do you understand what they mean by that?"

"I don't want to."

Linux moved a hand over his mouth to cover a smile. But Jacob was sharp enough to catch his response, and it made him angry. "Alban was a *centurion*, and it didn't stop *him* from becoming a follower of the Way."

"I was not laughing at you, Jacob. I was thinking how very similar we are, you and I. And Alban too, for that matter. We were all forced into trades and lives that were not of our choosing."

"You did not *want* to be a soldier?"

"To be honest, Jacob, I was never given much of a chance to ponder the question. My elder brother— Well, let's just say that if I stayed at home, my life would have ended long before I was ready. Besides which, every second-born brother and beyond in my clan has served in the legions. It has been the tradition for generations. I had this drummed into me since I was far younger than you are."

Jacob said idly, "I wish *I* had been ordered into such a fate."

His attention was on a cloth-walled tavern in which skewers of lamb were grilling on open coals.

"How are they feeding you, my boy?"

"I'm always hungry."

"So was I at your age." Linux steered Jacob into the shade and said to the tavern keeper, "Two portions of your finest."

When the serving dish was placed before them, Linux spoke again. "You sit and enjoy the feast. I have a simple matter to attend just down the street. Wait here when you are done."

The boy nodded, a morsel of lamb already up to his mouth.

When Linux resolved the matter with the silversmith, paying a delinquent soldier's bill himself, he returned to find Jacob had devoured both portions. "Another?"

He could see the lad was tempted. But Jacob finally shook his head. "I wish I could, sire. But I couldn't hold another bite. Not right now." They both smiled.

Linux pushed the platter to one side. "And now to business. I want to speak with you man to man."

"Sire?"

"You heard correctly. I am in need of your service. It is our tradition to find a trusted ally when . . . pursuing a matter of some delicacy."

Jacob stared at him for a while, eyes narrowed. "You are speaking of Abigail?"

"Yes—"

"But she is . . ."

"She is what?"

"There is another suitor, sire." Jacob's words now tumbled over each other.

The news struck Linux like a blow to the heart. "This is not good. A Judean, no doubt."

"Yes, sire. He is very . . . rich. Abigail . . . is waiting . . . to see what Alban will say. Yes, you see, Alban and Leah are considered our guardians," Jacob said, finishing in a rush, looking around furtively.

Linux leaned closer. "Don't worry—Abigail herself told me that Alban would be coming soon. Would you speak to him about this? Ask him if—"

"It would be my honor!" Jacob's perspective on the whole matter seemed to have suddenly altered.

"Wait, lad." Linux had known so few reasons to smile recently, his face felt stretched into uncomfortable lines. "First you're supposed to ask what I will give you in return."

"I need nothing, sire. I would do this with . . . with joy!"

Linux felt his throat constrict. He wondered if he had ever been so young, so trusting. "Well then." He coughed and said, "Here is what I will do for you. Speak to Alban, and to the . . . to your leaders if you feel it is proper. In return, I will attempt to find a place for you within the garrison."

The light that burned in Jacob's face was so intense it was hard to meet the boy's gaze. Jacob whispered, "Oh, sire . . ."

Linux rose to his feet, found it necessary to cough a second time. "Come. Let us get you back to work. It likely will be for a short time only."

CHAPTER

ELEVEN

EZRA KNEW SAPPHIRA DID NOT WANT TO RETURN. She had already presented his case to the elders of this new group. They had not responded. His sister feared that for her to now bring her brother to them without a formal invitation would be disrespectful, an affront. Ezra, however, did not care and felt he had waited long enough.

Ezra also knew Sapphira's husband had placed the first tract of land up for sale. Ezra had been very angry to learn of this. Land within the Jerusalem walls was priceless, a family heritage to be treasured, not bartered. But at least Sapphira was in no position to object further when he insisted she return with him to the compound.

His businessman's experience told him he was making a mistake. To take up his pursuit again with them, and uninvited, was to reveal his impatience, the depth of his desire for this woman. And if the years in his chosen profession had taught him anything, it was that an impatient trader was one who could be forced to pay far too much. Though he knew this, he pushed it aside.

He did not consider himself a rash man. His every step through life had been measured, considering every decision in light of the future. But not now—not with this . . . this orphan, this serving girl, this washerwoman. Even listing such evident flaws had no effect on him. This fact alarmed him, but this too was not enough to deter him from his quest.

He conducted his business while another part of his mind remained trapped by the fleeting glimpse of an impossibly lovely woman. His dreams were repeatedly broken by a whisper of hunger he had not known since his wife's death.

He wanted this woman, this Abigail, for his own.

As soon as they entered the compound in the city's old quarter, the place where the dead prophet had supposedly first reappeared to his so-called apostles, Ezra knew something was amiss. Several groups, heads circled together, were murmuring about something, expressions strained.

The two took places at the courtyard table, yet no one seemed to even notice them. Ezra said to his sister, "Perhaps you should find out what is happening."

She returned soon enough. She pointed to the group clustered in the shadows by the kitchen alcove. "Word has come that several of the apostles were arrested and taken before the Sanhedrin—"

"What of Abigail?"

"She has gone to visit her brother. Jacob is apprenticed to a carpenter."

He tried to hide behind a merchant's mask. But he could feel the bile twisting his features. "When will she return?"

"No one will say. I doubt they even heard me." Ezra could see that the news of the arrests troubled his sister along with the followers enormously. "Did you hear why they were arrested?"

"Something to do with a healing." It looked like Sapphira's

attention was torn between her brother and the distress that swirled about them. "Another miracle."

Ezra bitterly disliked hearing his sister state such drivel so calmly. But Sapphira seemed too preoccupied to notice his grimace. "Perhaps you should mention that I have connections with the Sanhedrin, sister." When Sapphira did not respond, Ezra reached across the table and tapped her elbow. She turned, and he continued, "If they would only respond to my most reasonable request for the hand—"

A shout drew them both around. A group of men was entering through the main portal. At their center a burly man, dressed in a commoner's robes, held himself like a prince. The courtyard's sunlight shone upon him, and this man exuded such a force that for the first time since coming face to face with Abigail, Ezra's attention was fully directed elsewhere.

Sapphira murmured, "That is Peter."

The hand stroking his beard was massive, twice the size of Ezra's. Yet the man contained a gentle demeanor, along with an aura that unsettled Ezra in a way he could not explain. "Go and see what is happening," he instructed. With her penchant for the latest news, Sapphira gladly joined the others.

The courtyard was filling rapidly, excitement clear in the voices. Another man, a spindly character Ezra found vaguely familiar, was skipping about the courtyard, arms waving in excitement. They all watched him with amazement.

Then Ezra realized where he had seen the man before. The recognition drew him up so swiftly that he overturned the bench upon which he had been seated.

Ezra said to no one in particular, "That man dancing. He's the cripple who begs at the Beautiful Gate."

Though the courtyard was full enough that people were pressed in around him, space was made for the dancing man. Ezra righted his bench and stood upon it. Yes. It had to be the same man. Ezra recalled seeing him years ago, when he was still a student. Ezra could recall the man being carried into the area and deposited in his place, probably by clansmen who claimed a few of his coins for their trouble. People were saying the man had been deformed from birth.

The man's chant suddenly rang in Ezra's ears. As to be expected, the man was again asking for alms but using a very special word.

A young man standing beside Ezra said to his neighbor, "*Zadaka.*"

That was it. The word literally meant a righteous gift. It had been the favorite term of Ezra's teacher, an invitation for the listener to do a certain thing, not to help the one asking, but rather to help himself. A zadaka was, in its purest form, an opportunity to bless the doer through a godly act.

Ezra stepped off his bench and demanded, "Were you there?"

"I was," the young man answered.

"Could you tell me what happened?"

Another on the man's opposite side said, "I was just asking the same thing."

"And I will tell you both." His face looked like it possessed the same internal illumination as the man his sister had called Peter. "We were going to the Temple yesterday for the afternoon prayers, as usual."

This in itself immediately told Ezra a great deal about the group. Most observant Judeans were content to pray the morning and the evening services. The teachers often said that the afternoon prayers carried a greater sense of divine connection, because they were the hardest to observe. People could more easily find time to address the Holy One at the beginning and the end of each day, but to stop in the middle of activities and pray, this signified a special calling. Ezra himself rarely took time to pray the afternoon service. He took a merchant's view, telling himself he would pray twice as long at sunset, when he had set down his work for the day. But these men went often enough for afternoon prayers to call it usual.

The young man went on, "The man you see there was as he always was, laid out on his mat by the gate called Beautiful. He called to Peter, asking for the zadaka. This time, Peter stopped. We do not carry money with us, and Peter told the man as much. Then he said to him, 'But I will give you from the best that I have. In the name of Jesus the Messiah, rise up and walk!' "

This was the first time Ezra had heard the dead prophet referred to as the Messiah, and he could feel the hair on the back of his neck rise up, as though the command had been directed at him as well. He should perhaps have felt a greater indignation, even fury. Granting this Jesus the title of Messiah went against everything he had ever learned. Yet the story of the dancing beggar left him so shaken he could not utter a sound.

The young man was continuing, "We went on to prayers, and the man you see there came with us, entering the Temple as a whole person for the first time in his life. He danced and he shouted, and the crowd he drew grew to an enormous size. Peter began preaching to them until the guards arrived and took us all before the Sanhedrin."

A group, including Ezra's sister, had gathered. Someone demanded, "What did the Temple priests say, Samuel?"

"They were very angry," he said. "They put us in the hold overnight, then brought us back before them this morning. They ordered Peter not to speak of Jesus again." The young man called Samuel shrugged. "They might as well have ordered him to stop breathing. Peter was direct, as only Peter can be. He told the Sanhedrin that it was *they*, along with Pilate, who crucified Jesus. Then he recounted what the prophet had said, explaining how everything had happened as the Holy One had ordained, just as had been prophesied in the Holy Scriptures. He invited the Sanhedrin—" he paused for effect—"to join with us in worshiping our Lord as Savior."

Ezra felt himself backing away from the man. Such words were a blasphemy. He could no longer see the joyful beggar, which made it far easier to weigh the young man's words from the perspective of a lifetime of worship and study. To expect the Sanhedrin to accept this dead prophet as the Messiah was *insane*—and worse.

Samuel was saying, "Peter told the Sanhedrin, did they think this miracle was perhaps the work of his own hands? If so, how did he happen to pass by this very same man repeatedly and only now, this time, work the miracle? The answer was that this was the work of the risen Lord, through his Spirit, which resides in the heart of each believer." The young man must have noticed Ezra's reluctance, because he turned to him and said, "You are new to us. Perhaps you also would join with us in knowing our risen Christ?"

Ezra's reply held a calm he did not feel. "Another time, perhaps. Today I come only . . . only to listen and to learn."

The young man started to say something further, but then merely nodded and turned back to the others.

Ezra sought out his sister, who was talking excitedly with several of the other women. The one known as Abigail was nowhere to be seen. He touched his sister's arm and said, "We must go."

His entire being rebelled against what he had just witnessed. Part of being successful in business was having the ability to see beyond veils of deception, the flicker of a cunning eye, a meaningful exchange of glances. But there was none of that in what he had encountered here. Of that he was certain.

Ezra discovered the crowd was now spilling out into the cobblestoned plaza. He passed several discussions, some in debate, others listening avidly as the prophet's followers invited them to join and know the presence of the Holy Spirit for themselves. Ezra lingered for a moment at the edge of one such group, until the speaker looked directly at him and asked if it was time for him to enter through the narrow gate. The merchant motioned abruptly to his sister, and they left the tumult behind.

C H A P T E R

TWELVE

THE NEXT DAY A SUDDEN SQUALL sent the Old City shopkeepers scurrying to protect their wares. In the stalls surrounding the Lower City gates, sheep and goats bleated their panic as thunder crackled and lightning flashed. Children shrieked in fear and ran to find their mothers. Abigail could not remember a storm sweeping in as quickly or as turbulently. This one would have the locals reminding each other of it for months to come.

The cobblestones turned instantly slippery as the rain pelted down and people rushed for cover, sliding their way across the rain-polished stones.

Abigail, again on market duty with Hannah still sick, was caught in the downpour. Her overloaded basket impeded her progress as she tried to hold her own among the rushing throng. She was almost to the courtyard when two youths knocked into her as they ran past, sending her spinning and reaching for empty air in her effort to stay upright. One of the boys must have noticed and swung back toward her. But it was too late. Abigail crashed against the raw corner of the stone wall, then went down with a little cry while her basket flew from her hand, scattering its contents across the rain-slick street.

At first she was only embarrassed. She was now in a puddle, being further pelted by rain. She felt her clothing cling to her, sodden and mud-splashed. The fall had dislodged her shawl so that one side dragged into the water as well. Tendrils of hair stuck to her face, and the wind caught at her braid, whipping it back and forth.

"I'm so sorry. So sorry," the boy said. "I did not see you in the rain."

He offered a hand, and numbly Abigail took it and got to her feet. It was then she realized her leg was throbbing . . . again. Looking down she could see the edge of the puddle was tainted by blood. Her blood. The boy must have noticed it too.

"You're hurt."

"My leg," she managed. Abigail wanted to assure him she would be all right, but she wasn't certain it was indeed the case. "I should be all right. But I'm afraid I will need help getting home."

He nodded. Abigail held her basket as the other boy joined him in gathering up what fruit and vegetables they could. The sloping street rushed with little rivulets, carrying the ever-present dirt and grime.

One of the boys took the water-logged basket from her. "Where do you live?"

"If you could just help me to the courtyard up ahead, I will be able to get someone to assist the rest of the way."

"I am so sorry," the other boy repeated.

Abigail tried for a smile, even if a bit wobbly. "I have a brother about your age," she offered. "I'm sure he would have also run for cover from the storm."

Abigail took the offered arm, leaning heavily on the young lad, and pointed the way to the courtyard.

By the time they made it to the entrance, the wind had abated and the rain slackened to a mere drizzle. The sun would soon be shining again as though the whole incident had never taken place. But Abigail knew the harm had been done. Once again the fragile scar tissue had been broken. She prayed that Martha or one of the Marys would be there to help her cleanse and bind the wound. She was no doubt facing another long recovery.

———

Two days later, Abigail's leg again throbbed painfully. Martha muttered her dismay as she bent to clean the red and swollen area. Abigail disliked being a burden to this overworked woman. She hid her discomfort from the cleansing as best she could. Jacob hovered close by, his concern obviously pushing aside whatever else had driven them apart. Abigail did not ask questions about where he had been and why, and Jacob volunteered no information.

When the wound was again bandaged, Jacob led her home, quietly scolding that she should have remained where Martha could care for her a few more days. The wound was still open beneath its bandage and needed more time to heal, he told her, sounding more like a man than a boy. Abigail admitted inwardly that he was likely right, but she did not say so.

When they reached their small abode, Jacob insisted that she sit down on the only stool in the room. Abigail did not argue. Her leg burned with pain, and she could tell it had begun to bleed through the bandages once again.

Jacob laid out her pallet and eased her down. She felt exhausted as she mumbled her thanks. Jacob started a fire, and when the pot had boiled made her some tea. Abigail sipped it appreciatively. The warmth soothed her soul if not her body. But it was Jacob's tender concern that brought the most comfort. To have her brother back again was an answer to her prayers.

The walk to the Temple a couple days later was more difficult than Abigail had foreseen. She did her best to conceal her distress and her limp from those with her. Jacob claimed the place by her side. If she so much as looked down at her feet, his steadying hand came out to her arm. She was comforted by all his anxious attention, but she felt she should be caring for him. It was Jacob who had been coming home after a long day of work, gathering sticks for the fire so preparing a simple supper would not cause her undue exertion. They normally had taken their meals at the compound, but now Jacob stopped daily for food supplies provided by Martha. And Jacob made sure Abigail applied the healing ointment and wrapped her leg with fresh cotton each day.

Though not yet able to determine how far she was from full recovery, Abigail had insisted she attempt the walk to the Temple for afternoon prayers. It had been too long since she had joined the other followers for this time of worship and devotion together.

Yet as she walked, Abigail wondered if she was doing the right thing. She knew if her limp was obvious, she would be turned away. But she sorely needed this access to her God among the rest of the believers. She felt useless, a burden. Jacob was carrying most of her responsibilities at home, and the women at the compound were doing her share of the work for the evening meal. The tasks of selecting the fruits and vegetables from the markets already had been given to others. And of course with her re-opened wound, her overseeing duties in answer to Martha's needs had hardly even begun.

She was so busy with her own conflicting thoughts that she had not been listening to Jacob.

"He's a fine man," she heard him say for her ears alone.

Abigail nodded. She was sure Jacob's assessment was correct, though she knew not of whom he was speaking.

"He's nothing like that rich old man. He does care for you. He has told me so."

She nearly stumbled in her shock. "What . . . what are you saying, Jacob? What are you talking about?"

"You have not been listening."

Abigail fumbled, "Not . . . not totally."

"Linux. I'm speaking of Linux."

"The *Roman?*"

Jacob stopped midstride. "Why do you say it like that? You make it sound like . . . like a curse."

Abigail flushed. "I had no intent of doing so. I'm sorry."

"He is sincere in his quest," went on Jacob rapidly. "I know he is. I see it in his eyes."

Yes, Abigail too had seen the young officer's intense, bold eyes as they swept over her face. The very thought made her shudder. Though he had the power to draw her attention, she wanted no part of him. It was impossible. And he was an outsider. A pagan. He likely paid court to some Greek or Roman god—or many gods, if he had a religion at all. And he did not believe the truth about Jesus. No. She wanted no part of him whatsoever.

"I will not even speak of it," she said, her voice as firm as she could make it.

She felt Jacob stiffen, but he did not withdraw his supporting hand under her arm. "I think you would do well to at least consider it, Abigail," he was saying now. "You don't want to find yourself in the home of that pompous merchant, no matter how much money he has under his tunic."

Abigail flinched at Jacob's second reference to the possibility of her marrying for the merchant's money. *Ezra, wasn't it?* She had been told more about the one who sent his sister to plead his case. No, she certainly did not want to find herself in his home, even if his children did need a mother.

Subconsciously her limp now became more pronounced. Surely neither of the men would desire a woman who was crippled. Perhaps, just perhaps, her recent tumble would be her deliverance. God sometimes worked in mysterious ways, didn't their prophets say?

She spoke again to her brother, her voice now calm, placating. "We will discuss this with Alban when he arrives. He will have the solution, don't you think?"

Jacob only nodded, but by his expression Abigail knew his thoughts were elsewhere. Would he still insist that Alban help him to become a legionnaire? Abigail remained hopeful Jacob had given up his burning desire. Had accepted reason and the counsel of their elders.

Making up her mind quite suddenly, Abigail said, "I think I will rest here while you go on. My leg is not as strong as I thought."

Jacob led her to a low wall and brushed away the debris. "Are you sure? I could take you home."

"No, the rest will do me good. I can pray here. I'll return when I am able." She motioned him on with the others, and Jacob turned away.

Up ahead she could see Peter with several of the apostles along with a crowd pressed in around them. Abigail could almost hear his words as he talked with them. He would be telling about the Messiah's coming to earth. He would quote, as he often did, from the ancient prophesies and explain how each one had been fulfilled in Jesus of Nazareth, whom the Jews had crucified. He would invite them to join with the followers for further discussion and instruction. And all the time his deep voice would be challenging, drawing, lovingly leading them toward the kingdom of God.

Those were the very things she herself should be concerned with, but there she sat, her injury her excuse for not joining the group at the Temple. She was worried about being forced into an undesirable marriage. One of her suitors was certainly unwanted. And the other was unthinkable. Could her injury possibly save her from such a fate? She knew her culture well. An unmarried woman had little position or power. But she would gladly forfeit any future as wife and mother and be content as she was.

Please, God, just let me serve, she prayed silently as she sat, hardly aware of the crowd that streamed by, but her words brought no feeling of peace. No sense that he was listening. She couldn't have explained which pained her more—a troubled heart or an injured leg. But even as she struggled, a quiet voice inside whispered that here was a new opportunity for her to trust her Savior.

Again she prayed. Not merely for wisdom, but for submission. Would she ever be ready—and willing—to let God work out the details of her future? *Even if it was with* . . . But she shook her head and pushed herself to her feet. She would not let herself even think about it. *Help me trust you, Lord*, she prayed, her lips moving silently as she limped back home.

C H A P T E R

THIRTEEN

GAMALIEL WAS WAVING HIS ARMS over his head. "Those people are impossible!"

Ezra, seated in a carved chair set within the chamber's shadows, felt the wind against his face. He watched the breeze push the curtains back and forth, casting occasional blades of sunlight across his sandaled feet. The heat was enough for him to shift his chair back from the sun. "You are speaking of the dead prophet's followers, yes?"

"The Sanhedrin released them on the condition they not speak the name of this dead prophet in public. And what do they do? They turn the Temple forecourt into a teaching platform for their heretical ideas! They were back there this morning, proclaiming that this Jesus of Nazareth is the Messiah! The *Messiah*!"

Gamaliel was normally a placid man who showed the world a gentle smile. Now, however, he stormed about the chamber, arms in the air. One of his students hovered in the background, a slender man with a thin, dark beard. Gamaliel was a popular teacher, with a way of encouraging his students to excel beyond their own expectations. Today, however, the student looked rather frightened.

Gamaliel pointed at the young man and ordered, "Tell him what you saw, Titus."

"It is as the teacher says," he began hurriedly. "I was going to the Council on an errand, and there they were. They had taken over Solomon's Porch."

Ezra grimaced. King Solomon had erected a structure in the Temple forecourt from which he could say his prayers, situated as close as anyone who was not a priest could come to the Holy of Holies. But Solomon's Temple had been totally destroyed by the Babylonians, and the returning exiles built a replacement that was rather modest in comparison to the original. Herod the Great commissioned an expansion and restoration project which included a new Solomon's Porch, located on the east side of the Temple. The cedar roof was supported by a high, three-aisled colonnade. This shaded area was perhaps ten paces wide and four times as long. Teaching at the Temple was only on a strict order of hierarchy. Solomon's Porch was limited to pronouncements by the Sanhedrin or one of their appointed scribes.

Ezra asked, "By whose authority did they address the crowd from the Porch?"

"They claim not to need earthly authority," Gamaliel replied grimly. "Why should they, when they declare the dead prophet is Israel's long-awaited Redeemer?"

At a sign from Gamaliel, the student went on, "The one called Peter was preaching. The crowd was enormous. Peter told of the beggar's healing. He claimed that such power was at work within all believers. That all could be healed and made to rise up and stand before the Lord their God."

"If it was the beggar at all," Gamaliel muttered. "If he was indeed healed."

"It was the beggar, and he was healed."

Gamaliel spun about to face Ezra. "How can you be so certain?"

"It was the same man we have passed by since our youth," Ezra said. "And I know he was healed because . . . I watched him dance."

Gamaliel tugged hard on his beard, his fingers clenched tight, his hand pulling his face down into a deep scowl. "You saw this?"

"A few nights ago."

"Why did you not inform me?"

"Because I am not ready to make my full report." Which was only partly the truth. "I am to meet with one of their senior leaders tomorrow. After the meal that ends the Sabbath. An apostle, he is called."

Gamaliel continued to tug upon his beard. "Do you know how many they have added to their ranks since we last spoke? Thousands. They are spreading faster than we can count. How do we know this? Because they carry on the same absurd practice as that other dead prophet, the one they called the Baptizer."

Ezra shifted in his chair. This was new.

"Our spies have seen them gather at the Pool of Siloam before morning prayers. There are hundreds of them standing and waiting to be immersed. We hear the same thing is happening at the river Jordan. And more still along the Sea of Galilee. Every morning it is like this."

The student, Titus, added, "They enter the Temple still dripping from their immersion."

"Sacrilege!" Gamaliel muttered.

Ezra decided nothing was to be gained by pointing out that the Pharisees liked to enter the Temple with their beards still dripping wet from the ritual baths, an outward show of their piety. Such public demonstrations, and the way many of them looked down on those whom they considered not to be pious enough, was one reason why Ezra was glad he had never become a priest.

"I had heard they share everything," Ezra said. "I went expecting to find that many joined only for the free food."

"And?"

"It was nothing of the sort. They share with each other and with all who come to them. But there was no sign of people gathering merely because such things were on offer. You understand what I mean, yes?"

"I understand."

"They were preparing the evening meal when I arrived, so this would have been the perfect moment to see the hordes descend for a handout. It was not so. They moved together as one. It reminded me . . ."

"Yes, go on."

"I mean no offense by this. But I was reminded of our time as students. The way we were enveloped by our teacher's household. Surely you remember how we were all considered part of his family."

Gamaliel said nothing.

"The calm was . . . Well, it sounds strange, but a genuine force. The sharing was real. This is fact. You and I may not like it. But I tell you this is so."

Gamaliel was quiet for a long time. "I must admit I believe you," he finally said. "There are others I have spoken with. They all describe it similarly as you have. As a living force."

"When the beggar arrived and began to dance, there was excitement, yes," Ezra recalled. "But there was also the calm of people who had witnessed many such wonders. Those with whom I spoke did not claim these powers for themselves. There was none . . . Forgive me, old friend, I do not mean to offend. But you know how I view some of the Sanhedrin, their manner of putting their religiousness on public display. As the beggar danced, one of the followers invited me to join their community. He claimed that the Holy One's own Spirit would be breathed into my heart as well, and his power would reside within me."

"This is why I asked you to go and observe," Gamaliel said. "You speak the truth, even when it is precisely what I did *not* want to hear."

"Whether it is the truth or not, I cannot say. But it is what I saw, and what I felt."

Titus cautioned, "Master, the hour."

Gamaliel glanced at the evening shadows, and Ezra also looked out the window. The trumpet announcing the Sabbath's commencement would soon sound. Gamaliel asked, "You meet with their leader when, precisely?"

"After sunset tomorrow." Ezra felt his entire body resonate with the prospect. His sister Sapphira had received formal confirmation that Abigail was both unwed and not yet betrothed, which was a clan's way of saying that he might make a formal request. Which he intended to do at this meeting. But such news could not be shared with Gamaliel. Not when the priest was in a position to issue an injunction.

The young woman's face and form shimmered before Ezra's eyes once more. The only way he could suppress his anticipation was to clench his jaw.

But Gamaliel obviously was far too concerned to notice. "I have a very bad feeling about all this. You must inform me of everything you learn, do you hear? And without delay."

———

How was he supposed to explain this twist and turn of fate, Linux wondered, even to himself? He was walking a rutted lane leading to the valley beyond the Jerusalem boundary, led by a silent Judean. Linux wore a commoner's garment. His only weapon was the traditional knife at his belt. His sandals were of untreated leather. His hair was oiled and tied at the nape of his neck in a simple leather thong. His brother would find his appearance mildly amusing. Linux, the man who lusted after the family's power and wealth, walking through the night like a peasant.

The one who guided him carried a torch, as a servant might. But there was no air of servitude about him. He walked with a shepherd's ease, moving lightly over the uneven terrain. The road they followed seemed more a trail, rocky and twisted. Twilight cast the route in shadows. The sky glowed a soft rose over to the west, while overhead the first stars appeared. The trail turned steep once they entered the valley below the Mount of Olives. On the next hill, the coliseum, a massive monument to Roman power, caught the sun's final ray. As though the empire mocked him and his motives for his journey this night.

The man spoke for the first time since meeting Linux outside the Temple gate a few minutes before sunset. "That is our destination up ahead."

Linux responded formally, "I am grateful that you would take such trouble on my account."

"I saw you once before. When you arrived at the wedding celebration of Alban and Leah and gave them your horse when they had to depart suddenly." He brought them up the last steep incline toward a walled enclosure.

"Have you heard exactly when Alban will be arriving in Jerusalem?"

The man hammered on the stout oak door with his free hand. "You might be out of uniform, Roman. And you might be here at Peter's invitation. But Alban is a friend, and I know not your motives. I tell you nothing."

Linux nodded, accepting both the man's words and his own position as seeming interloper. The door was opened by a stout gentleman in the robes of a wealthy Judean. He gave Linux's tall form a single glance and said, "You bring a Roman?"

"At Peter's request."

"He said nothing of this to me."

"Ask him for assurance if you wish."

The man stepped back and motioned the two inside. "If you are certain—"

Linux did not move forward. "I do not wish to enter any home where I am not welcome."

"Then you are truly peculiar, for a Roman," his guide said.

The stout Judean pushed the door open wider. "If Peter wishes it to be, then so it shall be. Welcome, Roman."

"My name is Linux, and I am grateful for your hospitality."

———

Abigail winced as she set the heavy jar of water on the wooden table. She wondered how much longer she would be able to stay on her feet. Her leg was not healing as she had hoped. That much was apparent. Why? She had been praying. Had been trusting God for healing, and still the open gash oozed putrid discharge and the skin around the wound spread a flame of red in an ever-increasing circle. Ever since last night, the pain had been throbbing to each beat of her heart. She felt flushed, and she could feel the fever when she touched her brow. Tears squeezed from under her closed eyelids as she steadied herself against a nearby wall. Was she wrong to attempt to hide her misery? Should she confide in Martha? But wouldn't that show a lack of faith on her part?

Now her heart was fluttering with another fear. For Jacob had brought the news that this very night, in the evening hours, Peter planned to meet with two men. Both of the men she had come to fear would be together. . . .

She knew they were not seeking counsel from Peter on becoming a follower. No, they would be coming to barter. To haggle over which one would obtain her as his bride. Her recollection of both men was vivid. Their hungry eyes told her all she needed to know. It was not love she saw when each man looked at her. It was not the expression she had seen on Alban's face as he gazed at his new bride, Leah. No, it was desire. Raw. Open. And utterly appalling to her.

And she was helpless.

Or was she?

God knew of her plight, she was sure. Hadn't their Messiah said he knew when a tiny sparrow fell? But she had not received any discernible answers when she had prayed for his help and direction. Why?

If only she understood what this was all about. Until now, marriage had not been a frightening thought. *But to one of these two men?* Why was her faith being challenged in this way?

The sound of a firm step on the stair drew her head up, and she straightened her shoulders and quickly snatched a corner of her shawl to wipe at tears. But Abigail had not been quick enough in her recovery to hide from Martha's knowing eyes.

"So which is it," the woman asked with directness. "The leg? Or the men?"

Abigail sniffed, then shrugged.

"Both, I take it."

There was no need to agree . . . or attempt to argue. Martha understood her too well.

"Sit," said Martha as she lowered herself to a bench and patted the spot beside her. Abigail moved slowly across the room.

"Now—let's see that leg."

Abigail hesitated for a moment before lifting the hem of her robe.

Martha grimaced. "The bandage is soaked through. Remove it."

Abigail leaned forward and began to slowly unwrap the filthy cotton. Even before she finished, she felt Martha stiffen beside her. "This is not good. The redness reaches nearly to your knee."

Martha took over the unwrapping from Abigail's fumbling fingers. "Mercy, child. This is a mess you have here. How long has it been like this?"

"It . . . it just keeps getting worse instead of better."

"Why have you said nothing?"

Abigail shrugged again. What was there to say? She felt duty-bound to carry her share of the work load. Plus there was something she was almost afraid to acknowledge to herself, that confessing her worries might reveal her lack of faith. Or, to be truly honest, was she hoping the damaged limb would keep these two undesirable men from seeking marriage with her? In truth, she did not know the answer.

But Martha was already on her feet, pulling Abigail to a standing position. "It's to bed with you. You shouldn't be on that leg at all. No arguments. Why, I can't believe what I am seeing."

Martha continued to explain herself as she led Abigail toward a small room near the kitchen. "There is a time for prayer and a time for action. Right now, action is appropriate. First we tend to this wound. Then we pray. Or in this case we will pray as we work. And while we are at it, we will add a prayer about those two men as well. Actually, I don't think God approves of either one of them any more than I do."

C H A P T E R

FOURTEEN

THE COMPOUND'S OUTER PORTAL opened and a long-familiar face beamed at him. "*Shalom*, Ezra bin Simon. Shalom. Welcome to my home."

"You are opening your own door these days, Isaac?"

The merchant only smiled more broadly. "Many things are changing, Ezra. We live in an age of . . . well, miracles."

Ezra had known the merchant for over a decade. The family had long dealt in incense and wares from the East. Because Isaac's brother was a skilled carpenter, the family enterprise also imported fragrant woods, and had branched out to other locations. Isaac had bought more land and set up workshops around this area where his brother and apprentices fashioned ornately carved chests and inlaid boxes.

Isaac's home stood just outside the city gates in the Kidron Valley. Tradition had it that part of the city's original boundaries had included this land. But when the Judeans returned from their exile five hundred years before, they shrank the borders, holding the city walls to the hilltops. It meant that a merchant like Isaac could own a compound large enough for storage areas as well as his brother's workshops, something that would have been impossible inside the city's walls. Yet according to Temple dictates, he and his clan officially resided within the holy city.

As he was led inside by his good-humored host, Ezra continued to digest the startling news that one of Jerusalem's senior merchants had joined this new sect. Isaac clearly sensed what Ezra was thinking, for he turned and said, "At first I was as you are. Two servants within my home had become followers of Jesus. One was the woman who had raised me after my own mother's death. I would trust her with my life. Of course I went to investigate."

Ezra felt another shiver of anticipation touch his gut, though the sensation had nothing to do with what the merchant was saying. Ezra had known this sensation every time his mind turned to the young woman. He asked politely, "How long ago was this?"

"Four months, almost five." The stone path led them around a cluster of date palms, past a shallow pool surrounded by desert flowers, and onto a flagstone patio, where a series of tables had been set beneath torchlight. The area was already rather crowded with other guests.

Isaac asked, "Is your sister not coming tonight?"

"No, her husband is not well." For as long as Ezra had known him, Ananias had suffered from occasional fevers. "Sapphira did not want to leave his side." He did not mention her reluctance to approach the leaders once again.

"We shall pray for his swift and full recovery."

Ezra bowed in formal thanks, but before he could speak the traditional words, he noticed a man seated against the opposite wall. "Who is— What, may I ask, is *he* doing here?"

Isaac's good humor vanished. "The man was a surprise to me as well."

"You invite Romans into your house?"

"No, Ezra. But I opened my residence to Peter and our clan for this meal to celebrate the Sabbath's close. And Peter invited this man to join us." Isaac lowered his voice. "If you want my opinion, I think he has come with a certain young woman in mind."

Ezra stared at the Roman. *Surely not,* his mind raced. Yet what man could see Abigail and not desire her? Already he felt jealous. He had no intention of losing her.

He was struck by a sudden thought. Perhaps the Roman had been invited as a ploy, to raise her dowry. *Of course.* It was a shrewd move. Ezra's respect for these people heightened. Once again he was pressed by logic to withdraw. Here he was, ready to haggle with a *Roman* over a washerwoman. But he would not willingly concede. What did the cost matter now?

The merchant gave no indication he had noticed Ezra's calculating squint. "Every time a woman appears from the house, the Roman turns. When it is not her, he goes back to waiting. He speaks to no one."

Ezra could not keep the jealous ire from his voice. "Who *is* he?"

"The name is Linux. He is one of the tribune's officers. Abigail's guardian is his friend."

"Another Roman." The news from Jacob that Abigail's fate was held in the hands of a Roman married to a Judean from Italy had not been welcome. *And now this.* "You admit Romans into your ranks?"

"Alban is counted as a God-fearer."

"And this one?"

"Peter asked that I admit him. He is here. I know nothing more."

Ezra's glare burned with such intensity that the Roman must

have felt it. He turned in his seat, facing Ezra and his challenging expression straight on.

Isaac touched his arm. "Come. Let me introduce you to Peter."

———

From his position at the far wall, Linux watched their host lead a Judean around the various groups of visitors and across the courtyard. He was undoubtedly a Judean merchant prince. The man might live under the full weight of Rome's occupying army, but Linux was certain he was a leader among his tribe. The newcomer, tall and strong, followed their host across the courtyard with a stately bearing. The man had wrapped one length of his formal robes about his right arm, as a visiting dignitary might when approaching a king. He was led to a group of the clan leaders speaking intensely with one another. Linux, on the other hand, had been left on a lone bench set alongside the wall. He noted that the other man's approach caused something of a stir. Conversations halted and eyes tracked the man's progress. The Judean might have been aware of the attention but gave no sign, undoubtedly accustomed to it.

The man reminded Linux of a slighter version of his own brother. Haughty, born to power and the subservience of others, accustomed to getting whatever it was he craved.

So this is the other man seeking Abigail's hand. Of that Linux had no doubt.

Further, Linux sensed the man had seen him and knew he was there on the same quest. The Judean stopped and looked at Linux once again as the two men approached the people gathered near the far table. The man's obvious stare was not because Linux was the lone Roman among this Judean gathering. The man saw Linux as a rival.

The expression could have been taken straight from his

brother's face. This man might be leaner, his face covered with a neatly cropped beard, with some grey in the jet-black hair, and his eyes might be as dark as onyx while his brother's were a flat brown. But the expression was identical. Lofty, superior, brutally cold. Linux knew it well. He should. He had been seeing it all his life, whether in person or in his dreams.

When the man turned away to follow their host, Linux sipped from a cup someone had set before him on the table. No one was seated on either side of him. Linux was as isolated as he could possibly be, yet surrounded by this intense gathering. The guests talked quietly among themselves and ignored him entirely.

He stared at the newcomer as he bowed toward a young man who had risen from his place at a table not far from the main one. The merchant spoke in a low voice, no doubt making his case for Abigail. Linux sipped again from the cup. He might be a Roman offi-cer, but in this case he was utterly defenseless. The Judean merchant had every reason to dismiss him and his common suit for Abigail's hand with one contemptuous glare. Just like his brother.

Linux turned away and quickly searched the throng for a single glimpse of Abigail, even though he knew she would not be appearing. In his heart of hearts he also knew he should not have come.

He could almost hear his brother laughing at him.

The evening was not going as Ezra had expected. To begin with, he was not speaking with Peter at all.

Instead, he was directed to a table slightly apart from where the big man was now seated with his associates. This alone would have been enough of an affront to have Ezra objecting. His place had been at *every* head table since he had taken his father's position as leader of their merchant clan. He was known in the marketplace, he was known to the Romans, he was known in the Temple. Yet here he was, seated in the shadows off to the left of the head table, waiting his turn.

The man now serving as his host was the same young man who had spoken with him in the followers' courtyard several days back. His name was Stephen, and he carried himself with a quiet fervor that left Ezra even more unsettled than he already was. Once the man had acknowledged Ezra and motioned to a place beside him, Stephen had returned to a spirited conversation with others seated with them. Now and then Ezra picked up words and phrases that came directly from the Torah, but the full sentences were lost among his own uneasy thoughts and the stirrings about him. Ezra had known Pharisees who spent their entire lifetime arguing over a single passage of Scripture. To anyone but their select group, the issue was meaningless. To the dedicated, it was as vital as life itself.

It was not Stephen's quiet passion that disturbed him, but the contrast between him and most of the religious Judeans he had known.

For the Pharisees and their followers, these arguments over Scriptures held the same power and importance as the way they dressed, the rituals they followed for prayer and for eating. All of this was intended to *divide*. To *separate* them from the rest. Either a person was part of their exclusive group or he was an outcast. Others might call themselves Judeans. They might consider themselves the Chosen, the followers of the One True God. But if politics or habits or interpretation of the Holy Book did not follow that of the Pharisees, they were doomed.

Stephen could not have been more different than they.

When he once more turned back, Ezra took the opportunity to ask, "Are you perhaps a member of the Sadducees?"

The younger man gave Ezra his full attention. "Not now, not ever," he answered with a slight shake of his head. "I believe in the afterlife and the union with the risen Lord. As do all followers of the Way."

Which was why the Sadducees in particular were so infuriated with this sect, Ezra realized. The Sadducees were convinced the afterlife did not exist at all. Man lived, man died. The candle was snuffed out. Finished. A very Greek philosophy, it was one that found favor only with the highly educated, the rich, the well traveled. The average Judean despised the Sadducees for this and for how they had allied themselves with the Romans.

Ezra said, "I meant no offense."

"None taken, my friend."

"It is your name. Stephen is very Greek."

"It was given to me by my master."

Ezra leaned back and surveyed the man more carefully.

"I was born a slave," Stephen explained. "I received my freedom as a gift when my master died. He passed away a believer also, praise to the Lord above."

Ezra said slowly, "You brought your master into the clan of this prophet Jesus, and in return he granted you freedom."

"I am sorry, but you do not understand." Stephen pointed to where Peter's head was bent in close to a cluster of people, all craning forward and listening intently. "Peter is saying the very same thing to these new believers. It is not within my power to bring anyone to faith in Jesus. Only the Holy Spirit can do this. All I can do is introduce the concept and suggest that if indeed what I am saying is true, then they should pray to Jesus and ask that he enter into their lives and reside in their hearts and minds."

Ezra said, "Peter is speaking to new believers?"

"Yes. This takes precedence over everything." Stephen waved

a hand around. "Everyone here knows how important you are. But these require instruction."

"Of course." But Ezra's matter-of-fact response belied his awe at what he was hearing. Peter did not look like a man intent upon drawing wealth or power from his new allies. Ezra now said, "I have heard that Peter told the Sanhedrin the power of miracles was not his at all."

Stephen nodded and smiled as though Ezra had finally realized a crucial point. "It is vital for these new believers to understand that this is not a cult following any man. We seek the risen Lord. Our allegiance is to him alone. All power *derives* from Jesus and *resides* in him."

Ezra studied the young man seated next to him. "Yet Peter performed the miracles."

"No, my friend. No. I am sorry, but the truth is this. Peter opened his heart and mind to the Spirit's movement and acted as he was directed. Nothing more. We are merely hands and feet for the Spirit's use."

Ezra tugged at his beard, then stopped when he realized he was duplicating Gamaliel's actions during their last discussion. Ezra knew his Scriptures. He knew that everything the young man was saying came straight from the prophets. Which only unsettled him more.

Stephen said, "Our meal is delayed. It is often thus when new believers are being instructed. Will you take tea, perhaps?"

"Tea, yes. Thank you. It was a long walk here."

"One moment."

After the young man departed, Ezra allowed his gaze to roam over the crowded patio. At his position on the opposite wall, the Roman remained alone. A torch burned in a tall iron stand rising to his left, but an overhanging branch cast the Roman's face in shadows. Ezra was certain, though, that the man watched him. He turned away. The Roman was isolated, and this was Ezra's home ground. The sect might be new, and the woman's fate might be controlled by men whose interpretation of Scripture differed from his own. But these were his people just the same. They were here for their Sabbath's end meal together. And he was a Judean of wealth and power.

The Roman did not stand a chance.

CHAPTER

FIFTEEN

After Martha had cleansed the wound with water and spread the healing balm and new strips of cloth over it, she eased Abigail to a pallet on the floor and covered her with a light cotton wrap. "Now," she exclaimed, straightening and wiping her hands on the sides of her outer tunic, "now we take time to pray."

She knelt beside Abigail, her bones creaking in protest, and folded her hands. "Lord," she began, "we come to you in the name of the dear Savior, our Lord, asking for healing for this your child. You see our need clearly. We have nothing to offer but ourselves. You have asked us to pray in faith, knowing and believing that you do all things well. Reveal to us your purpose. Work out your will. Help us to accept what you desire to give. In the name of our Lord Jesus we pray. Amen."

Abigail murmured her own amen.

Martha pushed herself to a standing position, again brushing her hands on her plain tunic. But she wasn't done. "Now—this problem of the two suitors."

Abigail sensed that the older woman wanted her to speak. But what was she to say? Could she voice her fears?

Martha lowered herself to a stool. She finally said, "I know how I would feel were I you. In the first place, I don't care for either one of them. One is wealthy and successful, and thinks he can have anything he wants because he always has. The second man sees himself as a prince whom any maiden would desire. But just because he looks handsome and holds Roman power does not make him an acceptable match.

"Secondly, neither of them follow our faith. Though it is true that God can use a godly wife to bring a wayward husband to faith, it is my opinion that our Lord would prefer they start yoked equally as followers. You can better serve in other ways, to my thinking."

Abigail whispered, "But I have asked and prayed ever since . . . well, ever since I have known. I still cannot see his will for me."

"Perhaps there is something here we are missing," Martha mused. "I cannot advise you in this. Only God knows the plan he has for you. We must continue to pray for his will to be done. He has promised to answer, and he keeps his promises. So answer he will—in his own time and way. Whatever your future holds, this I know. He will not desert you. Your duty, my dear, is to seek his will and to walk in his way."

Abigail was well aware of the tears on her cheeks and dripping on the pillow placed under her head. Of course it was as simple as Martha had expressed. And yet so complex. So frightening. Why could she not hold to a stronger faith, and trust God to lead her?

Martha placed her hands on her knees and pushed herself up from the stool. "So that is what we pray for. That God will give you the wisdom and the faith to look beyond this moment. To know that whatever lies ahead, he has prepared the way. And he will have you ready for it as long as you are faithfully following him."

As Martha began another prayer, standing beside the pallet, for the first time in weeks Abigail felt a stirring of hope.

———

The silence surrounded Linux like an unseen force.

He found it strange to use *silence* to describe how he was feeling in a courtyard full of commotion and conversation. To Linux it seemed as though the noisier the various table groupings became, the more profound the stillness.

He wanted to leave. And yet there was something at work here. Something that *invited* him, drew him to remain—almost against his will.

Linux leaned back against the wall and shut his eyes. Instantly his head was filled with painful images. All of them centered upon Castor, his older brother.

Castor had always been the lesser son in terms of abilities, natural gifts. Linux was stronger, more handsome, more competitive, skilled with a sword. Linux had always led the hunt, had beaten his brother at every game. Linux had even won the greater share of attention from their father. But when it came down to it, all that was to no avail. Castor, the elder brother, was the prince, the one born to rule. Everyone knew that and sought to remain in his good graces. Even their parents.

Linux learned to hide behind a sardonic twist of humor. Laughing away the acid flames of fury. Pretending that everything was fine, he could handle all such matters and still come up laughing. That proved to be the finest weapon against Castor. Linux played the fool, and gradually his brother began to ignore him.

When he first met Alban, Linux was astonished to find within the fierce Gaul the heart of a true brother. Alban's own brother had conspired to kill him, and Alban wore his rage like a badge of honor. Until, that is, Alban had come to follow this Judean prophet. And started using words that had struck Linux like fists. Forgiveness. Salvation. Messiah.

Linux lifted both hands to rub his face. He found himself trapped and abandoned to a fate that mocked his laughter, that ridiculed him with bitter spite. Never before were the mental images so clear, the motives behind them so vivid. Because here, in this crowded court-yard where the internal silence was so powerful he could not even hear the tumult surrounding him, Linux recognized a bitter truth.

This hatred of his brother ruled his life.

He was dominated by the futility of life's unfairness. Castor was not merely flesh and blood. He was the barrier to everything that Linux deserved. It was Linux who was born to rule. He was, in truth, the family's prince and heir. He should be the one seeking favor in Rome. He could rise, he could ascend, he could become . . .

Oh yes, he hated his brother with every fiber of his being.

Only now, in this Judean night, did Linux realize how help-less his position truly was. Beneath the crackling torch that cast shadows upon his closed eyelids, Linux saw that he was chained to his wrath. It imprisoned him, and he had no chance of ever finding fulfillment, another way to move forward. Everything he did, all that he might achieve, would remain as ashes because of this fiery rage. Even the woman he wanted to claim as his own, the reason he was here this night, would likely be consumed by it.

Linux felt a hand come to rest upon his shoulder. He opened his eyes to find a smiling young man who said, "Peter will speak with you now."

———

Even when Ezra had been invited to join the senior apostle, it did not proceed as he wished. For as he was ushered to the head table, the young man he had been speaking with, Stephen, went over and brought the Roman forward as well.

Ezra had endured such exchanges before, and he loathed them. Two merchants brought together and forced to sit across from one another. The buyer then could sit and smile and observe the pair struggle over who would win the business. Ezra felt his position within the market and the Judean culture should grant him a greater degree of respect and deference. Especially under these circumstances.

Then he noticed the Roman's face. Though he wore a commoner's clothing, the man had served in the military, perhaps still did. That much was clear from his angular form, his evident strength and bearing. Yet he approached the head table seemingly mired in deep confusion.

Peter was in the process of rising to greet Ezra when his eye also must have been caught by the Roman. The apostle, in the process of stretching out his hands to Ezra, stopped and walked around the table. He drew the Roman down onto the bench across from where he had been sitting. By his own hand. A Judean seating an oppressor. And smiling as he did so. And laying his hand on the Roman's shoulder before returning to his place. Only then did he offer Ezra the traditional greeting, all the while his gaze resting upon the Roman.

Nothing could have prepared Ezra for what happened next.

When the three were seated, Peter waved Stephen down next to the Roman. He asked, "Your name?"

"Linux."

"I am Peter and this is Stephen." He spoke with the rough edge of the country born. Yet his manner was just as Gamaliel had described when Peter had stood before the Sanhedrin. His bearing held none of the subservience such a person would be expected to show his visitors, a senior merchant and a Roman officer. "May I ask, are you a God-fearer, Linux?"

The legionnaire wiped his face with a trembling hand. "I remember hearing the same being asked of a friend of mine. In my mind, I mocked him for taking the question seriously."

Peter seemed to accept the words without reproach. "Do you wish to be free from your chains, Roman?"

Ezra felt his mouth drop open in astonishment. For a Judean to speak thus to a Roman officer was unimaginable. Such an offense could result in Peter's death.

Yet the Roman nodded slowly, as though he had almost expected the question. "My friend asked me the very same thing."

"This is the God-fearer who once was a centurion and now is Abigail's guardian, yes?"

Ezra stiffened. Everything became clear in a flash. The Roman was cunning, he had to give him that. Since this Linux could not beat Ezra on normal Judean terms, he was appealing to Peter as an ally of the sect. Very wily indeed.

But Peter was asking, "Do your chains have a name, Linux?"

The Roman's gaze dropped to the table. "Castor. My brother."

"And what did your Roman friend, this Alban, ask you about your brother?"

"He said . . ." The officer's swallow was audible. "He asked me what I would say if I was granted the power to . . ."

"To what?"

Another swallow. "Forgive."

"And your answer?"

"What he asked was impossible."

Peter turned his head and exchanged a long glance with the young man seated across from him. He then addressed Ezra. "And you, good sir. You too have come with motives of your own."

These people continued to astonish him. Ezra had never heard such a comment as an opening gambit to a negotiation. And Peter's piercing look gave him the feeling that the man knew what he was going to say before he spoke. He searched hard and fast for something else, another response than the one he had planned, which was to suggest the man name his own price for the young woman's hand. An absolutely outlandish proposal for a washerwoman and an orphan. But with the Roman clearly having captured the center position, what choice did he have but to put his desire clearly on the table? Ezra replied, "I seek the hand of Abigail in honorable marriage. Tell me the amount you require."

He could tell the Roman's head had swiveled toward him. Ezra resisted the urge to turn and meet the man's challenge, keeping his eyes fastened on Peter. A moment later, Ezra sensed that Linux had dropped his focus back to the table before him. And he heard the man's sigh.

Ezra wanted to shout his triumph. Something about the Roman's abject state had him certain that he had already won.

Peter held Ezra's attention a moment longer, then asked quietly, "Is there no other reason why you came?"

It was Ezra's turn to nod slowly. The man was observant indeed. "I was sent by Gamaliel, the Pharisee. He wishes to know if you and your . . . group . . . if you are a threat to the Sanhedrin, and the good order of the Temple."

" 'The good order,' " Peter repeated softly. He waited a moment longer, then asked more quietly still, "Is there no other reason why you are here this night?"

Ezra leaned back. "What other . . . ?"

Then it struck him. It was as though his entire world was canted slightly, pulled a fraction off its normal course.

Ezra looked at the Roman. The man remained locked in some internal discourse, his features cast in tragic shadows.

Ezra realized it was not about the woman at all. Not anymore.

This gathering, this night, this discussion. He was being asked to join the sect. Not only that, this senior apostle was speaking to the Roman about the very same thing.

Ezra knew a few Roman God-fearers, of course. Most had been in the country all their lives. A few others had been raised by a Judean servant and had adopted the Judean God in deference to a woman loved and revered since infancy. The laws governing such people were very clear. The Scriptures included numerous calls from the prophets and even the Lord himself for Judeans to be a witness to all the nations.

But this . . .

He was stunned by everything he had gotten so wrong. This meeting had nothing to do with what he had expected. He had come as a merchant, prepared to negotiate. He wanted something they had. He discovered he was willing to pay as much as was required, though he had not yet told Peter that. This was a new sect. They were growing by leaps and bounds. They needed money. They needed access. They needed . . .

Peter seemed to find in Ezra's face the information he had been seeking.

He turned away. And shut his eyes.

To Ezra, it seemed as though the entire night caught its breath. He had no idea how long the moment lasted. Perhaps a few seconds, perhaps an hour. Then Peter opened his eyes and said, "We shall meet again tomorrow evening. Come to our compound in the Old City after Temple prayers."

CHAPTER

SIXTEEN

THE NEXT EVENING, Martha arrived in the small room bearing a tray of food and drink. She set it down beside Abigail's pallet and lowered herself onto the stool. She reached out to smooth back the damp tresses from Abigail's face. "Try and eat a little," she said. "You must keep up your strength."

Abigail barely nodded. In truth, she had no appetite. "I . . . I still don't know. I know what I want, but I still don't know what the Lord wants for me."

"And you need not," Martha said with certainty. "Not yet. You simply need to trust, take each next step by faith. You will know what is right when the time comes."

Abigail nodded, tears starting again. She could feel Martha's worn hand smoothing her hot cheek. Martha's eyes held a promise that she would be there for as long as Abigail needed her.

At the sound of footsteps and a voice calling, Martha rose to her feet. Abigail could not see the visitor, but she recognized the voice as Stephen's. His words were unclear, but she saw Martha's back stiffen.

"But she can't," Abigail heard Martha exclaim firmly from the doorway. "It's impossible."

Stephen asked, "So what am I to tell Peter?"

"Tell him she is very ill."

"He may still insist—"

"Then I will tell him myself."

Abigail could see Martha push past Stephen and move out of sight.

Abigail stirred uneasily. She should have gone. She should have responded to the apostle's request. Now Martha . . . But she had no need to worry about Martha. She was no more intimidated by Peter than she was by anyone else. Still, Abigail wished no difficulties. Not for anyone in their community. But all she could do was to lie there and endure the pain—and wait.

———

Linux arrived at the torchlit compound where he had last seen Alban. He was directed to a long table where the Judean merchant was already seated. Linux had assumed he would again face his rival's hostility but seated himself and did his best to ignore the Judean's glare. Thankfully, none of the others milling about the compound seemed to share the merchant's antagonism, at least not tonight. Linux consoled himself that his desire to wed a Judean lass was not unique. Alban had accomplished that very thing. Why could Linux not do the same? So he had returned that evening with the intention of presenting himself and asking what they would have of him.

Instead, he found himself wracked by what felt like a lifetime of mistakes. Linux stared at the table before him. But what he saw was the vivid image of being trapped inside an olive press, the huge stone bearing down, squeezing out all the elements he so successfully hid from everyone, including himself.

Even in his withdrawn state, Linux noticed heads turning toward the doorway at the side of the compound. He had expected to see the man called Stephen returning with Abigail, but instead it was an older woman with stalwart demeanor and a determined look in her eyes who was quickly approaching. Peter rose slowly to his feet, his face concerned. "Martha. Is there some difficulty?"

"You asked for Abigail," she replied. "She is unable to come. She is ill."

"Seriously?"

"I fear so."

Linux felt his gut wrench. He sensed the man Ezra stir, but he did not look toward him.

Peter moved forward, deep lines creasing his face. "A fever?"

"Her leg. She injured it once again in the storm. It worsens with each passing day."

"Where is she?"

"Here. I insisted she remain nearby, where I can care for her."

Peter said, "Bring her to us, sister. It is not I who asks for her, but our Lord."

Martha hesitated a moment, gave an abrupt nod, and turned to leave.

Peter motioned to the group of men to find seats around the tables. Peter bowed his head. Linux had the impression that Peter was addressing his God. His lips moved, though no words could be heard.

Linux glanced at the merchant seated across from him. Ezra's eyes were wide with wonder—or alarm. The muscles of his jaw and neck were taut.

The wait might have been minutes or an hour, Linux could

not have said. He watched as others bowed their heads and prayed as Peter did. Martha and Stephen led Abigail into the courtyard. Her eyes revealed intense pain. One leg curled loosely, refusing to bear her weight.

Peter did not wait for her to come to him. He moved quickly, and Linux could hear his murmurs of concern as he crossed the courtyard.

The entire gathering was held by a tension that erased all conversation. The only sounds were the sputtering of torches. Then a quiet murmur filled the air. Linux realized many were again praying.

At Peter's direction, two men shifted a bench forward. Abigail was gently lowered onto it, but even so she cried out as her leg bent to her seated position.

Peter reached out a hand to her shoulder. "Forgive me, daughter, for not knowing of your plight. I had no idea how serious this had become."

Abigail's only response was to raise her own hand to grip his. Peter lifted his eyes heavenward, and his voice rose to a commanding level that all in the courtyard could hear. Linux heard him say, "Father, behold the suffering of your daughter, our sister Abigail. Touch her in your mercy, Lord. Release her from her pain. Bring healing in the name of your son, our Lord and Savior, Jesus of Nazareth. Amen."

Peter opened his eyes and gazed full and intently on Abigail as his free hand came to rest lightly upon her head.

"Be healed!"

The words were spoken quietly but with such authority that to Linux they rang throughout the courtyard. Amens echoed from many lips.

In the time it might have taken a lightning bolt to flash across the sky, Abigail's expression changed. First confusion, followed by a flash of wonder. No longer were her eyes filled with anguish. Her countenance relaxed. Her shoulders straightened.

"Look," she said in wonderment to Martha. "Even the scars are gone." Abigail's hand was moving up and down her leg.

Then she lifted her face toward the sky and tears overflowed her eyes. But it was clear these were no longer tears of pain but of joy. Her arms raised in gratitude and acknowledgment as she stood, unassisted. There was no need to explain what had happened. It was clear to everyone.

The crowd began to move—faces beaming in gratitude and wonder, arms waving their praise to God, voices crying out in thanksgiving.

Linux felt his chest unlock, and he breathed for the first time in what seemed like hours. *So this is a healing!* This was what they claimed to be the power of God. A shiver went through his frame. He wasn't sure whether to run from the place or fall on his knees.

Abigail was on her feet, arms lifted and her body moving freely in a beautiful dance of rejoicing. Her eyes glowed with an ethereal light, making her even more beautiful, though Linux would have thought that impossible a few moments before.

Ezra stood and pulled his elaborate robes more closely to his body, as though to wrap himself away from what had just happened. Linux wondered if he was about to rush out.

Linux turned his eyes back to the beautiful girl as she continued to express her praise.

"Healed. I'm healed," he heard her say over and over. The believers clapped and shouted their praise along with her.

Linux saw that Peter was back at the table. Though the man's face shone with thanksgiving, he neither seemed relieved nor surprised. Merely accepting.

He turned and looked directly at the two men, one seated and the other standing. Linux felt his soul had been laid bare.

The dark eyes flashed, yet in some unexplainable fashion, Linux also saw compassion.

But when Peter spoke again his voice was both strong and direct. Linux understood that here was a man of true authority. An authority outweighing the power of Rome.

"I know you both came seeking the hand of this young woman. That is not mine to give. She belongs to God. We shall pray. And we shall consult her guardian. And we shall seek to know her own desires. Until such time as we hear from them—from God, from Alban, and from her—no decision will be made." His steely eyes locked with first one, then the other. "And the decision will be influenced neither by wealth nor by power."

———

The moon was high overhead before Abigail could calm herself enough to sleep. The marvel of it all! The wonderful freedom from pain. The realization that her leg was now totally whole. Not only were the seeping sore and the red streaks gone, but so also was the weakened flesh, the taut, tissue-thin skin and the scars. She could walk now without the limp. Without the embarrassment of unwelcome attention. She was well. Whole!

She would no longer be concerned about a confrontation with Temple priests over a pronouncement of "unclean" at the Temple gates. She would have free and open access to the Court of Women. To worship with other believers. To join in prayers of thanksgiving or petition. It was as if she had been given a fresh start to become the woman God wanted her to be.

And with startling clarity came another thought. Her divine purpose was not limited by her appearance, the beauty her mother had warned her about. God could do anything with her life he desired. Her future would not be governed by her face or form. What difference did it make? God had worked a miracle. A miracle of healing for a reason. His reason. She no longer needed the injured leg to protect her from unwanted advances. No, God was directing her future. He would decide if she was to wed—and to whom. She was free. *Free.* The word was so glorious Abigail could scarcely contain the joy it brought with it.

Over and over again she poured out her emotions, her gratitude, in prayer. Thanks was not enough. Humbly and wholeheartedly, with pure and complete faith, Abigail placed who she was and all that she could ever become into the hands of God.

CHAPTER

SEVENTEEN

"THE NEW PRELATE HAS ARRIVED," Gamaliel declared. "Marcellus has taken over Herod's entire palace for himself. Apparently he intends to spend a great deal of time in Jerusalem. The Council is faced with dire threats on every side. It is the worst possible time to remain annoyed by a dead prophet and his rabble!"

Ezra nodded his thanks to Miriam, the priest's wife, who had brought him a mug of hot, sweet tea. "You are correct that these followers are spreading like an army of locusts."

"We thought it was over and done with when we demanded the prelate kill that so-called prophet, Jesus of Nazareth. But it has only grown worse. Far worse."

Gamaliel was in midsentence when a young man entered the room followed by Ezra's son, who had come with him on this visit.

Ezra disliked such talk in front of the boy, who was six and retained everything he read or heard like a sponge. He motioned to his son, who lingered by the outer portal beside Gamaliel's senior aide. His son glanced up at the slender young man in the black robes of a Pharisee scribe. Only when the young man nodded did the boy step forward and come to his father. Which was as it should be, for his son recently had begun his studies in this household, and he was now under the direction of this senior aide of Gamaliel—Titus, was it?

Ezra stroked the boy's cheek and said, "What did you study today?"

"We have started studying the psalms, Papa," the boy replied.

"Yes, most interesting. And can you remember anything you have learned today?"

"Of course!"

"So tell me what you liked best."

The young voice rang clear and high like chimes. " 'Why do the nations rage, and the people plot a vain thing? The kings of the earth set themselves, and the rulers take counsel together, against the Lord and against His Anointed. . . . ' "

Gamaliel visibly shuddered. His wife said, "Husband, are you—?"

"Leave us, please."

Ezra gestured for his son to depart with the scribe and Miriam. "I shall join you shortly."

When they were alone in the room, however, Gamaliel did not speak. In the distance, Ezra heard the cry of a water seller. The plaintive call through the afternoon heat seemed to make the silence even more oppressive.

Finally Gamaliel asked, "You went to their dinner marking the end of the Sabbath?"

"I did. I also met with them again last night."

"And yet I had to send Titus to find you."

"My apologies, old friend. I was . . ."

"Yes? Go on."

Ezra sighed. "It is complicated."

"I am listening."

He swallowed hard. "I . . . There is a woman."

Gamaliel turned from the window. "A follower of this dead prophet?"

"Yes. She . . . that is . . ."

Without taking his eyes off Ezra, Gamaliel moved behind the table piled high with scrolls and documents and seated himself.

Ezra realized there was no way to make this easy. "I want her for my wife."

"You have made a formal offer for her hand?"

"Through Sapphira."

"Do I know her family?"

"She is an orphan."

To Ezra's surprise, Gamaliel did not offer the objections Ezra would have himself offered a friend in similar circumstances. After all, he was a man of substantial wealth and position. Marriage was to be considered a contract to strengthen his position. Certainly no orphan, no serving woman, could possibly . . . All objections Ezra already had made to himself—to no avail.

Instead, Gamaliel asked, "She is a maiden of purity and modesty?"

"I am certain of it."

"She observes the Law?"

"As devout a woman as I have ever seen."

"You are already a man of great affluence and power. There will certainly be those who scorn you for making such a decision. But you have always charted your own course. And Miriam has been saying for months that you need to take yourself a wife. So I don't understand the problem. Your sister arranges the bride price with the girl's guardians and—"

"It's not as simple as you describe." Ezra took a very hard breath. "They expect me to join the sect."

Gamaliel's features went rigid. "Impossible! Think of the impact this would have upon our community, a man of your standing even considering such an act."

"It gets even worse." Now that he had started, Ezra felt as though he could not draw the words out fast enough. He described the night and the Roman and the encounter with Peter and the healing. By the time he stopped, he was panting, partly from not having drawn a decent breath and partly from reliving the experience.

Gamaliel stroked his beard, tugging hard upon the ends, drawing his face into a downward-sloping frown. "He healed the young woman."

"Yes."

"You are certain it was not a trick."

"Absolutely not."

"Perhaps they disguised her leg to make her look lame."

"She has limped every time I have seen her, since long before I made my intentions known. And I am a merchant who travels with my caravans. I know the rudiments of healing. This girl suffered from a terrible wound. There is a chance she might have died from it. The pain was such that at times she cried out."

"And after?"

Ezra wiped his face. "She wept in gratitude. She moved about with total ease—almost in a dance of praise. Like . . . like David dancing before the Lord. And she lifted her arms to heaven and called out her thanksgiving over and over."

"So." Gamaliel's fist gripped his beard and tugged harder still. "We have another miracle."

"There is no other way to describe what I saw. I have relived it countless times, both awake and in my sleep."

"And then the one they call an apostle—" Gamaliel grimaced at the word—"he invited you to join them."

"No. It was not . . ." Ezra struggled to explain. "Upon my arrival, a young man named Stephen said something that mirrored words I had heard my own sister speak. How each of us comes for our own reasons."

"Comes where?"

"To be with them and listen to their message. What Stephen meant was that our motives are wrong. Our thinking is wrong. But if we come . . . with an open heart and mind, we will see the rightness of their declarations." He finished in a rush, feeling his explanation had not conveyed what he intended. Or what Stephen intended.

Gamaliel did not object as Ezra might have expected. After all, he had just told a senior Pharisee and a serving member of the High Council that he was in error in his assessment of a religious matter. Instead, his friend merely sat and wrestled with matters beyond his ken. Ezra knew Gamaliel's sleep would now be as disturbed as his own.

Eventually Ezra rose and went in search of his son. When he returned to bid his host farewell, he found the priest still seated behind his table, still staring out the window, still stroking his beard.

CHAPTER

EIGHTEEN

LINUX SAT IN WHAT HAD SERVED as Pontius Pilate's hall of judgment. The new governor of Judea, Marcellus, had turned this into
an assembly room for those seeking an audience. The large hall
had three entrances—one to the gardens, one into the hallway
connected to the palace entrance, and the last into the prelate's
private quarters. All three doors were flanked by armed legionnaires standing at full attention. Through the outer door Linux
could see workers demolishing the wall that had divided Herod's
garden from Pilate's. More construction noise came from the private chambers.

"The governor is certainly wasting no time." Horus, master
of the Caesarea harbor, had sidled up next to Linux. "The same
day I learn his ship had set into Joppa, I receive orders to present
myself."

"You have nothing to worry about," Linux said.

"So you've had a word with the soothsayers about my future?"
Horus used the sleeve of his dress tunic to clear sweat from his

forehead. "If he's so pleased with my work, why didn't he land at Caesarea and bid me meet him there?"

"His ship was blown off course and damaged by a storm." This much Linux had learned from the sergeant who had brought his summons. "Marcellus intends to make Jerusalem his principal residence. At least for the moment. So you have been sent for, as have I."

Horus studied him closely. "Speaking of storms, you remind me of a green recruit sailing through his first hard blow. Are you ill?"

Linux drew himself up straighter. Two days had passed since his last encounter with the apostles. He had scarcely slept. His nights were a battleground. One moment he was consumed with desire for the beautiful young woman. The next, he was back in the compound, feeling the force of the apostle Peter's words. They struck at him like hammers in the dark. *Be healed.*

Not to mention the voice he had heard just before the miracle had taken place. And miracle it was. Linux had no doubt of that. He had seen more than his share of tricksters and mendicants. The man Peter was nothing of the sort. The man had asked for nothing, save that Linux give his allegiance to a dead prophet. This one whose power had swept through the compound, silencing even the sputtering torches. This one who had spoken to Linux from beyond the grave.

Linux realized his friend was watching him. He searched quickly for what they had been talking about, and came up with, "The prelate Marcellus has just one interest in Judea."

"And that is?"

"Money."

"And you know this by what means?"

"He told me. We met in Rome, remember? My guess is he will insist that you increase port charges and ensure that every ship pays its full amount of duty."

Horus bristled. He was a stumpy man who in earlier years had earned a reputation as a brawler. "I keep honest books and demand the same from every captain who enters my harbor."

"Take that attitude with the governor, and he will feed you to the fish," Linux warned. "Present yourself, bow to the prelate as you would the emperor, and assure him that every boat, right down to the meanest fishing rig, will pay its full share of customs. And when he offers you extra men, do not give a single lift of an eyebrow. You and he both know he is placing spies in your midst, but instead thank him for aiding you in carrying out his orders."

The harbor master's response was cut off by an attendant calling his name. He wiped his face once more. His voice was gruff. "I owe you for this gift of wise counsel."

Soon after the harbor master left the chamber, another familiar figure appeared at the garden entrance. Tribune Bruno Aetius carried himself with a sulfurous air. He jammed his helmet down hard upon his head and stomped across the marble-tiled gallery. Linux liked the man, and knew he deserved far better than the new prelate had probably offered. He showed what respect he could, snapping to attention, slamming his fist to his metal breastplate, and bowing low.

Tribune Bruno Aetius growled as deep as an angry bear. "The man has only arrived in Judea. Yet already he knows enough to demand why I have allowed the situation to descend into chaos."

"Your head is still attached to your shoulders," Linux observed. "So I can only assume you did not tell him what you thought of the question."

"I was tempted, I give you that. Sorely tempted indeed." The tribune mashed his helmet harder still. "The prelate wishes for me to depart for Damascus with all possible haste. As if I would serve under him a moment longer than necessary."

"I will miss you, sire," Linux said, and meant it. "Jerusalem will be poorer for your departure."

Bruno Aetius inspected the younger officer. "Come with me, Linux."

"Sire?"

"I have need of good officers. My guess is I'll be reassigned to the Parthian borderlands. You can sit out the madness that is soon to be sweeping the empire."

"Lower your voice, I beg you."

Bruno Aetius stepped in close enough for Linux to smell the garlic on his breath. "You were in Rome. You know I speak the truth. Madness is on the wind. It blows like a pestilence over this land."

For some reason Linux once again heard the words that had rocked his world. *Be healed.*

The tribune took Linux's silence as agreement and stepped closer still. He hissed, "When you arrived here, you served a man who knew the value of soldiers. Pilate fought for Rome in Germany. He was an officer in the emperor's corps. He lived without a care for the trappings of power. He knew the worth of men he could trust. You think this new prelate will hold to any of that? Look around and tell me what you see!"

Linux glanced about the chamber. Pilate had preferred it because it was austere in the military manner. Now benches lined the bare walls—all filled. Merchants clustered together, while their servants stood at a discreet distance holding samples of their wares. A group of Temple priests, Sadducees by the cut of their gaudy robes, murmured quietly in the corner. Other than the guards by each door, he and Bruno Aetius were the only military personnel.

Linux said softly, "I will think upon what you have said."

"Don't take too long." Bruno Aetius backed away. "I leave for Damascus in a week."

Linux watched the tribune march across the gallery. His mind was suddenly filled with an image of a lovely young Judean lass. Such thoughts had no place here, in this moment of danger and uncertainty. Yet he knew in his heart of hearts that he would be going nowhere until he knew for certain what chance he had with her.

He was so intent upon his musings, he did not notice the servant until the man touched his arm. "The prelate will see you now."

———

The new governor of Judea received Linux in Herod's most luxurious hall. Many of the overdone trappings were gone, the luxury piled upon luxury, but the gilded thronelike chair remained. The prelate Marcellus was surrounded by the same cluster of advisers that Linux had met in Rome. They eyed Linux with the cold cynicism of hyenas sizing up their next meal.

Linux came to attention before the throne and saluted the prelate as he would the emperor. "Linux Aurelius reporting as ordered, sire."

"Ah. My able servant and soldier. We meet again in my new home."

"Allow me to add my own welcome to that of all Judea, sire."

"Spoken like a true prince." Marcellus wore the uniform of a Roman officer, including a gold breastplate embedded with precious stones, as were his wristbands. His silk tunic was dyed purple, a shade restricted by royal decree to those holding imperial power, and normally worn only inside Rome's borders. "Will you take refreshment?"

"Thank you, sire. I was served in the antechamber."

Abruptly the prelate rose from his chair. "Walk with me, Linux."

His advisers rose like a gaggle of fowl, adjusting their fine robes like birds shaking their wings. Marcellus gave them a slit-eyed smile. "Alone."

The order was so unexpected, the entire group froze. Were his situation not so grave, Linux would have laughed out loud.

"Come, Linux." The governor of Judea exited the audience chamber, ignoring the soldiers who saluted his passage, and led Linux down the steps and into the palace gardens. "Is it always so hot here?"

"You have arrived in the dry season, sire," Linux replied stiffly. "I'm afraid the worst heat is still to come. August can be unbearable. Some Septembers are equally bad. It would be advisable to spend those weeks in Caesarea, where the sea air is much cooler."

"You see how much I do not know of this land, and how important is your counsel." Marcellus bent over a bell-shaped flower and inhaled. "I am of a mind to reward you."

"You are too kind, sire. But it is an honor to serve your lordship. I have no need of—"

"Nonsense. A trusted ally is deserving of special attention." The prelate led them further down a curving stone lane, until the palace was lost from view. "Perhaps I should have your brother disposed of."

Linux felt his legs turn to stone. "Sire?"

"Did I not mention that I know Castor? No, perhaps not. He is a foul pest, wouldn't you agree? That child he took as a second wife would certainly not miss him." The prelate leaned over another flower. "It was so kind of Herod to make a gift of his garden, wasn't it?"

"I . . . that is . . ."

Marcellus glanced back at Linux and smiled knowingly. "Come, come. We are both men of the world. You can't possibly expect me to believe that you have never wished your brother would depart for an early grave."

Linux felt as though his senses had never been so sharp. Every leaf shone in utter clarity, every flower. A hot wind touched his cheek, a breath of warning. And he knew, in that crystalline moment, that he was being offered a choice. The stone path at his feet shone as though washed by ghostly hands. One direction led to a future he could only see in the most hazy of terms, the other to an awful realization of his every desire.

Linux realized that the prelate was waiting for him to respond. The words slipped from his throat. "And in return?"

His moment of utter clarity vanished. The world became as it had been before. Hot and dusty and dulled by hate and desire.

The governor gave him a reptilian smile. "Come, my new adviser. Let us see if this lovely garden can offer us a bit of shade."

Marcellus led him deeper still into the green enclave. Linux could not help comparing this man to the predecessor he had once served. Pontius Pilate wore the uniform because it suited him. On the new governor, however, the military trappings mocked his evident weakness. Marcellus was a man shaped by idleness and indulgence. The arms which emerged from the tunic were the color of flour.

They passed one fountain, another. The workers hammering down the dividing wall faded into the distance. They arrived at the fountain furthest from the palace. The outer border was rimmed by date palms planted so tightly their branches formed a basket-weave overhead. "Sit here beside me, Linux."

"Sire, I am most grateful. But I think more clearly on my feet."

"As you wish." The prelate adjusted his robes before settling onto the fountain's stone rim. "A man of your abilities cannot possibly wish to live the remainder of his days here in this pestilent province with its quarrelsome folk."

"The tribune Bruno Aetius has invited me to join his officer corps and travel to Syria."

"I do not wish it, do you hear?" The man slapped the stone with an open palm. "I forbid you to accept his offer."

"I hear and obey, sire." As Linux bowed he heard a door slam shut in his brain.

"Besides which, your place is not in yet another hot and dusty war-torn land. Your place is in Umbria."

The way Marcellus spoke the word *Umbria*, it sounded like a song. Linux was flooded with a yearning so strong that he shivered.

Very little seemed to escape the prelate's eye. He gave Linux a tight smile. "Or, if you prefer, Rome. After all, with your brother out of the way, you would rule the family holdings. A prince of Umbria would be expected to spend time in Rome. A seat on the Senate would be his for the asking."

"Transfer of power from one brother to another is not guaranteed by Roman law."

The prelate was not at all disturbed by Linux's statement. "I can guarantee that the emperor would appoint you guardian over your brother's children."

"How is that possible, may I ask?"

"Do sit down, Linux. I dislike having to look up at you."

Reluctantly he settled down onto the fountain's edge, but well out of striking range. Marcellus had given no sign of carrying even a dagger. But the man emanated a palpable flavor of doom. "Forgive me for speaking openly, sire."

"Why do you think we have removed ourselves to this station? Say whatever is on your mind."

"A guarantee is easily offered when there are no witnesses, and the emperor is in distant Rome."

"I carry a document bearing his own seal. All I need do is supply the words."

Linux leaned so far back he felt the fountain's splash upon his neck.

"As soon as we return to the palace, I will show you the scroll." The prelate was not a patient man, and when Linux remained silent he slapped the stone once more. "I command you to answer!"

"I have known men of nearly limitless power who will not sleep alone," Linux said slowly. "Yet here we are, with neither guards nor advisers. I am thinking that the task you have in mind for me is as grave as it is dangerous."

"Are you afraid of danger, Linux?"

"No, sire. Not when the threat bears a purpose that a simple officer's mind can understand."

"There is purpose indeed. But not military. My intent lies within the realms of power." The prelate slid over the stone, closing the distance between them. "Sejanus demands to be made consul. The Senate desperately seeks to refuse him that post. But they need someone else to hold that position. Someone they can trust. I wish to claim it for myself. I wish it with the same passion as you wish for your brother to vanish from this earth."

Linux nodded. The consuls of Rome acted as bridges between the emperor and the Senate. They also served as high judges of the Roman empire. Their power was second only to the emperor himself.

Marcellus went on, "My allies within the Senate have said that I would be acceptable as consul. But only if I can pay their price, which is enormous."

"Forgive me, sire. But I am utterly without funds. And I doubt that my family could possibly—"

"I don't wish to give you a princedom merely to beggar you. As consul, I will need trusted allies even more than I do here."

"Then what—?"

"Do you know the amount that foul priest Caiaphas and

his father-in-law, Annas, paid me to retain the position of high priest?"

"I had heard it was their weight in gold."

"That and more. They paid without a quibble. Do you know what that means? The Temple treasury must be huge. Large enough to satisfy even the Senate's impossible hunger for gold." Marcellus dropped his voice to where it joined with the fountain's music, a soft murmur of poison. "Find a way to bring me the Temple treasury, and your brother will not last another month. Agree to be my thief, and you depart for Umbria with the guardianship decree in your pouch. Marry the widow or dispose of her, adopt the children or lock them away forever—no one in Rome will care either way, of that I can assure you."

The man's expression carried the heat of a branding iron, one that scalded the inner reaches of Linux's heart. "All your dreams and more are here on offer. If you agree to be my chosen man."

CHAPTER

NINETEEN

IT HAD BEEN SUCH A SATISFYING MORNING. The intense heat, of course, had added to the strain of working since before dawn in the kitchen and distributing the meals. *A chance to just sit and relax for a few moments . . .* But neither the heat nor her weariness could erase the joy that filled Abigail's being. Both legs were strong and ready to take her wherever she wished to go. Besides the healing itself, what a marvel it was to be directly touched by the Lord.

But she had to admit the hours of work left her body aching from her neck to the soles of her feet. Many of the women were considerably older than Abigail. She felt responsible to carry as much of the load as she could.

She had kneaded bread for the ovens and set it to rise. Then, having decided after all that she preferred to make her own selections, she headed for the market stalls. She hoped the fresh garden and vineyard produce would already be laid out by the time she arrived. There was no waiting, and she was able to quickly fill her two baskets and start back. As she struggled through the streets, the heavy load slowing her steps, the roosters had awakened, admonishing their flocks to also get busy.

By the time she made it back to the compound the bread was ready to be baked. It was needed for the first meal of the day.

From then on the day sped forward without slowing for a moment. It seemed to Abigail that every day brought new people to the compound who needed provisions. Peter had ceased trying to keep count of how many were being baptized into the community of believers.

It was true that only a few of the followers of the Way actually met and ate at these central quarters. All over Jerusalem and stretching into the surrounding villages and farms, other groups were housed.

But in the morning and afternoon many came to the compound for their daily rations of food to prepare in their own kitchens. A cart and additional donkey were purchased so more food could be brought from the market. That was now how much of Abigail's day was spent. Her new assignment to aid overburdened Martha included managing the distribution of the food—it had to be sorted, portioned, and handed out to those who came.

Responsibility for keeping track of donated funds and outgoing expenses was Stephen's. He showed the same open heart to everyone, both those giving and those in need. Abigail found herself in awe of his calm demeanor and his giving heart. Particularly this day, when God's presence seemed so very close to her, she enjoyed a prayerful calm as she saw to her myriad tasks.

That afternoon, as usual, Peter and another apostle prayed over the food and funds coming from volunteers, asking the Lord to bless it and increase it as needed. Abigail had never had to turn anyone away from the distribution table empty-handed.

Abigail watched the last of the afternoon crowd hoist their

baskets and head back out into the street. She heaved a sigh, thankful that another day was nearing an end.

Seated at the central courtyard table, Stephen wrote his last entry and rolled up the scroll of his records. He nodded to her. "You look hot and tired."

"I am both. But weariness is nothing like the pain—"

"The entire gathering has spoken of little else besides the miracle." He motioned to the bench opposite his, now cast in afternoon shadows. "You should take a moment and rest. Have you eaten?"

"I don't remember." They both laughed, and she added, "Not since daybreak."

"You must keep up your strength if you are to care for others."

Abigail nodded and went into the shadowy cooking alcove to pour herself a mug of goat's milk. She returned to the table. Though the compound remained a center of activity with people still coming and going, this one spot was both public and yet somewhat isolated. "Will you take anything?" she asked before she sat down.

"Not for the moment, thank you." He fingered the corner of the scroll. His usually tranquil expression held a look of concern.

"Is . . . is something the matter?"

"God always supplies. His miracles abound, as we have been so profoundly reminded." He nodded toward her with a smile. "We are indeed blessed by his abundance. I need only see you moving so well about the compound to be reminded of these truths." But his face was grave again.

"Yet something troubles you, I can see it."

Stephen leaned across the table and murmured, "We have almost nothing left. Not even a few coins to pay for tomorrow's supplies."

"We have no money?" Abigail could not believe her ears.

He simply shook his head.

"What will we do?"

Stephen ran a finger along the edge of the scroll, as though tracing the accounts of each passing day. "We wait. We trust." He straightened his shoulders and said, "Then we marvel when God meets the need."

Abigail hesitated, then confessed, "I wish my faith were that strong."

His smile returned, and all his features seemed transformed by that simple act. "Do you know, for weeks I would sit here working and praying and worrying. And then God answered my prayers by bringing you."

Abigail was so shocked she could not respond.

"Indeed. What a wonderful reminder of his power, seeing you walk across the courtyard, smiling despite your weariness. With your wound utterly healed." His dark eyes shone with renewed purpose. "We have God's promise. You have helped me remember this."

She lowered her eyes, not wanting Stephen to see her doubts. What would they do to feed the people if the money did not come? So many followers depended upon them.

She managed what she hoped was a confident smile. She too must allow faith to guide her thoughts and expectations. A brief nod, and she replied. "Please tell me . . . when it happens. I will rejoice with you."

Stephen stood and tucked the scroll under his arm. "I will," he promised. "We will not have long to wait. Funds are needed for the morning purchases."

———

They had just finished evening prayers, including some fervent requests for "God to supply all our needs," and a weary Abigail was wrapping her shawl about her shoulders when Stephen approached her. "I have news," he said, the shine in his eyes saying even more than his words.

Abigail allowed herself to be guided to one side of the courtyard, a few steps away from the bustle of departing worshipers. "It's already happened." His voice was low, but his expression was clear in the glow from the courtyard torches. "The money. For tomorrow. For many, many tomorrows. It's here."

"But how . . . ?" There were so many questions. "Where did this . . . this miracle come from?"

"I was just putting the accounts away in the locked chest when the Levite Joses, a Cypriot— Do you know him?"

Abigail felt almost overwhelmed by Stephen's excitement. She forced herself to think. "The apostles call him Barnabas?"

"Yes, that's the one. He sold a property, and this very evening he set the money at the apostles' feet."

"What—*all* of it?"

"Everything. We have enough for months to come." His voice held a quiet triumph. "Another wondrous sign that God is taking care of us."

Abigail murmured words of thanks she scarcely could hear herself. When the young man moved away, she looked down toward her healed leg. Why had she ever doubted? It was just as Stephen said. The Lord promised. The Lord supplied.

Abigail continued to find wonder in the smallest of acts, such as picking up the baskets and heading off to market. Or knotting the day's coins in the corner of her shawl, and smiling with Stephen over the miracle of money for all their needs. Now it was up to the community of believers to spend the funds wisely.

Stephen nodded a farewell to her as he and Philip started off in the donkey cart to transport supplies to those in greatest distress. As reprisals against the followers of the Way grew in intensity, there were more and more who needed such help. Many had lost their jobs because shop owners feared Temple reprisal if a follower was found in their employ. Looks of contempt were cast on them when they were recognized in the streets—or even curses, spitting, or handfuls of dust. It was clear their increasing numbers had the whole city on edge.

Abigail was mentally busy with all these concerns as she moved from stall to stall, selecting, bartering, and filling her baskets. When the task was accomplished she was happy to head for the compound.

She stopped at the well to draw water to wash the vegetables and then carried the pail to the clay trough. Thankfully, the trough and the stone bench alongside it were still held in shadows. The cobblestones surrounding the well reflected the sun and created even more heat.

And then there's Jacob. . . . Her brother was a study in contrasts these days. He was overjoyed by her healing. Yet he remained extremely troubled. Abigail knew it was at least partly his yearning to join the Roman army. Yet she also sensed that Jacob was upset with her. Why, she had no idea. But sometimes she found him watching her, his face veiled in anger and frustration. Occasionally he would bring up Linux as a possible suitor, and when she pointed out that Peter had insisted they wait for Alban, he would fume in silence.

She was so taken up with her concerns about Jacob that she was halfway through her task at the trough before she realized a man and a woman nearby seemed to be arguing. She heard the woman say, "The land was given to *me* to arrange the betrothal."

Abigail's hands, holding a leek, stilled. She recognized the voice as Sapphira's, a member of a wealthy Judean clan. Wife of

Ananias, both of them part of their group. And she was sister to Ezra, the merchant who sought her hand. . . .

The voice came from the other side of the stone wall providing her shade. A teahouse fronted a narrow ledge that overlooked the city's ancient walls. Abigail had passed it any number of times but had never been inside. Sapphira must have been seated right beside the wall.

She heard the man say, "Which gives them even less right to demand any part of such a gift. Especially after they have refused your brother's entreaties."

Abigail was certain the voice belonged to Ananias. She started to move away, but something held her in place. Fear, certainly. There had been no word from Ezra since Peter had said he would pray and consult with Alban before making any decision about whom she might wed. But Abigail had no doubt such a powerful man could make trouble for them all. And especially for her.

Sapphira was saying, "It was not a gift, really. He paid me with the land."

"A payment of sorts, I suppose. But what's important here is that the land belonged to us. Ezra placed no conditions on it, and neither should anyone else."

Abigail frowned, bewildered. What could they be arguing over?

"Well, it's sold. You took care of that in a hurry." She sounded angry. "I'm not sure it was the wisest thing to do. Such property would only go up in value—but it's gone."

"And it brought a good price."

"That's not the point, husband. We find ourselves in a dilemma. You know what Barnabas did. And what others are doing. Whatever they receive from such transactions, they give. They will expect the same from us."

"Why do they have to know?"

"Why? It's not a matter of why. They will, that's all. Does any land in this city change hands without the world knowing about it? No. Of course not. Everyone will have heard of the sale before this day is out. If you hadn't sold it so hastily we . . ."

Abigail tried to concentrate on the vegetables, but the voice on the other side of the wall could not be blocked from her hearing.

"All right—so maybe I acted in haste. I did not think of this . . . this situation."

"I don't think you thought at all."

A bold statement for a woman to make to her husband. But Sapphira sounded too angry to be guarding her tongue.

"So what do we do?" Ananias had lowered his voice in defeat.

"Well, we have to give it. We will feel their disapproval—and maybe worse—if we do not."

"But . . ."

"But?"

"That's a great sum—"

"Of course it is," Sapphira said. "The property was worth a small fortune."

"I know. I know. You've told me that several times. But do we have to give it all?"

"What do you mean?"

"Nobody will know the price we got for the land." Ananias spoke more swiftly now. "I could give them double what Barnabas did. We would still retain more than half."

"I suppose—"

"Then it's settled. I'll bring in the bags of silver in the morning and give them to the treasurer, Stephen. No, no, I'll give them directly to Peter."

The voices faded away as the couple must have left the teahouse. All Abigail could think of was the excitement this additional amount would bring to Stephen. He had a great responsibility in caring for the needs of so many people. And the two had said this gift would be twice what Barnabas had brought. Abigail was tempted to run and tell Stephen right away. But, no, that wouldn't be right. This was not her secret to tell. She never should have heard the conversation in the first place. She would let Ananias and Sapphira be the bearers of the good news.

But she couldn't help but smile as she dumped the water from washing the vegetables and carried the baskets of clean produce toward the kitchens.

———

The next morning Abigail was busy in the kitchen with Martha, her sister Mary, and two younger girls when they heard a commotion from the courtyard.

"What is that?" asked Mary, lifting her head.

"What?" Martha's hearing was not as keen as it once had been.

"I heard some noise. It sounded like a . . . like a muffled scream."

"I heard it too," Abigail agreed, wiping her hands on her robe. "But it wasn't really a scream. It was . . . I don't know. I've never heard anything like it before."

When they heard nothing further, they shrugged and continued their meal preparation.

It was not long until Philip appeared in the kitchen doorway, his face as pale as chalk. He told them, his voice hushed, that Ananias had come with money from the sale of property. He had presented it to Peter, claiming it to be the full amount of the sale. Instead of praising him, Peter had condemned him. Not for his generosity, which was commendable, but for his lie.

"The land was yours," Peter had told Ananias, his eyes flashing fire. "The money was your right to keep. But you have lied to the

Holy Spirit." And right on the spot, Ananias had collapsed on the cobblestones. They could not revive him, and he was dead.

The women struggled to accept what they were hearing. But Philip was not finished with his report. Even more frightening, when Sapphira had arrived, the whole scene was repeated.

They were gone. Both of them. In only the matter of a few hours. Peter had ordered some of the men to take them out of the compound and bury them.

The group of women stood aghast. Abigail felt faint. So that was the result of the conversation she had partly overheard. The shocking turn of events sickened her.

———

Abigail wrestled with her troubled thoughts the rest of the day. What had just happened? Was their God really that vindictive? As she moved about the courtyard serving those who came for their daily supplies, she saw the little clusters of whispering people, eyes wide with both wonder and fright. Word had traveled quickly. People dared not even ask questions or express their concerns.

Peter was not seen until evening prayers. He rose and addressed the entire gathering. Abigail had never seen the compound so full, or so silent.

"Brothers and sisters," Peter began, his booming voice drawn to a husky murmur. "You all know of the sudden deaths today of two of our members. It was not for the good they were attempting to do that they were struck. No. The God we serve demands an open and honest heart. It was not to me that the lie was told. It was a lie before a holy and just God. God sees the heart. He knows our thoughts. May this caution each one of us to be honest in all our dealings. We cannot"—his voice rose then—"we cannot deceive God."

Peter looked out over the crowded courtyard. His voice rang with fervent pleading. "If we are to fight evil in our world—as we are called to do—we cannot harbor deceitfulness in our hearts. May God give us the courage and the strength and the wisdom to live as he wants us to live. He is a *holy* God. And he is also a God of love. He desires only our good. He will show us what we each must learn from this experience today."

Abigail and Jacob did not speak as they walked home that night, but Abigail reflected on Peter's words all the way back to their small quarters.

EZRA WALKED BEHIND THE SERVANT past the sentries and out the Dung Gate, his questions held tightly inside. He had not spoken since Ananias's servant had arrived with the appalling news. Despite his panic and his dread, he would not shout such news to the city. If it was indeed true. *And why?*

The servant had appeared at Ezra's door, his face still wet with tears. He had been sent alone by Ananias's family—no one else could bring themselves to face him. The servant, a follower, had related all that had happened, everything he had witnessed from his place among the gathering.

Even as the servant had related the news, Ezra had reshaped the words into something more acceptable. Clearly the servant had witnessed something that had shocked him to the core. This much was certain. Yet Ezra's mind refused to accept what the servant had told him. His sister dead? Her husband also? Within hours of each other? Impossible!

A drover shouted a warning at Ezra and prodded his sheep

toward the gate. Ezra stepped off the road, stumbling over the uneven earth. The ground did not seem stable beneath his sandals. Nothing was as it should be.

Ahead of him, the servant took the turn onto the lane leading south into the Kidron Valley. Ezra demanded, "Where are you taking me? Where is Sapphira?"

The man pointed ahead, his hand trembling. He did not speak.

When the man's destination finally struck home, Ezra stopped as if struck dead himself. The reality of where they were headed condensed the heat and the sunlight until it held him fast. He had to struggle to breathe.

The servant stumbled forward another few steps, then realized Ezra no longer followed. He returned and stood before the merchant, panting in exhaustion and fear.

Ezra heard his own breath punching out in tight gasps, as if he had just run far into the desert. He blinked and stared about him. Finally he said, "This is the potter's field."

The man stood silent, his eyes lowered to the stones at his feet.

In the distance, a crow gave a lonely cry. A rock clattered down the hillside behind them. Otherwise, there was no sound except their strained breathing.

Ezra licked dry lips. "Tell me again what happened. From the beginning."

"The apostles had gathered. Followers were coming before them and offering donations. Ananias stepped forward." The servant sounded utterly shattered. "He stood before the apostles. He laid money at their feet. Peter asked if this was everything he had received from the sale of the land. He—"

"Wait." Every word was a struggle to get out. "What right does Peter have to make such a claim?"

"Barnabas also sold land. He gave the entire amount."

Ezra blinked, dislodging sweat. Or perhaps he wept but was too stunned to realize it. "This other man gave everything he made from the sale of his own property to the apostles?"

"Barnabas is a leader among us. He performs miracles. The Spirit is strong in him. The people look to him for leadership. He casts a gentle shadow." The servant's words carried a numb and toneless quality. "I think, that is . . ."

"Go on."

"My master and mistress wanted to gain a similar respect within the community. I believe . . . they sought to wield the same influence."

Ezra winced, and another droplet of sweat or sorrow fell to the earth. This was very much like his sister. Sapphira always wanted to have everything her way, but never understood the price that had to be paid. Her entire life, she had been given whatever she wanted. The sacrifice and the labor were paid by others. Of course she had sought to have this power without paying the price.

Ezra felt his grasp upon the world slip away, as though he had been laid to rest in the same grave as his sister and brother-in-law. It was indeed true. Sapphira was gone.

The servant went on, "Peter was the apostle who spoke. When Ananias insisted that he had given everything, Peter accused him of lying not to the apostles but to the divine Spirit of God. Peter said that Ananias was under no obligation to give anything at all. But he had turned his donation into a treachery against the Holy Spirit. As he said this, Ananias was struck down."

"Who struck him?" Ezra could feel the rage in the base of his gut, ready to uncoil and lash out. It was good to feel something, anything at all. "Who dared strike my kin?"

"N-no one, sir. No one was even close to him."

"They threw a stone? A stave, an arrow, a . . . ?" He stopped because the servant was shaking his head back and forth, denying Ezra a target for his anger even before the words took form.

"No one touched him." The servant might have been trembling with shock, his voice dulled to a simple moan. But he was utterly certain. "No one threw anything. No one moved at all. He just fell down. Dead."

"That cannot be."

The servant did not respond. His gaze remained fastened upon the rocks at his feet. But his hollow expression suggested that he saw the event happening again. Over and over and over.

"What happened next?"

"Several of the young men were instructed to . . . to pick up the body and bring it here." The servant's swallow was loud in the dry, silent air. "Then your sister arrived in the compound. Peter asked her the same question. She gave the same response. Peter condemned her for lying." His voice was now barely audible. "She fell and breathed her last."

"And then?"

The servant waved his hand toward the sunlit emptiness. "The same young men brought her here as well."

Ezra tried to take in the field before him. But he felt like he was looking through a veil. Not that he needed to see it clearly—he knew what lay before him. The potter's field was Jerusalem's recent burial ground for commoners and the poorest of the poor. A lone tree grew by the furthest boundary marker, its limbs stunted and stained by the field's nameless crop. The yellow earth was tilled into dozens of mounds, hundreds. His sister was buried somewhere out there, her grave unmarked.

Ezra turned his face to the sun and allowed the tears to rise and fall. He slammed his fist into his other hand and groaned out the only dirge that would mark his sister's passage. "They will pay for this."

The atmosphere within the community remained subdued. Besides the appalling deaths, it sounded as if attacks on their members within the city were becoming sharper and more frequent.

Abigail felt increasingly vulnerable as she went about her duties. Jacob was on edge as well. As they made their way to the compound for evening prayers, she was startled when Jacob gripped her shoulder and shoved her hard against the wall. He stepped in front of her, blocking her vision and shielding her with his body. He snarled over his shoulder, "What do you want?"

A stranger's voice said, "Please—I mean you no harm. I have been sent."

Jacob remained tense and guarded. "Why are you lurking in the shadows if you mean no harm?"

"I was told to find you but to remain unseen. I assure you, I am no danger to you. I've been sent by Alban."

Jacob's voice rose. "He is here?"

"He is not far away, and he wishes to see you."

Abigail dared take a peek around Jacob. The stranger seemed harmless enough. She prayed he was telling the truth. "Where is Alban?" she asked.

"At the south camp. He wishes you to meet him there."

Abigail pushed past Jacob. "You will take us?"

"It is why I came."

"Then let us go."

As they started off, Abigail clutched Jacob's arm. "How we have prayed. And now when we need him the most, he . . ." She could go no further. In spite of her resolve to push aside the fear that had crept into her heart from the recent events, its dread left her shivering. Tears veiled her eyes until she could scarcely see where they were headed. *Alban has come!* whirled through her mind.

As Alban had warned them in his letter, he had changed much in the two years since their last meeting. Abigail would have been hard-pressed to recognize him had she passed him on the street. But his voice and firm embrace convinced them that he was the man they had been waiting for.

Alban drew them quickly into his tent and pulled the flap across the door. The flickering torchlight illuminated a bearded face that looked both leaner and darker than Abigail recalled. But the eyes belonged to Alban.

He was dressed in a plain tunic, with a simple band around his waist and a headpiece very much akin to that of a Bedouin. A short sword hung from his belt and a long knife from the other side. Abigail had no doubt that he could wield both with skill. She watched him pull the weapons out and lay them on the table beside a battered shield. And saw as well how Jacob followed the moves with undisguised longing.

"Jacob, my boy. I can't call you that anymore. Look at you. You are nearly my height. How could you grow like that?"

It was true. Jacob was now only half a handsbreadth shorter than the older man, though still much slighter in build in spite of muscle developed from his work lifting heavy wood.

"And Abigail. How Leah would love to see you. She misses you so. Every day she speaks of you."

"She is well?"

He grinned and nodded. "More than well. She is counting the weeks until we are blessed with a child. And sewing little garments. Already she has filled the cradle with soft blankets—and the whitest of sheepskins for him to lie on."

Abigail laughed softly. "Him, you say."

"It is a habit. If it is not *he*, then *she* will be greatly loved. I

hope she will be as beautiful as her mother. And as pure of heart."
He waved them onto cushions by the tent wall. "But you. Are you
keeping well?"

Abigail and Jacob looked at each other and laughed. "Yes,
Alban, I am more than well," Abigail said. Then both she and
Jacob described her healing, with many questions along the way
from Alban.

"Thanks be to our Lord!" he exclaimed when they were finished with the story.

"Now, tell me what else has been happening," he said. "Are
things well with the brethren? I hear many have been added to
the numbers."

"That is true," Abigail said. Then she glanced again at Jacob.
The deaths remained a shadow that stained his features.

"Has there been trouble?" Alban looked from one to the other.
"Has Rome struck against the followers with its heavy hand?"

"No. Not yet. Though daily we see Jerusalem becoming more
frenzied, chaotic."

"The Sanhedrin, then?"

"They are angry with us over the preaching and teaching. In fact
they put some of our number in prison a short while ago. But we all
pray for courage as Peter admonishes. The teaching continues."

A moment of silence turned awkward. Alban pressed, "Will
you not tell me what is wrong?"

Abigail hesitated. Where was she to begin? So much had happened, so many things crowded into her mind.

She gazed about at their surroundings. Torchlight shone on the
tent walls, casting a comforting glow over the threadbare carpet and
low wood table with the simple brass utensils. The water pitcher
and mugs were once-fired clay, with no adornment whatsoever.
When Abigail had first come to know Alban, he was a centurion
and one of Pilate's chosen men. He and Leah's betrothal ceremony

had been held in Herod's palace. Yet here he sat, dressed in the garb of a caravan guard, sitting amongst poverty almost as abject as her own.

And one look into the man's face told her that here was a truly happy man. Content, serene, calm in his faith. All that she was not. She saw no doubt, no worries about the future, no regrets over things that were not as he might have preferred. How she wished for Alban's strength!

When she did not speak, Jacob said, "Two men are vying for Abigail's hand in marriage. Peter put them off, saying you are her guardian and the matter would be settled when you arrive."

Alban showed no surprise over the news. "Do you wish to marry one or the other?"

"No, I do not," she said quietly but firmly. "Neither of them."

Jacob shifted restlessly beside her. "Well, I think she should give serious thought to—"

Abigail cut him off. She had no interest in Alban knowing one of the suitors was his old friend. "I have already told you I do not wish a marriage to *either* man."

Alban looked toward Jacob, but he merely scowled at the carpet by his feet. Alban said, "Perhaps we should wait and discuss this more on the morrow. It certainly is not something we can settle tonight."

Abigail sighed her thankfulness. She would prefer to discuss this without Jacob present.

Alban's calm gaze shifted from one to the other. "There is more, yes? I sense—"

"I work for a carpenter." The heat of passion lifted Jacob's voice. "It is loathsome. I detest it."

"You want to do something else. I see that. Do you have an idea of what you wish for your future?"

"You know I have," Jacob shot back. "Nothing has changed. I want to do what you have done."

"You still wish to join the Roman legion."

Jacob sent Abigail a look, one so strong she found herself holding back from the torrent of arguments that filled her mind. He turned back to Alban. "You offered to help me."

Alban sighed. "That was a different man who said that."

"Just the same, there was once a time when you considered it a worthy profession. And I still feel that way."

Alban nodded slowly. There was a measured pace to his words and motions, one Abigail did not recall from earlier times. *As though the desert has worked itself deep into the man's bones. . . .* And prayer as well, she added. He was far more thoughtful, and much deeper. His copper eyes held the depths of a Bedouin well. "Perhaps that too should wait for tomorrow, Jacob," she said. "It is getting late and we have traveled far. I am weary, as you must be also, Alban. Perhaps we will all see things more clearly with the morning light. Now—"

But Jacob was not finished. "Something terrible happened at the compound. It frightened me." He glanced at Abigail, revealing how the shadows had returned to his features. "I . . . I don't even know if I want to go back."

Alban studied her brother. The flickering torchlight had turned the young man into someone far beyond his years. Abigail felt more than ever the threat of losing him. He was growing into his own person, and handling the traumas of life very differently.

Alban asked quietly, "What happened?"

"Two people were killed. Or died. Or something . . ." Jacob picked at a thread in the carpet. The words tumbled out as he recounted the story of Ananias and Sapphira.

Alban did not take his eyes from the boy's face. Jacob's eyes grew ever wider with disbelief, doubt, concern, and awe. By the time he was done with the tale, his shoulders were shaking.

Alban reached out a hand of comfort. "Do you wish to stay here for the night?"

"Oh yes. Could we?"

"There is room." He rose smoothly to his feet. "I'll gather extra pallets and blankets from the caravan owner. Wait here."

Abigail shut her eyes and rocked back and forth. She was thankful they would not have to sneak back through the streets in the darkness to their small dwelling. They would feel safe here.

Alban rounded up extra bedding. "I'll spread my pallet outside under the stars, right across the entrance," he told them. "Try to get some rest."

———

Dawn was a silver hue on the eastern horizon when the three left the caravan site and entered the city's south gate just as the first rooster crowed. Alban wore the same simple garb as the previous night, covered now by a robe worn by many desert folk against the night chill. Abigail could see his eyes searching every shadow, watching carefully for any movement that might be meant to catch them unawares. And she knew that under his folded robe, the sword remained at his side.

He asked, "Will Peter be there when we arrive?"

Jacob shrugged. "We never know. Some mornings he goes off alone to pray."

"Whom would you suggest we speak with?"

"Maybe John. Or James. Or even Nathanael," said Abigail.

"Stephen. You could talk with Stephen," cut in Jacob. "He's a good man. I can talk to him. All my friends like him too."

"I do not recall a Stephen. Is he a leader?"

Jacob shrugged again. "He is always busy looking out for people. He watches everything and cares for everyone. Isn't that right, Abigail?"

Abigail was surprised at Jacob's words. She'd had no idea Jacob was observing Stephen so closely. And, oddly enough, what Jacob had just said rang so true. "Stephen truly lives to help others."

"Stephen and Abigail work together," Jacob explained. "Abigail helps distribute food for those who have need, and Stephen supervises the donations coming in and everything that is purchased. And he keeps all the records. . . ."

Alban laid a hand on the boy's shoulder. "As we walk the market lanes," he said in a low voice, "we should perhaps keep silent so as to not draw attention to ourselves. We will continue our discussion when we arrive at the compound."

Jacob nodded and was quiet for the rest of the journey.

———

Peter was not there. Abigail could tell that Jacob felt relieved. The lad swiftly volunteered to find Stephen. She was happy to sit and talk with Alban in the brief interlude. While they waited she told him more details of her healing. Just talking about it altered her mood from the evening before. By the time Jacob and Stephen appeared, she felt more like herself.

Alban and Stephen were introduced and greeted one another in the custom of brothers of the Way, with an embrace and a kiss on the cheek. Jacob moved up by Alban and pressed in as close as possible when they all took seats. Abigail could tell how much her brother had missed his friend and guardian.

"I have been told that an unusual event took place recently," Alban began.

Stephen's already dark eyes deepened as he nodded. Abigail,

who was watching him closely, realized he had been shaken by the incident too.

When Stephen did not speak, Alban went on. "May I hear your assessment of the matter?"

Stephen looked thoughtful. He hesitated as though arranging or sorting his thoughts. Alban did not hurry him.

"I was not there. I did not see it happen, but I have heard much from those who were there. It seems . . ." He hesitated again. "It seems that Ananias attempted to deceive and was punished. Severely, I admit. When it was found that Sapphira conspired in the deception, her punishment was the same." He shook his head.

"So Peter himself did nothing?"

"Peter? No. No, Peter did not so much as lift a hand toward them—save rebuke them. The *doing* was God's."

"So what do you make of it?"

"I have spent the nights since trying to find an answer to that question." He shifted on the seat and looked directly into Alban's eyes. "I do not know the answer. So I have returned to the things I do know. We are children of God. God is holy. He is merciful. But he is also just. He does not delight in punishing his own. So this . . . this indiscretion was serious in the eyes of God. More serious than we as his creatures might have made it to be. Had God ignored it, would one lie have grown into two? Multiplied many times over? What would the end have been? Total disregard for who God is? Would we, as his people, eventually lose all proper holy fear?" Stephen looked down at his hands folded on the table in front of him.

"I have come to the conclusion that God, as a holy, just God, had to act as he did," he said finally, lifting his head to look directly at Alban. "Had he allowed this deceit to go unpunished, more of his children would eventually have perished than the two we lost. The evil lurking in our hearts will take over if left unchecked. God has given us a reminder of whom we serve. Just as he did in the days of Moses, when God gave the painful instruction to destroy some in order to save more. In a way, it is encouraging, blessed, to realize that we are serving Moses' God. He has not changed."

Abigail listened with her full attention. How wise the words. How beautifully he had expressed what she needed to hear. How deep his faith. She looked at him with new respect.

Alban was nodding, but Jacob seemed not to have been listening. He still looked drawn tightly within himself. Abigail prayed that Alban might be able to get through to her distraught brother.

Abigail pushed her worries about Jacob aside. She had listened. She had heard every word Stephen had spoken. A wonderful truth engulfed her. She was safe. They were all still safe. As long as they followed the ways of God, they had nothing to fear. He was holy—but he was just. And as long as they followed their godly leaders—like Peter, like Stephen—they would remain protected and on the right path.

An unfamiliar stirring in her heart made her lift her head. She had always admired this calm, helpful man, but now she felt drawn to him in a way she had never experienced before. She lowered her gaze before her eyes would reveal her secret.

CHAPTER

TWENTY-ONE

LINUX MOVED THROUGH THE STABLES attached to the Antonia Fortress, his mind on Umbria.

Normally he did not allow himself to daydream about the home of his youth. But since meeting the prelate earlier in the week, he had been unable to clear his thoughts of such recollections. They crept up and snared him night and day.

The heat was fierce, especially inside the stalls, and the air was crowded with the smells of horses and leather and men. Linux wiped the sweat that beaded on his face and recalled those summer showers from childhood, gentle as a baby's murmur, too heavy to be called mist yet too light to fall like winter's downpours. The rain silenced the world. Linux had loved walking through it, listening to the water condense and drip from every surface. The world of Umbria was so gentle, even the hills were softened.

Linux stepped into an empty stall and swept the hay off the rear wall, patting the stone with both hands. He wondered fleetingly if Abigail would like Umbria. Could he transplant such a beautiful desert flower to Italy? Would she thrive or pine for the hot sands of her world like he did for the land of his birth?

He heard footsteps creak the floorboards overhead. Linux stood utterly still until a voice on the verge of manhood called, "Sire? Linux?"

"Down here in the stables." He stepped from the stall, brushing straw from his hands. He heard the boy tread lightly down the stairs. "How are you, lad?" he said as Jacob came into view.

The boy was troubled. Linux could see that much from his silhouette moving toward him. His shoulders were pulled together and he was tilted slightly, as though young burdens had become too heavy for him to remain fully upright. "What are you doing, sire?"

Linux knew Jacob had long proved himself to be a safe pair of hands when it came to holding secrets. "I am on an errand for the prelate. I needed to wait until the stable master and his men broke for the midday meal."

"Can I be of help?"

"You can keep me company, how is that?"

Jacob climbed up on one of the barriers separating the horses as Linux moved into the next stall and began scraping away the detritus covering the stone wall. "Alban has arrived," Jacob said.

The news brought Linux's head up. Alban was back! Yet the lad's expression was anything but joyous.

"You don't sound happy about it."

"After Alban left us, I quarreled with Abigail this morning. Again. I hate it when we fight."

"I was never much good at squabbling with women myself." The stones had not been touched in years and were covered with a thick layer of old straw and dust and refuse. Linux spied a wooden rake used to clean the stalls and scraped away at the stone. "Do you want to tell me about it?"

"I can't remember my birthday. She did not want to tell me when it was."

The family tragedy captured in those words halted Linux for a moment before he moved to the next stall. "Abigail does not want you to know the day you were born?"

"I will soon turn fifteen. That is the age of joining the legions."

"Ah. Of course. Keep an eye out for anyone coming in the entrance, will you?"

Jacob swiveled about so as to face the stable entry. "Do you think I can become a legionnaire and also be a good believer?"

Linux moved to the next stall and scraped away the filth. "You're asking the wrong man."

The flies buzzed around the horses not being used for duty that day and slumbering through the heat. Linux hurried from one stall to the next, chased by the knowledge that the stable hands would soon return.

By the time Linux had worked his way down the enclosure, he feared his memory had played tricks on him. Either that or the information had been nothing but idle gossip.

When Linux had first arrived in Jerusalem, he had served under a tribune whose family had lived in Judea since the time of Herod the Great. Linux had revered the officer and enjoyed his tales of bygone days. One night after several goblets of ale, the tribune had told Linux how the old Judean ruler had fashioned a special gate for himself through the Temple wall. Herod the Great then could enter the Temple compound without being forced to join with the common folk. In truth, however, he had done it because the Temple priests despised their ruler. To the Sanhedrin, Herod the Great was not Judean at all, but rather a Hasmonean, a desert tribesman who had taken Judean citizenship merely to claim the throne. Fashioning a private entrance into the compound was his way of establishing a claim and a power separate from the priests.

Linux had recalled the tale in the middle of yet another sleepless night. He was still uncertain whether he was going to act upon the prelate's offer. But in order to give himself the time and freedom to make that choice, he wanted Marcellus to think he was at least trying to fulfill his charge.

Suddenly Linux discovered he was scraping dirt off an ancient portal. "It truly exists!" came out in a hoarse whisper.

"Sire?"

"Nothing. Keep a sharp watch on the entrance."

"The lane is empty of all save heat and dust, sire."

"Good lad." Linux stood in the rearmost stall. The space was filled with broken tools and saddles. The rear wall, masked by dust and years of disuse, contained a wooden portal. Linux used a rake handle to clean off enough to be certain what he faced. He prodded the door, and the wood gave off a hollow clunk.

Linux leaned a bundle of tools against the now uncovered wood and started back toward Jacob. The closer he came, the more evident was the boy's distress. "What's the matter?"

"Something terrible has happened."

His first thought was that the new prelate had moved against the sect. It was logical enough. Win favor with the Sanhedrin by wiping out this troublesome group. Linux felt his chest gripped by a very real fear. "Abigail, is she—"

"She is fine, sire. Well, not fine. But she is all right." Jacob kicked at the wooden slats. "As all right as any of us are today."

"Tell me what happened!"

Jacob continued to kick the wooden barrier. "Peter killed a man."

"What?"

"And his wife."

"Surely not. Peter is the respected leader of your clan."

"I was not there, but I heard. Peter spoke to them and they died."

Linux stepped up close to where Jacob sat upon the railing. "Start at the beginning and tell me what happened."

Jacob related what he had heard. When the lad finished the tale, Linux tried desperately to sort through what he had just been told. "So two members of your clan lied to the leader about money they had gained from selling land that was theirs to sell."

"Abigail and Stephen say it is the Holy Spirit that killed them. They lied to God, not to Peter." Jacob rubbed his face with his hands. "I don't understand what they mean."

"Nor do I."

"Abigail says . . ."

"Go on."

"She says our Lord demands that we be true to him in our hearts." Jacob's voice rose. "But my heart says I want to be a legionnaire!"

"And so you shall."

"But Abigail says I can't. Not and be true to my God!"

"Have you spoken with Alban about this?"

"I tried. Last night and again this morning. He told me to wait. I fear he may agree with Abigail." He looked down at the floor. "What if he says no?"

Linux rose to his feet, one hand gripping the lad's shoulder. "I think it's time the two of us had a word with our friend. But first, you and I will visit the baths."

———

An hour later, Jacob led Linux toward the southern gates. The city baked as though on a red-hot anvil. Most of the market stalls they passed were shuttered and the lanes largely empty. The few people they passed flitted from one spot of shade to the next.

A pair of dogs lay directly in their path, panting hard, unwilling to lift themselves out of the way. Linux stepped over them and continued on. Once again he was a lone Roman walking along Jerusalem's streets. But no one even bothered to glance his way. Today the heat was his shield.

His thoughts weaved and shimmered like the sunlight reflected off the cobblestones. He recalled Abigail dancing with joy after she had been healed, her face filled with an ecstasy so intense it stunned him still. He heard again the power in Peter's voice, and felt anew the desperate longing he had known that night.

He remembered the palace gardens and the shimmering fountain and the way the daylight had glinted in the prelate's eyes. Now, as he walked the empty lane, Linux heard the governor inviting him to carry out a mission, a theft from the Temple. Would he be stealing from the Judean God? Though from what he knew of their religious leaders, they likely had stolen the gold themselves.

Jacob, beside him, took a hard breath, and Linux was drawn back to the empty lane. Clearly the lad carried an immense burden. "Steady, lad."

"I was thinking about that dreadful day. They'd sent me on a delivery. When I left, everything was fine. When I came back . . ."

Linux finished the thought for him, seeking to make the concept real. "They were gone."

They continued on in silence for a time, then Jacob added, "Everything seems so confusing. For months and months I've longed for Alban's return. Now he's here, but nothing seems to be any clearer. Like everything is tied up in this terrible confusion. . . ." He shrugged. "I don't know how to say it."

Linux gave that a long moment, then offered a confession of his own. "I first came to Judea five years ago this summer. I feel like I've spent five years waiting for something to happen. Waiting for my time to come." He glanced over. "Do you have any idea what I'm talking about?"

"Oh yes, sire. I have felt the same way since going to work for the carpenter."

"Now I'm getting hit from all sides. First my brother pulled me back to Umbria and reminded me of all I have never been allowed to claim as my own. Then Rome . . . feeling the empire taking a turn that, well . . ." Linux stopped. He could not finish that confession, not even to this lad. "Then I return to Judea and see Abigail once again. Now the meeting at your compound and the healing."

Jacob turned toward him. "Do you ever have the feeling that all these things are somehow connected?"

"Jacob, you might as well have taken the thought from my own head."

"But that's impossible." He searched Linux's face. "Isn't it?"

"Logic says yes. My heart . . ."

Jacob nodded slowly. "I feel so afraid, and I do not know why."

"It is the sign of a strong man, to confess weakness." Linux cast a look around him. "Where are you taking me?"

Jacob pointed toward the city wall. "Alban awaits beyond the Pool of Bethesda."

"But . . . that is the caravan site."

"Yes, sire. Alban is serving as guard."

Linux was still digesting that bit of news when they passed beneath the Damascus Gate and entered bedlam.

The dusty plain beyond the city gate was divided into parcels, each containing a different caravan. Two of the merchants were readying their convoys for departure. The drovers shouted and whistled, the animals complained, the dust swirled. Jacob led Linux along a rutted path to the northernmost campsite. The noise was somewhat less there, and the dust blew away from them.

In the shimmering light Linux saw what might have been a

familiar figure. Only this man, bearded, was dressed in peasant robes, tied about his waist with a cloth belt. His feet and lower legs were white with chalky dust. He was bent over a horse's rear leg, scraping away at the hoof with a curved blade. Only when the man glanced up, waved, and hurried toward them was Linux certain the man was Alban.

Even Alban's smile was different. Broader, stronger, more open than Linux recalled. Linux accepted the man's rock-hard embrace. "How the mighty have fallen."

"Hello, old friend. How are you?"

"Better than you, or so it would seem."

"Are you certain of that?"

"I am the one still wearing the uniform of a Roman soldier."

"Indeed you are." Alban called to the drover holding the horse's reins, "Walk him around a bit and see if the limp eases up."

Linux asked, "You doctor horses now?"

"It gives me pleasure to heal." He clapped Jacob on the shoulder. "Come, let us find ourselves a bit of shade."

They entered the shelter of a Bedouin tent. Jacob hovered at the borders, glancing uneasily from one face to the other. Alban asked, "Won't you join us, Jacob?"

"I . . . I don't . . ."

Alban sighed. "Go and fetch us some water, please."

When Jacob had departed, Linux said, "He is sorely troubled."

"As are we all."

Linux noted the grave set to his friend's features. "So your leader really killed those people."

Alban was long in responding. "The news was awaiting me when I arrived yesterday. I could scarcely believe it myself. I have spent the entire night praying about it."

Linux was beset by several impressions, one piled on top of the other. Alban appeared immensely calm. His features were stretched taut with exhaustion, which was scarcely a surprise, since he had trekked for days and perhaps weeks with the caravan and then spent a night without sleep. Even so, his voice remained steady, his eyes clear. More than that, he spoke with Linux as though they had been apart for only a few hours rather than over two years. Linux asked, "Has your God answered you?"

"Perhaps." Alban's features drew back in a dust-creased smile as Jacob reappeared bearing a sloshing leather bucket. "And what a welcome sight, Jacob—both you and the water." They both chuckled, and Jacob came up with a weak smile. Alban accepted the ladle, handed it to Linux. They both drank their fill before handing it back to Jacob.

Linux spoke once more. "I thought your God was a God of peace."

"He is the Lord of all things." If Alban noticed how Jacob kept his focus upon Linux, he gave no sign. "Only time will tell whether my impressions are correct. As far as I know, our Lord has spoken to no one to explain what happened. But I will share with you what I think, if you wish."

"Does this God of yours speak with you often?"

"No. But he makes his will known. His Holy Spirit moves among us. I'm practicing listening and hearing and obeying."

Alban refilled the ladle and drank again. Then he settled back and stretched out his legs. Linux knew his friend would wait all day until he himself said the words. "Speak, then."

"You have heard of the miraculous healings Peter and the other apostles have performed, yes?"

"I have seen one."

Jacob said, "He was there the night Peter healed Abigail."

"Ah, then you know that the power is real. You *accept* this."

Linux gave a reluctant nod. "I know what I have seen."

"Then why, may I ask, do you not wish to pray with me and find answers for yourself?"

Linux found his nod moving to a slow rocking of his entire body. He stared out into the sunlight. Out to where the donkeys brayed and the drovers pushed the camels to their feet.

Alban nodded himself, as though Linux had given the answer he expected. "Abigail's injury happened the month before Leah and I were married. Yet Peter only prayed for her healing the night you and that other man came seeking her hand. What is the merchant's name?"

"Ezra," Jacob supplied.

"Why did God wait until then, do you think? Is it possible God wanted to reveal to you his power? To help you understand that he is who he claims to be? To strip you of any excuse that you might think you have to reject him?"

"We were speaking," Linux said, "about the death of two people."

"We are speaking about *miracles*. Peter did not heal Abigail, Linux. The Lord our God performed a miracle of healing *through* Peter. The apostle allowed himself to be used. He sought to hear when the Lord spoke, and to do his will." Alban glanced at the lad seated by the entrance. "Just as all of us should seek to serve our Lord."

Linux saw Jacob wince and lower his head. He felt a flare of protective anger. But he resisted the urge to lash out in the boy's defense. "Would you commit murder if your Lord ordered it?"

Now Alban was the one who dropped his gaze. He looked in physical pain, and his voice sounded uneven. "I have asked myself the same question all night long. When I arrived I spoke with several who had witnessed the event. Peter did not order the two to die. Nor did he touch them. He condemned them for lying, not to himself, but rather to God and his Spirit. As soon as Peter said those words to each, the man and his wife collapsed there before the gathering and breathed their last."

"He didn't touch . . ." Linux glanced over at Jacob, who was staring at Alban. "I don't understand."

Alban began drawing in the sand at his feet. "I told you before, God has not spoken with me directly. I have prayed for guidance, I have begged for illumination. And I have talked with Stephen. But I don't . . . I can only tell you both what my heart is saying. I think a time of great trial is coming. A time of testing. A time of division." He continued to draw in the sand. "I fear we believers will be tested . . . unto death."

Linux leaned back so as to study his friend from head to toe. "How you have changed."

Alban gave no sign he had even heard. "I believe the Lord performed this fearsome sign so we would clearly understand that choices must be made. Either we are fully with him, or we are with the world. We will soon be forced to declare our allegiance, and in doing so, we must accept that the world may then cast us out."

Linux protested, "But it was your own leader who condemned those two!"

Alban nodded slowly. "Yet it was the Lord who caused this dread miracle to take place. And for what purpose? That is the question we must ask ourselves. Miracles carry a great many messages. God did this for a *reason*. Or maybe more than one."

Outside their tent, men shouted as a neighboring caravan began to move. Linux watched the long procession slowly take aim for the Judean hills. He felt a sudden lurch in his chest, as though he too was about to embark on an unexpected voyage, one whose destination he could not fathom.

He could feel Alban's gaze on him. Linux turned and looked directly into his friend's eyes. He had the distinct impression that

Alban knew what he was about to say, was merely waiting for Linux to shape the words.

"I wish . . ." Linux licked dry lips. "I wish to wed the woman Abigail. I ask you to speak to her on my behalf."

Alban turned to Jacob and said, "Would you go and tell the caravan master where I am? I promised to accompany him into the city this afternoon."

Jacob looked like he was going to argue but eventually shrugged and left. Linux said, "He does want to become a legionnaire."

"I know full well what Jacob wants. What I'm waiting to hear is that he is seeking the Lord's will for himself."

Linux looked beyond Alban's commoner's clothing, the dust, the marked changes from what he had been when they had first met. "Who exactly are you?"

"I should be asking you that question," Alban said. "And until I know the answer, I cannot help you with your own request."

Linux squinted against what felt like a rebuke. "After all I did to assist you in getting the woman *you* wanted. Were you so honorable in seeking your own bride? Everyone knows you saw her as a mere stepping-stone to higher position."

"I have forgotten nothing," Alban replied quietly. "Ambition certainly ruled my desires. But things have changed. *I* have changed. I am not proud of those original motives. But thankfully I moved off that path to one that leads in a totally different direction." He paused and looked directly at Linux, then said, "Abigail is also on this new path, this new life—mine and Leah's."

"You are saying I cannot be a part of that world?"

"My dear friend, nothing would give me greater joy than to count you among us. Is this what *you* want?"

Linux clenched his teeth and did not reply.

"Abigail is a follower of the Way. Until such time as you too have become one of us, I cannot fulfill your request."

The bile rose in Linux's throat. He had imagined many routes this discussion might take, but never had he anticipated such an outrageous condition. "Aren't your eyes open? Have your ears been dulled? The followers are considered a growing threat to Rome! If you cared for this woman as you claim, you'd know that she would be much safer with me!"

"Safe perhaps, but exceedingly unhappy. Her faith means everything to her. That you do not share it—"

"Might I remind you that my intentions are honorable. I would not demand she forsake her faith. I love this woman."

"Love?" Slowly Alban shook his head. "No, Linux, I see desire."

Linux rose to his feet, the dust of defeat coating his throat. "This pompous, narrow religiosity does not become you."

"This faith," Alban replied quietly, remaining seated where he was, "this all-encompassing faith."

"I had thought you to be a worthy friend. Now I see only a bigoted fool, unwilling to accept the inevitable." Linux stomped back into the sunlight and almost collided with Jacob.

One look into Linux's face, and all hope fled from the boy's features. "He refused you too?"

Linux resisted the urge to lift his fists to the heavens and shout his rage. "When you are ready, come to my quarters. I will do for you what I can."

CHAPTER

Twenty-Two

The family of Ananias gathered at Ezra's house for the formal period of mourning. He had made the offer because his own home was larger, and because his children were in no state of mind to be transported back and forth through the crowded Jerusalem streets. The death of their aunt had revived all the tragic feelings they still harbored from the loss of their mother. Ezra knew he was not a good enough father. Though he took them with him on his various travels, he did not spend enough time with them. He was fond of them, as fond as any father could be who also ran a trading empire. But he needed a wife who could be a mother to—

His thoughts ran in this direction only to collide with the fact that it was the clan of this woman Abigail who had *caused his sister's death*!

And it was only because of this woman that he'd had any contact with these so-called followers at all. Well, it was true that Gamaliel had asked him to investigate the group. But perhaps if he had not become so involved. Perhaps if he had resisted Abigail's lure, he could have turned his sister away from this fate. . . .

Ezra knew these thoughts and the guilt were not founded in reality. But he could not stop them any more than he could keep at bay his uncoiling rage.

He focused upon the man seated across the table from him. They sat in a private chamber of the home, away from the large group of mourners whose cries could be heard through the walls. Ezra spoke in a voice he did not even recognize as his own. "They are a threat, and they must be crushed."

Gamaliel had come each day, joining with the family in the formal kaddish, the prayer for the recently departed. The senior Pharisee and member of the ruling Council stood shoulder to shoulder with Ezra and the other elders. His presence had done much to quash murmurs and gossip about the unusual circumstances of the deaths.

Here in the privacy of this chamber, the Pharisee's doubts and hesitation were given freer reign. "Did you know even Titus has joined them?"

Ezra started to lash out, tempted to tell his oldest friend that his minor troubles had no place in this chamber today. But he stifled the outburst before it took form. Ezra was doing that a great deal these days. Everything seemed to bring him to the brink of losing his normally formidable control.

He had to search to recall of whom Gamaliel spoke. Then it came to him. Titus was the slender bearded student, the trusted young man who had been teaching his son. Gamaliel had sent Titus out also to gather information on the sect.

Ezra could hear the repressed anger grate in his voice as he finally said, "I am sorry to hear of this betrayal. But I fail to see how that news has a place in today's discussion."

"Yes, of course you are right," Gamaliel said contritely, stroking his beard. "Even so, I wish to tell you what happened. Titus came to me a few nights ago. He said he had searched the Torah and searched his heart. He found that the message being brought to the people by these so-called followers had spoken to him. He was joining them. He asked my blessing. Of course I told him it was out of the question. I warned him that if he took this preposterous step, I would cast him from my household and erase his name from the members of the scribes' community. That was the word I used. *Preposterous.* Even so, Titus merely bowed and departed. I have not seen him since."

"You can't possibly be suggesting there is any parallel between this dreadful act that caused my sister's death and your student joining the sect. There must be *revenge* for their barbaric actions, whatever your aide—Titus, is it?—might be doing."

Gamaliel looked at his friend, his face creased with deep lines of anguish. "Logic says that we must strike. As do many on the Council. But . . ."

Ezra felt the rage uncoil, lifting him from his seat. The fire in his gut sparked flames to his words. "You cannot *possibly* be thinking to *defend* this rabble!"

Gamaliel seemed to struggle to his feet, moving like a confused old man. "I must pray and study further on this."

"They have murdered my sister!"

"Your dear Sapphira is most certainly dead," Gamaliel said, his voice reed-thin. "But by whose hand?"

"You *cannot* be serious!"

"All I know is what I have heard. From a dozen different sources. Eyewitnesses." The elder Pharisee's feet moved slowly across the stone floor. "A man accused them of lying. Two people who had conspired in a dishonest act fell down and breathed their last. What does this suggest to you?"

Ezra pounded the table with both fists. "It *suggests* nothing! It *demands* revenge!"

"Pray." Gamaliel did not turn back toward Ezra from the doorway. "I must pray."

———

Abigail feared that there would be no sleep for her this night. Never had her world made such a dramatic turn for the good in such a short time. Not in her wildest dreams or her most heartfelt yearnings would she ever have dared to wish for such reversals.

It had begun at an evening meal she had planned in Alban's honor. Yet even as she had carefully prepared the roast of lamb seasoned to Alban's liking, she had a growing sense that much more was at work this evening. There had been no further discussion of the offers for her hand in marriage, though Alban's time with them was quickly coming to a close. Abigail knew that conversations and decisions were still ahead. As she worked, her mood vacillated. First with pleasure anticipating the evening ahead, then with concern. *Surely Alban will not assign me to a life with either of them. . . .*

The meal had gone as Abigail had hoped. The invited guests conversed animatedly about what God had been doing in their midst. Alban talked about what was happening among the believers in Galilee, how the numbers were growing there as well. Many villages and cities between Jerusalem and Capernaum were also reporting additional seekers of the Way.

Even the threat of continuing opposition did not dampen their enthusiasm, though everyone around the table knew the threat of persecution hung on the horizon.

When the tables had been cleared, Martha insisted that she and others from the kitchen finish the cleaning up so Abigail might spend the time remaining with Alban before his departure. Abigail quietly sat down at one end of the table, a mixture of emotions making her tremble.

It was Peter who introduced the subject. "You are aware of course, Alban, that two individuals have asked for a marriage to be arranged. I have given my word that nothing will move forward without your consent. I cannot let the time of your departure arrive without making good on my word."

"I understand."

It was clear to Abigail that Alban was no more anxious to make the decision than she herself. He cleared his throat, an action Abigail guessed was a stall for time. When he spoke it was to Peter. "Would you offer your thoughts on these two men?"

Peter was direct as always. "One is Ezra, a high-ranking merchant, rich as the world counts richness. An older man, but well respected in his community. He is the father of two young children. Maybe a bit on the pompous side. But undoubtedly well able to care for a wife and, I should suppose, do so with an amount of honest concern for her well-being. The other man is your friend Linux. A Roman. Not a bad sort for a Roman. If I remember correctly, it was he who helped you escape a few years back."

Alban merely nodded. Abigail could feel her heart pounding against her arms folded across her chest.

"But neither of these is a follower. Nor is Linux even a God-fearer. Ezra is most stubborn in his refusal to join us. In Linux, I see hints of change. But at this point, he too remains among the nonbelievers. Given those circumstances, I am not able to recommend either one of them."

Alban nodded again. "It is as you say. Neither man is suitable for Abigail."

"It is agreed, then. I shall tell both men that you have not accepted their offer."

I am safe. Abigail's hands dropped into her lap, and she lowered her eyes also so they would not give away her relief.

Alban rubbed a point on his ankle where the sandal straps must have chafed. "It may not be quite that simple. Both men have power and influence. Both represent groups looking for reason to destroy us. I would not want to unnecessarily make cause for further conflict."

"And you have a suggestion?"

Abigail felt her stomach tighten.

"I think it might be wise for Abigail and Jacob to return to Galilee with me."

Abigail saw her brother sit forward and look around, eyes wide in protest, then sink back into the shadowed recess where he was seated. She knew Jacob would fight this idea with all his being.

But Alban must have noticed Jacob's response. Abigail saw the sorrow that filled Alban's eyes as he glanced briefly at her. He continued, "I will see if I can make arrangements with the caravan driver. We are not prepared to transport a young woman, but perhaps—"

"There could be another way." Peter was stroking his beard, his fingers curling to rake through the thick growth. "You could give her in marriage to one of ours. We have several who might be suitable."

Abigail's spine stiffened in shock. Was she to be given to another man, someone else she did not know, in whom she had no interest? *And what of love?* She forced herself to sink back against the cool stone of the wall behind her, her whirling thoughts causing her to barely hear the ongoing discussion of her future.

"Yes," Alban was saying. Clearly the idea was pleasing to him, and he leaned forward, arms folded on the table. "Yes. That could be done. We could celebrate their betrothal before I leave. So there would be no further question."

Abigail wanted to leap to her feet and shout a refusal. But, like Jacob, she did not utter a sound, just pushed back further against the wall and tried not to weep. She could not, would not, challenge the authority of her guardian.

But Alban was speaking again. "I met a young man that impressed me greatly. What can you tell me about this fellow Stephen?"

Stephen? Abigail wanted to run and hide. *Please, please,* she cried inwardly, *don't thrust me on Stephen. He is a fine and honorable man, but far too sensitive and caring. He would feel obligated to marry me just to save me from an unsuitable union. You don't know Stephen. A man of great faith which he puts into action daily. He totally gives of himself for others. . . .*

Abigail stopped breathing. She had just listed the qualities she would look for in a husband.

"Stephen," Peter was musing aloud. "Yes, Stephen. I couldn't have chosen better myself."

Abigail's thoughts became such a jumble she could no longer sort out what was being said. Stephen was called, and she drew back in embarrassment as he stood before the elders, even as she found herself yearning to hear what he might say.

Alban laid out the circumstances. He then asked Stephen outright if he would be willing to agree to a betrothal to Abigail.

Though her head was lowered, Abigail watched Stephen take a small step back. Then he turned and somehow found her in the shadows. Abigail saw a tenderness in his gaze, an expression she had never seen before.

"I can think of no greater honor for any man," Stephen replied. "But, sir," he said, turning back to Alban, "I have nothing to give. I am a poor man that God has called to serve. I have nothing to offer in return for such a gift. Nothing."

Alban was quick in his response. "Indeed, you have everything to offer that I wish for Abigail. Faith. Uprightness. Integrity. Good will. What are the world's riches in comparison to these? And if I'm interpreting correctly, you could also promise her love."

"Yes," said Stephen simply. "I have already learned to love her. She serves with a heart of compassion. She desires only what God is pleased to give her. Yes, I would love her."

Abigail closed her eyes and let the wonder of the moment wash over her. Stephen had expressed love for her. Before them all, he had declared his love.

There followed a spontaneous celebration of sorts. With the help of a learned elder, Alban and Peter drew up papers. Stephen was not a bit hesitant to sign the document. Abigail was drawn forward by a smiling Martha. Her down-to-earth strength provided a heartwarming validation. Abigail stood before Peter, Alban, and Stephen with a confidence she did not quite yet feel. But when asked if this betrothal was what she wished for herself, she replied, "It is."

Peter thumped the table. "It is settled, then. On the morrow your betrothal to Stephen shall be announced."

Martha put a strong arm around Abigail, and other women came forward to embrace her and offer their blessings. Abigail felt as though their words and their heartfelt joy spilled over her like an anointing. Her eyes were so filled that when Alban stepped in front of her, she scarcely could make him out.

But it was the strong but gentle voice of her guardian that said, "Abigail, I wish you the same joy and contentment with Stephen that I have found with my Leah."

She heard herself thank him, saying something she hoped made sense. Still, she could scarcely believe it. The man she had learned to admire, the man whose steady faith had helped her own to grow, was to become her husband.

Only two things marred her happiness that night. Leah was not present to share her joy.

And Jacob had vanished into the night.

CHAPTER

Twenty-Three

For the first time since he had arrived in Judea, Linux found himself without enough to do. In light of the "special assignment" he had been given, the prelate had relieved Linux of all regular duties. He still had not officially accepted the task of moving the Temple treasury into Marcellus's possession, though he had discovered the secret doorway into the Temple grounds.

Tribune Bruno Aetius was leaving Antonia Fortress on the morrow, and he was taking most of his officer corps with him. The news was passed on by the tribune's adjutant. The officer apologized, saying that the tribune had intended to speak personally with Linux. But he had been called away on an urgent matter. "The Zealots have attacked one of our outlying garrisons," the adjutant explained. He then said, "The tribune wishes you good fortune."

"Please pass on my wishes for a safe journey, which I offer you as well."

He was a clean-shaven man a few years younger than Linux. "The tribune would like me to remind you that his invitation to join him in Damascus still . . ." He halted midsentence when a shadow filled the doorway. "Yes, what is it?"

"The prelate's compliments. He asks if the officer Linux is present."

"I am."

"Governor Marcellus asks if you are prepared to present your report."

"Not yet. But soon—"

"The prelate reminds you that this matter is most pressing."

"Give the governor my respects, and tell him I hope to have my report ready in two days. Three at the most."

The prelate's household guard saluted and departed. The adjutant studied the empty doorway and quietly remarked, "Do you find it interesting, Linux Aurelius, that the prelate's own guard arrives just as we were about to speak of the tribune's invitation to you?"

Linux did not respond.

"I see," the adjutant said dryly. "Very well, I will make sure the tribune receives your . . . reply."

Linux saluted and left, passing through the fortress courtyards, where iron rang upon iron. Linux stood and watched young recruits, sweating in the summer heat and learning Roman warcraft. He tried to tell himself he had no choice in the matter, that the prelate had ordered him to remain. Even more, the prelate's messenger had just revealed how closely Linux was being kept under observation. But Linux knew full well that if he wished, he could slip away in the night and join the tribune in their march to Damascus. Once there, he would be under the protection of a man who had every reason to despise the governor of Judea and ignore his protests. No, Linux intended to remain because . . .

He found it impossible to even think the woman's name without his heart lurching. *Abigail.* His disappointment at Alban's refusal to help him had hardened into a calculated rage. That morning, in the midst of another sleepless dawn, Linux had made his decision. He would go to Marcellus and agree to the task. He would steal the Temple gold for the prelate.

But only after Marcellus obtained the Judean girl for him.

Why would the prelate refuse the request? After all, the man had already formally assigned Linux the guardianship over his brother's family and promised Castor's assassination. What difference would it make to the governor whom Linux married?

But first Linux would give Alban one final chance to help him, possibly diverting him from having to complete a theft that made him more than uncomfortable.

The last thing Linux expected, however, was to find his friend standing in the shadows across from the fortress gates. His heart gave a tight lurch. "Alban? I thought you were keeping clear of the city. What are you doing here?"

"Waiting for you, of course." He pushed himself off the wall and left the shadows behind. "The stable master said you had been called in by Bruno. How is the tribune?"

Linux waved that aside. "Do you have news of Abigail?"

"I do." Alban took a long breath. "I came because I wanted you to hear this from me. Knowing your heart, this is not easy for me to say. Abigail is betrothed to one of our own."

Linux felt his heart heave more violently, as though it sought a way out of his ribs. "You cannot let this happen."

"It already has, old friend. The young man's name is Stephen. He is a good man. In time, I think he may well become a leader among the believers."

"And if I became one? What then?"

Alban clearly had not expected this. "Would you do this truly?"

"Answer me that question. You owe me this much," Linux pressed. "Would you reconsider if I joined you?"

"It is not a . . ." Alban stopped and sighed. His head dropped and his eyes clenched shut.

Linux realized with yet another start that his friend was praying. There was no other explanation for the sudden silence. He started to shout his demand that Alban respond. But he was suddenly caught by the recollection of an unseen presence filling a Judean courtyard, strong as the torch flames, strong as the night. Linux realized he was feeling that same sensation again. For some reason, the realization filled him with remorse as real as a physical pain.

Alban lifted his head. He looked at Linux with a calm that unsettled Linux as much as the news about Abigail. Perhaps more.

Alban said simply, "Come with me."

"Where are we going?"

"There is something I want you to see."

The empty lane fronting the fortress spilled into a major market thoroughfare. They turned left and followed the avenue up to where it bisected the main artery passing before the Temple gates. Linux tried to avoid this thoroughfare whenever possible. It was the area where overt hostility, resentment, and an entire society's chafing under the Roman heel was concentrated. If ever a riot were to start in Jerusalem, it would be here, where the crowds were worst, the religious fervor highest, and the Temple guards eyed every passing Roman with undisguised loathing.

Yet Alban passed through the throngs with ease. Though many cast silent daggers toward Linux in his legionnaire's uniform, few if any seemed concerned by Alban. He moved easily up the tightly packed lane, then turned away from the Temple toward the Old City.

He pointed Linux into a side alcove. "We can wait here."

Linux sat beside him. "You have become one of them. A Judean."

"The correct term is God-fearer. And, yes, I have."

"So why couldn't I—"

"I ask that you wait, my friend. Everything will be made clear."

Linux stifled his irritation with an impatient sigh and settled back against the wall. Alban glanced up several times to the sky overhead. Linux realized the man was noting time's passage by the sun. "What are we waiting for?"

"The afternoon prayers."

"You mean, inside the Temple? Then why are we here?"

Alban lifted a hand. "Patience. It won't be much longer."

But it seemed to Linux that the waiting was endless. He thought of a dozen different arguments he could force upon his friend. He thought of racing to the prelate's chambers and demanding that Marcellus act immediately, before the betrothal could take place. His mind grew more frantic by the minute. Until finally Alban said, "It is happening."

"What is?"

"Look and see for yourself."

Linux squinted into the sunlight. If anything, the avenue seemed more densely packed than normal. A sudden gap in the throng allowed Linux to see the crowds were not increasing, but rather the avenue itself was becoming obstructed. And how this was taking place caused his hair to stand up on his neck.

People were laying out pallets containing the very sick. Others were supporting the aged and infirm down the lane, settling them into places against the opposite wall. The process continued until one side of the avenue was completely full. Yet there was no crying nor wailing, as would have been expected from such a gathering of beggars and others who clearly were in pain and distress. Instead, they simply waited, their friends and families along with them.

"Why do they gather just along the one side? There's room—"

Alban raised his hand. "Wait."

"For what?"

"The answer to all your questions and demands. Here it comes."

The avenue grew very still. Even the wind became hushed, or so it seemed to Linux, as though the entire city caught its breath. In that moment, he spotted a procession headed toward him. At its front strode the tall bearded leader Linux recognized from the courtyard, the man who had healed Abigail. The man's name was Peter. They called him an apostle. His gaze had unsettled Linux mightily. He still recalled it in the midst of his nightly distress.

But the Peter who strode toward him now was a man transformed.

He seemed to have grown in stature. Not that his physical form had increased, but rather his inherent power was so great it seemed impossible that *any* physical shape could contain it. His face shone with an ethereal light.

And as he passed, people began to shout and rise up and cry aloud. And *dance*.

Peter did not look at anyone directly. Nor did he reach out and touch them. Instead, he merely continued to walk toward the Temple. And his shadow passed over those who had been set along the avenue, on the side opposite the sun.

One by one the people rose up from their pallets, revealing faces transformed by the same ecstasy that Linux had seen in Abigail's features. Once again Linux was beset by the same painful longings, as though this exhibition of miraculous power illuminated the dark musings of his own heart.

Alban turned to him, his eyes holding the same ethereal light as Peter's. "This is not a question of becoming a follower so that you can claim a woman as your own. This is a question of your *life*. Do you wish the Lord Jesus to be central to all you are, all you do? Do you wish to be transformed? Do you wish to be healed on the inside?"

The pungent force turned bitter in Linux's heart. The darkness he had wrestled with, the longings and the anger and the years of bitter struggle all joined together and swamped the sudden fire of longing. His mouth tasted ashes as he said, "You won't help me, then."

Alban's expression turned tragic. "Brother, that is *exactly* what I seek to do."

CHAPTER

TWENTY-FOUR

ABIGAIL ROUSED FROM A NIGHT of conflicting dreams. So much had happened, and so quickly, that her mind could not take it all in. She had suddenly gone from a young woman being wooed by two objectionable suitors to betrothal with a man she deeply admired.

The betrothal ceremony was to take place following that evening's prayer service in the open courtyard to allow room for friends to attend. There would be little of the usual celebration, though Martha had insisted that the guests be served a refreshing drink. But the legal and religious rite would be full and complete. From this day forth, she would be known in the community as Stephen's wife—even though there was yet no date set for the marriage to be consummated.

Abigail knew with certainty that the day ahead of her would change her life.

But there was a cloud in her sky. A darkness that dragged down her soul even on this day when she wished to feel only happiness.

Alban and Jacob were still in disagreement. And there was little time left to settle the dispute. Alban would be leaving for home soon with the traveling caravan. Already feeling the stress of being so long away from Leah, Alban was anxious to return. Though the coming baby was not due for another two months, he was concerned about her welfare.

Alban had invited Jacob to join him, declaring that there was plenty of work on his small farm for both of them. They could be partners, and Jacob would be in charge whenever Alban acted as guard for a caravan. He would even school Jacob in becoming a caravan guardsman if the boy desired. But even that promise could not persuade Jacob.

Abigail could imagine Jacob's cynicism as he weighed "carpenter" against "farmer." He had his heart set on becoming a legionnaire and hotly declared that if Alban would not help him, he was sure Linux would.

And with these angry words, Jacob had once again fled.

Alban had gone after him and searched well into the night, but the boy's knowledge of the back streets and alleyways made him impossible to find.

When Alban had returned, exhausted and worried, he informed Abigail that it was very late and she should try to get some sleep. He made sure she was safely in her quarters, promising to be at the compound in the morning to see if Jacob might have returned.

But Jacob did not return. Abigail had stayed awake far into the night listening for his footsteps.

Now as the sun rose, she knew that she must also. She dragged herself from her pallet and prepared for her walk to the compound. She would be late for morning prayers if she did not hasten.

———

Abigail was breathless as she entered the courtyard. Already a crowd had gathered, and Thomas was giving them all a word of encouragement. Abigail found a place at the back and rearranged her shawl over her dark hair. She was listening intently to the words being spoken when she felt someone brush against her side. She turned, hoping with all her heart to see her brother. But it was Alban who stood beside her. He looked haggard and weary. His eyes asked the question, and Abigail shook her head in answer.

They began their prayer time together. Many voices lifted in fervent entreaty, asking for wisdom, for courage to live their faith, to speak boldly whenever given opportunity. They prayed for their leaders. For those who daily came together as one. For those on the outside who still needed to hear that Jesus was the Christ, the Messiah they had long awaited.

Abigail became aware that the spot beside her was vacated. Alban was no longer there. She looked around. He was over beside the east wall, kneeling at the bench placed there for weary travelers. His hands were folded, his head bowed in prayer—and his shoulders were shaking.

Abigail was quick to leave her place and go to him. He was weeping. *Weeping over wayward Jacob!* A moment of anger swept through her. How could Jacob do this—to her? To Alban? How could he so hurt this man who had saved his life? Alban had given him his freedom when he was fully within his rights to keep him as a slave. Alban was his guardian. Jacob had no right to rebel. Not by law, nor by conscience.

Abigail knelt nearby, her own tears falling between her fingers onto the bench. She moved a bit closer to say, "I am so sorry. So sorry my brother has not obeyed. That he has treated you with disrespect when you did so much for him. I—"

"No," he said as he turned to her and shook his head. He rubbed his hands across his face. "No, that is not what brings me sorrow. The boy owes me nothing. Nothing. He has been only a pleasure to me for these many years."

"You saved his life. . . ."

Alban waved her comment aside. "I feel . . . I feel deeply that God has a plan for Jacob's life. He does not belong to me. And that is what troubles me. Jacob is not rebelling against me. I fear he is rebelling against God. I would gladly say, 'Follow your dream. Become a legionnaire,' if it were that simple. But I've been there. I know where it leads. What demands are made on a soldier of Rome. And the days are darkening. I fear for the future. I fear the time is coming when the orders from Rome will demand . . ."

He looked into Abigail's eyes and stopped. "Forgive me," he said. "I do not mean to frighten you. But I sense the tension building. We must be ready for the future—whatever it brings. We must cling to our faith with each breath we take. Being a legionnaire hardly encourages that, Abigail. That is why I weep. Though I can endure separation from Jacob, I do not want to lose him as a brother in Christ. His soul, Abigail. It is his soul that is of utmost importance."

Abigail felt a hand on her arm and looked up to see two of her dearest friends close by. They didn't ask if they could help. They simply knelt beside her and joined in prayer.

———

In the early afternoon Abigail and three others left for the Freedmen's Synagogue. It was a bit of a journey, and Abigail had never been there before. She knew it was located near the Damascus Gate in close proximity to the market used by the caravan masters. It was an extremely unfashionable district and one that women, particularly young women, were discouraged from visiting unattended.

But today was different. She had been invited by Stephen. As he had explained earlier that morning, the crowd was made up of freed slaves who were not welcomed in other synagogues. In many cases they felt cast out, despised and rejected by the very society they had once served. Abigail felt elated that Stephen had invited her to observe this work in which he had been engaged. She could hardly wait to hear him speak to this long-ignored sector of their city.

She expected Stephen to meet her with a new glint of anticipation in his eyes, maybe a little quicker step, but he greeted her with the same proper formality and sincere concern with which he greeted each of the women who accompanied her. She could not help but feel a twinge of disappointment. But she pushed the feelings aside. After all, this was Stephen's ministry to people who sorely needed someone to care. To nurture both body and soul.

It wasn't until after Stephen had finished speaking and was moving through the crowd greeting this one, reaching a hand to that one, stopping to pray with another, that understanding began to dawn on Abigail. He had not brought her to the meeting simply to observe his work. He wished her to *share* in his work.

She glanced about her place in the women's section. There were so many needs surrounding her. Old women with age-dimmed eyes felt their way through the crowd with walking sticks in hand. Ill-clad mothers, clutching infants wrapped in ragged garments, hoped for a meal for another day. Orphaned children hung about the door, not even daring to set foot in the sacred place, but hoping with eyes that pleaded for a small coin or a piece of bread. There were the lame, the obviously abused. The broken. How could she hold herself apart from these people?

Abigail also began to move through the group of women. At

first she tried to imitate Stephen. Walking. Talking. Praying. Placing hands on those who longed for human acceptance. And then, something happened. It was no longer all about Stephen. It was not even about Stephen's ministry. It was God's Holy Spirit ministering through her hands, her feet, her lips. It was God who had brought her here on this day. To see the need. To realize that in his name she could bring them blessing. To do what he wished her to do for these discarded ones of society. People that he loved, had died for. People he had come to save.

The very thought nearly overcame her. She had never dreamed the Spirit could use her. But she saw it in the eyes of those she touched. Those she prayed for. And she had never felt more alive.

————

The evening was both exhilarating and difficult. Abigail was delighted to have Alban there for the betrothal ceremony, so far the most joyous occasion of her life. She could only imagine that it would, sometime in the future, be surpassed by their wedding night when she and Stephen would truly begin their life together.

But Jacob was not there. And that grieved her in a way she could not have expressed. He had not only disclaimed Alban, he had disclaimed her as well. She prayed over and over that he still clung to his faith in God.

She tried to keep her fears and disappointment at bay as she received blessings and best wishes from the many people who had gathered to hear their vows.

After the crowd had gradually dispersed, Stephen was finally able to approach her in a moment of private conversation.

"I wish you to know, Abigail, that I feel deeply honored you have agreed to become my wife. I had never dared to hope that God would bless me with such a life mate. I admire your deep devotion.

Your commitment. Your compassion for those about you, and I promise that I will do my best to care for you, Abigail, always."

But even as he spoke such touching and fervent words, Abigail could sense a tension.

"I do not know how soon we can be together," he said. "I pray our wedding celebration will be soon. But our world is being tried. We are being tried. There is much opposition to our faith. It grows even as our numbers grow. The most important thing for us is to hold strong to the faith. To share with our brethren the truth that we have been given—and as much as I would wish to be with you, Abigail, to give you my full time and attention, I love God even more, and I must be obedient to his calling. I pray you understand."

Abigail nodded. His words had only made her respect him more. "I understand. And that is exactly what I would wish you to do. What I would expect you to do. That is the reason I have learned to respect you as I have. I have seen your faithfulness. That God is first. That must be so—for both of us."

CHAPTER

TWENTY-FIVE

IN ALL THE YEARS EZRA HAD BEEN ENTERING the Temple gates, since he was fourteen, he had never before felt like an outsider. His sister's death—and its unbelievable circumstances—made him feel somehow unclean, contaminated. Which of course was ludicrous.

He had been fetched from his home by one of Gamaliel's black-robed students. This tall young man, bearing a document carrying the Sanhedrin's official seal, he did not recognize. The courier requested that Ezra accompany him immediately to the Temple. During the period of mourning, an observant Judean normally did not leave his home. With Gamaliel present every morning, it was certain the Sanhedrin knew full well what was happening in Ezra's household. Only the most vital of issues would have moved them to draw him away.

In truth, Ezra was glad to go. The house had become packed with people who had multiple motives and used the opportunity to petition him, knowing none would be turned away at such a time. Only a few were actually there because they truly lamented the loss of Ezra's sister and brother-in-law. The women of Ananias's family sat on low three-legged mourning stools and moaned from time to time, their wails now dampened by time and fatigue. The family gathered before the dawn prayers and remained there all day. Ezra's household staff kept the courtyard tables full of food and drink. The visitors came and came and came. Many pressed his hand and murmured the traditional words of mourning, "May God comfort you together with all the mourners of Zion and Jerusalem." Yet even as they spoke, Ezra could see the ulterior motives in some gazes, the desire for him to remember them and the fact that they had paid their respects at this tragic time.

Ezra had heard a term used by several mourners when they thought he was out of hearing range—*suspect*. Their meaning was clear enough. No one was certain precisely what had happened, why the family was caused to suffer, what hand the husband and wife had themselves played in their demise, and ultimately, who was to blame for this.

In truth, deep in the secret recesses of his unspoken thoughts, Ezra had his own suspicions—that his sister and her husband had done precisely what the apostle had denounced them for.

But even if that were true, he quickly told himself, the apostles had had no right. None at all. And they would pay. Along with as many of their followers as Ezra could include in his revenge.

Such were his thoughts as he entered the Temple compound through the Hulda Gate. And drew to an astonished halt. "What is this?"

"This is why Gamaliel decided you must be disturbed," the student Pharisee replied grimly. "Come. There is more to see."

He fell into step beside the young man. "What is your name?"

"I am Saul."

"Where is your home?"

"I hail from Tarsus. But I always have considered Jerusalem my true home. And this Temple its heart." Saul eyed the crowds with grim distaste. "But not these days."

Ezra glanced at the sun's position, wondering if perhaps he had lost track of the time. But no, afternoon prayers were not scheduled to begin for at least another two hours. So why were the crowds so immense?

The young Pharisee murmured quietly and pressed forward ahead of Ezra. Bearded men grumbled as he pushed through, but when they saw he wore the robes of a Temple Pharisee, they moved away, granting them space. Ezra felt sweat trickling down his spine as he threaded his way through the jammed courtyard, and it was not only from the heat. In the distance he could hear the bleating of animals in the sacrificial pens. But he could see nothing save a multitude ahead and behind and to either side.

Finally they arrived at an opening. An invisible perimeter held the throng in a large circle. Ahead of them, jammed together as tightly as the group through which he had just passed, was a second ring. There appeared to be an invisible barrier keeping the two crowds apart.

Then Ezra realized what he was seeing.

Solomon's Porch, near the Beautiful Gate, was directly across from the Temple wall closest to the Holy of Holies. Beyond the Temple rose a smaller structure where the Sanhedrin met as the Temple Council. The space between the porch and the Temple and the Council building was utterly filled by this second crowd.

There in Solomon's Porch, in the space traditionally reserved for senior Pharisees and Temple scribes, stood several of the apostles. Beside them was the young man Stephen. Ezra could hear his clear voice ring out, easily heard by both groups, telling about the Scriptures related to the promise of the Messiah.

Ezra was filled with such wrath he could no longer make out any more of Stephen's words above the ringing in his ears. He turned to Saul and hissed, "I thought the Council had forbidden them from speaking!"

"The Council has done that and more," the young man said. "Have you seen enough?"

"More than I ever needed to," Ezra muttered.

"Gamaliel bids you join him in the Council building."

But the crowd was so solid they were forced to weave their way back to the front of the Temple, through the money-lenders' tables, past the Temple priests accepting supplicants' payments for sacrifices and around the northern side, through the section reserved for foreign God-fearers.

Finally able to breathe freely again, Ezra asked, "Those followers do this often?"

"Every morning, every afternoon, every evening. Before and after prayers. They come, and the crowds gather. They speak. They leave. Each time we hope it is over. But the next day it is the same again. And every day the crowds grow larger."

"And there is this division between the followers and everyone else," Ezra observed.

"That is new. Before, those who were curious joined the others, at least for a time."

"When did this change occur?"

Saul looked at him a moment, then said, "This week."

Beside him, crates holding doves were stacked higher than his head. The sound of their wings beat in time to his heart. "Word has spread of . . . of my sister's death?"

"The entire city speaks of little else. The people are afraid now. They fear the apostles' ability to see within the human heart. They look and they listen, but from a distance." Saul tugged at Ezra's sleeve. "Come, the Council is waiting."

Ezra heard the tumult even before he entered the chamber. The young man pushed through the doors, and the noise assaulted Ezra from every side. The Council chamber was a large space, almost as broad as his home's interior courtyard. Even so, it seemed scarcely able to hold everyone. Ezra recognized important Pharisees and many Sadducees, joined by senior Temple guards and other city officials. All of them seemed to be shouting at once. The Council table was on an elevated dais, and every chair was filled. The Sanhedrin argued back to the group, and with each other. Even so, as soon as he saw Ezra, Gamaliel stood at the table and motioned for him to come forward. The sound of the voices quickly died away.

Gamaliel asked, "You have seen?"

"I have." Ezra felt his nails digging into his palms. "These people must be *stopped!*"

Instantly the group roared back into argument. Caiaphas, the high priest, called for silence. Reluctantly, the group obeyed. Caiaphas turned to the senior guards and said, "Arrest the leaders."

The next morning a trembling Abigail gathered for prayer with a larger group of the followers than usual. Word had arrived the previous evening of more arrests. Their leaders, including Peter, were in prison awaiting the Sanhedrin's decision.

A cold dread clutched Abigail's stomach, holding her captive to doubts and fear. She sensed the same panic in those around her. They all were knotted up in confusion and worry that only prayer could untangle. Would the Messiah's promises about the future ever be fulfilled? Or would this same fate eventually claim them all—prison, perhaps even death?

And so they prayed. Earnestly. Fervently. And at length, humbly. Pleading for wisdom. Pleading for boldness, for endurance, for God's power. What of their little ones? Should at least some of the families flee the city?

A sudden calm filled Abigail's being—like a fresh wind of God's blessing. A sense of peace leaving a warm inner glow.

Abigail lifted her head to see if others were feeling it too, but then the sound of quickly tramping feet carried into the courtyard. Peter and the other jailed apostles appeared at the gate!

The believers as one rushed toward the men, shouting their welcomes and praising God. A barrage of questions finally made Peter raise his hands and gesture for them all to be seated.

"I have never seen anything like it in my life," he began. "There we were, shackled and waiting for morning to come and our fate to be determined, and suddenly I felt, more than saw, this presence in the cell with us. At first I thought I was dreaming, but I quickly knew it couldn't be so. I could see the solid walls, feel the damp beneath me, and hear the guards telling each other crude jokes to pass the night hours.

"This . . . this heavenly being, this messenger of the Lord, appeared and motioned for us to follow. We walked right past the guards—I don't think they even noticed us. Then the angel opened the prison doors, without even a whisper of clanking iron. We walked out into the night. It had been raining, making our cell even more miserable, but now the stars had never looked so bright. The air smelled fresh and cool. I stood there blinking, wondering if I was having a vision.

"Then the angel turned and relocked the gate—and he was gone. Just like that." Peter waved a hand. "In a blink of an eye, he disappeared."

He paused to look around at their attentive faces, then said, "We just stood there and stared at one another."

John put in with a chuckle, "I think he would have stood there until the sun came up if James hadn't said, 'Well, I guess we might as well go home.' " They all laughed in response to the wit, but the sound was also full of relief and joy as the followers celebrated the moment with pats on the back and embraces.

"So we did," finished Peter, his usually serious face also lighting up with the humor of it all.

Abigail looked around the group. Where there previously had been doubt and fear, she saw expressions of thanksgiving. She could sense the release of tension—felt it herself.

Her eyes sought out Stephen. He was pressed in close to the group that had been delivered from their jailers, obviously captivated by every word of the report. Now and then his head would nod in agreement or his lips would form an amen.

But Peter was not finished. His face was again sober. "They will not be happy when they discover we are gone. They have already warned us to stop teaching. But, brothers and sisters, God has given us a message to be proclaimed. There is no time to waste. We cannot, must not, disobey our Master."

"What will you do?" The question on everyone's tongue was voiced by someone Abigail could not see.

"We will go to the Temple court and teach," Peter said, moving as if to be on his way.

"And by this evening you will be back in prison," spoke up another member of the group.

"That will be fine," another called out. "They get arrested, and God's angel turns them loose." Several voices joined in laughter.

But Peter raised a hand for silence. "Brothers and sisters, it matters not. Perhaps the next time they arrest us we will not be delivered. Nevertheless, we must do as we are commanded. Pray that all of us will continue to have boldness to preach the Word."

C H A P T E R

TWENTY-SIX

EZRA HAD HURRIED TO THE TEMPLE as soon as the morning kaddish was recited. The streets of Jerusalem were painted in a soft dawn glow. The air was sweet, cleansed and perfumed by a rare summer shower that had lasted until nearly dawn. The sky was now clear, the breeze light. It would have made for a fine walk along familiar streets except for what awaited him up ahead.

He entered the Council chambers to discover the entire Sanhedrin already gathered, along with many of the same city elders who had yesterday jammed into the room. Gamaliel gestured him over, looking very troubled. "The guards should be back with our prisoners at any moment."

"Something is amiss?"

"I am beset by troubling—" The Pharisee broke off as the chambers' doors slowly opened. Three guards stood on the threshold looking ashen.

The high priest demanded, "Where are my prisoners?"

The men looked at each other, then the bravest one said, "Sire, forgive me. But they are gone."

Caiaphas leapt to his feet, his face terrible to see.

The senior guard quickly said, "My men were on station as always outside the prison. The doors were locked. But when we went in this morning, the cells were empty. All of them."

"Your men fell asleep!"

"Sire, that was my first thought also. But these are my best men. I would trust them with my life. And they give me their solemn word that none of them slept an instant."

"How am I—?"

The high priest was cut short by the outer doors slamming back. A wide-eyed guard rushed between his cohorts and shouted, "They are back!"

"Who? Where?"

"The prophet's men, the apostles. They are back on Solomon's Porch! They are preaching to the crowd!"

Ezra, stunned by the news, looked around the room. None seemed capable of speech.

Then the high priest shouted, *"Bring them to me!"*

"Wait!" Gamaliel's voice carried such authority the guards turned back as one. The Pharisee turned to the high priest and urged, "We must take great caution."

The high priest's face turned almost purple with rage. "These men were arrested on my authority, they escaped from prison, and you tell me to use *caution?*"

"Precisely." Gamaliel turned to ask the guard, "How large are the crowds?"

"More than yesterday, sire. Thousands come to listen to them."

"Just as I feared. If we go out and strike them a second time in public, we may be faced with a riot. Imagine what would happen, several thousand people rising up inside the Temple compound. It would give the Romans precisely the excuse they seek to invade our sacred area and take control."

The high priest slumped back in his chair, his mouth working before he managed to say hoarsely, "Bring them here, but use no force."

The guards stood uncertainly until the high priest's son-in-law, who shared the Council's most senior position, snapped, "Carry out your orders."

———

The chamber waited in absolute silence. Ezra thought he could hear his heart beating. Time moved by at a tortured crawl until finally the doors opened once more. The guards shepherded in a small group of men. The high priest demanded, "Is this the lot?"

"All who were speaking this morning, sire."

"Shut the doors and guard them well." The high priest glowered at the men standing before him. "We, the High Council of Judea, ordered you never again to speak in the name of your dead prophet!"

The one who seemed to be the chief among these apostles, the broad-shouldered one who was said to be a fisherman from the Galilee, replied, "We must obey God rather than orders from men. Jehovah has raised Jesus from the dead and declared him the Messiah, to bring Israel to repentance. We are witnesses of all this, as is the Holy Spirit, the one God has given to those who obey."

Ezra felt as though a veil were suddenly lifted from his eyes. It was not the man's words, which were outrageous to all the learned men gathered within the Council. And certainly it was not the way this man spoke, which was quite common, as befitting his heritage. But rather there was something about the man himself, a power so great it silenced the entire chamber.

The place was suddenly filled with strident voices, all of them calling for the apostles to be put to death.

Above the din, one voice again called out, "Wait!"

It was the power of Gamaliel's reputation, as much as his voice, that silenced the room. The high priest said, "Speak."

"I ask that you remove these men from our presence."

The high priest motioned impatiently to the guards. "Do as he says."

When the doors closed behind the departing men, Gamaliel said, "We have seen our share of false prophets and impostor messiahs. These are perilous times, and our people can easily be led astray. But what has happened in the past? The teachers were killed and their followers dispersed."

"What are you saying?" Caiaphas visibly was controlling himself with great effort.

"Only this. I advise the Council to let these men go."

Ezra watched his friend with a mixture of trepidation and awe. Was the man mad . . . or heroic?

Gamaliel's next words were drowned out by the tumult. He waited quietly until the room returned to silence, then said, "If their purpose and actions are those of mortal men, they will fail. But if it is from God, how can you possibly stop them? You will only find yourselves fighting against our Lord Jehovah!"

To Ezra's astonishment, the entire Council around the head table looked subdued. The only voices that rose in protest belonged to the people crowded about the room. Those with the power to judge and condemn were clearly being influenced by what Gamaliel had just said.

Ezra forced himself to swallow his own protest. What good would it do? He was not a member of the Council. Ezra looked over at Gamaliel and felt the bitter wrath rise anew. He had been betrayed by his oldest friend.

Ezra stood in silence as the apostles were brought back in. The high priest sternly ordered them never to speak the name of Jesus again, then commanded the guards to take them out and publicly flog them.

Ezra left the chamber immediately after the apostles were taken away. He heard someone call his name. But he did not turn around. His mind and heart were clenched in the rage-filled certainty that it was not over. And vengeance would have to come from another source.

———

Linux drifted in that vague state between waking and sleeping. Every time his slumber grew deeper, his dreams were filled with images of Alban's eyes imploring him to understand, to accept, and of people lining one side of the street. But in Linux's dream, he too was lying there, trapped upon one of the pallets with all the other sick and maimed and insane. Waiting for the shadow of a bearded Judean to fall upon him.

Somewhere toward dawn he was aware of a furtive sound, of a shadow passing over his bed. He knew he should open his eyes and investigate. But nights of broken slumber had left him exhausted. As the sounds drew him further awake, he decided that if it was a thief, he was welcome to what little there was to take if Linux could just have a few decent hours of rest in exchange.

Later he awoke to brilliant sunlight, the sun filling the room. He lay as he was, staring at the dusty footprints meandering across the floor and ending at his bed. "Who is there?"

"Only me, sire."

"Jacob?"

"Yes, sire."

"Why are you under my bed?"

Jacob rolled from underneath, dragging a filthy cover with him. The blanket smelled of horses and sweat, which suggested he had found it in the corral and brought it up with him. "Please don't send me back, sire. I am an excellent servant, as you know. I can see to your needs until—"

A voice from the other room demanded, "Who's that I hear speaking?"

Jacob's face tightened in very real fear. He scrambled back under the bed as hesitant footsteps sounded across the adjoining room.

The old servant, Julian, limped into view bearing a mug. "Are you given to conversing with ghosts now?"

"Not unless the ghosts possess filthy feet and eat for ten."

"Ah. The boy you were telling me about."

"None other." Linux sat up in bed, accepted the mug, and kicked a heel under the bed. "Come out, Jacob. Let Julian have a look at you."

The elderly man, a former legionnaire, stared at the boy. "Is that sawdust I see in your hair?"

"He's been apprenticed to a carpenter. He is not happy about it."

"I hate it all," Jacob said with a nod. "Please, sire, I beg—"

"Let me have a swallow of tea before you restart your entreaties." Linux indicated the boy with his mug. "Bring the lad something to eat."

Julian eyed the boy with distaste. "I suggest a bath first."

"At that age they can live for weeks without a wash. They do need constant feeding." When Julian stumped away, Linux said to Jacob, "Has something happened?"

"I ran away when . . . well, I left. Yesterday I returned to work because I needed to eat. Then I learned . . ." Jacob's words emerged in reluctant stages. "I'm afraid."

This was new. The boy had always shown courage. "What of?"

"The Sanhedrin has arrested the apostles."

Julian stopped suddenly as he returned with bread and cheese. Linux shared a look with his aged servant and said, "When was this?"

"Yesterday afternoon."

"Do you know the charges?"

"They were preaching from Solomon's Porch."

Linux again looked at his servant, who shrugged. Linux gripped the boy with the hand not holding his mug and lifted him to his feet. "Come, sit at the table."

The boy wolfed down his food and talked between bites. Julian leaned against the doorpost, watching with a soldier's wary eye. The lad did not stop either talking or eating until the plate before him was polished clean.

"Let me see if I have this straight," Linux said. "The ruling Judeans treat this patio area beside their Council building as hallowed ground, which only the senior teachers may use for their proclamations. But the apostles have started using it as their own personal station."

Julian put in, "Sounds as if they were deliberately seeking to provoke the Council."

"Not exactly," Jacob replied, idly rubbing his belly. "They feel the Sanhedrin no longer is able to speak for God. The religious leaders' aim is to hold to power, not help the people."

"And how about the apostles? Whom do they speak for?" Linux asked.

"The apostles have been assigned their authority by the Lord," Jacob replied. "The Spirit fills them and they speak. For them, it is only logical to address the nation from a platform of authority like Solomon's Porch."

Julian's eyebrows rose. "Did you think all that up by yourself?"

The youth shook his head. "But I listen. And Abigail speaks of little else these days."

"You haven't said why you ran away." This from Linux.

"Alban wants me to go work for him in Galilee. But I want to stay here and become a legionnaire. Abigail says I must go with him. And the leaders . . ." Jacob's features drew down. "I don't know what to do."

Linux thought of Abigail now bound to another man, and he wondered if he would ever be free of that gnawing desire. When he did not speak, Julian asked, "Let's go back a moment, lad. The folks who want you to leave Jerusalem for the north, they're the same leaders who were arrested by the Sanhedrin?"

"Yes, but the apostles are free again."

"The Sanhedrin's already freed your leaders?"

"No, sire. An angel came in the night and freed them. This morning they went back to the porch again."

"They are still preaching from the restricted area?" Julian's face could have held either bewilderment or affront. "The Sanhedrin will hand them their heads."

Linux was bewildered himself. "Why do they seek to provoke the Council?"

"They do not care what the Council says or does. They follow the edicts of our Lord. But I . . ." He drifted to a halt and stared unblinking at his empty plate.

"You can see ahead to the day when the Sanhedrin will punish you all," Linux supplied quietly.

"Abigail says all this is happening for a purpose." Jacob looked from one man to the other. "She says we must be strong and trust in God. She says we are being cleaved away from all that is unclean, all that is not of our Lord. I don't understand what she is saying! All I can see is . . . death."

Linux rose to his feet. "You were right to come here, Jacob."

Julian demanded, "Where are you going?"

"Out to learn what I can."

Julian's age and infirmities kept him from moving fast. But he managed to step in front of Linux to block the doorway. "Think carefully over what you are about to do. If the prelate is anything like the rumors I am hearing, you do *not* want to let him think for one instant you are on the side of people he may decide to put down."

Linux stepped around his servant. "You will frighten the boy," he said, his voice low.

"Now is as good a time as any I have ever known for remaining well hidden, utterly silent."

"Stay with Julian—I will be back," Linux said to Jacob. As he reached the stairs, he heard a voice calling his name from below. "Here!"

The prelate's household officer climbed the stairs and looked about the stable chambers with obvious disdain. "Governor Marcellus sends his greetings and invites you to join him at the arena tomorrow."

Linux had heard officers in the fortress speak of the prelate's coming games. Some were eager, but most treated the affair with scorn. The majority of the true warriors had little time for the arena. The smell of blood upon the sand only brought back the battles they preferred to forget. But Linux knew an official command when he heard one. "Please thank the prelate, and say I shall be honored."

The subaltern saluted, then offered, "There is a man lurking down below. He has the look of the caravan about him. Or perhaps that of a thief."

"Thank you. I shall go down directly."

But when the officer had departed, Jacob leapt forward in panic. "Alban has come to take me back!"

"He will take you nowhere."

"But he is my guardian! He can order—"

"You are under the protection of a Roman officer. I will go and see what he has to say."

Downstairs he found Alban standing in the first stall, currying a horse and speaking with a smiling stableboy. Alban brushed the gleaming flank in long strokes timed to his words. As Linux approached, he heard Alban talking about Rabbi Jesus. Linux stopped outside the stall, listening as his old friend murmured in easy tones that would calm both horse and man. He felt a sudden burning rage at this Judean God who was keeping him from the woman he wanted. He had a dozen reasons why Alban should be helping him in arranging this. Instead, they invoked this dead prophet's name as if erecting a barrier between themselves and the rest of the world. But he knew in an instant that was as unreasonable as his rage—the woman was promised to another, and if these people wanted to build barriers to keep people like him out, why would they risk their lives by returning to the porch?

Alban handed the brush back to the stableboy and invited him to come sup with them that night. He patted the horse's flank, lifted his head to look at Linux, and walked over. "There are few things I miss about my years as a soldier. But I admit such fine horses are a far cry from the nags a caravan guard rides."

"What do you want?"

Alban must have heard far more than Linux's query. "Old friend, old friend."

"It's a simple enough question. What?"

"I came for Jacob. I heard his voice upstairs, so please don't deny that he is with you."

"I deny nothing. Why should I? He is here of his own volition."

"I need to have a word with him."

"He wishes to become a legionnaire. A goal you instilled in the lad yourself. A most excellent goal."

"He is a Judean and a follower of the Prince of Peace. His future is among his own."

Linux could no longer hold back. "Like the woman you refused to me. So that now she is betrothed." Bitterness filled Linux's mouth so he could scarcely form the words. "Jacob has no interest in speaking any further with you."

"Do not refuse me this out of revenge. He is in danger."

Linux turned away. "Jacob has made his choice. As you did."

"Wait!" Alban's hand fell upon Linux's shoulder. "Tell Jacob I fear for his life. There is more trouble on the wind."

"This is nothing Jacob does not already know," Linux said, shrugging off the hand. "I could have saved Abigail and her brother if you had been the friend you claim to be!"

"Abigail is the betrothed wife of a man she has come to love, doing the Lord's work. Of that I am certain. We are now talking about the boy. You have heard about the events of yesterday?"

Alban's gaze kept Linux where he was. "You mean the imprisonment of the apostles? Jacob told me."

"Last night an angel of the Lord freed them. Today—"

"He told me that as well. I can accept a youth speaking of such nonsense as though it actually happened. But you, a former legionnaire, a former *officer*, should take more care in the gossip you repeat."

Linux half expected an argument. In fact, he would have welcomed it as an excuse to break things off cleanly and forever.

But Alban's gaze only deepened. "From where you stand, old friend, your words make sense. But hear me out. We followers of the risen Lord are seeing these kinds of extraordinary happenings on a daily basis. We are *surrounded* by miracles. To have a messenger of God free our captive leaders is amazing and indeed unbelievable—yes, I agree. But from where I stand, it is only the next event in a series of miracles that started upon the day of Pentecost, when tongues of fire settled upon us and I heard the message of truth spoken in the language of my homeland by someone who had never heard a word of it before this."

Linux felt the vague stirrings deep in his soul, a reflection of what he had first sensed in the dimness of a Sabbath courtyard, and then again while watching a man's mere shadow bring the ill and maimed to health.

Alban must have sensed the change, for he leaned closer still. "Join with us, Linux, and know this same power to heal the pain in your heart, that which goes far beyond physical pain."

Linux felt himself torn, as though the invitation were in truth a blade that could cut him off from everything he had ever known and leave him with something totally unfamiliar and even frightening. And yet . . . He wrenched himself back. "You make less sense with every word you speak." But his voice sounded weak in his own ears.

Alban looked at him a long moment, then sighed. "Tell Jacob I would have him come with me to Galilee. He can travel as a caravan guard and see the world from a very different vantage point than he's had before. I should have done this before. But I thought it would be better not to separate him from his sister—that he would learn more of what it means to be a follower of Jesus in the company of our apostles. But I see I may have been mistaken. Tell him . . . Tell him I must leave in two days. I hope and pray he will come with me. He knows where to find me."

CHAPTER

TWENTY-SEVEN

As Ezra entered the Temple gates at the side of Gamaliel, the air smoldered between them. Gamaliel had declared it was finished, he would clash no more with his oldest friend and closest adviser. Ezra was silent, seething with all that he had not said.

The Temple guards saluted Gamaliel, but he did not respond. Inside the compound, he aimed for the throng between the Temple and the outer wall. Though nearly noon, it was as though the people of Jerusalem had arrived for their dawn devotionals and never left.

As they approached the horde, Ezra had a sudden image, one of such piercing clarity he felt for a moment as though he actually had been transported back to the days of his youth. He was reliving a day when he and Gamaliel had moved through a similar throng, so caught up in their argument over a passage of Scripture they had not even noticed how the crowd parted and then closed in behind them to follow. The two headed for their teacher, the senior Pharisee waiting for them upon Solomon's portico. That day, the teacher stepped to one side and motioned for Gamaliel and Ezra to continue their dispute. They had launched back into their heated discussion, so passionate they failed to realize the entire gathering was listening. Finally Ezra had looked over and seen their teacher, instead of being irate that they were usurping his podium, smiling. He came to them and gripped their shoulders. He announced to the listeners, "I leave my life's work in able hands." And the crowd had laughed and applauded.

Now the Council's lead Pharisee turned and looked at him. Gamaliel's countenance was so somber, so reflective, Ezra wondered if he had been recalling the same event.

Gamaliel said, "I will argue with you no longer, Ezra. I will simply explain to you as I am able the basis for my concern. Will you honor me by listening to what I have to say?"

Why should I, he wanted to retort, *when you refused me the same honor?* But all he said was, "I will listen."

"Come, then." Gamaliel started through the crowd.

If anything, the gathering was more impenetrable than the previous day. A murmur ran ahead of them, and the crowd parted, pressing aside until the robes of the men they passed became two dark walls. Normally they would be greeted as respected merchant-scholar and Council elder with murmurs of respect. Today, however, these men were silent, their eyes burning with a scalding rage. Their anger was not directed at Ezra, however. He walked in the wake of wrath being poured upon Gamaliel. Undoubtedly news had spread of his comments before the Council, how he had stayed the hand that would have unleashed their fury against the followers. Now Gamaliel walked forward, his face to the stones at his feet, giving no sign that he noticed anything at all.

But Ezra saw. He absorbed the crowd's wrath like an elixir that might someday ease his own burning wound.

As yesterday, they arrived at the same stretch of empty stones.

On the other side of this impossible divide was a second group, one that occupied the entire length of Solomon's Porch.

"And so they grow," Gamaliel murmured.

"Which is only one more reason for the Council to act," Ezra hissed.

Though he had not intended for his words to be heard further than Gamaliel's ear, the men closest to them began muttering their angry agreement.

Gamaliel gripped Ezra's arm and pulled him forward. They crossed the empty space and came to the rear of the gathered throng, straining to hear what the men upon the porch's top step were saying.

Gamaliel said, "Try and look beyond your loss, old friend. For all our sakes, I beg you to see what is happening. We, the religious Judeans of our oppressed nation, need to stand united more than ever before. We are beset by dangers on all sides. The Zealots, the Romans, the Hasmoneans—they threaten to crush us utterly. If ever there was a time when our nation needed a messiah, it is *now*."

"You can't possibly be suggesting—"

Gamaliel halted him by pushing in so tight Ezra felt the man's beard brush his ear. "I beg you to stop your arguing and *listen*. The prophets speak of this time, when the Chosen One of God will cleave us apart, separating the believers from those who will be cast into the outer darkness. Have you ever in all your days seen a time when the division has been clearer? Have you ever known a time when miracles rained down from an empty sky, when the prophets' words were so clearly being fulfilled?"

Ezra felt the man's grip on his arm. "But the teacher they follow is *dead*."

"Is he? Are you so certain of that?" Gamaliel's eyes carried a piercing quality. "Have you bothered to hear what they are saying? They spoke their news again yesterday, standing before the group that had threatened them with death. They follow a messiah who departed so that the Spirit of God could breathe upon them all, a messiah who lives *within*."

Ezra shook his arm free and took a step away. "I cannot believe what I am hearing. You, of all people."

Gamaliel made as to reach again for his friend, then stopped, gripping only air. "I beg you, think upon what I am saying. For your own sake. For the sake of our nation. *What if they are right?*"

The man's desperate entreaty stretched his features into lines of genuine agony. Ezra had never seen his friend in such turmoil. For a single moment, Ezra felt as though the Temple courts were filled with an otherworldly wind, one so powerful it punched through his skin and his muscles and his bones, causing his very soul to shiver.

Then he caught sight of the crowd on the other side. If anything, their rage burned more fiercely still. Ezra felt it reach out and rekindle the wrath in his own heart. The world settled back into place. The summer heat drenched him.

Ezra walked back across the empty divide. They did not so much make room as enfold him. He caught one final glimpse of Gamaliel standing at the border of the other group, staring at the flagstone floor, his features caught in confusion and sorrow.

Then the crowd drew Ezra away.

———

Abigail glanced up from drawing water and saw the familiar figure in desert garb. "Alban, how wonderful! I thought—"

"I really can't stay long." He carefully scanned the courtyard before easing himself down on the well's stone wall. "I actually shouldn't have taken the time. My duties are elsewhere."

"Surely you can spare a few moments for something to eat."

"I have not eaten since before dawn. That does sound most appealing."

"I will run," promised Abigail.

Alban's chuckle surprised her. "Walk, please. I will not disappear that quickly."

She was soon back, carrying a cup with fresh well water and a plate of Martha's flat bread wrapped around goat cheese and spring onions.

"Now," she said as she placed the food on a nearby table, "come and eat, please. What brings you here in the middle of a working day?"

"Jacob."

Her heart leapt. "You have found him?"

"He is with Linux." Alban took a bite and followed it with a long draught of the cool water. "It appears he wishes to stay there."

Abigail's spirits sank as fast as they had soared. "I do not like the sound of this."

He nodded. "It concerns me also. Not only over his choice of companion, but also over his safety."

"What are we to do?"

He shifted on the bench, chewing thoughtfully. "There is more, Abigail. I worry about you as well. There are rumors everywhere. The caravan masters tell tales over the campfires. People whisper from house to house. The Sanhedrin grows increasingly irate over how the followers continue to daily grow in numbers. Even the Romans fear the pot could soon boil over."

But Abigail's mind was fastened on her brother. "There must be something you can say to Jacob—"

Alban interrupted, "You also must come with me to Galilee. You can help Leah care for the new baby."

Abigail looked upon her friend and guardian with a little smile. "Have you already forgotten, Alban? I am betrothed."

"Stephen can come for you when he is ready. This likely will settle soon, and it will be safe for your return. Or Stephen too can come with us now. There is much work—"

"Stephen already has his responsibilities here. He cares for the distribution to the most distressed among us. He speaks at the Freedmen's Synagogue. Oh, I wish you could hear him, Alban. The people love him, and he loves them. He wouldn't be able to leave, I know. His place is here. His calling is here. And now my calling is to serve with him."

Though clearly still very concerned, all Alban said was, "You sound very sure of your way forward."

"I have prayed long and hard, Alban. I too have heard the rumors swirling about. I know the situation is uncertain, but God remains the God of power. I belong here with Stephen. Where could we be more safe than where God has placed us?"

Alban reached forward, then dropped his arms. "My dear Abigail, I wish you could hear the beauty in your words."

"If there is anything in what I say, it is only what God has instilled in me."

"I will tell Leah." Alban rose to his feet. "She of course will be disappointed, but she will also understand."

Abigail stood as well. "What are we to do about Jacob?"

"Have you seen him at all since—?"

"No. I heard from the master carpenter that he returned to work one morning, then vanished again. He has not been back to our quarters. I am very concerned." She hesitated, then confessed, "There is an ongoing battle in my soul. Why is it so easy to trust God in some things, and yet . . . I fear I keep reclaiming my burden for Jacob."

"God has not forgotten him," Alban assured her. "Continue to pray. It may take a while, but I am certain the divine answer will arrive. Along with Jacob."

———

That evening Abigail was preparing to depart for the little place she called home when Stephen stepped out of the shadows.

"I worry about you going out in the darkness, Abigail. It isn't good that you travel alone. Especially now—"

"I walk most of the way with others. It is only in the last alley that I am alone."

"I am thinking I will speak with Peter and see if you can have a room here above the storage bins."

"Oh please, Stephen. There is no cause for concern."

"But I worry." Indeed, his voice and concerned expression told her more than his words.

"And I am deeply grateful. But I truly would like to stay where I am for the time being."

"Promise me you will walk with the others, and maybe there are a few who would walk even that alley with you. I will ask among the believers." She attempted further protest, but he raised a silencing hand. "Do be careful. I would not wish to lose you," he said, now with a twinkle in his eye, "before I have even claimed you."

She smiled, then turned serious. "Remember our Lord, Stephen. The same one who led our leaders out of prison is the God who walks with me every night."

He smiled too. A very tender smile. "Of course. May God go with you."

CHAPTER

Twenty-Eight

Linux and Jacob climbed the road out of the city, skirting the Mount of Olives. The people headed in the same direction made for jovial companions. The opposite side of the road told a different story. The Judeans straggling into Jerusalem mostly came from the surrounding villages, many of them extremely poor. Also, a vast number of those headed into the city looked unwell. The worst were transported on donkey carts or pallets swinging between poles resting on strong shoulders. After climbing each rise and seeing the city walls appearing once again in the distance, the pilgrims' renewed hope seemed to wash over even the neediest ones.

Those headed away did their best to ignore the impoverished Judeans. Everyone on the road walking with Linux was either Roman or allied to the rulers of Judea. They were on their way to the amphitheater built for just such occasions. Judea's new governor had declared this a day of celebration.

The walls of Jerusalem and the gleaming Temple roof finally were blocked from view when they rounded the Mount of Olives.

Soon after, they turned onto a paved road heading north. From that point on, the day belonged to those who swore allegiance to Rome. It was a relief to no longer share the road with the maimed and the sick. For a few brief hours they could ignore the city behind them and a people seething with resentment. Rome ruled over a hundred different tribes and races. Yet none had continued to chafe so long under Roman dominion as the Judeans.

It was at this point Linux realized something was bothering him. He stepped off the road and turned around.

Jacob looked at him with questions in his eyes.

"A moment." Linux bounded up a steep rise to where he could see the two roads intersecting. Further in the distance was the road from Caesarea. All held a constant stream of the sick and poor and distressed.

Jacob had followed and now stood beside him. "What are you looking at, sire?"

Linux did not respond. His attention was held by the sea of humanity streaming into the city. He recalled how Peter had walked the avenue to the Temple. As his shadow had fallen on those sprawled along the east wall, they leapt up from their beds of affliction and praised their Judean God.

"Sire?"

Linux glanced at the youth by his side. Jacob stood in his shadow, his face showing his bafflement. Linux felt his gut wrench with a vision of what awaited them at the road's end. *What influence am I having upon Jacob?* Instead of his shadow bringing health and life and joy, the young man who trusted him was being led toward . . .

"Enough," Linux muttered to himself. "We go."

The road to the amphitheater recently had been brushed clear of the worst signs of its neglect. Even so, it was clear to Linux the lane had not been used in a very long time. Pontius Pilate had been contemptuous of provincial games. He had also loathed Jerusalem. The arena road had seen little use in nine long years. Between it and the city sprawled one of three camps used by Judeans returning for the festival seasons. Today the camp was empty save for stones used as border markers and the burn marks of old campfires. The road served as a natural boundary, for no observant Judean would dream of coming a step closer than necessary to the arena and the blood sports it represented.

The new prelate had brought with him a Roman's lust for blood upon the arena sands. He had proclaimed a three-day festival of games and frivolity to celebrate the new emperor.

As the Roman stadium loomed before them, Jacob interrupted Linux's thoughts. "I have been approached by the Zealots." A hint of pride could be heard in his tone.

Linux stopped in his tracks and stared at Jacob.

"At least, I think it was them," he said. "They sought me out through a friend. They asked what I was doing, spending time with you." Jacob's face was turning red. "I said you were my friend. They didn't like that at all."

Linux gripped the sleeve of Jacob's tunic and drew him off the crowded lane. "What exactly did they tell you?"

"They said that there were better ways for a strong young Judean to spend his days than . . ." Jacob's gaze dropped to the ground.

"Go on, my boy. I have been called worse than whatever name they might use."

"They said the Roman dogs had only a brief time left in Judea. And you would flee with the others."

"Did they?"

"They said they could offer me purpose and direction. One in keeping with my heritage. But that if I came with them, I would never return." Jacob's expression was very solemn. "I told them I wanted to be a legionnaire. They . . ." He kicked at a stone.

"Yes? Go on."

"They spat at the dust by my sandals. They said that such actions would cast me out forever from the Judean clan."

Linux could see Jacob was in great conflict over this. He knew all the arguments that were available to him. How the Romans ruled the greatest empire the world had ever known, how joining the legionnaires would make him part of the most powerful army on earth. But all Linux could think of just then was how Peter's shadow fell upon people lining the Jerusalem street, and they rose from their distress and they danced.

Linux steered the boy back onto the road. "Come, lad. The day awaits."

The lane was by now lined with makeshift stalls. Greek merchants selling sweetmeats, roasted meats, carafes of rough local wine, fruit, and rice. Colorful paper parasols were used by the commoners to shade against the sun. Closer to the arena, vendors gathered about the gambling stalls, vying for customers by shouting their odds over coming events and gladiators. Competing fans jeered and booed as bets were placed against their man.

Surrounded by the wealthiest and most powerful people in Judea, the two aimed for the southern gates, where the prelate's standard flew alongside the emperor's. This entrance was flanked by the consul's own household guards. Linux returned their salute and entered the shaded passage. The stone walls glistened from a recent cleaning and smelled of lemon and thyme. He reentered the sunlight and started down the stairs toward the governor's stand. Then he realized Jacob was no longer beside him.

Linux hurried back to where the stairs had emerged from the stadium shadows. Jacob stood at the entrance, his mouth agape as he stared around the stadium.

For Linux, the amphitheater was like a hundred others situated around Roman provinces. It crowned a hill just northwest of

Gethsemane and the Mount of Olives. Unlike the theater built southeast of Jerusalem or the hippodrome to the southwest, this stadium was a multipurpose affair. Large enough to hold the region's entire Roman population, along with a number of its Hellenistic allies, with the additional rows of wooden seats erected above the initial stone structure. The result gave it a steep and somewhat unfinished look, as though someone had started building and then lost interest midway through the job. Compared to the coliseum of Rome, though, in which four such provincial arenas could have fit, Linux did not find it all that remarkable.

Linux gripped the boy's shoulder and felt him start as though coming awake. "Come."

"The stadium touches the clouds!"

"Not quite."

As the two descended the stairs, Jacob kept his gaze fastened on the arena sands. "Look—two bears dancing on their hind legs!"

Linux hardly glanced at them. "Astonishing."

"And there, those men leaping up, forming a human pyramid! How do they ?"

"They are tumblers, and they spend their lives in practice." Linux moved to look into the royal enclosure. A brilliantly colored awning offered shade against the sunlight. Three sentries stood beside wooden pillars decorated with flowering vines. A pair of incense burners spiced the air. There were a half dozen people already seated, eating and laughing and giving scant attention to the performances in the arena. Linux made sure the consul was not yet among them. Then he turned back to Jacob. "Come, we have work to do."

Beneath the arena's sandy base was a netherworld of dimly lit chambers. The stone walls trapped all sound, and the place rang with such clamor it was impossible to identify any single noise. The few windows were all set high on the outer walls, and sunlight fell through tightly barred openings. Torches sputtered and fumed along the dim hallways. The larger chambers were sectioned off into cages holding all manner of beasts—hyenas, tigers, bears. And men.

Three ramps led up to barred doors, through which slits of sunlight and the crowd's tumult poured. Beyond the third one, Linux entered the quarters set aside for the arena's chief officer. The burly soldier bore the seared features of a former desert dweller. His name was Crasius, and his voice was hoarse and low, no doubt from a wound that creased his neck. "You are late."

Linux pointed Jacob into a dimly lit corner. "Where are your men?"

"This is genuine, the offer you told me about?"

"Gather your men," Linux said. "I want to say this only once."

The officer seemed ready to argue. But in the end he rose and stumped to the doorway. Clearly the men had been waiting for his signal, for at his shout eight legionnaires swiftly filled the chamber. Crasius settled back into his leather-formed chair and barked at Linux, "Be quick about it."

Linux reached into his shoulder sack and slowly extracted the scroll bearing the governor's eagle. "I need a team willing to do whatever it takes to accomplish the prelate's will."

"What is the task?" Crasius growled.

"You will only know upon the day. And only if you agree."

Another man laughed, a rough snarl. "What kind of deal is that?"

"The kind that will free you from this place." Linux waved the scroll so that the eagle glinted in the torchlight. "The task bears great danger. But in return for carrying out the prelate's orders, you all will be restored to your former ranks and positions. But not here. You will be sent to a more . . . shall we say, hospitable place."

The soldiers surrounding the chamber's walls bore the mark of mercenaries, with cruel eyes and leering features and brutal strength. No doubt brawlers and thieves and brutes, they lived by force alone. They had been assigned here as punishment for a variety of crimes, though deemed too valuable to kill or maim outright. It was hoped a stint in the arena's bowels would teach them to obey. Only just reopened, it meant these men faced months and perhaps even years imprisoned here in the cellar teeming with animals and noise and odors. And fear.

Linux added, "And you will be paid well. In gold."

"Words are cheap," Crasius sneered.

"You will have this in writing. And your first payment upon agreement."

"This can only mean we aren't expected to survive."

"There is great risk. But also great reward."

The officer pointed at Jacob. "What's the boy doing here?"

"He serves me. And he plays a vital role in this assignment." Linux rose from his seat. "I go to see the consul. I expect your answer within the hour."

When they returned to the royal enclosure, Linux settled Jacob by the front railing. "Wait for me here. Enjoy the show. We have work to do later."

"Yes, sire." Jacob's attention had already been snared by more performances upon the arena sands.

"I will be back soon."

Linux climbed the enclosure stairs and bowed toward the figure on the miniature throne. "My sincerest gratitude for today's invitation, sire."

"Ah, Linux. Excellent." Marcellus, on an elevated dais to bring him to eye level with those standing about, was seated on a gilded chair at the center of his shaded enclosure. Now that the prelate had arrived, the royal patio was crowded, the prattle brittle with forced gaiety. Marcellus looked annoyed. "I was wondering what was keeping you."

"Forgive me, sire. I needed to see to one other matter before I could make my report."

"Your report? Ah, yes, of course. . . . Yes, well then. You mean you found what you required in the arena?"

"I did, sire." Linux was baffled. He assumed the prelate had ordered him here to grill him about the Temple treasure. Instead, Marcellus gave every indication of having forgotten the matter entirely.

"That's all fine and good. But something else has come to my attention, and I wish for your counsel." He motioned to the steward who hovered by his shoulder. "Bring Linux a chair."

Several heads came around at this. Linux watched in amazement as a second gilded chair was placed upon the dais, an honor normally granted only to visiting royalty, close allies, or intimate members of the prelate's own family.

Marcellus must have noticed Linux's astonishment, for he said, "And should not I choose to seat a trusted adviser? Is that not well within my rights? Or am I breaking another custom of these pestilent Judeans?"

The steward replied smoothly, "Indeed it is a most worthy act by Your Excellency." He held the chair's high back and nodded Linux into the seat.

Linux eased himself down, as though testing the chair's ability to hold his weight. The prelate swished the air with an ornately carved fan, its handle fashioned from ivory and gold. "I have been in this country less than a month, and already I despise it."

The steward approached once more, this time offering Linux a jewel-encrusted goblet. He started to wave it away until he saw the cautionary glint in the steward's eye. Linux accepted the goblet and placed it, untasted, on the chair's arm.

Marcellus said, "Please tell me that this land improves with time."

"I wish I could, sire. And perhaps your experiences will prove rather in contrast to my own."

The steward bent over the prelate's shoulder and murmured, "Sire. Your visitors."

"Oh, very well. I suppose I have no choice." The fan moved faster still. "That pesky tribune has finally left for Damascus, and my own commander is still out somewhere on the sea between here and Rome. So you must act as my adviser."

Linux bit back his immediate response. There were several higher-ranking officers still present within the Antonia Fortress. "I stand ready to obey, sire," he said instead.

"My adjutant informs me of your current living situation. Really, Linux, residing above the garrison stables? It is disgraceful that an officer on official duties for the governor sleeps in chambers not fit for a Judean goatherd." Another flip of his fan. "No doubt it's the work of that despicable Bruno Aetius. We are well served to have him gone."

Linux opened his mouth to explain, but again did not speak. What was he to say, that his friend, a disgraced centurion who had joined the followers, had chosen it? That Linux liked the freedom, while granting him a proximity to the Antonia Fortress and to other soldiers? That all his life had been spent in just such a situation, close to power, yet isolated?

Marcellus went on, "I can only assume there are suitable apartments within the soldiers' fortress?"

"Indeed, sire. But they are reserved for the tribune and his staff."

"Oh, nonsense. I am prelate, am I not? The tribune serves at my discretion." He used the fan to summon his steward. "Inscribe an edict. As my adviser on military affairs, Linux Aurelius is to be granted the fortress apartment of his choosing. And he is to select a staff from among the soldiers. An appropriate stipend is to be added to his pay. And any other of the usual benefits."

Linux's head was spinning with the sudden change. He watched the fan flip back and forth, knowing with utter certainty that the largess could just as swiftly be stripped away. He managed a weak, "I am most grateful, sire."

"Good, that pleases me." Marcellus said to his steward, "Show in the Judean visitors." When Linux moved to depart, the fan waved him back.

The arena's chaotic din formed an echo for the clamor in Linux's brain. He stared around him, yet saw nothing. He sipped from his goblet but could not name what he drank. He did note Jacob, stationed behind the patio's front pillar, appearing very disturbed by something. But there was nothing he could do about it now.

The steward had returned, leading two Judeans in formal robes. As soon as they came into view, there was no room in Linux's world for anything else.

The older Judean walked forward with a regal bearing, the trailing edge of his robes draped over his left arm. He bowed, lifting his left arm higher still, as though attempting to keep his robe from touching the patio's stones. "Thank you for speaking with us, Excellency," he said, his tone as stiff as his bow.

"I fail to see why matters related to your Judean Temple could not wait for my next regular audience," Marcellus said testily.

"Were it merely a matter related to Temple affairs, sire, we would not even have dreamed of troubling you on a day of such festivities."

"Oh, very well, very well." He indicated Linux. "I suppose you must know my military adviser, Linux Aurelius."

"An honor that has evaded me until now." The elder bowed a second time.

"I am Verres."

"Verres is my emissary from the Council. . . . What is it you call yourselves?"

"The Sanhedrin, Excellency. Though I do not have the honor of counting myself among that select group. I am merely their spokesperson."

"And who is this you have brought with you here?"

"My associate, Ezra, a representative of the Judean merchant community. We thought a voice from within the trades might illustrate to Your Excellency just how serious—"

"Yes, yes, I understand all that. But why is this compatriot of yours dressed this way?"

The Council's emissary faltered. "Sire?"

Linux tore his gaze away from the face of the second man and explained quietly, "Verres is a Sadducee, sire. Ezra is a Pharisee."

"And why exactly should this be of concern to me?"

"The Sadducees are Hellenized Judeans and dominate the Council. The Pharisees are a minority on the Council, and consider the Sadducees to be their, well—"

"Their enemy." The second man spoke for the first time, his dark eyes boring down hard on Linux.

Both Marcellus and Verres looked from one man to the other. The prelate demanded, "You know this man?"

"We have seen one another," Linux said, keeping his tone even. "Though we have never been formally introduced."

"Well, well. How fascinating." Marcellus was evidently pleased by indications of hostility among the three. "All right, Verres. You may proceed."

"As your adviser has correctly stated, Excellency, we Sadducees and the Pharisees tend to disagree on almost every point. And yet this matter is of such crucial importance that it overrides centuries of disagreement. We come to you today, united by our deep concerns over a new threat to Roman rule."

Ezra's black robes were both severe and elegant, fashioned from a light fabric drifting about him in the breeze. He stood with his hands tucked inside the opposing sleeves. "A threat to us all."

"Indeed so." Verres glanced at his associate, then went on, "We speak, sire, of those known as the followers of the Way."

"Ah, these disciples of the dead prophet. What's his name?"

"Jesus of Nazareth," Linux supplied, listening intently.

"You know this group?"

"I have had contact with them, yes, sire."

"And they are a threat to Rome?"

"From everything I have observed, sire, they are ruled by edicts of peace."

Verres exclaimed, "Excellency, please, I must be permitted—"

"Wait," the prelate barked. To Linux, "Go on."

"Their leader did indeed declare himself to be the ruler of the Judeans. But he also was scourged and then crucified without ever calling for violence by his followers."

"So this group follows a dead man."

"They claim, sire, that Jesus has been brought back to life by the Judean God."

"Preposterous!"

"Exactly, sire," Verres said immediately. "And yet the common folk are drawn by such outrageous claims. As a result, very deep divisions are being created within our community."

Marcellus gave the pair a calculating look. "As deep a division," he asked silkily, "as exists between your two groups?"

Ezra replied, "Worse. Far worse."

"Yet if this group holds to edicts of peace," Marcellus pressed, "what threat could they be to Rome?"

"Through the disruption of your peaceful rule, sire."

"Utter rubbish!" Marcellus bounded from his chair. The two Judeans retreated a pace, granting the prelate room to pace. Linux noted how both Judeans kept their backs to the arena, clearly determined to have nothing whatsoever to do with the Roman concept of sport.

Marcellus snarled, "Your Council and your elders and your Zealots are a *constant* disruption! I am beset by your demands and your stiff-necked arrogance at every turn! And now you insist upon wrecking my festivities with claims that a group of peaceful Judeans is a threat to Rome!"

"Because they are, sire."

Linux was astonished at the man's boldness.

"Nonsense. They are a threat to *you!*"

The emissary from the Sanhedrin did not back down. "That is true enough, sire. They accuse us, your ruling Council, of being responsible for this so-called prophet's death. They use his blood as a means to divide your subjects and turn them—"

"Enough drivel! I have heard all I can bear! Begone, the both of you! And the next time you seek an urgent audience with me, have a care that it is over a true emergency, else I may decide to create one of my own!"

The Judeans bowed a final time and backed quickly from the patio, their eyes fastened firmly upon the stones at their feet. Even after they had departed, the observers continued to hold their breaths. The prelate paced for a time before settling back in his chair. He snapped, "More wine."

The steward had the goblet in front of the prelate before the words were hardly spoken. The prelate drank, grimaced, and tossed the goblet aside. "Not this Judean swill. It turns my stomach. Bring me something from Rome!"

The steward vanished.

Linux knew he should speak, offer some word of advice or counsel. Yet now that the Judeans were gone, his thoughts were filled with the sound of a sweet name, one he would never be able to claim as his own. How could a woman he had only glimpsed a handful of times have so captured his heart? He sighed.

Marcellus mistook his sigh and said, "I could not agree more. These Judeans and their constant complaints are a plague upon my peace."

Linux stared blindly at the sunlit arena. His mind sought futilely for some way to right the situation. But Abigail was betrothed to another. He was surrounded by the ashes of forbidden dreams.

"Still," Marcellus said, almost to himself. "There may be something to the Judeans' complaint, I suppose."

Linux's attention gradually came back into focus. He turned to look at the prelate.

"It would certainly do my standing no good if this group did prove to be a threat, and it became known I had been warned and did nothing." The prelate's expression tightened. "In the meantime, I suppose we must postpone any further actions on the . . . the project you and I discussed. If their threat of revolt is indeed true, such an action might shove them right over the edge."

Linux felt an invisible weight lift from his shoulders. "As my prelate commands."

"You have told no one?"

"Not a soul, sire. There was no need, not until the day you ordered me to move."

"Hold all your plans in abeyance. We will speak on it again once this latest problem is behind us." Marcellus turned to the steward hovering by his elbow. He accepted the new goblet, tasted, and moaned. "Ah, the sweet taste of Rome. Rome! May she conquer all pestilent barbarians and rule them with splendid dignity!"

Linux rose from his chair as expected and lifted his own goblet. "To Rome!"

The rest of the gathering took up the toast, each vying to shout louder than the next. The prelate nodded to the roars as though accepting his rightful acclaim, which Linux supposed in a way he was.

CHAPTER

TWENTY-NINE

As SOON AS THE PRELATE'S ATTENTION was recaptured by the arena, Linux backed away, bowing as he did so. To his relief, the prelate did not demand that he remain. The steward immediately lifted the chair from the dais and carried it away. While the other guests gathered about the prelate to fill the air with their further empty accolades, Linux went to find Jacob, who was attempting to conceal himself behind a pillar. His shoulders shook and his hands covered his face. Linux nudged the boy forward and discreetly departed.

They returned to where the arena road joined with the main thoroughfare to Jerusalem. Jacob did not speak, and Linux did not question him.

Linux had paid little attention to the games themselves. The sport of blood had never held him. Linux had a warrior's scorn for gladiators and the maiming of man or beast as entertainment. But for Jacob, a young Judean lad with no concept of Roman games, it clearly had been a terrible shock. The boy's occasional shudder indicated the level of his distress.

The road traversing the Mount of Olives was still crowded with the people wending their way into the city. Linux and Jacob joined the silent throng and let those about them set the pace. For Linux, it was a decidedly odd sensation, to be enveloped within a Judean crowd that paid him no mind. Their attention was firmly fixed upon what lay ahead. In truth, he did not mind becoming mired within this motley group. There was a certain comfort to becoming simply another person trudging along the road, enduring the midafternoon heat and desert wind.

The beautiful face of Abigail weaved in and out of the light and heat, and his heart was pierced anew with what would never be his. And yet he was also pierced by the fact that he had twisted a human desire into something that festered and drew him into dark thoughts. His bitterness and anger had fueled a readiness to undertake an extraordinary theft from the Judean Temple. And to what end? So the new prelate, a man who served an emperor Linux knew to be truly evil, would murder Linux's brother. And in doing so, Linux would have added his own name to the scroll of evildoers. He would carry his own portion of this plague. He could clothe his actions in whatever words he might choose. He might call it vengeance. He might claim merely to be an obedient officer, or maybe a better leader. But it changed nothing. Linux had almost become what he most despised about his own empire.

Linux gripped the boy's shoulder more tightly and kept him on the road. Jacob still had not spoken, and Linux could not tell much more from the lad's expression than that he was devastated by something he had seen.

Linux started to speak, but what could he say? That everything would be all right? How could he utter such a lie, when he himself had been ready to use this Judean youth to carry out a horrendous crime against his own people? For that had been Linux's plan. He would have granted Jacob his dream of being a legionnaire by corrupting the lad, by twisting his ambition into deeds as dark as those the prelate had prescribed for Linux. He would have sent Jacob into the Temple, where Linux was excluded, to see where the doors hidden inside the stable opened within the Temple compound. The distance from the Council building, and where precisely within that structure was the treasury. Jacob would pace around the treasury building, taking prescribed measurements, and report on how many guards stood duty as the Temple was shut for the night.

Linux was filled with a shame so bitter he too began to falter as he walked. His only defense against life's bitter dregs had been a cynical quip and a sardonic smile. Now even these were being stripped off.

Then, between one step and the next, it all fell away.

Not that his troubles vanished. But their ability to grip him, to clench him and blind him and choke his heart, all this had simply dropped from his soul. And for the first time since that night in the Judeans' courtyard, Linux could *see*.

That sense of revelation beyond his own ability to reason or perceive was precisely as it had been on that bewildering night. He looked around at the dregs of humanity surrounding him and saw himself as no less needy than they, as utterly helpless against the inner torments. He carried what he had seen up the final rise and through the gates and into Jerusalem. He no longer held himself aloof from the supplicants who walked this harsh road with him. He did not care what the city dwellers thought of a dusty Roman officer trundling along with all the others, his hand resting upon the shoulder of a sad Judean lad.

They arrived upon the broad avenue leading from the Old City to the main Temple entrance. He steered Jacob to the side, where they leaned against the eastern wall. An elderly couple stood nearby, so frail they seemed to remain upright only by leaning upon each other. On Jacob's other side was a gaunt young girl on a makeshift pallet.

Gradually the sun lowered to shine directly into his eyes. The afternoon wind funneled hot down the avenue. Linux hardly noticed. He could no longer even say why he was there. Only that the old ways and all he had brought himself to no longer held him. Linux felt if he were to release the boy's shoulder, he might well be swept away, only another meaningless bit of debris blowing hither and yon through the street.

His thoughts kept returning to the night in the courtyard. Standing here now, Linux realized he had been fleeing from the miracle for which his heart yearned. He had hidden behind the pain he had felt over Abigail. He had allowed himself to be tempted by the prelate's dark plotting. They had all been barriers to the truth. His wound was better hidden than Abigail's had been, but no less in need of healing.

Linux recalled once more the brilliant expression of the apostle as he had cried out with a voice so powerful it split the night air. Despite the afternoon heat, Linux shivered anew at the force of those words. *Bring healing in the name of your son, our Lord and Savior, Jesus of Nazareth. Be healed!*

The crowd stirred about him, their heads all turned toward the left. Linux pushed himself away from the wall. He had no clear idea of why he was there, but he too watched the large man coming toward him on the avenue.

"Linux?"

Peter's shadow fell upon him, and the man reached out to grip Linux's shoulder. The apostle looked into his face, then said, "The door remains open to you."

———

As the procession of believers continued on, Alban planted himself in front of the lad standing next to Linux. "Ah, Jacob, I've been so worried. Where have you been?"

When Jacob did not respond, Linux leaned in close to the lad. His voice was hoarse. "I want you to listen to me very carefully."

Jacob stood straight and wiped his dusty face with a sleeve.

"You have no place among the legions of Rome. What you saw back there in the arena is the clearest possible reason why."

"What has happened?" Alban's alarm was evident.

Linux lifted one hand for silence and continued to speak directly to Jacob. "Alban wants to take you with him to Galilee. You must go."

"But, I—"

"No," Linux said, his tone unmistakable. "You do not want it. You would not find your dreams there. What you want does not exist. Behind the glitter and the pomp and the power lies the brutal force, the might of a godless empire, and all too often, death."

"Listen to him, lad," Alban murmured. "He speaks truth."

"Go with him to Galilee," Linux said, then straightened with the slow motions of an old man.

Alban asked once more, more quietly this time, "What has happened?"

Linux tried several replies, then said simply, "I was wrong. About many things." He began to turn away.

"Wait." Alban gripped him by the arm. "Old friend, will you pray with me?"

Linux found himself no longer able to protest. He simply stood, head bowed. Alban held on to his arm and began to speak. Linux heard no words clearly. He felt as though a cool rain had begun to fall on him. Washing away all he had believed was inevitable, all that was impossible to change.

Finally Alban stopped speaking. He leaned closer and said,

"Listen to the Spirit's voice within you, my friend—he will guide you the next hour, the next day, and into the future."

———

The storerooms felt stifling in the morning heat. And the dust from the grains made Abigail's throat hurt. She wished there was another way to weigh and portion the daily distributions. But this was part of the service she gave to the community of believers. Morning by morning she encouraged herself with the thought that this was the task that God had given her, and she was privileged to be serving him. And not far away from Stephen.

She was just opening another sack to measure out a portion for a family of four when she heard noise in the courtyard. It was not the usual soft chatter of children, the shuffling about of those coming for supplies, or a guffaw from one or another of the men. These voices were loud with sounds of frustration. Even anger.

Abigail felt fear up and down her spine. The compound had been filled earlier with new rumors of Judean religious leaders meeting with the Romans, seeking to stem their rising numbers.

She looked around the door and saw some of the followers in an animated discussion with Peter and James, the natural brother of the Lord. Abigail watched for a time, then returned to filling sacks with grain. Whatever it was, Peter would handle it for all of them.

The conversation outside gradually diminished. When Abigail looked out again she saw Peter and James, arms around the shoulders of their visitors, as James led them in a prayer. Clearly the situation, whatever it was, had been resolved.

Stephen and two young boys came for the filled sacks. The heavier task of moving them from storage to the courtyard was always done by the men. Stephen hoisted sacks on the boys' backs and turned to lift his own.

Abigail dared to whisper, "What was that about?"

Stephen put the sack down and moved a bit closer, his eyes showing concern. "The Hellenized Judeans are not happy with the distribution process. They don't feel their own widows and orphans are being properly and fairly cared for."

If anyone would know the truth of their concerns, it was Stephen. She asked, "What do you think?"

Stephen said carefully, "Whenever I am present, we are vigilant to give the same allotments to all who approach us."

"But when you are absent?"

Stephen turned and stared out the storeroom's open doorway. "The widows and orphans from the freedmen's group are perhaps the most vulnerable among us. Many come from outlying provinces. They include many former slaves, with no funds or income or place to stay. We help care for all their needs. Especially those without gardens, fields, or vineyards of their own."

"And families to help," Abigail said softly.

He looked at her. "If everyone had your giving heart and caring spirit, this situation would vanish."

She studied the man before her. Stephen always gave careful thought to another's circumstance. Her heart swelled with a sentiment so new it took her a moment to name it—pride in him and for what they might soon share.

Abigail asked, "What can be done?"

"Peter says the apostles who are teaching and healing should not be pulled away from those callings. There is a meeting planned for tonight. It will be decided then. Peter says he feels that the task is too great for one man. He is suggesting that others be sought out. With more working together, the needs will be met."

"What do you think?"

"I agree," Stephen said. "It really is a large responsibility, and I cannot be several places at once. I trust it will make your load easier as well. I fear you are doing far more than your share."

She smiled. "God gives me strength."

"But more hands will be welcomed. Have you ideas of who would work well at this ministry?"

Abigail did, though she did not then express her thoughts. "They will draw lots?"

"That is the usual way. But tonight they may just be announced."

"No matter," Abigail said. "However they are selected, there will be much prayer beforehand. God will direct toward those who are the best ones for the task."

"That is right, of course. A good reminder, Abigail."

He gave her a smile and turned back to the pile of filled sacks. The two boys were already returning for their next load.

———

That evening Abigail sat with the women and listened as Peter explained the situation. "We must not fail to give our full attention to the spreading of the Good News and to prayer. But we must also care for those who are in need. That, too, is God's commandment to us. We must be careful not to neglect that task.

"I have spent the afternoon in prayer, as have other apostles, and now we are ready to act. We would like you to select seven men—men who are full of the Spirit and wisdom—and we will turn this responsibility over to them."

The entire assembly held silent for a time, and then nods and smiles went around the gathering.

"Please organize yourselves into seven groups," Peter said to the men. "Then pray that God will direct you to the person who is equal to the task. When your group has agreed on one person, bring that name here to us."

After a pause of slight uncertainty, the men began to form themselves into circles. Peter stood to count the groups, motioning for some to join others as necessary. In a surprisingly short time, all were arranged as instructed and the sound of voices in prayer lifted over the courtyard.

Abigail and the other women also prayed that the Lord would guide in the selection. She saw one man move to where the apostles were sitting, murmur something, then return to his place. Rather quickly others followed, and Peter wrote their names down.

Peter stood, and everyone turned to face him. "God has revealed the names of seven men who are equal to the task," he said, looking at the papyrus in his hand. "These men will together be responsible to see that those who are in need have supplies, fairly given. We do not wish any to feel slighted or to be in need. The men will oversee the tables, and if there is a requirement from someone who is unable to come to the table, they will see that a delivery of supplies is made."

Peter looked around at those in the courtyard. "I will read the names." He paused to clear his throat, then lifted the papyrus.

"Stephen."

Abigail felt her heart lurch with pride and joy. She looked toward Stephen, already knowing where to find him in the crowd. The moment his name was called he sat a bit straighter, his hand went to his face, and he bowed his head. Already he was praying, she knew, for God's help and direction.

Peter continued reading, "Philip, Prochorus, Nicanor, Timon, Parmenas, and Nicolas of Antioch."

Oh good, there is at least one Grecian among them, she noted as the names were read. *It will be easier for the Greeks to feel they are being treated fairly.* She could hear murmurs of assent.

Peter called the seven to come forward for their commissioning prayer.

Abigail scarcely knew the others on the list, but Stephen had been named first. Did that mean he, the keeper of the records, would be the one truly in charge?

If so, it was to be an enormous task. But she was sure he would do it well. And she would pray for him.

But at the moment she could not wait to speak with him.

———

There was opportunity for only a brief meeting before Abigail's companions would be leaving the courtyard for the night.

Stephen sought her out, and she lifted her face, slightly embarrassed. "I am pleased you have been chosen, Stephen." She wasn't sure if that was a proper statement, but she did want him to know how she felt.

He did not respond as she had expected. "It is an overwhelming assignment," he said. "One I do not feel worthy to perform."

She didn't know what else to say to him.

"I felt it was a gift from God that I was assigned as the keeper of the records," he continued, his voice low. "Me, with my background, trusted to serve in this way . . . So new to the faith. I owe such a debt of gratitude. To Jesus Christ my Lord. To the apostles. To the followers who put my name forward."

"You are more than able to do it," Abigail said, though feeling rather helpless in the face of his uncertainty.

"But to be chosen tonight and added to the ranks of our leaders . . ." He frowned at the cobblestones. "I feel very unworthy and unprepared."

Abigail pulled her shawl across her face in preparation for

her departure with the others. Then she reached out and lightly touched his arm.

"You were not chosen tonight simply by the insight and knowledge of our fellow believers, Stephen. The Lord was with each group as they prayed and discussed their assignment. 'Full of the Spirit and wisdom'—weren't those Peter's instructions?"

CHAPTER

THIRTY

LINUX SLEPT BETTER than he could remember. He awoke to the sound of Julian moving about in the adjoining room. As his feet touched the floor, the aging servant appeared in the doorway and announced, "There is tea. And hot water for shaving. And a soldier in praetorian dress arrived this morning bearing a scroll from the prelate."

Linux nodded his thanks and went to the bronze mirror by the door to shave.

"You look . . . well, different this morning," Julian observed as he brought in the breakfast, the scroll tucked under his arm.

"That is precisely how I feel," he said, the razor-sharp knife scraping over his face.

"Good to hear. You've been rather off your feed of late."

"An illness," Linux replied quietly.

"One brought back from Umbria?"

"No. This ailment I have carried with me for far longer."

"So it's gone, then," the man said, placing the items of food on the table.

Linux took a moment to study the image reflected back at him and wonder if the change was there for all to see. "I can only hope so."

The scroll bore the prelate's crest. As promised, it assigned Linux chambers in the Antonia Fortress, a staff, and an increase both in stipend and rank. Julian's eyebrows rose as Linux read the inscription aloud.

Linux was just finishing breakfast when Alban's voice called, "Permission to enter?"

"Please. Come."

Alban climbed the stairs and entered. "How are you, old friend?"

"I feel better than I have in a long time, though I can scarce believe it myself."

"Believe it," Alban said firmly. "Believe also that it does my heart good to hear the news."

"But I thought you were leaving today."

"The caravan master has decided to put off our departure a few more days." Alban started to say something more, then stopped and finished simply, "It is for the best."

Linux had the distinct impression that Alban wanted to say something about Abigail. But he did not press. "How is Jacob?"

"He has agreed to accompany me."

Linux rose to his feet. "I would like to speak with him."

"That is why he came." Alban followed Linux from the chamber, then halted him at the top of the stairs. He said, "There is another man with us."

Linux noticed his friend's hesitation. "Who is this one?"

Alban took a hard breath. "His name is Stephen."

"Do I know this man?"

"You have seen him. Several times." Another breath. "Stephen is Abigail's betrothed."

"You brought that man here? To what end?"

"We prayed for you last night. Afterward Stephen came to me and said that God had spoken to him. About you."

Linux stared back at Alban, stunned into silence.

"It is customary to offer new believers instruction from one of our leaders," Alban added.

Linux nodded slowly. Not just in confirmation, but rather to give himself time to take in the words. "Your God told this man to offer me instruction?"

Alban smiled briefly, then corrected, "*Our* God."

"There is much to learn," Linux said. He searched himself and found only the same calm he had awakened to that morning. "He is sincere in this wish to teach me?"

"Come and determine for yourself."

———

Word came by way of a young boy. Abigail felt herself tremble as she was summoned into the courtyard to speak with him. The youth looked as nervous as she felt. She assumed this was his first task of such importance, and the way he tightly held his fist told her that he clutched coins for his service.

"Yes?" she prompted.

"A man, Alban, asks you to come back to your quarters. He is waiting to speak with you," he said in a rush.

Abigail's hand flew to her breast. *Jacob.* "Is . . . is my brother well?"

"Your brother?"

"Jacob. My brother. Is he—?"

"I cannot say," the lad said with a shake of his head. "I have given you the message just as it was given me."

Abigail fought for composure. "Thank you. You may go."

He whirled and ran from the compound.

Abigail also hastened her steps to the kitchen. Already she was out of breath. "I must go, Martha. Alban must have news of Jacob."

"Is he well?"

"I . . . I have not been told."

"Go and God be with you," said the older woman.

Abigail almost ran out, wrapping her shawl about her.

By the time she reached her street she felt sick to her stomach. Both because of the hot sun and because of her uncertainty about what might be ahead. But as she hurried up the alley she saw Alban sitting in the shade of the lean-to.

And Jacob . . .

He was not far off, leaning against the building's wall.

Abigail whispered a fervent prayer of thanks as she rushed toward them.

Alban rose to his feet, but it was Jacob who moved toward her. "I am sorry," he began. "Sorry for making you worry. I shouldn't have left with no word."

She managed to control her emotions as she stood in front of him. "You are here now. That is all that matters. You are here." She reached out a hand, and he grasped it tightly.

She could not read Jacob's expression as she looked into his face. Something new was there, something she could not identify.

Alban finally spoke. "Let us go inside."

Abigail followed numbly, hardly recognizing her own humble abode. Alban motioned her to the one stool while he and Jacob settled on a floor mat. "Linux seems to have done me another favor," Alban began.

"Linux?"

"He has sent Jacob back to us. Jacob now sees that some dreams are meant to be handed over to God. To be remolded and redirected in keeping with his will. Sometimes our plans do not fit with the plans of God. Linux helped . . ."

Alban stopped, and he and Abigail looked at Jacob, who was staring straight ahead at the empty gate and the road beyond. His attention seemed to have been given to something, to someone, beyond the present, beyond Alban's words.

Then Jacob spoke. "Linux only told me what I already had realized. I saw it for myself." He hesitated as though even the telling was too hard for him.

"Where were you?" breathed Abigail. "What happened?"

"The arena."

"You were *where?*" Abigail could feel anger surging inside her. "Why were you in such an evil place?"

"Linux had taken him there—perhaps unwittingly," Alban explained. "Or perhaps to show him what being a legionnaire really means."

"It truly was awful," went on Jacob, his voice nearly inaudible. "Six soldiers, they called them gladiators, were fighting. Two already were dying in the sand. And the people were shouting and laughing and yelling for more blood. They used this . . . this horror like it was a game. For their amusement. Death. And pain. And suffering. I could hear the fighters groaning and crying out to their gods. They were frightened to die. And they were frightened to live. I could tell.

"That's when I knew I could never be a Roman soldier. I thought . . . I thought their assignment was to keep peace. To serve the law. To fight the enemy. Not . . . not to fight each other in an arena filled with screaming people. Not die in a heap in the sand with flies swarming all over. I knew then that I could never be a soldier. It was wicked. It was wrong."

The lad turned an ashen face toward them. "And I had been approached by the Zealots. They showed me another side to being a soldier. Different, yet the same. If I joined the legionnaires or the Zealots, most likely I would be forced to fight other Judeans. And kill them. And for what?"

Jacob covered his face with his hands. Abigail was sure that he was seeing the horrible scene all over again. She slipped off the stool and knelt beside him, drawing him close. "It's all right, Jacob. You are here now. Safe."

For a time Jacob huddled within her embrace. When he pushed back, Abigail didn't know if the trace of tears on his cheek were his . . . or hers.

Jacob took a deep breath, then another. Alban spoke softly. "Who was in that arena, Jacob?"

The boy shook his head. "I do not know who they were. They were torn and bloodied and lying on the ground. Some were still crying or groaning, and calling out to their gods." He looked down. "And I prayed. I knew I needed to pray. For them."

Jacob was swallowing, fighting to control his deep emotion. "I asked God what I should do. I asked him to guide me. I had always wanted to be a soldier, but I knew I couldn't be a legionnaire or a Zealot. I didn't know what to do. So he . . . he showed me."

Abigail found it hard to wait for the boy to reveal the Lord's answer. It took him a moment, but at length he lifted his head. "I'm going with Alban."

Alban said, "The caravan master has almost completed his business here. We should be leaving within the week. Until then, Jacob will remain with me and learn of his new responsibilities on the road as a caravan guard."

Abigail felt enormous relief, but also mourned inwardly, *What will I do without Jacob?*

She forced the thought aside and even managed a slight smile. "I shall miss you, brother."

"But you must come too," Jacob said quickly. "You can't stay here."

"I must stay here," responded Abigail. "I am betrothed. To Stephen."

"If he wants to claim you, he can come too. He should go with us."

"His calling is here. He has just been appointed—"

"God can use him wherever he is," Jacob argued. "Galilee needs believers, too, does it not, Alban?" The boy was practically pleading.

"Indeed it does. But each of us must serve where God has placed us. If Stephen feels God has asked him to serve here, then stay here he must until God provides different guidance. You have now decided to be a soldier of our God rather than a soldier of Rome, and God is now your authority. He will give the commands, and you must learn obedience. That is also true for Stephen.

"And I must stay with him," Abigail added. "We will serve God together. There is much need, and Stephen is a good man. He is totally dedicated to our Lord—and the people. He wishes only to give his life in service. And I—"

"But . . ." It was obvious Jacob was sorely troubled.

"What is it?" prompted Alban.

Jacob bowed his head, and his shoulders were shaking as though he had taken a chill.

"There is more?"

Jacob lifted his head, but his eyes were tightly closed. "When I was praying in the arena, I had a dream. A vision—or something.

Instead of the gladiators, I was seeing . . . our people. Believers of the Way. Followers." He opened his eyes and looked at Alban.

"It was our people in the arena," he said, his voice hushed. "I knew it. As real as if they were actually there. And the crowd was still cheering and laughing and calling for blood."

Jacob turned to Abigail. "Please. Please, sister, come with us."

Once again Abigail wrapped her arms around him. "Jacob, I love you dearly. Though it is very hard to see you leave, I am glad you are going with Alban. To be with Alban and Leah—and the baby. But I cannot go. My place is here with the man I have come to love. He needs me. If . . . if suffering lies ahead, then that too is in God's hands. Don't you see? He knows what is ahead, and he has not shown me, at least yet, to leave for Galilee."

She ran a hand through his unruly hair. "I will tell Stephen of . . . of what you saw, and ask him to be watchful. He will warn the others."

Alban asked softly, "And what did God say must be done?"

Jacob raised his head and looked at Alban, then Abigail. He said, 'You must be ready.' "

CHAPTER

THIRTY-ONE

LINUX CLIMBED THE NARROW LANE into the Old City. Accompanied by a young lad whose name he did not remember, Linux was being escorted to his next meeting with Stephen. Though the world had shifted beneath Linux's feet, and he now saw things through different eyes, he was still a Roman entering an ancient Judean realm. To be led by a distinctly Hebrew lad was a sign, to any who noticed, that Linux came because he was invited.

As soon as he entered the plaza, the memories swept over him. So much had happened here—Alban's wedding, their fleeing from Herod's wrath, meeting Abigail, and now this. For a brief instant Linux was tempted to turn back.

Ahead waited the young man with gentle but searching eyes, the one who was betrothed to the woman Linux still thought of with a pang through his heart. How could he, a Roman officer and by blood a member of the aristocracy, come to such a man for instruction? Yet the force that had drawn him this far remained with him still, a growing determination to see this to completion.

The boy pushed open the inner doors through which Linux had spoken to Abigail. . . . Could it have been only a few weeks ago? So much had become packed into those ensuing days. The youngster spoke to Linux for the first time since meeting him where the fortress lane intersected with the main avenue. He said, "Wait here."

The interior courtyard was crowded. Many people, mostly women, surrounded the central table so that the boy could not squeeze through. He called, "Stephen?"

"Here."

"The Roman has come!"

All eyes turned Linux's way. He searched the faces for a glimpse of Abigail. He knew it was futile, but he could not help himself. All he saw were weathered features, ancient eyes filled with at least curiosity, some with hostility and fear.

Stephen must have found a way through the throng. He smiled at Linux. "Welcome, welcome. Perhaps we would be more comfortable speaking outside."

Linux allowed himself to be drawn back into the outer plaza. Stephen explained, "I am helping with widows from among the Hellenized community. You understand that word?"

"Judeans drawn from around the empire."

"We want to be sure they are treated fairly by the local community of believers."

"Why you, may I ask?"

"Why indeed? I wanted to decline their request, but . . ." Stephen led him to a bench shaded from the afternoon sun. "Sit, please. Now tell me. Why are you here?"

"You sent for me."

"Yes, yes, of course. But listen to what I am saying. *Why are you here?* What has brought you to this point, that you would sit with me this afternoon and speak of matters related to our Lord?"

Linux resisted the urge to squirm. "I dislike speaking about myself."

To his surprise, Stephen did not press him further. He may not have expected an answer. "I would like to offer a suggestion, Linux. Stop me if what I say does not apply. You came because you have found yourself trapped. There are forces at work in your life over which you have no control. You are a man of power, of influence, of wealth. And yet, you feel helpless."

Linux could not have been more surprised. "How—?"

"There are others who have experienced similar trials. Here, let me tell you the thoughts of one such person. Another man of power, a king. This comes from our holy texts, and it is called a psalm." He shut his eyes and began to recite, " 'Save me, O God! For the waters have come up to my neck. I sink in deep mire, where there is no standing; I have come into deep waters, where the floods overflow me. I am weary with my crying; my throat is dry; my eyes fail while I wait for my God. Those who hate me without a cause are more than the hairs of my head; they are mighty who would destroy me, being my enemies wrongfully; though I have stolen nothing, I still must restore it. O God, You know my foolishness; and my sins are not hidden from You. Let not those who wait for You, O Lord God of hosts, be ashamed because of me.' "

Linux could barely speak. "Why are you telling me this?"

Stephen opened his eyes. "I would like to introduce you further to our Lord God through the holy writings. David was a man chosen by God, anointed as king, and yet he too suffered. As do we all. And here is the key. Our God has been with us all along. Our God awaits the moment when we turn to him and ask his forgiveness, his blessing, his anointing, his peace."

Linux looked around the empty plaza. A pair of sparrows fluttered down from the empty sky, drank from the well, and flew away. Somewhere in the distance a donkey brayed. Through a window behind him, Linux heard a child laugh. "I understand none of this, and yet it calls to me."

Stephen nodded slowly, rocking his entire upper body in the process. "This is true of all of us. It is a huge change, from unbelief to knowing God's presence, from perception of only what we can see, hear, and feel to a new realm, the spiritual world. We enter into this like infants.

"Listen to me, Linux. I do not meet you out here, away from the community of believers, because you are Roman and excluded. I meet you here so that we are not distracted by all else that goes on inside. We do not sit here and speak because you must be pros-elytized into one temple sect or another. You are here because you *already* know God. He has touched your heart. Is that not so?"

Linux's swallow was loud in his own ears. He nodded. "Yes."

"So he has touched you, and yet there is much you do not yet understand. How are you to fathom all that is happening? What shall be the direction from inside for what you think? How you shall live? Where you will go? The answer, my new brother, is found within the sacred texts. Together we will begin to study them, you and I. You will learn to speak with God directly. And you will discover how to listen to him speak with you."

Ezra brooded as he watched his children play with the maid-servant. She had been personally selected by Miriam, Gamaliel's wife. Seventeen, the girl came from a poor but very religious fam-ily. Tonight she had fed the children, then brought them into the room where Ezra pretended to work. The candlelight cast their young features in ruddy shades, and their laughter filled the usually somber chamber. His little girl walked over to where his chair was set by the open window and pulled at his sleeve. Ezra lifted her up and placed her in his lap. The child smelled fresh, and her voice sounded clear and sweet. She allowed herself to be held for a few moments, then squirmed her way down and returned to play with the servant and her brother.

The maidservant was attractive enough, with a pleasant face and a lilting voice that soothed and encouraged as she interacted with the two children. Yet Ezra would never dream of seeking such a one as his wife. How could he have permitted himself to be ensnared by that orphaned washerwoman, one belonging to a sect that held such power over its members? He shook his head at the agonizing memory of his sister.

His gaze moved to the drapes drifting in the evening breeze. The bottom of each drape was sewn around a lead weight, and the material was as sheer as a bride's veil, meant to keep out the night creatures but let in the air. Ezra listened to the sound of the drapes sliding across the tiled floor, in time to the music of his children's laughter. He recalled other nights in this room. When his wife had been with child, she had liked to come and sit here to watch him work, her hands cradled about her, a faint smile on her face. The way she had looked at him, her eyes filled with maternal love, had left him feeling as though he was the most blessed of Judean men. He shook his head once more at another agonizing memory.

His head servant appeared in the doorway. "A man is at the gates, sire. He wishes a word with you."

"It is late. Tell him to return tomorrow."

The servant glanced at the maidservant. "He comes from the house of Gamaliel."

"You may show him here." Ezra rose from his chair. "Ask to his needs. If he wishes food, order the cook to relight the fires."

Ezra nodded toward the young woman, and she trailed behind with his son as he carried his protesting daughter to bed. This night he wanted to remain close to her a moment longer. Only later did he wonder if perhaps he had a foreboding of the change to come. He went into his son's room and spoke with him of the day now gone and the one yet to come. As though either of them might have guessed what lay ahead.

Finally he strode back across the courtyard and along the pillared walkway to his chamber. He stood for a moment in the shadows and observed the young man inside. Saul of Tarsus carried himself with such tension that the air about him seemed alive. He was striding back and forth in front of the shelves of scrolls along the north wall, the section which contained Ezra's collection of the Torah, the biblical law. The broad-shouldered man held himself erect in the manner of one who has known hard labor. This was no pale scholar who had lived his days hunched over ancient scrolls in a synagogue.

Ezra stepped through the doorway and said, "I was hoping you would come."

THE ANTONIA FORTRESS WAS DESIGNED in a series of square blocks, each surrounding its own interior courtyard. Passages were long and narrow, as though Herod the Great feared his troops might revolt, and so built the fortress and adjoining palace in a manner that sections could be isolated and thus more easily defended. The most sumptuous apartments, and the tribune's private offices, lined the outer wall facing Jerusalem's southern hills. The light was better there, and the rooms were protected from both the city and the soldiers' din.

Linux selected an apartment that probably had housed a senior servant. It overlooked one of the secluded interior courtyards. Julian made his way from room to room, poking into corners and muttering, but he did not object outright.

Two days later, the tribune that had been sent to replace Bruno Aetius arrived from Rome. Lucius Vitellus Metellus was a staunch supporter of the Senate and a man well accustomed to sailing with the political winds. He sent for Linux, who appeared each morning in the tribune's outer office and sat waiting.

The tribune passed through from time to time, normally surrounded by aides and clerks. Because the tribune ignored Linux, so too did his staff.

Each day, just prior to the midday meal, a senior aide emerged and ordered Linux to report again the next day. Linux saluted and left.

In truth, he did not count these mornings as squandered time. For each afternoon he met with Stephen, and the young man continued Linux's instruction. The material Stephen introduced, and the implications of what Linux heard, left him requiring these empty morning hours to reflect before the afternoon's lesson.

Stephen separated his instruction each day into two parts. First, he introduced Linux to writings of the Judean prophets, and what they had to say about the Messiah's coming. Gradually Stephen built up an image of the Messiah—who he was foretold to be and what his role on earth would encompass.

Stephen's second lesson of the day was about a follower's personal behavior regarding prayer and the commandments—both the traditional ones handed down by Moses and, more recently, Jesus' interpretation of them.

It was very hard for Linux to say which of the two was more jolting.

The tribune's antechamber was as vast as Linux's entire apartment, an ocher rectangle twenty paces wide and fifteen long and ten high. Two square windows set in the fortress's thick outer wall gave the impression of light having to burrow its way inside. The morning sun fell in two brilliant pillars upon the polished stone floor. Often Linux rose from his seat to stretch his legs and pace. The distant green and gold Judean hills seemed to follow his movements, as though the country itself monitored his progress.

The process of thinking his way through these lessons forced him to inspect the very core of his life. The more he studied with Stephen, the greater became his certainty that these hours spent captive in the new tribune's outer hall, intended to humiliate an officer close to the consul, were actually graced to him by . . . *by whom?*

It took Linux four days of sitting and pondering and pacing to finish that sentence.

Graced to me by God.

"Linux Aurelius."

"Ah . . . yes?" Linux started as though coming awake, and realized he had paced over into the antechamber's furthest corner. He swiveled about. "Yes?" he said again.

"The tribune will see you now."

"Oh, that is, thank you."

Linux straightened his tunic and followed the aide through the tall double doors. He halted before the tribune's wide table and saluted. "Linux Aurelius reporting for duty, sire."

The tribune did not look up from the scroll he was reading. "I suppose you have lodged your complaints with the consul by now."

"Complaints over what, sire?"

The tribune was a narrow man. His shoulders seemed scarcely broad enough to support the standard legionnaire's breastplate. His wrists were slight as a young girl's, his fingers long and supple like a musician's. Hair wispy, neck far too long, head elongated. Only his nose was at odds with the rest of him, a protuberance of astonishing size. "I have kept you waiting because I have been forced to deal with myriad crises since my arrival. Affairs far more vital, I'm afraid, than taking the report of a young officer whose role I have yet to fathom."

"I am here to serve at the tribune's pleasure," Linux replied. "As for keeping me waiting, sire, I have been grateful for the time."

The tribune's eyes were of a light shade of grey, so pale as to appear colorless. It was a trait of the Metellus clan, along with their grandfather's rather frail build. They even took pride in it, claiming that real leaders were those who merely purchased brawn and steel, and controlled both with ruthless brutality.

"Grateful? To what end?"

"Since returning from Rome, I feel as though I have been trapped inside a whirlwind, one not of my own making. It has been a time to sort through everything."

The tribune set aside his scroll. "I'm not certain I approve of my officers spending so much time thinking. Your role is to serve. Your leaders will do the thinking. Too much thought from subordinates leads to dangerous directions and threats against Rome's proper course."

Linux knew the tribune sought a quarrel. He knew also he should have been more worried about it. Yet it seemed as though the sentiment growing in him over the past days was only now truly visible. Here, in this moment of great danger, could he search inside himself and name this new experience? What he felt here was peace.

"Well, do you not have anything to say for yourself?"

"I stand ready to serve at my tribune's pleasure."

"Do you? *Do you?* And tell me what have you been doing that our consul would reward you with an apartment and staff that should have been the *tribune's* prerogative to grant?"

"I have served the consul in the tribune's absence, sire. If you wish, I shall gladly give up my chambers this very hour."

"But that does not answer my question, does it? What service have you performed for the consul?"

"That is for the consul to say, sire. I have been ordered to speak to no one about my duties."

Tribune Metellus leapt to his feet. "I countermand that order!"

Linux took great comfort in the steadiness of his mind and tone. "Sire, I am no threat to you or your command."

"So you say," he spat out as he began to pace. "Why should I believe that?"

Linux chose not to answer as he watched the man stalk about. The tribune's breastplate was fashioned from a sheet of gold, embedded with precious gems. The finery flickered a silent warning as he passed back and forth through the sunlight. "I do not know what to do with you, Linux Aurelius. I was warned about you by your brother. Castor is a friend of mine, did you know? He had quite a lot to say about how dangerous, how untrustworthy you might prove to be."

In the past, such evidence of his brother's poison would have sent Linux into yet another rage. This time he found himself at an astonishing distance from those previous responses to even his brother's name. Though he stood at attention while Tribune Metellus deliberated over Linux's future, he felt only calm.

If he had been searching for confirmation that this new direction was real, and the God behind it was as genuine as Stephen and Alban had claimed, it was this.

Abruptly the tribune stopped, swung around to return to his desk, planted his fists upon the scrolls, and said, "You are dismissed. Your fate will be decided in due course." As Linux left the room, the military leader of Judea shouted after him, "Decided by me, do you hear! Not by the consul! By *me*!"

The sensation of being surrounded by an invisible protective barrier was even more powerful once Linux left the tribune's chambers. He found himself going straight out the fortress entrance and walking directly through the crowded city. He entered the Old City and climbed the stairs to stand in the plaza. He panted softly from the speed with which he had traversed the city. Linux watched the widows gathering at the other end, knowing he was not expected and might not be welcome at this time. But he could wait if need be. He could wait all day.

Then he saw her.

Abigail was playing some game with a group of very young children. Her laughter was just as free as theirs, almost as lilting and high. It was her laughter that had turned Linux around, though he had never heard it before. He was sure no one else would laugh in such a manner, with the clarity of a starlit winter night, and a beauty all her own.

How was it possible, he wondered, to know such sorrow and loss for a woman he could never have, and yet also be surrounded by such peace? How could he feel as though his world had crumbled once more, and yet know at some higher level he was where he should be? In this tragic moment, filled with impossible desires, he could still breathe normally, his heart at rest.

For the first time, he freely accepted the meaning of the word *miracle*.

Abigail must have noticed him then. She straightened slowly, the laughter draining away. He was sorry to have caused the moment of unbounded joy to end. He watched her adjust her shawl over her face, then turn and speak to one of the older women. Together they crossed the square and nodded a formal greeting. "The blessed Lord's greetings to you, Linux Aurelius."

He nodded in return. "My sister Abigail."

"I'm sorry—Stephen was not expecting you until this afternoon."

"Something happened this morning. I wanted, I needed . . ." He stopped. It was not Abigail's reserve. Nor was it the older woman who observed him with such concern, even fear.

Linux turned his face away. He knew the women expected him to continue, yet in that moment it was all he could do not to give in to the furious craving clawing at his soul. He had the will, the power, the means to carry her away. . . .

Linux clenched his fists to his sides and shut his eyes as tightly as he did his hands. More than the sun baked down on his upturned face. There in the silence, he heard another voice. One so new he could not truly fathom the language. Only that it spoke to him, a whisper beyond his ability to hear. He could sense that this new voice sang to him, wooed him back.

He turned away. Not physically. Nothing about his outer form changed. He remained as he was, his face turned toward the sun, his entire being locked in conflict. Yet it was over. He knew he would take no action, no matter how great his hunger. He sighed.

"Linux, are you . . . ?" The question was no more than a whisper. He lowered his head and opened his eyes.

Abigail and the other woman both backed up a pace. He could see the conflict in Abigail's eyes. She did not know whom she faced—a Roman officer or a fellow believer. He could tell she wanted to offer him the peace with which they all greeted each other. He also knew it was more than a simple greeting. It was real. He had no question of that now. The peace and the power both existed within him. And he accepted that he was part of them. *And yet . . . A follower who has a new life, a new purpose, a new peace. But who cannot have her. . . .*

"Please do not concern yourselves," he finally said with a sigh. "I will sit and await Stephen."

He did not have to remain there long. Though, in truth, actual time counted for little. He sat and watched the sparrows drink from the fountain. The boldest bird flitted over to perch beside him on the bench, tiny eyes brilliant in the sunlight. When Linux did not offer anything to eat, the sparrow eventually fluttered away, its wings making a quiet whirring in the empty air.

"Linux, forgive me for keeping you waiting. I had no idea you would be here until . . . Is everything all right?" Stephen hovered beside the bench, the sun turning him into a silhouette. Rays of light shimmered about tousled hair.

Linux sighed and licked his lips. "No. Definitely not."

Stephen settled upon the bench next to him. "May I help?"

Linux's ears turned the question into a condemnation. He could not stop himself from comparing his own conflicted state to the man's clear-eyed conviction and gentle nature. He felt so ashamed he could no longer meet Stephen's gaze. "You already have."

"Are you able to talk about it?"

Linux would like to have said no. But the words seemed to well up of their own accord. "I have a . . . a great problem. Two voices struggle within me. Two directions. Two forces." He twisted his hands, then wrenched the air before his face. "I am being torn apart by the power and the—"

"The temptation," Stephen said quietly. "The fact is, you are aware now that you cannot walk in two opposite directions at the same time."

Linux dropped his fists and stared over the now empty plaza. He was not certain how he felt about having his innermost conflict so clearly understood.

"It is time I introduced you to some wonderfully vital concepts that guide a believer's life," Stephen said. "About sin, and repentance, and redemption."

C H A P T E R

THIRTY-THREE

ABIGAIL HAD RETREATED TO THE UPPER ROOM for some solitude before her afternoon responsibilities began. She could not have said why she crossed over to the window. Perhaps her troubled thoughts had drawn her to look out on the courtyard below. Maybe she needed the picture to distract her, or to assure her that everything was as it had been. She studied the courtyard with its well, the surrounding walls with scattered seats where she and others often took refuge from the day's heat. People she knew and had learned to love like family were passing back and forth on various duties of the day.

Yes, it was there. All there just as it had been. Surely the God they loved and served would keep it so.

Three small girls played with a kitten in the shadows of a wall. A woman carried a jar of water from the well. Two younger women washed fresh vegetables in the trough, while a pair of older ones sat in the shade grinding wheat into flour for the next day's bread. Four men and two young boys rebuilt a door to the courtyard across the way. At a corner table out of the sun, two men talked while another wrote on a tablet.

But Abigail's eyes lightly skimmed over the scene. It was all familiar—and comforting. Then in the far corner she spotted two men deep in conversation. One of them was Stephen. Her heart instantly took on a faster beat. She recognized the other as Linux. She realized Stephen was again schooling the man in the faith.

She watched as her betrothed reached out a hand and laid it on the other man's shoulder. And then she saw both men bow their heads. She could tell that they were praying. Praying fervently.

Abigail's own prayer joined the men's.

Perhaps this was the way to safety. To bring their oppressors—one at a time—to accept the Messiah as their own.

"So be it, Lord," whispered Abigail. "Thy will be done."

Abigail carried the courtyard scene and the two men praying with her through the day as she went about her duties. It was not until after the evening prayers that she had opportunity for a brief time with Stephen. They sat across from each other at an empty table.

"I saw you in the courtyard with the Roman."

"Linux is proving to be an able student."

"Does he . . . well, does he ever speak of trouble ahead for us?"

Stephen shook his head. "We study the Scriptures and talk of faith, not of the world."

"When I was called to see Jacob to say my farewells, Alban was waiting with him. The Roman—the one you spoke with—had taken Jacob to the arena. He saw horrible things. It was enough to thoroughly convince him that he could never become a legionnaire and serve God. He was deeply shaken." Abigail paused, shaken herself at the memory.

"But that wasn't all Jacob saw. As he left the arena to get

away from the dying men and the scent of blood, he says he saw a vision."

For a moment Abigail could not go on. She struggled to regain control.

"Suddenly the dead and dying lying there on the sands were . . . were followers. He could not identify any of them. But he knew clearly they were from among us.

"He . . . he prayed then. Asking God what we were to do, and he received an answer. God said, 'They must be ready.' Just that. 'Be ready.' "

Stephen's brows had begun to draw together as she spoke. When he realized she had finished her story he nodded. "I have had the same impression. The same message in a different way."

"What must we do? Where can we go? How can we protect ourselves from the forces of Rome?"

"I think it is not Rome that threatens us at this time," he said slowly.

"No? Then—"

"It is our own, Abigail. It is the Judean leaders who refuse to see Christ as the Messiah. The King we have been praying would come. They are the ones who challenge us and fear the power that God has placed in our hands. They fear . . . because they do not understand."

"But surely . . ." But before Abigail even finished the thought she knew he was right. She had observed the scowls and flashing eyes, heard the hissing under their breath when a group of followers encountered them in the streets. Yes, Stephen was right.

"If there is trouble with our own countrymen, then Rome wouldn't hesitate to step in. They will not tolerate unrest. Rioting. Then indeed we may be caught in the middle."

Stephen's words were so solemn they made Abigail shiver. "I will tell the apostles," he said. "We need to pray as never before."

"Then you think it is possible? There could be trouble?"

He spoke gently now, even laying a hand lightly on her arm as it rested on the table. "Abigail, we have had no illusions. They killed our Lord. Peter has told us from the beginning that Jesus said we would face persecution. That they rejected and hated him, and we would face the same. We should not be surprised."

"Then . . . you are not afraid?"

"I am terrified."

"You think death—?"

"I am not afraid of death, Abigail. I am afraid that I might draw back and not be bold in proclaiming the gospel." He hesitated, then said, "And I am afraid that I might not stand firm. That under the heel of the enemy, in pain, I might deny my Lord."

Though her heart quaked at such a prospect, Abigail said with utter certainty, "I cannot for one moment imagine the stalwart and dedicated man I know would ever even consider denying his Lord."

He smiled a bit crookedly. "Have you heard Peter tell his story? He thought he would be willing to go to death if necessary, with our Lord. But when our Christ was taken, Peter failed to stand with him. He denied him, Abigail. It broke his heart. But it also perhaps made him into the man he is today.

"But Peter also warns us, continually, that we are not able to stand in our own strength. We need God's presence with us. We must pray that God will keep us strong for whatever lies ahead and faithful to the end. And we must encourage one another. Daily."

Such words might have brought even more fear to Abigail's heart, but they left her comforted. Stephen was right. Their God would not desert them.

Someone else heard at least some of their discussion, for a man's voice said, "Well spoken, brother."

They looked over to discover Alban and Martha standing in

an archway where a torch cast deep shadows. Both Abigail and Stephen rose quickly to their feet, and Abigail exclaimed, "Alban, I thought you would be on your way by now!"

He looked at Martha, and they both exchanged smiles. "I had a talk with Peter, and we decided that I—and Jacob—would delay our departure in order to be here for the celebration."

Stephen said, "A celebration?"

"Yes, a wedding celebration."

Martha laughed. "Look at their faces."

Abigail dared a quick glance at Stephen and saw an expression on his face she had not seen before. She wondered if her own face carried the same look of awe and anticipation—maybe just a hint of concern. She did not trust herself to speak.

"Here comes Peter now," Alban noted. Instinctively Abigail reached to smooth her hair. Her robe was stained from her day's work, her hair untidy, and she felt she was not at her best after the long hours and long lines of needy recipients.

Stephen seemed not to notice. He gave her such a smile that it reached across the table between them and warmed her heart. Abigail took a deep breath.

Right then Jacob came bounding up to his sister, looking pleased. She was reaching to embrace him when Peter raised his hands to quiet those still in the courtyard and announced, "Alban will be leaving soon to return to Galilee, and we have decided to hold the marriage celebration for Stephen and Abigail tomorrow."

Abigail needed a moment to absorb it all. Could she be ready for marriage—tomorrow?

Peter was saying, "Traditionally a Judean bride does not know the day or the hour that her bridegroom will come to claim her, but since this bridegroom might find her with her hands deep in bins of grain, doling out food supplies for those who come each day, we are making this announcement in her hearing."

The group laughed and clapped, and Abigail shook her head and managed a nervous laugh herself. Stephen must have seen how stunned she was, for he moved around the table and quietly offered his hand. She felt his strength flow through the contact, the goodness of this man, and yes, the love.

"Tomorrow," she said, her voice trembling. "Let it be so."

She would be ready. She didn't know just what preparations she would need to make. But she would be ready. Of that she was sure.

———

It was a simple but joyful time. There was no need for anything elaborate. Many of the followers had gathered to wish the two well as they began their new life together. As Abigail stepped into the courtyard, she recognized so many—everyone she and Stephen had ever assisted, it seemed, their faces shining with unaccustomed joy. Today, everywhere she looked, Abigail saw only happiness. It was such a gift, this realization that their wedding was raising the spirits of so many.

Jacob hovered nearby, and Abigail reflected that he already seemed both straighter and taller. He reminded her of a lean and hungry sheep dog—his hair was as unruly as always, though he tried to force it into place with sweeps of his hand. Abigail clung to him for as long as she dared, glad he did not push her away in embarrassment.

He gave her a smile and said, "So my sister is to become a married woman. Does the good Stephen think he will be able to manage such an independent wife?"

Abigail heard chuckles around them, and she laughed too. She knew the comment was Jacob's way of expressing his love and care, and she hugged him once more.

He took her arm and led her through the gathering. "Where will you live?"

"Stephen feels we should live where I am now."

"I am glad that you will not be alone. I worry about you," Jacob told her. She wondered if she had seen just a flicker of sadness in his eyes, but he was smiling and nodding his satisfaction with it all. She struggled against the sudden desire to weep.

Then Stephen was at her side with a look only for her, then extending his hand to her brother. "Jacob, you are most welcome to share our simple home. The loft was yours, and will remain so. We will be glad to have you as part of our new family."

Jacob looked very surprised, and for one moment his guard seemed to fall away. Abigail saw his throat constrict as he tried to swallow. "That is most kind," he finally managed, and indicated Alban standing nearby. "But my path seems directed elsewhere at this time."

"As it should be," Stephen said with a smile. He waved at the sound of Peter calling his name. "But know that whenever you return, at any time, our home is yours."

Abigail gave Jacob one more hug. Then she stepped forward, moving through the smiling crowd, to her proper position beside her bridegroom.

The afternoon passed too quickly. Almost before she could totally comprehend what was happening in her life, the gathered group was cheering and throwing flowers toward the small platform where they had knelt when Peter prayed for them. She felt Stephen's hand seek her own. She now belonged to him. When she returned to her simple lodgings, she would no longer journey alone. She would never feel alone again.

CHAPTER

THIRTY-FOUR

SEVERAL DAYS AFTER THEIR FATEFUL nighttime conversation, Ezra met Saul at the Temple. One glance at the young man's face was enough for Ezra to know that he bore alarming news. "Several Temple priests have joined the followers' ranks," he spat out.

The shock pushed Ezra back a pace. "You are certain?"

"Gamaliel received word from the high priest this morning. I was in the chamber."

"What does Gamaliel say about this?"

"The same as yesterday and the day before and last week. We must determine whether they truly speak the word of God."

Ezra felt as though his insides were being twisted. He was losing his oldest and best friend. "He too is *joining* them?"

"I cannot accept that would actually happen."

Ezra forced himself to center his attention on the young man. He felt empty, hollow. "We should continue our discussions elsewhere."

"They are gathering again at Solomon's Porch."

"I do not need to see any more of that group," Ezra replied grimly. "Not ever again."

Ezra took the main thoroughfare into the wealthy district by the city's northwestern wall. This was the only portion of Jerusalem where Hellenized Judeans could safely gather. The broad plaza was filled with men and women wearing brilliantly colored robes. Ezra even spotted a few Judeans wearing Roman robes, their beards oiled and curled in the Greek style, smelling strongly of perfume. Ezra led Saul into a tea shop where three travel litters rested by the entrance, waiting for their owners' wishes. Ezra saw Saul's mouth curl in derision. Such conveyances were rare in Jerusalem these days, for many Judeans had taken to stoning these extravagant displays of wealth from shadowed alleyways.

The shop owner recognized Ezra and bowed the wealthy merchant into an ornately decorated alcove. Ezra ordered, waited until the curtain had been drawn, and said, "I do business here from time to time. We can speak freely and not be overheard."

Saul leaned across the table to declare, "This group must be crushed."

Ezra studied the man opposite him. Saul of Tarsus was the sort of Pharisee that Ezra normally avoided. Stiff-necked and bullish in his opinions, every pronouncement was made in the stubborn certainty that he alone knew what was right. Ezra and Gamaliel had been schooled under a very different philosophy. Their rabbi had insisted that only God could say what was truly the correct viewpoint, and such edicts were delivered through his prophets. This bred a certain flexibility in scriptural study, where the rabbi would present two different views of the same passage and order his students to find the truth in *both* commentaries. But such recollections only brought another piercing regret over this schism between Ezra and his oldest friend.

Ezra pushed all such thoughts aside and said what he had

decided upon just before dawn. "We cannot risk a direct attack upon the apostles."

Saul's beard jutted with indignation. "These leaders are the reason for all these troubles! Erase them and the crowds will evaporate!"

"Will they? Are you so certain of this? Was this not precisely the same argument the Sanhedrin used against Jesus of Nazareth? They crucified the man, and still their numbers grow." Ezra waved that aside, halting Saul in the process of further argument. "There is a greater problem."

Ezra related how he had traveled to the arena and how their warning against the followers had been rebuffed by the new prelate, Marcellus.

Saul's features darkened. He conceded, "If we attack them outright, the group indeed might revolt. The prelate could then blame us for the uprising."

"That we must avoid at all costs," Ezra agreed. The prospect had robbed him of more than one night's sleep. "If the Romans decide we caused a riot by persecuting the apostles, we would be the ones planted on Golgotha."

"What do you propose?"

Ezra leaned across the table and whispered, "We select from among the followers a leader, but one not from their top rank. We bring him forth on charges before the Sanhedrin."

"What charges? They are all known to be rigidly observant of the Law! That is the part—"

"I have thought of that. You have allies among the ranks of rabbis, yes? People who are frightened of what these followers represent?"

"They are most terrified," Saul said, his face grim.

"Bring the man before the Sanhedrin and have several of your cohorts level accusations against him."

As Ezra outlined what they might say, Saul began nodding with such vehemence his entire upper body was set in motion. "Such allegations are so grave the Council will be forced to condemn him."

"And thus we can start with one man, test their mettle, and then gradually attack the entire group." As Saul started to rise, Ezra halted him with a hand on his arm. "It would be best if you moved against them somewhere other than the Temple. We want to carry this out away from too many eyes."

"I know just the place, and just the man," Saul said, his dark eyes burning.

Ezra released the Pharisee's arm. "Go, then. There is no time to lose."

———

Linux walked along the now-familiar lane leading from the city center to the compound where he had first met Peter. The way was filled with Judeans racing against the hour to their homes before the Sabbath shofar sounded its haunting cry over the hills. Thankfully the fierce heat had lessened. A gentle wind blew from the north, casting a faint promise of fresh air and new beginnings. The sun crowned the western slopes, its ruddy light cascading over the rocky terrain as a hawk circled the forested hills beyond the city's borders.

Linux wore a simple tunic of rough weave and a belted cloak, the garments of most Judean commoners. He had purchased them from an astounded merchant earlier that afternoon, changing in the merchant's back room, and he now carried his Roman garb in a cloth satchel. Stephen had said nothing about his attire when he had made the invitation. But Linux had seen the looks cast his way by those who had overheard. He had no wish to draw attention to himself, or place his instructor in a position to draw disapproval from other followers. The commoner's clothing was his way of hiding in plain sight.

The new tribune had not contacted Linux further since their one brief encounter. Linux also had heard nothing more from the governor. Simply to give himself something to do and burn off restless energy, he had taken to helping train new recruits. It was a duty most officers of his rank and background—a former member of the prelate's personal guard—would have scorned. Yet Linux had never known such a time of constrained isolation. He was not made for enforced idleness. But his request for patrol duty had been turned down—by whom, and for what reason, Linux was never told. So he filled his hours and waited for his time of daily instruction with Stephen.

Linux arrived at the plaza to find the outer door standing open, a rarity in such uncertain times. He joined other late arrivals to slip inside, hopefully unnoticed. But his height and clean-shaven face, along with his evident foreignness, drew attention. One of the men standing inside the entrance moved toward him with a frown, but another touched his shoulder and murmured something Linux could not hear. He did not recognize the man who spoke on his behalf. The guard, still looking reluctant, nodded Linux inside.

Whenever he was among the followers, Linux always felt himself on guard. Even with Stephen he felt a certain reserve, but he put it down to the fact that Stephen was a Judean and he a Roman, and second, Abigail. Whether present or not, she had always seemed to cloud the air between them. But not today. Linux entered the courtyard and had an immediate sense of being fully engaged, within and without.

As though in confirmation of this change, Stephen's voice called, "Linux!" Linux watched him work his way through the crowd. "God's greetings upon you, brother. I wish you a blessed Sabbath."

Linux felt overwhelmed by the words. Though never before offered to him, he knew they were a traditional salutation, used by religious Judeans each week. "I wish you the same, Stephen," he said a bit awkwardly, not quite sure of the appropriate response.

"Come." Stephen led him to an empty place at one of the tables. He raised his hand, and those seated around it quieted. "This is Linux, a student of mine, and a God-fearer. I ask that you make him welcome." To Linux he said, "These are brethren from the Hellenized community. You understand that, yes? Good. Now you must excuse me. I am called to help with the distribution of the wine and the bread."

Stephen started to move away, then stopped and turned back. He settled his hand upon Linux's shoulder and said, "I am glad you came to share our Sabbath celebration."

"And I as well." Linux felt himself moved more than he could say, understanding that Stephen's words were for the others at the table also.

Stephen waited until Linux was seated to lower his head and move in close enough that Linux could feel the brush of his beard. "Signs and wonders. Do those words mean anything to you?"

"I don't think so. . . ."

Stephen's hand rose and fell. "I sense that God will speak with you this night, my brother. When that happens, I urge you to *listen*."

Abigail saw Linux enter the compound and watched her husband hurry over to welcome him. The Roman's very presence made Abigail nervous. It was not at all usual for a soldier to be welcomed to break bread with the brethren. What was Linux doing there? In spite of Stephen's regular meetings with the man, was it all a ruse to spy on them? Had he truly become a follower?

She felt unsettled about it all, and she prayed again for Stephen—for extra wisdom in his dealings with Linux, and for protection for them all. . . .

She noticed there were some others who shared her concern. Stares, shuffling feet, murmurs among the more conservative among them were signals of their unease. Even many of the Hellenized, who sat slightly apart, looked on with puzzled expressions.

But Stephen seemed to take no notice. He drew Linux forward to a seat among the Hellenized Judeans. After speaking with them a moment, he left to take his place at the head table.

Abigail glanced back at Linux. He looked slightly uncomfortable, then seemed to settle in, his eyes intent on Stephen and the others who were to serve with him. Stephen was sitting beside Nicolas, whom Abigail quite admired. Though he was a Greek, he had chosen to follow the Judean God, accepting that Jesus was the Messiah, whose death and resurrection brought forgiveness of sin to all who believed. In fact, the entire group had no problem accepting the sincerity of Nicolas. He already had been selected, along with Stephen and five others, to serve in the distribution to those in need.

She saw Stephen bend his head toward Nicolas and speak quietly. The other man nodded in agreement. While they talked, Stephen informally stretched an arm over the back of the man's chair, not quite touching his shoulders but showing to all that he considered Nicolas a true brother in every sense of the word. Once again, Abigail felt deeply moved by Stephen's boldness and his lead in declaring that the message was meant to be shared among both Jew and Greek. Her beloved was truly a wise and godly man. She felt her cheeks warm under their covering as she thought about their few but wonderful days together as husband and wife.

Abigail's attention was drawn back to the head table and the apostles, who seemed to rise as one. Peter nodded to Stephen to lead them in the first prayer. Then they broke the bread and shared the wine. Stephen, Nicolas, and other men took up the baskets of bread and the goblets of wine to serve each table of the gathered followers.

Stephen surprised her once again. As the others moved to serve the Hebrew believers, Stephen directed his steps to the Hellenized group. They would be served at the same time as their Judean brethren. And Linux was included.

Abigail studied not just the act but the soldier's response as he was served. It was obvious, even at this distance, that the man was deeply moved. She watched as he bowed his head and couldn't help but wonder what thoughts were going through his mind. Had he indeed been bold enough, needy enough, to reach out to their God as his own Savior?

———

Surrounded by those who had somewhat reluctantly made room for him, Linux watched the twelve apostles and seven others, whom Stephen had referred to as deacons, at the front table. Everything he saw and heard was new, but Linux had hungered for this. He did not know what it was exactly or why he yearned for it. But he recognized it as the same feeling he experienced before his studies with Stephen.

Unlike many Roman officers serving in Judea, his Aramaic was flawless. Some of the apostles spoke in Greek, most in Aramaic. Stephen was invited to pray. He did so in both languages, moving back and forth between the two with such fluid ease it was hardly noticeable.

Linux opened his eyes and lifted his head, noting that others also had been drawn by the man's words and were watching as well. Including Abigail, who was seated with the other women. He had not noticed her before, as the women's tables were at a distance from the main body and they wore almost identical shawls. But Abigail's face was not quite concealed, no doubt because she was so absorbed in what she was hearing. Her face shone with an inner light that matched the illumination on Stephen's features. She gazed at her husband with something akin to awe.

Her husband.

Linux had a sharp sensation of the night being torn in two. On one side of the divide lay all the feelings he had known for Abigail up to that point. The experience was both vivid and wrenching. The convicting reflections on all his impure thoughts and desires could not have been clearer. It felt as though some inner awareness had now been awakened. With each word Stephen prayed, the experience only grew stronger. On the other side, each of those desires and yearnings was being lifted up for inspection—not only his, he realized. Something else was inside him, something new. . . . He could only identify it as God. *Not merely the Judean God. My God.*

God was helping him sift and sort—those selfish and evil desires pushed to one side, the hunger for truth and holy living gathered on the other.

Linux saw with utter clarity that he had never loved Abigail. He had wanted her. He had lusted after her. He had desired to possess her. But *love?* What was love? What in his entire life had ever revealed what the word actually meant—until now?

Stephen and the others at the table broke the bread in the baskets before them, and one of the others then prayed about a broken vessel, a perfect sacrifice. Words Linux knew he should have understood, because Stephen had spent their last two sessions explaining what would happen during the communion service.

How they followed a pattern that had been set in place at their last meal with the Messiah during the Passover feast, the night before he had been taken from them. Linux knew all these things, yet he was unprepared for what was happening. Not there at the front table, as next the wine was poured and blessed and shared. No, what was happening inside *him*.

Linux glanced at Abigail. She continued to study her husband, and Linux saw there on her features a love so pure and intense that it left him shaken and ashamed. He was observing something so intimate, so revealing, he knew he was intruding even at this distance. He knew also he did not deserve such a love, had never in his entire life done anything to cause another person to care for him in such a manner.

He dropped his gaze to his hands, at that moment relinquishing the woman who had never been his to claim. He also turned away from the desires and wrath and lusts that were no longer a part of his world.

Making a space for a Savior's love that had been waiting for him . . .

Signs and wonders. Stephen's words returned to him. Linux now understood what the man had meant. For there was no question but what he had just experienced came from beyond him—a sign of his transformation, and certainly the wonder of it all.

Love so pure, so intense, burned away all he had been. No longer was he the second son, the princeling who would never make his rightful claim, the man of thwarted ambitions, the lonely officer trapped in a post and a land that hated him and all that he stood for. None of this mattered. Not in the face of this love.

Linux realized he was weeping. But he did not care. There was a rightness to the tears, to the exposure they meant among this gathering. For they were no longer strangers. All followers—just like him.

CHAPTER

THIRTY-FIVE

THE GATHERING DID NOT END so much as gradually disperse. His tablemates remained guarded, but several of them offered him cautious farewells as they took their leave. Linux remained where he was, more comfortable with his solitary position at the table than he'd ever been before. He felt a childlike ease, so protected, so accepted he could expose his most hidden weaknesses and fears and uncertainties and know all was well, all forgiven, all blessed. The stone he had carried inside was finally dissolving. Inner wounds were now open to healing light, and the gift of hope was like an illumination around him.

As he had promised earlier in the evening, Stephen came over, along with an older woman. But even as Linux rose to meet her and Stephen made introductions, the woman's name slipped from his mind. Abigail soon joined them. Yet even her presence did not erase the reality of his encounter with *signs and wonders*. If Linux had needed some evidence that the moment did indeed contain a miracle, it was this.

Stephen settled the older woman and Abigail on the bench opposite Linux, and then Stephen took his place next to his wife. And yet, and yet . . . even there Linux felt a calm acceptance. *That I might someday find such a love . . .* flashed through his mind.

Stephen clearly was willing to grant Linux as much time as he needed.

Linux said slowly, staring at his folded hands on the table, "Yes . . . yes, thank you, Stephen, for forewarning me about it. That moment—'signs and wonders,' you called it—did happen for me, I believe."

He lifted his gaze, and Stephen reached across to Linux's clasped hands, covering them with his own. "We do thank you, our Lord, for this gift to our new brother. Ready him—body, soul, and spirit—for whatever is to come." The women's soft amens echoed his own.

It was quiet for a moment, and then Linux looked at the three of them across the table. "I am hearing rumors around the fortress of . . . well, of possible troubles."

Abigail grasped the hand of Stephen on one side and the woman on the other.

"Nothing definite," Linux said, "but a number of the subalterns have developed associates within the Judean community. These might be stall owners where the Romans shop, or people the soldiers have helped out of danger, merchants who rely on soldiers, even a few priests and Temple guards. There is talk about the Sanhedrin being split among those who prefer to watch and wait and those who want to strike immediately."

"Our Lord will protect us."

Linux thought Stephen's statement was probably more for the women's sake than his.

Abigail asked Stephen, a tremor in her voice, "What if God is using Linux to warn us?"

The man gave that serious thought, then lowered his head and closed his eyes. Linux was flooded with the sense of the unseen not merely at work but *filling* the moment.

Linux glanced around the courtyard at the sound of voices. Individuals and groups looked to be praying. Some stood, while others knelt or sat. A few prayed with their heads covered by the traditional prayer shawls, while others clustered tightly together and laid hands upon those at their center.

Linux did not know what to think of Abigail's suggestion that he might be a divine messenger. All he could say of this moment was that it all felt natural, as if he belonged. The way they all prayed around the courtyard, the fact that Stephen still silently prayed, how the two women waited patiently for him to open his eyes. Both natural, yet a new world to Linux.

Finally Stephen looked at Linux. His voice was calm. "As you know, I have been called to serve the Hellenized community. I feel called by God to speak to my brethren at the Freedmen's Synagogue. The possibilities of danger do not change either of these callings."

"But what about . . ." Abigail stopped. It was a telling moment, for she closed her eyes and bowed her head as Stephen had done. And once again the table was circled by far more than silence.

Eventually she lifted her head, though her eyes remained downcast. She sighed, a quiet rush of sound.

Stephen asked softly, "You have felt it too?"

For a very long moment, Abigail did not respond. Finally she nodded. Once.

Stephen rose to his feet. He said to Linux, "Let me walk you out."

They wound their way through the dwindling people around the plaza. The night remained alive with far more than the flickering torchlight. By the outer gate, Stephen addressed a group preparing to depart. "You are going into the city?" At their nods, he asked, "Will you permit this brother to accompany you? I fear for his safety."

Two of the men wore the severely dark garb of the Pharisees. They started to frown, but the night was too potent even for them. One said, "Come, then."

"One moment." Stephen drew Linux aside. "I would ask a favor of you."

"Anything," Linux said, and meant it. With all his heart.

"If something should happen to me, will you see Abigail safely away from Jerusalem? To Alban and Leah?"

Linux felt a fist grip his heart. "You are thinking something . . . might?"

"These are perilous times," Stephen said quietly. "You have said it yourself. Alban and Leah are her official guardians. Take her to their home in Galilee. I would rest more easily knowing you have agreed to this request."

Linux heard a sound in his voice, almost of grief. "I will do as you have requested. But—"

Once again, Stephen would not let him finish. "May God shine upon you for this assurance. I am most grateful, my brother."

———

It had been too long since Abigail had last felt such an astonishing sense of God's peace. The morning was wrapped in calm, despite the many people who filled the compound on this first day of the week. It was as though they had come for a festival, though no holy days were upon them. Abigail could not shake the sense of the divine presence in their midst.

Through the proclamation of the gospel message and the power of the Spirit, she had seen great miracles that now were becoming common—miracles of rebirth, of physical healing—but she knew Stephen and the other leaders were looking for miracles of even deeper faith. Faith that would carry them through whatever the days might bring. That would give them boldness to continue sharing the Word. Not an hour ago, she and Stephen had talked about this on their way to the courtyard.

For the morning prayers at this dawn of a new week, an expectant crowd had gathered, seeking a new message from God. Perhaps one of the apostles had been given a word of prophecy from the Lord. A new understanding that would be unfolded to the group. If so, she was more than ready to listen—and to accept.

It was not one of the apostles, though, who stepped forward, head covered, and unrolled the scroll. It was Stephen. He read a portion from Deuteronomy then rerolled the scroll and handed it to the assistant, who would ensure its safekeeping. Stephen then reminded the assembly of the laws God had given to them through Moses. The importance of their gathering. Why God in his wisdom ordained that they should meet together.

"We need one another," he exhorted them. "We were not made to be individual worshipers. We are a body. Brothers and sisters. 'A cord of three strands is not quickly broken.' We draw upon its strength each time we meet.

"For those of us who believe in our Messiah, that cord now has new meaning. Our Father, our Savior, and the Holy Spirit who dwells within us and gives wisdom and guidance. Again, we need and accept the presence of all three in our lives. And at this time we come apart at the beginning of a new day, a new week, which was God's purpose in the festival gathering, and we present ourselves once more to God, not just as individuals, but as a community of believers. We draw strength and encouragement from one another. We share prayer for God's leading and direction. We ask for strength and courage, that we might continue to be strong in proclaiming the message of Jesus to all people."

Abigail felt the nagging fear again. *What if?* The enemy was out to destroy what they had become. The singleness of purpose, this sense of togetherness, this blessing of oneness. She couldn't imagine how she would ever endure. . . .

But even as those thoughts chased through her mind, a peace began to replace them. *I am here,* said a small but clear voice. In this moment she was not only safe, but focused upon the eternal, upon God. It was as though, for the first time, she fully understood through her own experience the words their Master had given, "The Kingdom is here. Now. *Within you.*"

Immanuel. God with us. With Stephen . . . She tried to clutch that promise close in her heart.

———

As members of the community left the compound to take up their tasks for the day, Abigail moved to where Stephen was praying with a small group. A new impression had arrived during her own prayers that morning. She waited while they finished the prayers and made their farewells. She fervently hoped Stephen might be able to offer some insight. Was it just her unsettled imagination, or was God's Spirit speaking to her?

When he turned to her, she began, "I need to talk with you, Stephen, but I do not even know what words to use."

Already a few of their workers were lined up, needing their instructions for the day. Stephen offered a few brief directions, asked for their patience, and drew her to a quiet alcove. "What is it, my love?" he asked as they sat on the bench there.

"A feeling. No, more than that. Well, perhaps . . ."

The setting was very much in keeping with the man Abigail was coming to know. Morning shadows within the recessed alcove offered them a sense of privacy though they were visible to everyone in the courtyard. She treasured his calm, an invisible strength she could feel every time they were close. Abigail found herself drawing greater clarity from his presence and said, "I wonder if perhaps God has given me a . . . a message. One that is directed at me."

Stephen had a certain posture he adopted when listening. Back straight, ankles crossed, hands folded, eyes unblinking in their intensity. "Why should God *not* speak with you, Abigail?"

"It's not that he shouldn't. It's only that he never has." Stephen made her feel that nothing else in the world mattered, including the passage of time. She allowed herself to rest against the back wall. "You know I have been troubled. Sometimes I feel as though I live almost constantly in fear. I know God is with us. And you will take care of me, Stephen, but . . ."

"You of all people have reason to feel uncertainties. Your experiences have taught you all too well how peace can be stripped away in a moment by events beyond your control."

"I want to have faith. Why doesn't God take away my fears?" She did not realize she had spoken up until people nearby glanced her way. She lowered her voice. "Why do I continue to feel as though my worries are in control?"

"Do you mean you would like for God to take away your memories also?"

"No, that is . . ." She looked at him for a long moment. "Perhaps sometimes. Especially at night, when I wake from dreams that terrify me. Though I haven't had so many of those lately."

They smiled at each other, and Stephen reached for her hand.

"I wish I could say that everything will be fine for you, Abigail. And for us. I would give anything. . . ." He turned to stare out at the plaza, his face a profile of light and shadow. He had never looked more tender. Or more vulnerable. "Perhaps God has a purpose for your keeping hold of your memories. And even your fears."

The tension she had felt building inside her suddenly found a release. "For days I've felt a growing desire to flee. Before our wedding, Alban had invited me to go to Galilee. At the time, I was certain I should remain here, where I can serve the community and stay close to you." She hesitated. "But now, since Alban and Jacob left, I have felt so afraid here. I have wanted you to take me away from here. I feel such a great tension in Jerusalem. And it is growing all the time. . . . Or perhaps I am imagining things."

"No," Stephen replied softly. "You imagine nothing."

"I know that God has given me a way to serve him here. But I admit . . . I admit I was ready to desert it if I could convince you to leave."

Stephen said nothing in response. He merely sat and watched her, his gaze luminous. She felt like he was giving her time to find the answer for herself.

"The warning Linux passed on to you," Abigail said, "captured all my fears and anxieties in one moment. But as I prayed over this later, I had the very clear impression that I needed to hear what he said, and then to face my fears. The instructions were so powerful, so vivid, I felt like I heard the words actually spoken to my heart. That I must lean on the promises that God has given. To let go of even life, if need be, and accept his calling."

She raised her face so she was looking directly into Stephen's eyes. "And perhaps . . . perhaps the hardest part, I need do that not only for myself but for those I have come to love."

Stephen responded with a nod that required his entire upper body. As he rocked, he watched her with a gaze as powerful as the morning sun.

Abigail took a deep breath and said what had now come clear in her heart. "I will not try to influence you to seek safety," she said, though her voice was shaking. "You must follow our Master—not a nervous wife's whims. I will continue to pray, but I let you go to fulfill God's calling, whatever that may mean for you. For us.

You are serving here. And as long as God allows, I will be here also. Serving with you. You are in God's hands. And God knows best. And if . . . if . . ." She could scarcely say the words. "If you are endangered, then I pray that God will make you strong. That, in faith in him, you will stand firm to the . . ." But she could not say the last word.

Stephen held her hand tightly and repeated quietly, ". . . firm to the end."

———

Later that evening, after they had returned to their little home, Stephen set the oil lamp on the small table and observed, "You look weary, my Abigail."

Stephen's tone more than his words brought Abigail's shoulders a bit higher, and she was determined not to add to his burden. The truth was, she was desperately weary. It had been a long and troubling day. Despite her prayers and best intentions, she continued to feel the tensions over the building opposition. Then there had been the strain of dealing with those in desperate need, including a newly widowed mother who had sobbed her desperate worry to Abigail over how she would care for her three small children. Abigail had tried to comfort, had spoken all the truths of God's care and provision, but it had drained her. How would she react in the woman's place? Was her own faith strong enough to carry her through . . . such a loss?

She pushed it all aside and turned to her husband with a smile. "It has been a long day. For you as well, I can see."

"How good it is of our Lord to provide the gift of sleep." He settled onto the stool, looking at her as she unbraided her dark tresses. "By morning we will be refreshed enough to face another day."

Abigail nodded and unwrapped the belt around her robe. At

the moment she did not want to think about what the new day might demand of her.

They prepared for the night in silence. Abigail spread out their sleeping pallet and coverings. Stephen blew out the oil lamp and stretched his lean form out beside her. Through the window Abigail could see stars, held firmly in place by the hand of God. A bright moon watched over roofs of nearby buildings. The slight breeze whispered against the curtain, cooling away the day's heat.

Abigail felt the soft sigh escape her lips. Trusting God at such a peaceful moment was almost easy. Stephen seemed to share her thoughts, for he murmured, "We are secure, my love. Our busyness sometimes keeps us from opening our hearts to God—and to each other."

Abigail turned to face her husband. She felt very comfortable with Stephen's reserved, calm nature. She understood and accepted that. She also had many personal thoughts and feelings she would have found difficult to share with another.

"I know you are weary, Abigail—but there are some things I need to say. Things I do not wish to leave unspoken for another day. Another hour. I find myself stumbling over my words. I do not express myself easily. Will I burden you further if I attempt to say them now?"

A slice of moonlight fell across Stephen's face, allowing Abigail a softened image of the man she loved. The day's hard labor and serious thoughts seemed washed away. Where his body touched her own, she felt his peace. She murmured her soft assent.

"I have always admired you, Abigail. From the first time I set eyes on you. You were so beautiful. So perfect that . . . that you almost frightened me. I would never have attempted to win your heart. Never. I had no right, no position from which to seek your hand. It would have been like . . . like a street urchin asking for a pearl."

Abigail held back a gasp.

"Then I was approached by our leaders. Would I marry you? You can imagine my shock. I struggled. I prayed. How could I? Would God really entrust such a lovely woman to my care?

"What I didn't know then, Abigail, was that I should not have been in such awe of your beauty. I should have been in awe of your spirit. Your faith. Your absolute commitment to God—and to others. Your striking eyes daily sought ways to serve. Your smile readily offered comfort, compassion, and encouragement." He lifted one of her hands in both of his own. "These strong, gracious hands continually minister to the needs of others, and your slender shoulders carry burdens far too heavy for them to bear. Even the healing of your leg has become a witness to so many.

"But it is your faith that I have come to treasure the most, dear one. Your confidence in God. Your trust in him—and in me—that gets us through each day. Yes, you speak of fear, but even amidst the fear you continue to serve. To trust. To believe God's promises."

She felt the tremble through her body. Stephen, more than anyone, knew of her fear. And he spoke of her unwavering faith. Did he know how fear gripped her at times, making her far from confident? Would he speak so if he knew . . . ?

"It is true we all have fears attack us," he was saying. "We do not speak of it—but it is there. In those times we realize more than ever that we need God. That is when we pray with the most sincerity. That is when he answers with the most fatherly compassion. His presence is most intimate, most precious, and most reassuring, in those times of fear."

Abigail felt his words flowing over her, into her heart. She was sorting through what she might say in response when he reached out to touch her face.

"Do you know what I fear, Abigail? Daily? Losing you. I have struggled with it ever since our betrothal vows. During morning

prayers, as well as with my last breath at night, I pray for your protection. Were it not for God's grace I would have snatched you away
from all this and fled long before now. You are my rock, Abigail.
You remind me of why the Lord's calling is so important in my life.
We must share his truth—to change our world. To make it a place
filled with love rather than hate. With peace, rather than war. With
mercy, rather than revenge. With holiness, rather than evil.

"As a man, that is my prayer—my desire—that through his
word the world will be a changed and safer place for you—and for
our little ones. I have always longed to have children. And could I
have envisaged the woman to be their mother, she would be exactly
like you. Strong, devoted to God. And beautiful. Only now, since
you have become my wife, do I begin to understand what love is.
What our Lord desires for *his* bride. *His* followers. Now I know why
he was willing to die."

Abigail felt the warmth of tears tracing their way down her
cheeks. She could not speak. Her heart was too full. She turned
her face so it rested upon his shoulder. God had blessed her with a
wonderful man. A husband she would never truly deserve.

I love you, her heart cried. *I love you so.*

And as soon as she wiped away her tears and was able to speak,
she would find the words to tell him so.

C H A P T E R

Thirty-Six

EZRA STOOD OUTSIDE the Freedmen's Synagogue. He was distantly aware of the sun beating on his head and shoulders and of the sweat trickling down his neck and spine. He knew there was shade beneath awnings to either side of where he stood. But in the most active portion of his thoughts, he was pleased with the discomfort. It suited the moment. It fit with his internal rage. He would have vengeance, the retribution his sister deserved.

"For Sapphira," he muttered. He ignored the nagging voice that told him these were true followers of the Law, that they had not caused her death, but in the divine unknown she had disobeyed God. And that the events he had set in motion were wrong—as wrong as Sapphira's lie.

Ezra pushed the thoughts aside. He was becoming adept at that, stifling such arguments before they could grasp his full awareness. Rage had become as constant a part of his life as the sun, the heat, his own ragged breath.

Saul waited on the square's opposite side, surrounded by a

cluster of dark-robed Pharisees. Even from this distance Ezra could see the brooding ire, the tension that dominated this group. Saul caught his eye. Ezra made a swift motion with one hand, signaling the young man to wait.

"Here they come now," a man beside him muttered.

"You may address me as sire," Ezra snapped.

The man stiffened. Ezra turned and looked at him. Whatever the ruffian saw in Ezra's face was enough to smother his comment. He said, "Yes, sire."

Ezra turned back. "Be ready. Move only on my signal."

He was surrounded by a dozen handpicked men. Most came from his warehouses and caravans, guards and former soldiers. Ezra suspected one was a spy for the Zealots. Two others worked in his countinghouse. They were all good with their fists, with clubs and daggers and swords. They all took his coin. They would do his bidding.

"All right. Do as we planned. Disperse among the crowd. Wait for my sign."

The men moved with the stealth of professional fighters, slipping in among the growing crowd standing in the synagogue's forecourt. Stephen clearly was the reason they had come. The crowd around the man was dense. But Ezra had studied these followers. He was increasingly certain they would put up no struggle. Protest, certainly. But when violence started, they would stand and weep, and they would make no move to protect their man. Just as had happened on Golgotha with their leader. Ezra and his gang should have no problem. And if they did, well, his men had weapons hidden beneath cloaks and lashed to their thighs.

Ezra searched through the crowd as he moved forward and saw no one bearing arms. His men knew what to do.

The Freedmen's Synagogue had been erected by Hellenized Judeans on pilgrimage to the Holy Land. Many had started life as slaves, while others had such heritage in their past. The synagogue was not far from the Damascus Gate and the stables used by the caravan masters. A marble structure built in an almost Grecian style, with a pillared portico similar to that of Solomon's Porch, had four broad stone stairs welcoming those who spilled out of the synagogue's forecourt. Stephen stood on the top step. A second crowd of women, most wearing head shawls, assembled on the side away from where Ezra stood. He wondered if Abigail might be among them, and his bitterness deepened.

But his resolve was shaken by what he saw next.

The man known as Stephen did not immediately address the throng. Instead, he knelt beside one pallet after another, laying hands upon ailing folk who had been deposited on the next-to-top stair. A group of other disciples joined him, encircling one after another, praying intensely, then moving on. Time after time the people lying there and others gathered about them shouted aloud in a joy so powerful it sounded almost like a cry. The crowd responded with shouts of their own.

Finally Stephen rose and began to address the crowd. Ezra found himself refusing to hear what the man was saying. Ezra pushed through the crowd, earning himself a few scowls, but most were too intent on listening to notice.

Suddenly he saw an image as strong as his ire. A veil had descended between him and the man on the synagogue's top stair. The veil was knit from his lies and his deceit and his rage. For an instant, one moment only, the veil lifted. And in that moment he *saw*.

Stephen's features were wreathed in a light so brilliant it turned the day dark. He spoke two words that Ezra could hear clearly. *Messiah. Love.*

Then the veil descended once again.

Ezra faltered. The hesitation was not merely in his thoughts.

He felt his very soul was being twisted and torn. He stood upon a divide as strong as the line drawn between those gathered at the synagogue. Once more he was granted a choice. . . .

But he had come too far. He had too much devoted to his anger and his lust for vengeance. He was, after all, a merchant. He knew what it meant to strike a bargain and move forward, against all the odds that might turn away lesser men.

He raised a fist over his head. "Blasphemer!"

He had not meant to shout quite so loudly. The noise of his voice startled even himself. All around him, men drew back as they would from an open flame.

But his men took this as not merely a sign, but a spur to action. Their voices rose at a pitch and fervor matching his own. The loudest cries came from the dark-robed rabbis surrounding Saul.

"Seize him!" Ezra shouted. "Take him to the Council!"

———

Abigail stood with the other women listening to her husband. She felt a little shiver as the still-unfamiliar yet wonderful term filled her mind. She held her arms around herself as she thought about how much their love had grown in such a short amount of time—betrothed only weeks ago, and now their marriage. . . . But, she told herself, she wasn't here to think about the wonder of all her recent blessings but to listen to Stephen preach.

He had begun the afternoon's teaching with an overview of Hebrew history, which she never tired of hearing, especially when he explained how it all pointed to their Messiah. But now he had paused and was looking out over his immediate listeners to a group of men further away. Abigail looked over at them too, and she was immediately alarmed at the expressions on their faces, the tense way they held themselves, as if they were poised . . .

Stephen's voice called out, "I invite you all today to recognize your Messiah, Jesus of Nazareth—"

Then she heard a voice scream, "Blasphemer!"

And it was like a rampaging flood, the chaos and terror the single word had unleashed.

———

Abigail watched in stunned horror as Stephen was dragged from the Freedmen's court, his arms gripped by angry men on either side, propelling him forward. Others grabbed at his robes, his sash, and even his hair. The crowd pushed and surged like a roiling storm, shouting words she neither understood nor desired to comprehend. Her legs could barely hold her upright. *What is happening?*

A boy nearby was backing away from the scene, his eyes wide with fear. He looked like he was going to turn and make a run for safety. Abigail recognized him from the compound.

She spoke quickly before he could make his dash. "What is happening, Levi? What are they doing?"

"I don't know!"

"Did you hear nothing at all?"

"They said they were taking him to the Council. I don't know why. I didn't . . ." And he was gone before finishing.

"The Council? Why?" But no one took heed of her questions. Abigail frantically searched about. Surely there was someone who could tell her, who could help Stephen! She did recognize some, but now they looked as horror-stricken and full of questions as she was.

"What has happened? Why Stephen?" she begged, pulling on a sleeve.

A shrug or shake of the head was all the response she received.

"Couldn't you stop them?" she implored when she came to a

huddle of men. Their only answer was to turn and walk away, their strides lengthening with each step.

At the square's other end two Roman soldiers lounged in the shade. For a moment Abigail felt a thrill of hope. She hurried toward them, but before she reached them a man in the dark robes of a Pharisee stepped forward and said something she could not hear. The soldiers looked at one another. Then one spoke to the other and shrugged his shoulders. The Pharisee turned away, and the two soldiers resumed their places, leaning against the stone wall. She could hear their crude laughter. No, they were not likely to help her. She swung around to address a few witnesses of the incident who still remained.

"What happened? What did he do?" she pleaded, trying to gain some understanding.

The one closest to her, his eyes still filled with fear, said, "We didn't see him do anything."

"Then why—?"

"I cannot say. They surrounded him and just grabbed him. He didn't even try to resist. It looked like they had it all planned."

Sickness swept through her, and she felt like she would faint. What could she do? Stephen needed help—*now*. The apostles were at the Temple for midday prayer. She knew they always lingered there afterward to hear Peter speak. The other women here would be as helpless as she herself. *What can I do? Lord . . .*

Yes, *pray*. The one word welled up within her. All she could think of was "Please help, God!" Over and over.

If only Alban . . . But of course he was many miles away.

Linux! Would Linux help them? He and Stephen had formed a friendship. Surely Linux would be willing to come to the aid of a friend. Abigail whirled toward the Antonia Fortress. She had never been there before. Had always been warned to stay well away from

Roman soldiers, but she did not stop. She simply pulled her shawl more closely about her, clutched her robe in her hand, and ran.

She arrived breathless and had difficulty making the soldier at the gate understand her words. "The officer Linux," she panted. "I must see him. Immediately. Please, sire."

But the fellow smirked and answered gruffly, "Afraid you're too late. He's left on some mission."

"Where?" pleaded Abigail. "When will he return?"

"None of my business. Or yours." He smirked again. "I'm not his superior. I ask no questions. Now you'd best be gone. You don't belong here."

Abigail turned and staggered away. What was she to do now? *The Temple.* The Temple was nearby. She would check there. Perhaps she would find Peter—or John. Anyone who could help Stephen.

But when she arrived the courtyard was almost empty. The crowd, had there been one, had now dispersed. She looked toward the Council building, but it appeared to be empty. There was no milling crowd, no angry voices to be heard. She spotted a guard. As she approached him, she fought for control of her voice. She did not want him to think her a madwoman.

"Please. Could you tell me if the Council is meeting?"

"Haven't seen anyone go in for hours. And I've been here all afternoon."

Abigail was too distressed to express her thanks. Overwhelming fear gripped her. *Where have they taken him? And why?*

Her steps faltered, and she was afraid she would not even be able to make it back to the others. "O dear God," she sobbed, "may he be there when I arrive." The very thought gave strength to her weakened knees.

C H A P T E R

THIRTY-SEVEN

LINUX PAUSED IN THE VESTIBULE at the end of the palace hall, overwhelmed by disgust. Five doorways opened about him, revealing clusters of people in various stages of drunkenness and debauchery. Governor Marcellus was hosting a party to mark the emperor's birthday. Clearly his guests, many of whom had abandoned all pretense of modesty, had been drinking all day.

The governor's messenger had made it clear that Linux's invitation was in truth an order. Linux decided he would stay long enough to be noticed, then slip away. He kept his eyes on the marble-tiled floor as he moved through the least crowded room and out the garden doors. He remembered how Ezra and the priest had averted their eyes from the arena scene. . . . Could that possibly have been only a couple weeks earlier? It seemed like years, like a scene drawn from the memories of another man's life. Linux waved away a servant offering goblets of spiced wine. He took the stairs leading down to the palace gardens. Once the lush growth blocked his view of the palace chambers, his chest finally unlocked, and he breathed easy.

He stopped at a bench shaded by a trio of date palms. As he seated himself, he recalled a conversation from his childhood. His grandfather had died when Linux was nine. His grandfather had fought for nine years with Germanic legions. Afterward he had served as a Roman senator for thirty-seven years. As long as he was alive, his grandfather had sought to inject a soldier's rough care and instruction into the half-forgotten boy. The old man had taught how the original Roman virtues stressed discipline, simplicity, hard work, and an acceptance of personal responsibility for the greater good. Romans were expected to prepare for a life of politics, military, or both. Linux's grandfather had often gazed at the family residence as he lamented current changes.

Today, however, the fashionable word in Rome was *otium*. It was considered the proper way of life for this, the Imperial Age. The word had once meant, simply, a time of ease. Now it stood for self-indulgence, constant idleness, and the immediate satisfaction of every desire, no matter how base.

From the rooms behind Linux a woman screamed, and a pair of men howled in drunken abandon. Linux leaned over, fists on his knees and his eyes clenched tightly shut. He felt powerless, isolated.

He had not yet sought to speak with God directly. He had watched and listened as others had prayed over him, around him. Stephen had finished every lesson with a time thus in prayer. But now as he listened to the debauchery inside the palace chambers, Linux recalled how Stephen had responded to the threat of coming danger by reaching out to God. And how Linux had felt during that impossible moment.

He pressed his fists into his forehead. *O God, whom I have spent a life denying, whom I do not know well, still do I come and beg for your*

*help. Free me from this. I deserve nothing. Yet still I do ask. Free me
from the world that no longer has any place for me, nor I in it.*

"Linux Aurelius!"

Linux wondered briefly if the voice belonged to one of God's
invisible messengers. He lifted his head and blinked and searched
the empty path.

"I seek Linux Aurelius!"

"Here!"

A house guard stepped into view and saluted. "The prelate
commands you present yourself before him."

Is this the answer? he wondered as he slowly stood to his feet.

———

Abigail had not gone far when she heard angry shouts and
tramping feet. Even in her frantic state she realized that a mob
was on a rampage through the streets. She pressed herself into a
recess between two shops and pulled her shawl across her face. It
was as she feared—*Stephen!* He was in the center of the throng,
insults and worse still being hurled at him. His robe was torn so
that one side dragged in the dirt as he walked. She thought she
saw a bruise on one cheek, but she could not be sure. *Maybe it is
merely dust. . . .*

It looked like they were heading for the Council chambers.
Pharisees haughtily swishing their robes led the way. It was Temple
guards who now grasped Stephen's arms, and she saw chains dan-
gling from his wrists as though he were a dangerous criminal. *Oh,
my Stephen . . .* She caught the sob in her throat before it could
escape her lips.

She held on to the walls to keep herself upright and drew further back into the shadows until the mob had passed, then crept
out and followed at a distance.

More and more people seemed to join the throng pushing through the street. Their cries were now so loud, so demanding, that Abigail could hardly think. She knew she was helpless against such irrational rage. What could she do? Where could she go for help?

Again her thoughts turned to Linux. Somehow she *must* find him.

———

Linux felt a mixture of fear and excitement as he marched alongside the household guard. There was no question in his mind that up ahead lay an answer to his prayer. The timing was too precise. He had witnessed miracle after miracle. Though he had fought against the evidence of his own eyes, the time for resisting, for questioning, was over.

Did he have the strength to accept whatever lay ahead? Because he knew it came from God. Which meant that if there was danger or risk or even death, it was divinely intended. And this frightened him mightily.

At the same time, however, there was the sense of God being with him. Linux did not question this either. Not any longer. Here and now, he was certain that he lived in a time of signs and wonders. He was *part* of this time and these events. God, with his silent voice and in a mysterious swirl of measures beyond his control, was acting in his life. The concept thrilled him.

The servant bowed and announced, "Linux Aurelius, Excellency."

"You may approach."

Linux stepped from sunlight into shadow, and was momentarily blinded in the gloom. He marched forward and saluted. "You wished to see me, sire?"

"Indeed so. I am hearing reports that disturb me mightily."

Linux remained at attention, his eyes fastened upon a point against the far wall. But his peripheral vision took in a number of items. The raised dais held not one gilded chair but two. The second was occupied by Lucius Metellus, the new tribune of the Antonia Fortress. Linux replied, "I regret most sincerely that I might have disturbed the governor's peace in any way, Excellency."

"Peace, yes. An interesting word. It is an altogether too rare commodity in this dreadful land, would you not agree?"

Linux had no idea whether the question was addressed to him and so did not respond. Behind the thrones clustered the prelate's Roman sycophants, their colorful robes fluttering about them. They eyed Linux with the cold joy of an audience awaiting the arena's bloody entertainment.

Lucius Metellus continued, "I was warned before I arrived that maintaining peace in Judea would require a brutal hand. That no portion of my rule would be free of threat."

Linux marveled at how he could feel such dread, yet such calm, in the same moment. "I have maintained steadfast allegiance to Rome at all times, sire."

"Have you? Have you?" The prelate waved at the man seated beside him. "Do tell this officer your news."

"I have taken action to have you followed." The tribune's voice carried a reedy echo in the oversized chamber. "I know you have attended a gathering of this new sect."

The prelate asked, "What do they call themselves? I have forgotten."

" 'Followers of the Way,' " the tribune sneered. "Don't bother to deny it, Linux. I have two witnesses waiting outside the chamber."

"There is nothing to deny, sire."

"A Roman officer, consorting with some outlaw Judean sect," the tribune said. "It is unbelievable and revolting."

"Tell me what is going on here," the prelate demanded.

The answer appeared to Linux so clearly it might as well have been written in the air before his face. "Pontius Pilate was most concerned about them, sire. You yourself heard how they continue to trouble the Sanhedrin—"

"So you sought to determine whether they are a threat to Rome?" the prelate interrupted. "And are they?"

"Sire, they are drawn together by dictates of peace and brotherly love. Of that I am most certain."

The tribune countered, "I hear they are in alliance with the Zealots. And that you have become one of them."

Linux chose to answer only the first portion. "The Zealots are ruled by vengeance and war. The followers may share the Zealots' yearnings to reclaim Judea as their homeland. But they will not take up arms against Rome."

The prelate's hand relaxed. The fist stopped tapping the chair's arm. "Here is what I think has happened," he said. His voice had lost its icy edge. "I sought to reward a trusted adviser with chambers inside the fortress. The new tribune arrives and finds a man he assumes is a spy. A man loyal to me above all, and not the tribune. Is that not so, Lucius Metellus?"

The tribune scowled. "We both serve at the Senate's pleasure."

"A fitting response. And it was the Senate who ordered us to maintain peace in Judea. Peace at all costs. Which means that you, Linux Aurelius, who are guilty of nothing save loyalty, must pay. It is clear you cannot remain in your present station. I will not have our peace disturbed by further accusations, none of which bear more truth than this. The question is, what shall I do with you?"

The tribune fidgeted angrily in his chair, the advantage slipping away before his eyes.

Linux remained silent. But not out of fear. He simply waited. The prelate and the tribune were two very similar men. He did not need to look directly at them to see this. Though immune to the decadent behavior that surrounded them, they were captured by the lure of power. They shared the appearance of ascetics, yet this was merely a disguise. Both were so enraptured by the pleasure of holding raw force in their hands that nothing, no lust that captivated lesser mortals, could tempt them.

The tribune said, "You may not send him back to Rome. I forbid it. I will not have him spouting lies in the ears of senators and the like."

The prelate actually laughed. "You? Forbid?"

Lucius Metellus did not budge. "We both have enemies, Governor Marcellus."

The chamber seemed to freeze. The only sound was the soft tapping of the prelate's fingernails on the chair.

Then the answer must have come to him. At that same moment, the prelate turned back and asked, "Linux Aurelius, what is your wish?"

The tribune scoffed, "You would give this officer a *choice* in the matter?"

"I seek the counsel of all whom I trust. Speak, Linux. Tell us. What would you advise us do in this situation?"

Linux replied, "Assign to me the command of the garrison outside Capernaum."

The two men, and those watching behind the thrones, all gaped at him.

"What? Have you taken leave of your senses, Linux?" This from the governor.

"It would be an honor to serve as the prelate's rear guard. The Golan highlands have become a gathering point for both Parthian bandits and Zealots. They threaten the peaceful communities of that area, and the Damascus Road. This is a vital trade link, and must remain open at all cost."

Governor Marcellus took his time, his eyes moving up and down in inspection of the man standing rigidly before him. "You seek further action, is that it?"

"Sire, I seek only to serve."

"Well, I can think of no reason not to grant this officer his wish. Can you, Lucius?"

The tribune's scowl only deepened. "I still say he is not to be trusted."

"On that point, we must continue to disagree. Very well. Linux Aurelius, you are hereby appointed commandant of the Capernaum garrison. Prepare for your departure without delay." The prelate waved his hand. "You are dismissed."

THIRTY-EIGHT

WHEN SHE RETURNED to the Antonia Fortress gates, Abigail came face-to-face with another sentry. She quaked under the guard's hard expression. But she had no choice. She forced herself to step closer.

Before she could speak, the guard demanded, "Who sent for you?"

His accent was so harsh she had difficulty understanding his words. "No one, sir. I came—"

"Then you're free to be claimed by whoever wants you, is that it?"

Abigail felt her cheeks flame. "I seek the officer Linux Aurelius."

"An officer, is it?"

"Yes, sir. Do . . . do you know him?"

"Ordinary men not good enough for you, is that it?" He leered.

Abigail lowered her head, humiliation washing over her. "I seek him as a friend."

"Sure you do." He laughed crudely. "Heard that one before."

"Please, sire," begged Abigail. "My business with him is most urgent."

"Tell you what," he snorted. "I'll go call the man if you just pull away your shawl and let me see who you really are. Wouldn't want this officer fellow called out for some old crone, now would I." He laughed again.

At her wits' end, she was about to lower her veil when an officer stepped up to the gate. After glancing at the scene, he barked, "What goes here?"

"This woman says she needs to talk to Linux," said the sentry, backing off a step. "I tried to tell her—"

"Linux Aurelius is not here," the second man offered. He must have noticed that she was greatly distressed, for his tone gentled. "He is in audience with the governor. Do you wish to leave him a message?"

"No. No." Abigail backed away. The guard continued to leer at her from behind the officer's back. "I'm afraid . . . I'm afraid it will be too late."

She stumbled away from the entrance, managing to stay on her feet until she had rounded the corner into the confusion of the main thoroughfare. Then everything seemed to be tumbling about her. She lost the battle to stay upright and collapsed against the wall. Pulling her shawl tightly about her, she gave in to the sobs she had tried to hold in check. There was nothing she could do. As much as she wanted to cling to hope, she had the terrible sense that she would never see Stephen again.

———

Ezra stood at the back of the chamber, only one of the crowd jamming the Council building and spilling out the doors and down the broad front steps. Those inside kept shouting back through the doors so the mob outside could follow the proceedings.

Stephen stood before the Council, his hands chained before him. He was flanked by guards, with two more standing between him and the mob. He was being treated like someone considered a threat to the Council members themselves.

Ezra glanced out the doors to where the mob kept increasing. He turned back in time to hear the shouted accusation, "We heard his blasphemy against the Temple and the Law!"

When the words were called through the doors, the mob responded with the growl of an untamed beast.

"He claims that Jesus of Nazareth will destroy this place and abandon the customs handed down by Moses!"

The Sanhedrin's long table was placed on a dais at the back of the room, so from their throne-like chairs behind the table they could look down upon Stephen and out over the crowd, even out to where the mob continued to grow. Sunlight through the open doors cast their grave expressions into deep furrows. Gamaliel looked like he had aged overnight.

Stephen, by contrast, stood as if in an eerie light. His face was utterly devoid of worry or fear. To Ezra's mind, the young man did not seem to belong to this earth at all.

The high priest demanded, "Are these accusations true?"

Stephen began to speak in a quiet, respectful tone. There was nothing about his manner or his voice to cause alarm. Nor was there the volume required to have gotten the attention of the mob outside. Ezra was certain they could not hear him, and yet, in that first moment when Stephen opened his mouth, the mob fell silent. It was as though all the air was withdrawn from the Council chamber. There was no space for anything save the sound of this man's voice.

Stephen began by referring to the Sanhedrin and the audience in the most respectful of manners. "Brethren and fathers," he called them. It was the form of address a student might use before Judean rulers or the elders of his tribe. "The God of glory appeared to our father Abraham. . . ."

Ezra found himself drawn into the man's presentation. Stephen spoke as a rabbi might to a Sabbath congregation, beginning his statement by tying his point to the Scriptures and the Law. In a steady cadence, Stephen walked the listeners through their people's history, moving from Abraham to the patriarchs in Egypt, and from there to God's delivery through Moses. His voice only began to rise as he started to describe how Israel had rebelled against God, casting graven images while Moses went up to receive the Law. Stephen then spoke of the founding of the tabernacle of witness in the wilderness, and then Solomon's building of the first Temple. He concluded, "But the Most High does not dwell in temples made with hands. As the prophet says, 'Heaven is my throne, and the earth is my footstool. Where is the house you will build for me?' says the Lord."

It was at that point that the Council came fully alert. Though Stephen had given no indication of where he intended to go with his speech, they now knew. Attentiveness turned to alarm just before Stephen raised his hands and shouted, "You stiff-necked and uncircumcised in heart and ears! You always resist the Holy Spirit. As your fathers did, so do you!"

Ezra saw lances of genuine pain stab each of the men seated at the Council table. He felt again the power of his own guilt and regret and distress.

Stephen finished with, "You now have become the betrayers and murderers, you who have received the law by the direction of angels and have not kept it!"

Ezra himself felt the unified sense of outrage gripping those at the table. He knew he had been condemned along with the rest. Yet Stephen remained untouched. Instead, the illumination surrounding him strengthened further, as though all light in the chamber was drawn to this one man.

Stephen lifted his face toward the chamber's ceiling and cried, "Look! I see the heavens opened and the Son of Man standing at the right hand of God!"

These words unleashed both the Council and the mob. The chamber was filled with shrill cries demanding he be condemned to death.

Ezra backed himself into one corner as the mob rushed forward to snatch Stephen. The stone chamber reverberated with the force of their cries. He found himself shivering as though fevered.

His vengeance had finally been granted a fitting voice.

CHAPTER

THIRTY-NINE

THE SENSE OF FREEDOM Linux carried with him from the palace vanished the instant he arrived at the lane fronting the Antonia Fortress. There was Abigail crouched in the corner, her shoulders heaving. Linux knew in a flash that she had come seeking him, only to have her virtue threatened and humiliated by a rough-speaking sentry. She had then retreated. Yet something kept her there. Something so dire she could not leave. So there she huddled, too close to the main avenue for the guards to trouble her further.

"Abigail." He crouched down beside her. As soon as her tear-stained features came into view, he knew. "Why are you here?"

A stall holder across the lane called, "I've been over twice to ask what troubles her. She isn't saying. My guess is, one of your soldiers did her wrong."

Abigail gasped out, "It wasn't soldiers."

Linux lifted her to her feet. "Tell me what happened."

"Hey, you." The stall holder bravely shoved his way across the crowded lane. "It isn't right, a soldier handling a Judean lass."

Linux feared if he released her, she would collapse again. "I mean her no harm."

"And I'm telling you, she came away from the fortress looking like she'd been struck." The merchant was clearly ready for battle, now drawing hostile attention from passersby.

"Abigail," Linux insisted. "You must tell me if I am to—"

"The mob took Stephen to the Temple." It was more a sob than coherent words. "The guards bound him and took him before the Sanhedrin."

As soon as the man heard the Council was involved, he backed away. But Linux was not having any of it. "You. Stand where you are."

"I'm not looking for trouble with the Sanhedrin."

"And most of your trade comes from legionnaires. Do as I tell you. Stand by this woman, or I'll have your stall declared off limits!" Linux turned on his heel and raced back up the lane.

He flew through the fortress entrance and thundered into the open square used for weapons training. Thankfully, the sergeant on duty was a man whom Linux had helped train new recruits. He gasped, "I need a squad. Immediately."

The sergeant, a hard-bitten veteran of many years in Judea, said, "Trouble?"

"Perhaps. Speed is everything."

"All I've got on hand are these conscripts."

At least they were armed and wearing the standard enlisted men's leather breastplates. "Choose those you can trust and meet me at the main thoroughfare. Immediately."

Linux raced to the stables and took the one horse already saddled. When the stable master complained, Linux shouted at him with such vehemence the man retreated into a horse stall and did not reappear.

Linux emerged as ten men plus the sergeant trooped up the lane to where Abigail stood clinging to the side wall. The stall holder fled as soon as he saw Linux leading his horse up the path.

Abigail stared at them, uncomprehending. Linux moved in close enough to fill her vision. He addressed her in the stern coldness learned by every officer. "You will listen to me now. The life of your husband depends upon this."

She blinked, dislodging more tears. "It is too late."

"Perhaps, perhaps not. The faster we move, the more swiftly we know the truth." He helped her into the saddle, then turned to a soldier and ordered, "Hold fast to the reins."

"As you will, sire."

Linux turned to the sergeant. "Place your most trusted man as rear guard. I will lead off with you beside me."

"Where are we headed?"

"The Temple. The woman has brought word of a mob."

The young faces of the recruits stretched taut with alarm. They had all heard warnings of the Judeans' wrath if their Temple was in danger of being disturbed or desecrated.

The sergeant, however, made of sterner resolve, bellowed, "Form up! Five before the woman's horse, five behind. Ready? We move!"

Linux still wore the burnished dress uniform for his meeting with the prelate. His breastplate, belt, sword hilt, and leather fringes were all chased in gold. His helmet gleamed as if it were on fire. He was flanked by a sergeant who bellowed for all ahead of them to give way. The men marched in unison behind them. The horse snorted and pranced, its shoes sending up sparks from the cobblestones, and the people fled to each side before them. The wall from the Antonia Fortress to the main gates of the Temple was over a Roman mile long. They arrived puffing hard but made good time.

The sergeant's massive voice had alerted the Temple guards well in advance of their arrival. The normal contingent of six guards had been reinforced, and more came running through the gates as Linux and his men halted. Judeans in the area pushed as far away from the Roman soldiers and the gates and the coming confrontation as they possibly could.

The senior guard gripped his stave so that the wood trembled as violently as his voice. "What's the meaning of this?"

Linux stamped forward. He knew the sergeant and his men surged with him by how the Temple guards took a unified step back. "I have received word of a mob."

"Th-there is no trouble here, sire!"

"That is not the report I received. Of a mob seeking violence and revolt."

From behind Linux came a ripple of sound from the Judeans. Revolt was the one reason that granted Rome entry into the Temple compound. Despite all the Sanhedrin's protests and entreaties, every Judean governor had renewed the soldiers' authority to enter the compound at the first threat of revolt.

Linux snarled quietly, "Step aside or be cut down."

The Temple guard swallowed hard. But he held his ground. "They have g-gone."

"Gone where."

"Did not say."

"But you know." When the man hesitated, Linux bellowed, "*Tell me!*"

"T-to the clearing beyond the Dung Gate."

Linux felt the air freeze in his chest. The Dung Gate led to the Kidron Valley burial grounds.

"*No!*" Abigail's wail was so powerful she melted off the horse and would have collapsed upon the stones had the soldier holding the reins not caught her.

Linux demanded, "Did they have the one known as Stephen with them?"

"I know not any name."

"One of the followers! Did they take a follower with them?"

Something in Linux's eyes caused the man to quail. "P-Perhaps. Yes, I believe so."

"How long have they been gone!"

"An hour, per-perhaps more."

The silence was pierced with a single cry from Abigail.

Linux turned to the wide-eyed sergeant, uncertain what to say. A thousand eyes watched his utter defeat, the woman's broken weeping, the soldiers' indecision.

Then a woman cried, "Abigail!"

Abigail tore herself from the recruit and collapsed into the arms of an older woman Linux vaguely recognized. He heard Abigail say, "Take me to him."

"Child, the mob—"

"*Take me!*"

———

Ezra did not follow the mob. He led it.

Somewhere in the middle of the throng was Stephen, though not visible to Ezra. The crowd was simply too large. The people who surrounded the man waved their hands in the air and shouted their imprecations to the heavens as with one voice. From where Ezra marched, he felt they hollered in order to maintain their rage. As though if they were silent for a moment, the realization of what they were about to do might sink in and slow them down. For Ezra, however, no such drive was needed. The further he walked from the Temple compound, the greater grew his rage. As though all his frustration and all his fury and all his distress were finally ready to consume him.

They left the city by the Dung Gate and entered the Valley

of Death. The sun was so fierce that it seemed as though the day reflected their rage. Either that or the heavens were casting fierce judgment upon their actions. If the latter, Ezra no longer cared. He felt the still, small voice call to him from somewhere deep inside, as though that tiny part of him, the compassionate corner of his soul, had not been entirely stifled. But all around him roared the voice of rage, of vengeance. Ezra was so enthralled by the crowd's presence and power that he could acknowledge the small voice and yet not care what it said.

Elders assigned by the Council to witness the event clustered together by a grove of desert pines. At their fore was Saul of Tarsus. The young man's face was aflame with the same fiery vengeance that filled Ezra's heart. The elders dropped their cloaks of office by Saul's feet and moved forward as the crowd unfolded. That was how it seemed to Ezra. They were a human fist, cloaked not in their robes but in rage, and they flexed their fingers in preparation of doing away with the man who dared offend the Sanhedrin.

Stephen stumbled as he was shoved out into the breathless heat. The crowd bent to snatch up rocks, some in both hands.

Ezra felt his heart cry out, as though it were branded by the stone he now held.

Then he roared against the tide of regret and anguish that suddenly filled him, a piercing grief for he knew not what.

Ezra cast the first stone.

Stephen was struck hard. But he straightened, lifted his eyes and his voice to heaven, and cried, "Lord Jesus, receive my spirit."

The stones rained down upon him even as his face was lifted to the heavens, shining with that same light as in the Council chamber.

The last words Ezra heard him speak were, "Lord, do not charge them with this sin."

When they were done, the stones lay heaped upon the still

form. The crowd dispersed like crows flying from empty bones. The elders picked up their robes and walked away. The mob was now silent. No one met the gaze of his neighbor. They drifted away, until only Ezra stood at one side, Saul on the other.

Strange, Ezra thought, he felt no satisfaction. Only disturbance. The glow on the young man's face as he breathed his last haunted him. Almost as though, instead of inflicting intended pain, they had done him a kindness.

Strange. Strange and most unsettling.

The young man in his black robes walked over and stood staring down at what could be seen of the body. Ezra hoped the man would not voice regret, for the black wings of remorse hovered just beyond his own scarred vision.

But the young man only muttered, "And so it begins."

C H A P T E R

FORTY

ALL THE WORLD LOOKED YELLOW. The sun was a mere handsbreadth from the western slopes, hanging relentlessly in a sky spreading from gold to pale blue to a darker shade. The rocks and cliffs and even the stunted pines were all coated in the same summer dust. Even the people he saw up ahead bore the same unyielding color. By the time Linux arrived, the only sign of where Stephen had been murdered was a dark stain among the rocks. He could see the followers carefully, sorrowfully, moving his body toward an open burial cave.

Linux remained apart from those grieving by the cave's opening. His eyes were dry, yet his heart felt wrenched by tears only he could sense. Or perhaps not, for a pair of men approached, one of them the rugged apostle called Peter. "A tragic day, and a glorious day," the man said softly.

Linux did not understand the man's comment. And yet he felt it resonate within his breast. A gift of inexplicable hope in a moment so dark not even the summer sun could brighten it. "They are not done, I'm afraid."

The man standing next to Peter was another bearded apostle. Linux had seen him at the head table and heard him speak and pray, but did not know his name. The second man said, "Not for an instant do I doubt it."

"I have heard the soldiers speak of it. Rumors swirl about the streets and marketplaces. The Sanhedrin—"

"The Council is forbidden from taking human life," the second apostle said. "And so they send their minions."

"You should leave Jerusalem," Linux said.

He expected argument. Peter said softly, "I am called to stay."

The second apostle turned and said to Peter, "As am I."

Peter asked, "God has spoken to you as well?"

"As clearly as ever I have known his guidance."

Peter nodded. "So be it."

Linux realized there was nothing to be gained by disagreeing. In fact, he did not feel any need to do so. These men were being directed by the same God to whom he had now given his life. Linux had never felt this more strongly. "What of the others?"

Peter continued to nod, rocking his upper body in the stiff motion of a Judean in prayer. "We shall seek the Lord's guidance on this also."

Linux said quietly, "Perhaps your God has already spoken."

Peter looked at him, his eyes an unworldly combination of grief and peace. He corrected quietly, "*Our* God."

"Our God," Linux agreed, and told them of what had transpired at the governor's palace, and his appointment to the Capernaum garrison.

Both apostles studied him with the grave expressions of men

taking his words in deep. "We shall pray long and hard upon this," Peter said solemnly.

Linux replied, "As shall I."

———

Linux dreaded the visit he needed to make to the compound. He could only imagine what Abigail would be going through so soon after her excruciating loss. She deserved solitude in her time of grief. But the time and circumstances would not allow him that courtesy. Who knew what would happen next in this fever-driven city? Besides, he had made a promise to Stephen. A promise he planned to keep.

He was pleased that Martha was the one who first greeted him as he entered the courtyard. She looked drawn and somehow older. He had the strange impulse to embrace her and hold her close until she cried out all of her confusion and grief, as he would long to do if his own departed mother stood bereaved before him. But he restrained himself, not knowing how the woman would receive his condolences shown in such a manner. Instead he asked for Abigail.

Martha shook her head. "She is in seclusion."

"I understand that. And I respect it. But it is of utmost importance that I speak with her briefly. Could I ask you to convey that message to her, please?"

Martha hesitated, but at length nodded and with a deep sigh moved toward the stairway that led up to the rooms above.

She returned some minutes later. She came alone, and Linux feared that Abigail had refused to see him.

"She will see you in the kitchen. Come."

Linux thanked her and followed her.

He did not know exactly what he had thought to find, but

Abigail looked far more composed than he would have expected. She was pale and her eyes were red-rimmed, but she motioned him in and indicated a bench not far from where she sat. He could see Martha hovering nearby.

"My deep sorrow for your loss," he began and saw her eyes water. "I know this is untimely. I dislike disturbing you in this time of grief, but I have made a promise, and I pray you will allow me to keep it."

He hesitated, wondering if she was following his words. She looked so distracted.

But she nodded, indicating he should continue.

"The other day . . . Stephen came to me. He asked one thing. And I agreed. He . . . he said that if anything should happen to him, I was to take you to Galilee, to Alban and Leah."

Her head came up and her eyes met his. The tears now slid down her cheeks.

"He knew?"

"Perhaps. Perhaps he wondered—"

"And he went to minister as he always did. That is so like him. Like Stephen." She wrapped her arms about herself and lowered her head. He allowed her that time of fresh grief.

When she was able to look his way again, he went on, "I have just received orders that I am to leave Jerusalem. I have been granted charge over the Capernaum garrison. I need to depart in two or three days."

He waited for her response. Did she understand what he was saying?

"Two or three days?" she repeated. Then she shook her head. "I will not be ready to leave that soon."

"I understand."

Linux was trying to figure out how many days the tribune and prelate would give him before demanding he leave the city. Would it be enough?

"When would you think . . . ?" He let the question hang in the air.

She shook her head as though to clear her thoughts. "I . . . I do not know. I just know that I need time. Here. I cannot leave yet. I need to find a way through this among the ones I know. . . . I need to have time to say farewell. To be with these people who love me and encourage me with their prayers and strengthen my faith. I . . . I need them very much right now."

"I understand," he said again.

"It's not that I do not want to go to Leah. And Jacob. I do. And I will, God willing. But now is too soon. Too soon. Please."

She was almost pleading for his understanding. There was no way he could insist that she come with him now. "Of course," he said.

He stood. "I expect to leave two days hence. Three at the most. Should . . . should anything change, please get word to me."

"Thank you."

"And when you do feel ready, send word. I will come back for you. I made a promise. One I will keep."

She only nodded.

He didn't know what else to say. He could try some of the encouraging words he had heard others of the community say to offer comfort, but he wondered if they might sound empty. False. There was no way to say what he really felt. Her sorrow touched him deeply.

"I wish you God's peace," he did say, meaning it from the bottom of his heart.

She brushed back a curl that had escaped her covering. She nodded. "It will come. I know it will. Martha says it will take time."

He studied her one last time. She looked so pale. So small and alone. So sad. But there was nothing that he could do for her but pray. He knew as he turned to go that he would carry her forlorn image in his heart all the way to Capernaum.

He had stepped to the door when she said, "Linux."

He turned, hoping she had changed her mind.

"Thank you. Thank you for being a friend. To Stephen—and to me. And, Linux, tell them . . . tell them I am not afraid to die, if that is God's will."

He would have said something in reply but the words would not come. His mouth seemed too dry, his throat too tight. He nodded and went back out into the night.

———

It was not Abigail's deep grief that surprised her. She had lost a wonderful man. They had shared only a few weeks together as husband and wife. She was a widow now. A widow like many of those she served daily. Unclaimed. Broken. Destined for a life of solitude and perhaps a life of poverty. But even those thoughts did not devastate her. Abigail felt only the loss of the man whom she had come to respect so deeply. To love with all her heart. Her future looked so dark that it all seemed an indistinct blur.

The entire community had been so kind, so careful of her. Martha took charge, releasing her from her duties, coming often for times of prayer. Others sent messages of encouragement. With promises to pray. Abigail was given space and time.

No, it was not her grief that shook her world. She had expected and accepted this time of mourning as being hers to endure. It was after her few days of solitude when she again returned to her community for evening prayers that she felt the difference.

A dense pall of fear hung over the entire group. Previously

they had sensed that persecution *might* come. They had tried to prepare for it. Now it was real—raw and terrifying. If their enemies could do this to a man like Stephen, who sought only to serve his community and anyone in need, every one of them was in danger. All of them!

Little groups huddled in whispered conversation. Mothers stayed home from evening prayer to shelter children. Men moved furtively, casting glances to each side as they hastened through the streets. The whole community was wrapped in a shroud of tension and uneasiness.

Abigail had also noticed upon her return that quite a number of followers were missing. Were they in hiding?

She posed the question to Martha. The older woman shook her head, and for the first time in her life, Abigail saw tears on her cheeks.

"There is great fear," the woman said. "There has been much talk. A number of our group have left Jerusalem. Many more talk of leaving. Stephen . . . If they stay, will they be next? How can they protect their families?"

Abigail was not surprised by his message when Peter addressed the situation at evening prayer. "Brothers and sisters, we have been struck a crippling blow. One of our own, one whom we loved and deeply appreciated, has been cruelly taken from us. One who served his God and us with his whole heart. We miss him deeply.

"But let us not despair. Our Lord himself told us to expect to be hated even as he was hated. But we cannot let this distract us from our purpose. Our world still needs the Good News. Those who pose as our enemies still need the light. The light that can only come through Jesus Christ our Lord.

"The task is still before us and we must press on. We cannot let Satan defeat us because of fear. Our Lord would not want this. Stephen would not want this.

"Our brothers and sisters, may I remind you that Stephen—our Stephen—not only showed us how to live, but how to die. He died with forgiveness on his lips. He died praising God. He was ushered into the very presence of our Savior. Do we begrudge him this blessing? Do we mourn that he has received his reward while we still labor? I think not. We grieve because of our great loss. But now we must strengthen our hands and lift up our voices and carry on the task we have been given to do. May God keep us faithful until such time as we meet our Messiah once again.

"Let us pray."

FORTY-ONE

ABIGAIL COULD SCARCELY BELIEVE that two months had already passed. Two long, difficult months. Time during which she had found a measure of comfort by keeping both her hands and her thoughts busy with the care of others. They had lost some fellow believers, but others had come to join them. The Word was still being preached. There were still those who, in spite of the growing unrest and persecution, quietly and with deep faith joined the followers.

There had been incidents meant to remind them that they were being watched. Yet there had also been more arrests and darker threats and cruel floggings. The religious authorities had no intention of letting the group continue unchallenged. When any possible reason for an offense could be generated, they took full advantage.

Word slowly trickled back from Cyprus, Cyrene, and even Antioch regarding those who had left the city in search of safety. The previous day a letter had arrived from Damascus and was read by James, the brother of the Lord—welcome news of growing groups of disciples in that area. Their members had not cowered in defeat when they had left Jerusalem, but immediately they began to share their faith in the new locations.

These days, Abigail found great consolation in the community of believers. She tried hard not to think upon Stephen's death. It always brought tears and questions for which she had no answers. *How long did he suffer?* was the heart cry that was the most difficult to put aside.

But today, as she sat in her room following prayer, she reflected on how their numbers had grown in a way they could not have if they had all remained in Jerusalem.

This time Abigail allowed herself to give silent voice to her deepest questions.

Was this why, Lord? Was Stephen the seed that, when planted in the ground, bore fruit? Did you use his death to scatter us for your purposes?

Certainly Stephen had been faithful. Abigail had heard the full account of his triumphant entrance into heaven in spite of the hail of stones. He had died victorious, welcomed by Christ himself. His prayer had been answered. He had not denied his Lord.

What better could one hope for? What more was there to life than victorious death? Over and over Abigail came back to these truths.

With these thoughts came release from the veil of fear and doubt that had wound itself around her, threatening to stifle her faith. And now, in this instant, she found herself able to release Stephen. She would not wish him back, not when he resided in a far greater place. Not even now, as she faced an uncertain future alone, surrounded by worrisome news and fearful times. She found peace in the assurance that they had both served as the Lord wished.

With tears of thanksgiving upon her cheeks, she thanked her

Lord for relief of the dark despair that had threatened to consume her. There was reason to go on. And she had God's promise. And though she missed Stephen with all her heart, knowledge that the Lord was with her was enough.

———

My dear sister in Christ, Leah, Abigail mentally composed as she sorted produce for the day's distribution tables. Her silent musings had become somewhat of a habit. There was no way for her to communicate with Leah in reality, so Abigail expressed her thoughts, her feelings, in the only way she could. Silently. *I have so much I wish to share with you,* she mused on. *God willing, one day we will be able to see one another face-to-face, but for now . . .*

Our work here carries on. There are so many who need our help at the tables. Women like you and me, but with no one else in the community to care for their needs.

I have a small room here again and no longer live in the little lean-to that I had shared with Jacob and then my dear husband. I still miss them both. But with the death of my beloved Stephen, a part of my heart was lost also. He was a wonderful man.

But God is good. He has given me such special friends and a peace that I cannot even describe. It carries me through each new day.

There are still many dangers, but in a strange way, I no longer carry that intense fear. I have already lost what was dearest to me. What more can they take? Besides, they are much less threatening to women and children. It is our leaders who are in the most danger A young rabbi by the name of Saul seems to be our greatest threat.

But I do have something that I long to tell you. It—

"Abigail." A young girl suddenly appeared in the doorway, breathless. "There is someone to see you. You are to come now."

Abigail straightened and rubbed her hands against the towel at her waist. Who would be looking for her?

When she entered the courtyard, she stopped midstep, not expecting to see someone from her recent past. That world of yesterday seemed so far away. So disconnected from her life now.

Linux was seated on a shaded bench, a cup in his hand. Someone must have already served him. He rose and moved a step toward her.

She could not have put her feelings into words. She did not understand them herself. Here stood a man who had attracted yet repelled her—at the same time. She had feared him—then had come to trust him enough to search for him at the time of her deepest need. He had been an enemy—and the most loyal of friends. An outsider—and now a fellow believer. Most of all, he had been someone that her dear Stephen had taught, had led into the faith. For that reason alone, Linux would always have a place in her heart.

Abigail could feel the blood rush from her face, her heart pick up a more rapid beat. She feared she would not be able to speak.

"Linux," she managed to say.

"Abigail," he said with a nod. She thought his eyes appeared as haunted as her own must be. For a brief time neither of them moved. Linux was the first to recover. He stepped forward and motioned to the bench. "Please, take a seat here in the shade."

She walked to the bench. When she had been seated and had recovered her breath, she was able to ask, "When did you come?"

"I just arrived back in Jerusalem. I came straight here. I have word for you from Alban and Leah."

He withdrew a letter from inside his tunic. Leah accepted it with shaking hand. She would need to find someone to read it to her. She sat and stared at the parchment, caressing it gently. She blinked determinedly at tears. She would not weep. She had spent far too much time over the past two months in tears. She would not shed them now.

Linux waited patiently.

At length she was able to lift her head and turn to him.

"How are they?"

He gave a slight smile. "They are well. Jacob is helping Alban with the caravans. They travel north mostly, or in the area. It is still not safe. . . ." He let those words drop. "You should see their little one. A strong, healthy boy. They named him Gabriel. But I'm sure she will have told you all about him in the letter. Alban is strutting like a rooster. And the little one already adores Alban and smiles each time . . ."

Abigail had lowered her eyes. "I'm sorry," he said. "I am thoughtlessly rambling on when—"

"No—it's fine." She lifted her head. "It is so good to hear news of them. I have missed them all so much."

He nodded.

"And Leah?" she questioned.

He spoke more quietly this time. "Leah sends her love. She is well—and busy. She meets with the local women for study of Scripture and prayer. She . . ." He paused, then said, "She misses you. Is so sorry that she was not here when you needed her. She begs you to join them. I believe she thinks of you as her younger sister," he finished somewhat lamely. "She wants you to come back with me, to Galilee."

Abigail felt her heart constrict.

"And I cannot," she said, though the words seemed to tear at her heart.

"But—"

"I cannot. I wish so much to see her. And of course my dear Jacob. But I cannot go. I am needed here." She waved her hand toward the tables at the far side of the compound, busy now with servers and receivers. "There is so much—"

"Surely someone else can take your place."

Abigail straightened. "Perhaps. Perhaps I am not as necessary to running the distribution center as I tell myself. But it is more than that. I belong here. With my people. Serving my Lord. I would feel . . . I would feel like a deserter should I leave. Do you . . ." She turned to look directly at him. "Can you understand that?"

Linux nodded. "I can indeed."

"And Martha, she needs me. She has not been well. I fear if I were not here to help Mary care for her . . ." She let the thought drop.

Again they sat in silence. There seemed to be so much to say, and yet so little that could be said.

"That is your answer, then?"

"It must be. I have every reason to remain here."

"I understand." She didn't think he truly did, but that would have to be.

He stood. "I will return to Galilee in three days. If you wish to send a letter . . ."

"Oh—yes, I do." Abigail too was on her feet. She had so longed to write Leah all of the feelings of her heart. Somehow she would find someone who could put all of those thoughts in writing. *One of the young Greek widows, perhaps. They are schooled.* Her hurried thoughts ran on, but Linux was speaking.

"It has been good to see you again, Abigail. I have thought much of you—of your sorrow."

She nodded her gratitude.

"Stephen was a good man. A good teacher and a better friend. I shall always think of him with deep appreciation."

Abigail could not respond. She merely nodded once more.

Linux looked at her for a long moment, nodded at her, and turned to go.

Abigail stood and watched him as he walked from the courtyard. At the entrance he turned once more and lifted his hand. She raised hers in return. Then he was gone.

It was several minutes before Abigail could rouse herself enough to return to the storage area and her task. Her thoughts led her in many directions. She had just turned down an opportunity that would have taken her to Leah—yet in spite of her longing, her heart was at peace. She did indeed belong here. Here where she was needed. Here where she could serve. Here with her own people.

She entered the shed, its stifling heat nearly overcoming her, and bent once again to the routine of dividing up food portions. Even as she did, her mind went back to the letter she had been mentally composing to her dear friend. The letter that soon would be put on papyrus and delivered. Her hand went inside her robe to where Leah's letter was tucked. As soon as her responsibilities were completed, she would search out a friend who could read it to her. It was all she could do to wait.

I had to say no, Leah, her private message went on. *I do hope you will understand. I wanted so much to come. To see you—and meet your new son. But I could not. All of the reasons that I gave to Linux, our friend, were true. But I did not tell him the most important reason why I must stay here, among my people. You see, I have just made a discovery that has changed my world. It has been both so sorrowful and so joyous that at first I struggled. Now I feel nothing but intense wonder. Intense happiness. I can hardly believe it to be true. But it is. It is. And I am so happy. I cannot wait for the days to pass. My whole life has taken on new meaning. New excitement. With every waking hour I have longed to share it with you. And now the opportunity has come so I can.*

Leah, I am with child! Stephen's legacy will now continue in the next generation. I am so blessed!

One of the apostles, Nathanael, was teaching us one evening from one of King David's psalms, and I have made David's testimony my own. He wrote, "I am like a green olive tree in the house of God; I trust in the mercy of God forever and ever. I will praise You forever, because You have done it; And in the presence of Your saints I will wait on Your name, for it is good."

That is what I am doing, Leah, praising our Lord.

With love and prayers, Abigail.

Books by Janette Oke and Davis Bunn

ACTS OF FAITH
The Centurion's Wife
The Hidden Flame

SONG OF ACADIA
The Meeting Place
The Sacred Shore
The Birthright
The Distant Beacon
The Beloved Land

Books by Davis Bunn

Gold of Kings
The Book of Hours
The Great Divide
Winner Take All
The Lazarus Trap
Elixir
Imposter

All Through the Night
My Soul to Keep

HEIRS OF ACADIA *
The Solitary Envoy
The Innocent Libertine
The Noble Fugitive
The Night Angel
Falconer's Quest

* with Isabella Bunn
www.davisbunn.com

Books by Janette Oke

CANADIAN WEST

When Calls the Heart • *When Comes the Spring*
When Breaks the Dawn • *When Hope Springs New*
Beyond the Gathering Storm
When Tomorrow Comes

LOVE COMES SOFTLY

Love Comes Softly • *Love's Enduring Promise*
Love's Long Journey • *Love's Abiding Joy*
Love's Unending Legacy • *Love's Unfolding Dream*
Love Takes Wing • *Love Finds a Home*

A PRAIRIE LEGACY

The Tender Years • *A Searching Heart*
A Quiet Strength • *Like Gold Refined*

SEASONS OF THE HEART

Once Upon a Summer • *The Winds of Autumn*
Winter Is Not Forever • *Spring's Gentle Promise*

Seasons of the Heart (4 in 1)

WOMEN OF THE WEST

The Calling of Emily Evans • *Julia's Last Hope*
Roses for Mama • *A Woman Named Damaris*
They Called Her Mrs. Doc • *The Measure of a Heart*
A Bride for Donnigan • *Heart of the Wilderness*
Too Long a Stranger • *The Bluebird and the Sparrow*
A Gown of Spanish Lace • *Drums of Change*

www.janetteoke.com